**THE SEARING, SEX-FILLED BEST-SELLING
NOVEL WITHIN A NOVEL!**

*The madam called her Eva. She selected the Hebrew name
for its meaning—life; living. It was an appropriate choice.
For it would happen that the wee babe of a "dime-a-dance-
girl" turned pro would become a famous woman. But that
would be many years ahead—in another place, another
time. The madam sold her body; her daughter prostituted
her soul, never realizing each crucifying word she wrote
nailed her to a cathartic cross. From an elite Las Vegas
bordello to a prestigious New York publishing house—
what was the difference? Once a whore, always a whore.*

FAST FRIENDS

FAST FRIENDS

RUTH SMITH & SHARON LLOYD

PaperJacks LTD.

TORONTO   NEW YORK

AN ORIGINAL

PaperJacks

FAST FRIENDS

PaperJacks LTD.

330 STEELCASE RD. E., MARKHAM, ONT. L3R 2M1
210 FIFTH AVE., NEW YORK, N.Y. 10010

First edition published June 1988

ISBN 0-7701-0906-3
Copyright © 1988 by Sharon Lloyd and Ruth Smith
All rights reserved.
Printed in the USA

For all the people who have in one way or another willingly or unknowingly contributed to this work of fiction, and our special thanks to two of the smartest and most courageous men we know, Richard Curtis and Jim Connor.

PROLOGUE
1988

The theme music and studio applause faded. Mahalia Whittaker faced the camera. "Some of you may remember her from the most publicized trial in recent years, some of you may have seen the double-page ad in *The New York Times Book Review*, and some of you have braved the lines outside bookstores across the country to buy her novel, *Fast Friends*—and if not, you soon will." Mahalia dropped her teasers like pebbles into a brook and anticipation rippled through the audience. "Oh yeah, you know who my interview is with today."

America's leading talk show hostess leaned forward, her voice dropping to its familiar over-the-back-fence, secrets-trading tone. "You're just dying to know all the nitty-gritty details, aren't you? Me too, but first I must tell you that my guest's book contains graphic sex and violence. You may find the material offensive, and if so, it is certainly your prerogative to change channels. You've been forewarned; let's get down to it, folks. Welcome my guest, the hot—and I mean sizzling H-O-T—author . . . Eve Afton."

Beneath the sweltering lights, not a trace of perspiration marred Eve Afton's composure as the camera panned to her. She hiked the skirt of her Fendi leather suit and crossed her legs. The thin gold chain serpentining through her black stockings from ankle to thigh riveted the viewers for a moment, then was outdazzled by her brilliant smile. She'd been through much tougher inquisitions than Mahalia Whittaker's grilling.

"What we want to know—right, audience?—is do you do your own research? Just the sheer volume of *natural* sex acts in your book would take a-maz-ing stamina. What brand of vitamins do you take, girl?"

"One-a-Day, but I take them like my men: one every four hours."

"Eve, Eve, Eve. Shame on you! You're not being serious, and we *real*-ly want to know: Is *Fast Friends* just another sensational novel or are the main characters, as is rumored, based on real people? Did these things *real*-ly happen? Some people out there believe they did."

"Mahalia, Mahalia, Ma-halia! There is always speculation surrounding a book about powerful, ruthless, obsessive women. Everyone *wants* it to be true. It's the ultimate vicarious thrill, a safe chance to experience the dark side of their nature without risking anything more than a few dollars." Eve unwaveringly returned Mahalia's penetrating gaze. Promo was the name of the game. And she'd learned long ago to be quicker, slicker, smoother, smarter, and dirtier than the rest.

The minutes ticked, the switchboard jammed, the audience howled for the microphone like starving wolves tearing at a scrap of raw meat, and Eve remained as unruffled as ever.

"Hi, caller. Call-er?" Mahalia nodded impatiently.

"Yes. I loved Miss Afton's book and I love you, Mahalia." The hostess beamed. "But I'm disappointed you're allowing Miss Afton to get by with only admitting what is already public knowledge. Come on, Mahalia, you can do better than that." Mahalia winced at the static crackle.

"We thank you for sharing that with us, caller, and you're right. Eve, you have claimed repeatedly that all the rape, incest, bestiality, nymphomania, murder, treason, and treachery is pure invention and that, excluding your previous editor, the gangsters, evangelists, princes, politicians, pimps, and prostitutes you portray in *Fast Friends* are fictitious; but something strikes a chord of authenticity. I have to ask one more time: is there *any* resemblance to *any* person, living or dead? Do the three 'through-thick-thin-and-sin fast friends' *real*-ly exist? Is there even a shred of truth in your best seller?"

The practiced smile froze on Eve's lips and she waited, waited like the storyteller she was until her effect was spellbinding, waited until they were on the edge of their seats, holding their breath.

"I'm going to tell you, the American public, and the world." Eve faced Mahalia. "It's all true. Every bit of it."

CHAPTER ONE
1935
Monterey Peninsula, California

He smelled of fish and sweat, which wasn't unusual; practically every man on the Row did. He said little as he groped clumsily, which wasn't unusual; practically every man who paid for sex did. He wanted the works for his money and expected to find a piece of heaven in a living hell, which wasn't unusual. Practically everybody wanted to escape Cannery Row's stench one way or another, but few ever did.

If he had mentioned his name, Moni didn't remember. For her their names and faces had become a blur; only their preferences distinguished them; and only their cash up front meant anything. His money was on the battered bureau, his grimy clothes on the floor, his dick inside her. He was panting and thrusting. The bed rocked and bumped against the wall. And she, she was gasping, which he would doubtless assume was due to his expert balling. God! He was huge, a wild boar rooting and grunting and savaging her. Her head thrashed from side to side, her flame-colored hair whipping the stained pillow slip as she tried to catch a breath of air. She writhed beneath him, desperately struggling to alleviate the crush of his matted chest upon her bruised ribs. He was muttering about how good she was, not like the whore he had had last week, who was about as lively as a corpse. Moni feared she might truly die if he didn't climax soon. Come, damn you, come!

He heaved and she moaned right on cue. It was a wasted effort. The mountain atop her did not erupt, and she was beginning to believe that maybe he never would. Mother of God! Why had she agreed to take on this last john? What if she didn't make the rendezvous? What if Smoky decided to leave without her?

She panicked at the thought. She'd be trapped for another six months under animals like this one. The walls closed in. The light bulb dangling from the frayed cord shimmied precariously, casting shadows upon the fly-specked ceiling. Her back arched as she bucked and clawed her way from beneath the man. Nothing would prevent her from getting out, nothing. *Nothing*. Please, dear God, please, just this once don't turn away from me.

"Please, God, please!" she screamed as she raked her nails down the man's back and over his ass. His sticky semen shot into her, then oozed down her quivering thigh.

"You're good, Red," he grunted, at last crawling off of her and hastily pulling on his pants. He ran a hand through hair as slick as the oil-packed sardines that the cannery spat out daily. "Gonna tell my friends—but not too many. Wanna be sure you ain't too popular. Couldn't afford you if you were."

She gathered her thick hair and piled it atop her head, flashing him a haughty smile. "You couldn't anyway, buster. My price just went up. Beat it, will you? I got another appointment to keep."

No sooner had he shut the door than Moni was up and hurrying about the cramped room. She yanked the packed suitcase from under the bed and freshened herself as best she could. Hurry. Hurry! Smoky won't wait forever.

Quickly she pulled on a skirt and blouse over her lacy teddy, starting for the door without so much as a backward glance. The money, you idiot! She ran back to the bed, and dug under the mattress for the crumpled envelope that contained her savings. Reverently removing the cash, she rolled it into a wad and tucked it into her cleavage for safekeeping. She could still make it if she ran all the way to the dance hall. Smoky would wait. He had to. He knew how important it was to her.

As she tore down the decaying streets, her heart pounding, her life flashed before her: her family, as they had once been and were no more; her father's laughing Irish eyes before the Depression took its toll; her mother's undaunted spirit before Papa's suicide broke her heart and apathy smothered her will to live; her brother's devil-may-care attitude, until he was knifed in an alley over a penny-ante crap game. They were gone now, buried cheap and deep. She'd survived; not easily and not well, but she'd survived. She'd been young and enterprising and just stubborn enough not to give in. At thirteen she'd gone to work in a dance hall, obliging the drunks and the misfits by letting them fondle her for the price of a dime and the length of a tune. She'd developed early and hardened quick. She'd learned to say what they wanted to hear and not to flinch when they copped their feels. Had it not been for Smoky, her circumstances would have been intolerable, but he was different. He still had a spark of life, and he had seen the world outside the Row. He still had dreams, still had the energy to chase them.

From the night she'd danced her way to her first dollar, Smoky had been there; from the moment he'd given her her working name, Stardust, Moni had bloomed under his interest. Perhaps he was her first crush, but Moni hadn't the time or innocence to recognize it; instead she watched him run the dance hall, handle the staff, defer to customers, eagle-eye the books, bargain shrewdly with suppliers and oust troublemakers. But most of all, she watched

Smoky take the money to the bank, where it stayed, drawing interest for legitimate investments. She was getting an education and it was free—well, not exactly.

The suitcase burst open, spilling her meager wardrobe onto the muddy ground. She cursed, then scrambled to retrieve her possessions.

"Hey, Red, you running out of the Row, or for your life?" cackled one of her former customers as she crammed shut the bulging case.

Her green eyes narrowed defiantly. "Both." Now she ran even faster—away from the dampness that wilted the sheets and permeated to the bone, away from the stifling resignation that ate at the heart of the Row, away from the sorrows and memories that strangled your soul when the music stopped and the only thing left to hear was your own thoughts, and the only thing left to dance to was life's erratic rhythm.

Smoky had taught her so much—much, much more than the intricacies of running a seedy business, more than the economics of men paying for their lust. During the infrequent breaks, while she rested her throbbing feet, Smoky would talk of a distant paradise called Nevada. He claimed the desert air would warm the coldest of hearts, that you could breathe so deeply of the promise that there would still be some to spare. You could stretch your arms and touch the stars, and you could stretch your dreams and reach the moon. "And you, Stardust, could be a somebody if you keep your head and don't give away your heart. Do you think it takes a lot of gumption to build a future? Hell, no! It takes smarts. And what you have to be is special. Make 'em think what you got to offer is more than they can afford. Make them believe they are the exception, and then run, don't walk, to deposit their stupidity."

And that's what Moni Leah Afton intended to do. Expediently; expertly; earnestly.

Be there, Smoky, be there.

Moni arrived five minutes shy of her appointed time, but not her destiny. Smoky's black Packard was just pulling out, making its way back to Nevada's wide open spaces of promiscuity and fortune as she finally stopped outside the boarded-up dance hall.

"No, no, no! Don't leave me behind, Smoky!" But the Packard was disappearing around the bend, and Moni sank down to sit slumped on her suitcase, her head in her hands. There went Smoky. There went the dream. There went survival.

She jumped to her feet, grabbed the beat-up bag, and charged down the road. "You sorry son of a bitch. What would it have cost you—a few goddamn minutes? I'll see you in Nevada and charge you double the price, just like you taught me, bastard!" She yanked off her pump and hurled it at the dust. "I'll get where I'm going. I'll get every damn thing I ever wanted." She marched over to where her shoe had landed, put it back on her foot, and started walking.

CHAPTER TWO

On Monday, March 14, 1938, the Nazis goose-stepped into Vienna. Systematically, the Third Reich legions confiscated priceless works of art and commandeered all Austrian assets. Gold poured into the Bank for International Settlements and the powers immediately made paper transfers of the funds to the Reichsbank. The puppet chancellor-dictator Kurt von Schuschnigg was held in prison without trial, and all non-Aryans were pursued with a vengeance.

Sasa Bailesti crouched with his wife, Stephania, in a shadowy space between two buildings as German soldiers combed the city for Gypsies and Jews—the former to wear the brown triangle, the latter the Star of David, both marks of death. Before leaving his hometown in Romania to sneak Stephania across the borders so that she might see her aging parents one last time, Sasa had consulted the stars. He knew their mission was hazardous, but Stephania was young and homesick and Sasa was in love. And now they were being stalked like vermin, the smell of their fear so strong as to give them away. They dared not breathe, think, or flex a cramped muscle. But Sasa did flinch when he heard the guttural command, *"Halt!"* As Stephania looked helplessly into his black eyes, fear shimmering in her own, tentacles of dread curled around his spine and his bowels constricted. Pulling Stephania to her feet, he smiled bravely. "I am with you. Together we will face what we must. Do not let them see you cower. Be strong, be courageous, my love. We will survive."

In another part of the world on this same date, Fairfax Randolph Bennett VI celebrated his twenty-fifth birthday by marching into the New York branch of the Morgan Bank to claim his grandfather's legacy. Not only did he acquire a mother lode in gold bullion and titles to extensive lands, he overheard a conversation that began his association with the Bank for International Settlements and the fraternity composed of those American and European businessmen for whom the word *principal* had only one spelling and one meaning: money that drew interest. As the world marched toward war, an elite clique quietly grappled for profit and power. Suddenly armed with the means, Fairfax Randolph Bennett VI intended to be one of them.

He stopped at a pay phone after leaving the Morgan Bank and invited his parents and their lifelong friends, the de Ferrerses, along with their daughter, Anne, to dinner. Though it had been understood since birth that he and Anne would marry, he now intended to make formal the arrangement. There was no reason for him not to do so: he had the funds; Anne was beautiful, a young woman of breeding. That she didn't stir his blood was incidental. She would be proper and he would be influential. *How could such a match fail?*

While Fairfax Randolph Bennett VI and his fiancée dined at an exclusive seashore country club that evening, Sasa Bailesti and his pregnant wife were herded into a stifling boxcar and sent to Dachau.

CHAPTER THREE

Several blazing days, several hot men, and one cold night on the desert later, Moni had hitchhiked her way to the outskirts of Las Vegas. She had thumbed her way to fortune and now she thumbed her nose at those who dared to mock her determination. She knew something they didn't: she wasn't another woman gone bad. She had style and she had wiles. She looked like a china doll, and men would pay a king's ransom to see if she would break. She was a somebody with sex to sell and a future to build.

And build she did. Property was cheap along the barren two-lane blacktop road known as the L.A. Highway. She purchased a two-story stucco house with a tile roof for half its value from an old couple who thought the petite Californian mad for wanting to isolate herself in such a remote area. Her money talked, even if the anxious buyer said little about her plans. Her one condition was that they vacate within the week. She was in a hurry.

During that week, Moni scoured the adjoining counties for girls. She knew the type, knew the look. They had to have spirit; most important, they had to have potential.

She was going to run a first-rate establishment and needed girls who possessed the skill and ambition to grow with the business. She needed three or four to begin with, and she was determined that the group be varied. After all, men had their idiosyncrasies and particular tastes, and Moni intended to supply a seductive atmosphere and a variety for their pleasure. But her girls would be well served too. She offered those she chose an irresistible incentive: a percentage of the house.

The first to agree was a gregarious blonde by the name of Jewel. She had hard blue eyes, high firm breasts, and long, long legs. She liked the business but preferred women, a fact she neglected to mention to Moni.

The next recruit was nicknamed Abalone, because of her ear fetish. She was part Apache, part Mexican, and she always wore big dangling loops of silver and turquoise. She bragged that if a man inserted himself through her earring, he would last forever. If he was too big to fit, her services were free.

Then there was Constance from Kansas. Big-boned and borderline plump, she'd done time for nearly killing a john who'd disfigured her with a broken bottle. Unfortunately, he had been the mayor of Salina. She bore a scar on her right breast, and her specialty was bondage. Her intent was to skim as much as she made.

And last, but most special, was Lily, a devout Catholic from back East, who believed that communion should be taken through the mouth and washed down with fine champagne. The fragile brunette radiated class. She was a philosophy major and a fellatio gourmet. If Moni was any judge—and she was—Lily would be the hottest item at Moni's Place.

The madam had her four, but procuring customers for them proved to be not so easy.

Business was slow during the first few months. Once the house was renovated, the girls lounged away the afternoons, buffing their nails and bitching about their small incomes. Persuading them to cook or clean was next to impossible, and Moni knew she hadn't much bargaining power and even less money saved on which to draw. But she could bluff, and she did just that, with staccato orders and threats issued so fast and so fiercely the girls couldn't think quickly enough to argue with her. In the midst of one such tirade, Abalone, who had been hiding in the kitchen, waltzed into the parlor and announced that a crazy black woman was at the back door inquiring about work.

"Tell her I don't need anybody!"

"I tell her, but she won't vamoose. I theenk she *loco*."

"No, I isn't. No more crazy than you, wearing those flashy earbobs and hardly no clothes." A black woman with close-cropped hair and luminous ebony eyes spoke from the doorway. "My name is Vashon d'Williams. Porter down at the station tole me you ladies could be in need of some help."

"You were misinformed." Moni's tone of voice offered no encouragement.

"I isn't without references. It's just that I lost 'em."

"Sho 'nuff, sugah, ain't that a trag-e-dy?" Jewel mimicked. "Well, I don't suppose it would take you more than a couple of tricks to hustle up some more."

"I isn't a whore! I makes an honest livin', but I don't hold anything against those who got nothin' to fall back on 'cept their backside."

"Yi, yi, yi! I tell you she is crazy in the head. You theenk you better than us?" Abalone tossed her raven mane, shaking her silver hoops. Her eyes glittered. "Maybe I keek your skinny ass through the screen and teach you some manners. Miss Moni likes good manners." She smirked at the madam.

"You been eating too many 'dem chile peppers. They done scrambled yo' brains. Unless you want those hoops up yo' ass sideways, try to remember this isn't none of yo' affair."

Abalone took a step forward, but something in the

scrappy woman's eyes made her back away. Her bracelets jangled as she reared back and spat at Vashon's feet. *"Negro puta!"*

Ignoring Abalone, Vashon looked directly at Moni. "I can cook, clean, and sew better'n anybody you'll ever find. I keep my mouth shut and don' take a penny I hasn't earned. You won't never get into a bed that hasn't been turned down and won't never get up in the mornin' without coffee being brewed."

"I guess it would be too much to hope that you also know how to make café brûlot?" Lily asked, her attention momentarily diverted from the task of painting her toenails a glossy red. She puffed up another cotton ball between her toes and waited for the answer.

"I surely do. Tasted it while I was singing aboard a riverboat down 'round New Orleans. Liked it so much I done learned to make it, right on de spot."

"So how deed you learn about chile peppers?" Abalone challenged. "Meebe you also danced in a cantina in Veracruz?"

Everyone but Moni burst into laughter.

"I'm gonna tell you something right now, and you listen real close, 'cause I'm only gonna say it once and never again. I crept over the border before dawn yesterday mornin' and I ain't going back across tomorrow, the next day, nor ever. Where I been is where I been, and what I done is what I done." Vashon squared her frail-looking shoulders. "I'll tell you one more thing, wetback squaw: I been to places you never even dreamed about, and I could teach you a thing or two—that is if I had a mind to, which I doesn't."

Lily could see no reason not to hire Vashon. She could cook, clean, sew, and make café brûlot. Furthermore, it wouldn't hurt if Vashon taught her a few tricks from wherever it was she claimed to have been. Perhaps she knew something even more inventive than the champagne corkscrew.

"Now, Miss Moni, sugah, would you be wanting peach cobbler or strawberry shortcake for dessert tonight?"

Vashon was as good a bluffer as Moni. In Vashon, the madam recognized a little bit of herself, the part that was willing to give it all and go for broke. And she respected Vashon's spunk. A faint smile curved her lips as she inspected the prospective housekeeper from head to high-topped shoes. "Room and board and Sundays off is all I can offer."

"That's good, like to go to church on Sundays, but I's be needin' a dollar a week for personals." Cocking her head, she inventoried the madam from the top of her copper head to her open-toed pumps.

Moni nodded. "Since we don't have any peaches or strawberries, we'll skip dessert tonight."

"Oh, yes'm, we do. We's got both." Triumphantly Vashon opened her satchel and exposed the lush fruit. She then marched into the kitchen as if Moni's Place was hers.

Suddenly Moni felt like someone was on her side. It was the best feeling she had had in years.

CHAPTER FOUR

The Baroness Anna Marie Luedhof sat in her private box in the Vienna Opera House, listening to the final aria of *Carmen*. The appropriate mourning period having passed, this was her first public appearance since the baron's death.

From her box she was able to observe the hierarchy of the Third Reich. She was surprised to note how appreciative the German barbarians were of the performance, as though they understood the refined culture of their captives. She was not surprised, however, by their intermittent looks in her direction; of course the Nazis found her fascinating. She was not only an attractive widow but inordinately wealthy and a presumed collaborator. Little did they know that one of Europe's most renowned hostesses shared not one iota of her dead husband's pro-Nazi sentiments. In fact, she loathed and abhorred the sight of their uniforms, their rigidity, and their penchant for cruelty.

The crowd's applause registered and the curtain came down on the first act. She dreaded intermission, for now

Colonel Ludwig von Hanggler would descend upon her, polite as always, yet deadly as a viper. She would be utterly charming, though she knew the SS colonel suspected her loyalties and regularly attempted to expose her. Thus far, she had deflected his efforts. Now they would have yet another exchange of pleasantries, another sparring match. He did not disappoint her, and she would not disappoint him. Discreetly, she tugged the neckline of her taffeta gown lower. *Give him something other than his suspicions to concentrate upon.*

His knee-high polished boots clicked before her and his salute was straight-armed and expectant. "*Heil* Hitler!"

Ignoring state protocol, she extended her hand, enduring the feral graze of his lips upon her bejeweled flesh. "How nice to see you again, Herr von Hanggler. I trust you are enjoying the opera as much as I."

"Very much so, Baroness. And I enjoy it the more for your presence."

As his steely blue eyes assessed her, they did not miss the distracting display of cleavage. "My Führer wishes you to know that the late baron was held in the highest regard. His loyalty and devotion to the preservation of a pure and untainted Germany were a mark of honor. He is missed, and the Führer extends his hand in friendship and support should you require it. He also extends an invitation for you to dine with us this evening. It would be my privilege to escort you, Baroness."

"Ah, but I tire easily these days." She managed a look of regret. "Perhaps you will thank the Führer and explain to him that as I have not been out since Kurt's death, I have overdone a bit, but that I should adore dining with him soon. Tell me, *bitte*, who is the American sitting with your party?"

"Fairfax Randolph Bennett the Sixth. Relatively speaking, he is a newcomer, but the baron held him in the highest esteem. Their interests were similar."

"If the Führer's schedule permits, I should like all of

you"—she straightened a brass button on von Hanggler's uniform—"to dine with me at home Tuesday night. I shall call tomorrow to confirm."

"I shall look forward to the occasion of our next meeting. Good night, Baroness." Again, the click of the heels, the straight-armed salute.

May you march into the Danube and drown, you arrogant bastard! "*Auf wiedersehen!*" Once more, Anna had managed to circumvent the demand for fealty. As the lights dimmed, she turned her attention to the striking American.

CHAPTER FIVE

Things just kept getting better and better after Vashon arrived. The house sparkled, the cooking was sinfully good, and there seemed to be nothing that Vashon couldn't do. Moni often wondered when the tireless wonder slept. But the real boon was the girls' attitude. The griping stopped; they played ladies of the manor, and with this turnabout came an increase in business. Nothing major, just a steady trickle of repeat customers, but eventually the customers referred their friends and fellow workers. Still, Moni's Place was floundering.

Each month there was barely enough to meet expenses. Moni worried herself sick over the girls' extravagance and wastefulness. Vashon was her only source of support. Many was the time she bathed Moni like a child, then sat brushing her hair, stroke after stroke, easing her mistress's distress with poignant parables.

"Did I ever tell you 'bout the time I was stranded in Saint Louis? I was travelin' with a strappin' buck by the name of Nehemiah at the time."

Moni closed her eyes and leaned her head back on Vashon's knees, loving the tug of the brush through her hair. She had come to enjoy Vashon's tales. True or not, they were always entertaining, a blessed respite from reality. "No, I don't believe I've heard that one." She sighed contentedly.

"Well, let me tell you, chile, Nehemiah could play a horn. He had a talent for all kinds of instruments. He was down to his last dollar and I was so hungry that my stomach was touchin' my backbone. We come upon this blues joint 'n Nehemiah said he would take care of everything once the bossman heard him play. All I was thinkin' about was fried chicken and feather tickin'. The bossman wasn't interested in another black horn blower. Told us to get, 'n to use the back door this time. Well, this look come over Nehemiah—a look I won't never forget. He pulled out his trumpet, licked his lips, 'n blew for all he was worth. You nor that bossman never heard nothin' like it. Sent chills up 'n down my spine. It was the finest blow job a horn man ever did. Nehemiah was offered a spot on the bandstand, but before he could accept, this dandy-lookin' stud in a white linen suit who'd been sittin' 'n listening in the shadows walked over 'n said, calm as you please, 'You got a gifted pair of lips, boy. I'll pay you twice what this jiver's offering if you'll play for me.'

"Nehemiah wasn't nobody's fool. 'Now, why would I be turnin' down a guaranteed gig to blow for you?' he asked.

" 'Cause you'd be making the biggest mistake of your life if you refuse,' the man in the white linen suit said.

"Nehemiah couldn't make up his mind about the dude. He gave me a sideways look: should he or shouldn't he?

"To tell you the truth, I wasn't real sure. On one hand Nehemiah had a sure thing going with the blues joint, but there was something, something real special, 'bout the black dude in the white linen suit. I drew a deep breath 'n mulled it over; then I gave Nehemiah a nod. Still ain't real sure why, but there was a future in that man's voice, kinda deep 'n rich, and there was a sense of rhythm to his gait, like he heard Gabriel blowin', like he knew my Nehemiah had soul to share 'n God was wettin' his pucker. I felt that feeling once—only once—when I was young, 'n believed the gospels I sang had meaning. The notes Nehemiah blew reached down, *way* down, 'n pulled what was strong, what was gut, up from the depths that were tears turned to music, that was feelin' turned to wind—a wind that shouted, 'Alleluia, let me go, amen, brother!' ''

"Who was the man in the white linen suit, Vashon?" Moni asked excitedly.

"Are you sure you wants to know, Miss Moni?"

"Yes, tell me! I don't know if you're just one hell of a storyteller, Vashon, but I have to know. Who was the man? What became of Nehemiah?"

Vashon grinned. "The man in the white linen suit was someone you know, Miss Moni. You ever hear of Count Basie? 'N Nehemiah, well, he just become one of the greatest trumpet players you ever heard. When you lay yo' head back and let yo' mind trip through Count Basie's music, what strikes you? Ain't it the wail? Ain't it the soul? Ain't it the man I call Nehemiah?"

"Is he the sound that sets me free? Is he the bridge between what I am and what I long to be?" Moni sat up, realization dawning.

"Nehemiah is whatever you want, Miss Moni. He's the ache or the joy; he's the low or the high; he's the best or the worst. No one knows that better 'n me."

"And he's a success. But what happened to you in Saint Louis?" Moni turned to her confidante, her green eyes full of concern.

Vashon shrugged, as though the ache of Saint Louis and the betrayal of Nehemiah were of no consequence. "I tole him it didn't matter. 'N it truly didn't, Miss Moni. Something bigger than he and me was workin' that day. He was notes, he was music; 'n me, well, I was just listenin', I was just there that day. But I knows soul when I hear it. I knows fame when it comes knockin' at the door. I was smack dab in the middle of a starburst, 'n I knew I was only a way to make Nehemiah shine. You see, Nehemiah never had hope. He didn't realize his potential. A lot of us doesn't. Too many folk give up when it seems hopeless. Ain't no such word as 'hopeless.' Nehemiah, he's a somebody now. Folks flock around to hear him wail the blues. Funny thing is, I know the man. I know what he feels; I know where he aches. I know the times he's been spat on regardless of his talent because he's a man of color. We all got regrets, Miss Moni. We all wish we had one moment to do all over again. I want that moment to do. I wish I had that nod to give again. Maybe I would've changed my mind, maybe I would'na. I coulda let Nehemiah be a second-class blues wailer, but I saw a future for him, just as I sees a future for you. Nobody has the right to interfere. It's written. It's meant to be. 'N someday, Miss Moni, there's gonna be somebody who wails a tune as gutsy as Nehemiah. He's gonna look at you; he's gonna wait for a nod. 'N you sho' 'nuff will give it to him. He's gonna have a song to sing 'n you's the only woman who's gonna hear. Take a chance. Give him the nod, the freedom to be who he's supposed to be. It ain't easy, but you can't replace that wail. It's clear, it's pure, it's like nothing you never before heard or ever will again."

"Who are you talking about, Vashon? There isn't a man on this earth who plays a tune I haven't heard before. It's my business to know and not be deceived by lines and promises."

"Nehemiah became a great. He didn't really walk out on me; I turned my back on him. I thought he was a somebody who didn't need a nobody trailin' after him. You got sense, Miss Moni. When that somethin' special walks through your doors, don't turn your back."

"Listen to me, Vashon. Anybody that was ever special to me died, got killed, or left. I learned early on never to get too attached to anything or anyone, and that's my motto, that's my golden rule. So if Mister Man of the wails and the soul and the loving comes in the front door, he can waltz right on through, because no one is ever getting close to me. It hurts too much—I care too much—and there isn't anything or anyone who can ever touch me again. What I care about is what stays around if you protect it: money in the bank, land, anything that's negotiable, anything that's not subject to the whims of emotion. I got tired of aching a long time ago, and I'm not ever going to hurt again. The last disappointment I had was when my friend Smoky drove off without me, but I made it here anyway. As long as I live, I'm not ever counting on anyone, except myself.''

"Ain't natural, Miss Moni. Didn't you hear what I told you about Nehemiah? He didn't have any hope, he had a song to wail on the trumpet, and he wasn't even counting on himself. He was content with just enough dollars to get to the next place. Now I can see you ain't content with just a few dollars, and I can see you got faith in yourself, but what you can't see is what Nehemiah couldn't see, and what I told you most folk can't see. And that's that you never know when God's gonna decide to dump a bunch of good fortune in yo' lap. You gotta be aware so you can pick it up and handle it with care. Now, I helped Nehemiah, 'cause Nehemiah couldn't help himself. But, Miss Moni, I think you can help yo'self, so you's got to be awares, or dat good fortune gonna land on your lap and bounce right off on de floor, and you gonna be left singing yo' blues again 'bout how everythin' always be letting you down or runnin' off and leavin' you. You's got to be mindful. You's got to risk yo'self a little bit. Dat's de only way you's ever gonna get anywhere. All de grit and determination in the world ain't gonna do you one bit of good 'lessin' you get smart and never have to wish you had that one moment to live over that you woulda done different.''

Moni stood up slowly, her movements as deliberate as her carefully measured words. "I don't intend to have any regrets. Neither do I have any illusions about what men expect from a woman like myself. It isn't a nod, Vashon.'' She smiled ruefully, then moved over to stand before the long oval mirror. She laced her fingers through her hair, lazily lifting the silken strands and letting them spill about her face as she assessed the stunning shape reflected in the glass. These were her assets, this was her future: her body provided the only security she knew. "If Clark Cable himself walked through that door, I would be immune to his looks, his charms, everything but his money, because his money stays when he doesn't.''

Oh, chile, you isn't evah gonna know what hit you. Sometimes there comes along a man who is so special that you can't never get him out of your blood no matter what you does, a man like my Nehamiah, a man whose loving is like a fever. But Vashon kept her thoughts to herself as she turned down the bed and plumped Moni's pillows.

CHAPTER SIX

At the elaborate dinner party she hosted in her century-old castle high above the Danube, the baroness, who wore a diamond choker and a Worth gown of black silk, dazzled the German swine and her shrewd American guest with her wit, diplomacy, and an incomparable selection of wines.

Far away, in a tin-roofed shack on the banks of the muddy Loosahatchie River in southern Tennessee, Norma Mae Owen looped strand upon strand of peeling gold beads about her slender neck so that they tumbled down her flat chest. Slipping into her mama's tattered and stained crepe party dress, she stuffed rags in the bodice, and turned to study her suggestive pose in the tarnished mirror. Mm-*hm*. *Aren't I a fancy thing? 'Most as pretty as the ladies in the movie magazines*. Norma Mae sucked on the beads, hollowing her cheeks and slanting her eyes. "One of these days, I'm gonna be covered in gold from head to toe, and my gowns are gonna be made of the finest silk and satin. My breasts are gonna be bigger than Mae West's and men are gonna flock from miles around to come courtin'. And maybe I'll choose one and maybe I won't." She slung the beads over her shoulders, stuck out her rump, and wiped the streak of dirt from her cheek.

The twelve-year-old charmed no one but herself. She hadn't the vaguest notion what the word *diplomacy* meant and the only liquor in her corner of the world was bootleg moonshine. And although Norma Mae had never heard of a place called Vienna, she did have one thing in common with the baroness and her guests: an obsession with gold.

CHAPTER SEVEN

Valentine's Day was always slow for whores. Yet it was on that particular day in 1940 that Ben Randolph's shadow fell across the front porch of Moni's Place. Vashon, intent on her sweeping, first noticed his fastidiously shined brogues. The broom came to a standstill as she surveyed the man before her. He was different; just one look and anybody with a lick of sense would know it. His heavily starched shirt bore a monogram on one French cuff, and sunlight flashed off his solid-gold cuff links, causing Vashon to squint. Wasn't from these parts. She'd done some traveling, and she'd wager a week's pay he was East Coast. His hair was the color of wheat, his eyes the azure of robin's eggs, his hands those of a gentleman. Plumb handsome, that's what he was, a man of breeding. Showed in the bones: he was a thoroughbred. Power clung to him same as the fragrance of desire clung to Moni.

"I suppose you would be wanting the madam?" Vashon asked, careful to enunciate in the presence of such refinement. She was not about to refer him to Abalone, whose silver-hoop act had made her the object of widespread interest. It probably wouldn't be long before the crazy Injun changed her name to Princess Spread Eagle. In the last month she'd taken in twice as many men and three times as many dollars as anyone else. But the wetback squaw hadn't once tipped Vashon and was hardly aware that Vashon was now flavoring her food with spit before serving it! Jewel and Constance were out of the question for the likes of this gentleman, and besides, they wouldn't take kindly to being roused from the afternoon nap they'd taken to sharing together behind locked doors, under the guise of making a surprise for Miss Moni's birthday. Reminded Vashon of ladies in the South, always taking naps together, lying in their dark, hot rooms, under electric fans, wearing only their slips. She never could understand it. If she wasn't sleeping with a man, she wanted to be all alone, just her—and no slip, just the way God had sent her into this world.

At the gentleman's nod that yes, he wanted to see the madam, Vashon showed him into the parlor and quietly backed out the door. Then she raced pell-mell up the stairs and burst into Moni's room. "Hurry, hurry, Miss Moni, there's a handsome customer in the parlor, and he isn't one to be kept waitin'."

"Anticipation never hurt a man, Vashon." Moni continued to tally her ledger. "Have Lily serve him."

"Lily won't do for this man. He don't be wantin' a Lily."

"How would you know what he wants?"

"I jus' think you should come see for yo'self, Miss Moni, dat's all."

"You're making me lose my place," Moni muttered, not bothering to look up. "Quit pestering me and go get Lily for him. Pronto, *tonto*. . . ." As soon as the words were out of her mouth, Moni regretted using Abalone's insulting phrase. Vashon hadn't done anything to deserve it.

"I's nobody's fool, Miss Moni, but I get Lily. Pronto."

"I'm sorry, Vashon, I was just thinking about Abalone. I know you don't like her, but she paid your wages the last few weeks."

"Then I don't need no wages, even hard as I works and all that I does for you, till someone else can pay for my personals." Vashon crossed to the door. "You could pay me if'n you'd only go downstairs and take care of the gentleman, but I can see you's too busy countin' money to make more."

"Out!"

Accustomed to cataloguing all that surrounded him, Ben Randolph studied with amusement the parlor's most intriguing anomaly, a framed photograph of Franklin Delano Roosevelt. Someone had artfully scrawled *F.D.R.* The forgery was so good that all but those with the most personal knowledge would be fooled. Next to it was a small American flag and a crudely carved yet beautifully proportioned eagle. Native Indian art, he surmised correctly. He wasn't averse to a patriotic whore. In fact, it might prove—

Lily glided into the parlor, two tulip-shaped glasses and a bottle in her hand. She was more out of place in this raw setting than the small tokens of political fervor. Her dark hair, caught up behind one ear with a mother-of-pearl comb, cascaded against her cheek. Her fair skin bore no trace of the desert sun, her clinging flesh-colored satin gown no concession to the heat. She was elegant, beautiful, and cool. And Ben Randolph had not one whit of interest in her. After all, he had a wife who possessed the same qualities.

Lily was an expert at intuiting masculine responses. She knew immediately that he was not interested in her, but she was determined to have him. She was tired of the miners and truck drivers, the men with hopes, wishes, and nothing else. She wanted a man with clean hands and the sensitivity to recognize her talents. She wanted a man to move her

back to civilization and make her his mistress, a man who
could afford the clothes her taste dictated. She knew the
type and she knew what he wanted. Unquestionably he had
a wife who dutifully submitted to his lovemaking, making
her disapproval of such behavior quite clear by acquiescing
without participating. Certainly she would never do what
Lily did, or if she tried, she gagged until he shriveled up
and went into the library, removed the panel behind the
family Bible and genealogies, and read his collection of
erotica until dawn or the arrival of a young maid—which-
ever came first.

Upstairs, Moni stood, stretching, and rubbed the small
of her back. She went to the window to look at the sky for
a sign of rain, but her attention was seized by what she saw
parked below: *Isotta Fraschini*. Cannery Row had boasted
no such car, but Moni had torn a picture of one from a
magazine. Someday she intended to drive, and this was the
car she meant to have. It was a berlina transformabile, and
she was going to motor herself to see the world outside the
Row and Nevada. She was going to see some of the places
Vashon talked about; one day she was even going to have a
personal fireside chat with Franklin Delano Roosevelt. But
right now she was going downstairs to see the man who
drove the *Isotta Fraschini*.

Setting the glasses on the pedestal table, Lily expertly
opened the champagne with a soft pop. She slowly filled
both glasses, then picked up the cork and held it to her
ruby lips. Her tongue flicked out, licking at the swollen
head, and her hair fell forward as she rolled the cork lovingly between her hands, swirling it against her lips, gently
nibbling at it with her perfect teeth, circling it again with
her tongue, rubbing it against her face, over her throat,
then bringing it back to her mouth. She did not look at the
man.

From her discreet vantage point behind the screen provided for this purpose, Moni viewed Lily's enticement
ritual, saw the man's appreciation, felt but didn't under-

stand his lack of interest. She also felt but didn't understand a strange quivering within her, a tiny response—to him. She quelled it immediately. She had never seen a gentleman. Oh, yes, there had been some who masqueraded as such, but they were fluff to her bluff. She was no match for this man, and yet she had to do something to secure his patronage. She wanted to see him up close, wanted, just once, to talk to a man such as he. She could learn more from him in ten minutes than Smoky could teach her in a lifetime.

"Lily." Moni's quiet tone and look of dismissal was immediately understood by the philosophy major. Though Lily regretted forfeiting her ticket out, his immunity to her was evident, and the most she could salvage was her pride. "*Au revoir*," she whispered, making a provocative moue at him and tossing the cork in his direction.

Ben Randolph's first thought was how much he wanted to touch the petite redhead, to trace her delicate features with his hand. Her emerald silk dressing gown bore the mark of an expert seamstress; the padded shoulders gave her diminutive stature great presence, the open collar displayed a tantalizing glimpse of her perfect breasts, and the fitted waist and flowing length of the skirt as she swept into the room said she was in command. He knew instinctively that she had not chosen the gown, that someone had cunningly designed it to achieve its effect. Who? A lover? He didn't think so. Another anomaly.

"I'm Moni," she said simply, yet the woman before him was vitally alive. She crackled with energy. There was nothing blasé, nothing pretentious, nothing even politely phony about her. She was savvy, steeped in determination, wise to the ways of the world, and yet somehow innocent. She was the proverbial diamond in the rough, and he was a master gemologist. For an insane moment, Ben Randolph feared for his sanity. He visualized her in more elegant surroundings, a czarina in sable, her green cat eyes glittering like ice castles under the Russian sun. Here was a woman who could curse with the men and sing lullabies to a baby. He saw in her passion for life rather than propriety. The women he knew were molded by tradition, schooled by protective parents, governed by society's mores. It had snuffed the life from them. Not that Ben Randolph despaired of his heritage; on the contrary, his intent was to restore it to its full glory. Civilities, amenities, and comforts were as necessary to him as they were to anyone in his privileged circle, but they had stifled the zest in the women, trapping them in a web of manners and customs and ennui from which there seemed to be no escape. For a while it seemed that the Depression would free them; it brought out their backbone, gave them confidence in their resourcefulness, but they went about it quietly, still deferring to their shattered men. Now that the future appeared a bit brighter they were sinking back into the inertia of dependency. Dependency, he thought, was whoredom of a sort, born of pride and bereft of honesty.

He looked at the redhead before him and cherished her, worshipped her.

Stripped of control, Moni felt uneasy and instinctively extended her small hand.

"I am . . . Ben Randolph," he said, hesitating briefly. His specially designed monogram would not betray him, not here, not anywhere. Ben Randolph was not easily ensnared by his own ineptness or another's expertise.

Moni handed him the glass Lily had filled, nestling the bottle in the ice-filled bucket Vashon must have slipped onto the table. Picking up the other glass, she raised it to him. Ben Randolph studied her as she sipped, his own champagne untouched. Acutely uncomfortable under his scrutiny, Moni spoke first. "What would you like?"

"How much for a night?" he asked, intentionally talking her terms. He wanted her, and he wanted her as herself, not pretending to be someone she wasn't.

"Twenty straight, anything weird is negotiable," she replied, again in command. *They were all the same. They wanted one thing and they wanted to know how much it was going to cost them.* Green eyes taunted blue ones, her body enticed his; a cynical woman suddenly yearned and a powerful man teetered on the brink of an obsession.

Ben gazed deeply into Moni's eyes. "And you? Do you cost more?"

"A lot more."

Ben Randolph reached within his jacket and withdrew his wallet. "Will that cover a few days with you, madam?" He placed five crisp one-hundred-dollar bills next to the champagne bucket.

"That depends" she drawled throatily, "on what you expect for your money."

"Nothing perverted, I assure you; a guarantee of exclusivity is all." And then he smiled at her, a tender, charming, yet sad entreaty, and any thought she'd entertained of refusing him was forgotten. She couldn't exactly reconcile herself to wanting him, but neither would she forgive herself if she let him go.

Moni nodded. Pocketing the money, she picked up the champagne and led the way upstairs to her corner room.

From behind the screen, Vashon smiled. She had witnessed the exchange and she had seen the nod.

Muted twilight and a glistening film of scented sweat was all that sheathed their naked bodies. On him sweat smelled of rare spice and incomparable masculinity. Until this moment, she did not realize how very far she had come from the Row. Until him, she would not have believed it possible that she could actually enjoy the act and have no thought of an end, no thought of capitalizing on the lust she faked so expertly. She certainly wasn't faking now. She'd responded to him naturally and wantonly. Dear God! What had happened? What secret persuasion did this man possess? Whatever it was, it was incredibly subtle, yet very threatening. He rattled her, oh yes he did, but she had the presence not to let him see it.

She slid from between the silk sheets, gliding across the dusky room to the adjoining bath, where she turned on the taps in the tub. "Brandy?" she asked as she slipped into a black kimono and pulled the sash tight with a careless sort of ease.

Ben was impressed. He cupped his hands behind his head and smiled. "Will you join me?"

"If that's what you'd like." She poured two snifters, snuggling his between her breasts to warm it before passing it to him. She touched her sultry lips to her glass to test the liquor's temperature, then bent and transferred the pungent ambrosia from her mouth to his.

He couldn't stop himself. He reached up and grasped the nape of her neck, and in that instant their lips met, clung, and burned into each other, his tongue a key bent on unlocking the fortress.

She was as shaken as if the earth had undergone a massive quake, forever altering the land and the course of the future.

"You are magnificent, Moni," he said hoarsely, nibbling her soft lower lip, then marking her neck with his ardent signature.

Never before had she allowed a man to bruise her flesh or penetrate her defenses. *You make me think I am, Ben,* she thought. "So I've been told," she replied, taking his hand and drawing him up from the bed toward the bath. "Have you ever been bathed in desire? Have you ever been steeped in steam and stroked sure and slow? Have you ever wanted to groan with pleasure and fear you might die from the ecstasy?"

He was mesmerized by her husky contralto, beguiled by the languid sway of her hips as she led him to his second and most binding baptism.

Suddenly Moni wanted this man to make up for all that life had taken from her.

Do you denounce all others but me? She lathered the sponge and began to slick it over his furred chest.

Do you forsake life without me? Her possessive hand cupped his throbbing testicles, massaging, coaxing, demanding a sacrifice.

Do you believe in bliss? Ever so gently she palmed his foot and lowered her lips to his toes, taking them one by one into the warm, moist recess of her mouth and sending electric shocks up through his tense body to his spasming heart.

Do you believe a divine sin and a scarlet woman can give you a glimpse of heaven? Her wet hand slid the length of his manhood, back and forth, back and forth.

Yes, yes, madam, I do. Like Samson for Delilah, Paris for Helen of Troy, Antony for Cleopatra, and King Edward VIII for Mrs. Simpson, lust will make me denounce all others, renounce all else. I do forsake a life that does not include you. I do believe. I have glimpsed heaven, and more than anything in this world or beyond, I want you.

At the exact same instant she released his toes and traced the engorged vein of his erection, he reached up, claimed her firm ass and pulled her, kimono and all, into the tub on top of him. Water spilled over the edge of the footed tub, drenching the tiles and seeping under the door onto the parquet floor of the bedroom beyond.

"This robe is expensive, Ben," she said, laughing.

"I'll buy you ten more. I'll buy you whatever your heart desires. I will satisfy all your needs." He jerked the wet kimono off her shoulders and greedily sucked her ripe nipples until they contracted and peaked with craving.

Everything was wet and slick, but not nearly as slick as the crevice between her thighs to the touch of his probing middle finger.

"Don't do that," she begged. "I don't like it."

"Yes, you do. You're afraid of it, you don't want to relinquish control." He kept it up, moving his finger faster and faster, driving her mad.

"I mean it," she choked. "Stop it! I want to fuck."

"We will. I promise." Ben deliberately slowed, locating

the magical place every woman possesses but few discover. Two could play the game. Weakness it was called. Everyone had a point, everyone was vulnerable. The water swirled. Ben eased deeper beneath the caressing waves, clutching her hips and guiding her up, then inching her down, raising her a bit, then grinding deep, deeper still, until she wanted to cry his name, wanted to clutch him so tight he could never break her hold, wanted to whisper, *You are a canteen of cool New England water; I am the hot, parched sand of the Sierra Nevada. You are an oasis; I am so thirsty that I could not quench myself if I drank of you until there was not a drop left.*

Her words, had she uttered them, would have been inadequate. There was no way to say, *God, I am so hungry. You have put the food on my table, then yanked the plate from me. I have had the aroma of love and never the taste. I have taken all that you have dealt me without asking, but, God, I ask you now, I need, I want, I deserve this man.*

He plunged into her, rotating, withdrawing, entering, until she sobbed.

"Say you want me, Moni! Say I am the best you ever had," he demanded, all the while knowing that like so many before him, he had given his senses over to his balls.

She couldn't find her breath. She couldn't stop the friction of her body against his. But she could, and would, rephrase what it was he wanted to hear.

"You're fantastic, Ben." *You're motion and feeling; you're kind and suave.* "You're ready and so am I. Let's not analyze it. Let's not . . ." As her scalding lips slid down his chest, her thighs squeezed his. "Let's just fuck."

He wanted more. He wanted all of her. He wished to God it wasn't so, he wished he could make her climb his body, could get her out of his system. But she was like the mythology he had studied as a boy. She was Aphrodite, she was Venus, she was the red-haired woman of Nevada. No rhyme, no reason, just lust, gasps, a clinging body seeking release. And he did release her. He moved, turning and pounding her back into the procelain tub. He gyrated and thrust himself deep inside her until her climax became something she could never, no matter how hard she tried, forget.

CHAPTER EIGHT

On October 14, 1944, Field Marshal Rommel was given a choice between a public trial or suicide by poison, with the promise of a state funeral and immunity for his family. On the same day Anne De Ferrers Bennett, called Silver since birth, celebrated her sixth anniversary to Fairfax Bennett by selecting a wardrobe for her upcoming trip. The Desert Fox chose suicide, since the alternative was undeserved shame; the aristocratic blonde chose lightweight wools . . . since Paris could be cool in the fall.

"Fax, darling, who is this Baroness Luedhof you spoke of last evening? I don't believe I have heard of her." Silver's almond-colored eyes didn't betray the stab of jealousy she felt.

"I met her a few years ago in Vienna and dined at her castle before she fled to Paris. She serves as a directress on a board with me. I think you will find her interesting."

Silver stared at Fax's departing back. How would he know who or what would interest her? She knew so little of who he was, or what he did. Oh, yes, she was amply, even lavishly, provided for. Fax had made millions in munitions, magnesium alloys, and nearly everything else from which a legitimate fortune could be made during a war, but there were so many unexplained absences, so many undiscussed meetings, so many unfamiliar associates like this Baroness Luedhof.

"No, no! Place tissue between the folds, stuff the sleeves," she directed as one outfit followed another into her Louis Vuitton trunk.

She should have been elated, but she was depressed. She was not *interesting*. She had not been reared to be interesting; she had been schooled to be proper, to abide by the oh so correct etiquette of an era that was past. Her scintillating activities consisted of serving tea and scones while listening to her friends discuss their first babies and second pregnancies. The only thing she had accomplished was the proper monogramming of her silver and linens. The only item she had missed in the flawless training of her unimpeachable staff was the task Lucette now undertook—packing—so even the servants did not require much of her attention. Fax was absent so frequently that in his presence she felt as if she was only another adornment. He so rarely shared her bed that when he did she believed herself to be only another warm body.

Lucette sensed but couldn't understand madame's discontent. She had everything. "You are so *fortuné*, madame. To go to Paris with Monsieur Bennett." The young girl sighed wistfully, thoughts of her homeland mingling with admiration for her employer.

"Yes, Lucette, I am a fortunate woman," Silver agreed, wondering why she felt so guilty for resenting Fax's ceaseless endeavors to restore not only the Bennett family wealth but that of her parents, the de Ferreres. She was only ten years old when the market crashed, but she remembered what it and the subsequent Depression had done to their families. They'd come of age during the Roaring Twenties, with all the expectations such a time promised, and then were forced to live through the terrible thirties, their inheritances largely diminished, themselves wholly unsuited to the menial ways of earning a living. And so they had gone on, pretending the world hadn't changed. They continued to dress for dinner, but their collars and cuffs had been turned, their dresses cut apart and refashioned into newer styles. Overnight they had aged, become penurious. There was no more joyous laughter, no more lavish entertainment. Silver had been able to attend exclusive Bulwer-Lytton only because the sizeable De Ferrers endowment to the school had not been vested in Wall Street or deposited in the strictly national bank. There were quiet dinners and even quieter bridge games. Each Christmas one bottle was reverently removed from the depleted wine cellar, and one bottle of champagne was chilled for the New Year's Eve toast to a better year. Their one extravagance had been her presentation, and only because so many others were in the same position had it escaped being pitiful.

And so they would have continued had it not been for Fax. Silver *was* grateful. She *was* blessed. She smiled at Lucette. "But you are accompanying us to Paris."

"*Oui*, madame, but it is not the same. It is my role in life to work and it is your role to be a lady."

Fax disliked deceiving Silver. The trip was not to be exclusively the gala round of soirees, dinners, and balls he had led her to expect. It was a working trip, and she shouldn't be accompanying him during this dangerous and uncertain time, but he needed her to camouflage his activities. He was being watched by those purists in certain sectors of Washington who failed to comprehend that the same bank who funded Germany's war effort, the Bank for International Settlement, was also the correspondent for the Federal Reserve Bank, and that Roosevelt's economic sanctions under the Trading With the Enemy Act would produce benefits lasting well beyond the war years.

Prudent men looked to the future welfare of not only their families but their countries. That was true patriotism, that was true loyalty. Money endured, wars did not. He earnestly hoped Silver would enjoy herself. Her safety and amusement were assured, his high-ranking associates would see to that. He *had* neglected her, but he hadn't any choice, for like the De Ferrerses and Bennetts, both the Allied and Axis powers depended on him and his supplies.

CHAPTER NINE

"High dollar, she is," Vashon declared. "Just like her mama."

"Not yet, Vashon," the madam replied, bending and kissing the throbbing soft spot on the child's head. "But one day . . . one day." Her smile was a prophesy.

"You gonna tell him 'bout the chile?" Vashon raised an eyebrow as she smoothed the covers over Moni.

Moni's face hardened. "No," came the quick response. "This child is my responsibility—mine alone."

"Yes'm. It's just . . ." The black woman shuffled her feet and shifted her dark eyes.

"It's just that you're filled with curiosity," Moni supplied, staring out the open window at the highway stretching toward what would soon be the gambling mecca of the North American continent. "You're wondering how a woman as savvy as I am could make such a dumb mistake, why I allowed myself to get knocked up by a john." Again she smiled, only this time her ripe lips curved with a softness Vashon had never before seen. "He's special to me. I wanted to keep a part of him forever. And I have. The men come and they go. They pull on their pants, throw down their money, and walk away. Until him, I never cared. Except for a few, I couldn't even tell you their names, only their preferences and my price. But he was different. I knew it from the first. He's as fragile as I am hard.''

Moni pressed the fussing newborn closer to her heart. "Shh, my love. Mama's only a cry away. I promise you I will never be beyond a whimper from your need." Her pained eyes met those of her only ally, and she attempted to explain. "So . . . I keep a part of him—the best part, I am sure. Can you understand?''

Vashon shook her head. "He's been good to you, Miss Moni. He kept you afloat when you was goin' under. What's more, I think he truly cares 'bout you. Seems like you be making a mockery of his affection. I think you owe—''

"I owe no one! I especially don't owe you an explanation. Take the child. Tend to her and leave me be." Moni turned away as Vashon cradled her new charge and silently retreated toward the door.

"I'm sorry." Moni buried her auburn head in the pillow. "Sometimes I'm a royal bitch. I get paid to be.''

Vashon shrugged. "Don't bother me none, Miss Moni. I know you be twice as hard on yo'self. I surely am taken with this pretty babe. I think I'll spoil her—same as I do her mama.''

"Make sure the house runs smoothly tonight, Vashon. I don't want to be bothered. I'm tired . . . so damn tired.''

"Leave it to me, Miss Moni. Everything's gonna be fine. I'll see to it that the girls don't bicker and the gents behave. Don't think about nothin'. Don't do no good nohow.''

The door clicked softly, but Moni couldn't shut her green eyes, couldn't forget. She couldn't, or maybe she just plain wouldn't, dismiss the soft-spoken, gentle, handsome man who'd rolled over, pulled on his pants, and walked away like all the others. The father of her child.

Because for the first time in her twenty-eight years, Moni truly cared. From the moment he'd walked into her bordello on the outskirts of no-man's-land, she could not let go of him. It had been six months since his last visit, and with each passing day Moni's confidence in his return grew shakier.

Unwittingly, her gaze drifted to the bureau drawer. Inside was her jewelry box, with the gold wedding band Ben had carelessly left behind. She had known he was married for quite some time, but she knew little else about him. His business trips to Nevada were nearly as secretive as his private life, upon which he rarely and only minimally elaborated. Though Moni was curious, she never pried. She hadn't the right.

Her mind wandered. She recalled the lean years when Ben had subsidized her income. Had it not been for his generosity the doors of Moni's Place would have closed. Of course, Ben had had a selfish motive for backing her: to ensure that she remained his exclusive pleasure, involuntarily bound to him by indebtedness. Just as she had a price, so did Ben—understood and on demand.

Then as fate would have it the Japanese had bombed Pearl Harbor and supplied the means by which she could once again become her own mistress. Nellis Air Force Base and Magnesium of Nevada opened to serve the war effort. Fighter pilots and sunburned workers from construction camps filed into her establishment, a windfall in starched khakis and wilted coveralls. They built her bank account, all right, funding her addition to the house, allowing her to triple the staff, but most important, enabling her to invest in other lucrative ventures.

Twice in her life she'd been accused of being frugal and shrewd: first by her father, who'd taught her to play poker as she sat on his knee and was amused when she bluffed with a pair of deuces and then dashed to deposit her winnings in a carnival glass piggybank; then by Smoky, who'd tutored her in daily deposits and was not so amused when his star pupil charged him compounded interest each day he was late on a personal loan.

Frugality and shrewdness, and above all security, meant one thing to her: land. Lots of it, tracts and tracts and tracts. She bought at every opportunity and wouldn't sell at any price. Not yet. Her one risky move had been venturing into a new concept for tourists—motels. The result of that gamble was as yet unknown. Perhaps it was foolish or perhaps it was brilliant.

Again, her eyes fastened on the bureau drawer that held the eighteen-karat memento of Ben. What if his wife or the draft board had claimed him? What if he should never come back? And if he did, how would she explain her daughter? How could she both keep her secret and keep him? Tired, she was so tired of being independent and strong. Don't show what you're thinking; don't show what you're feeling; don't show your heart or soul, because they'll break both if they can. It was the nature of men. It was the way the world went round. God love you if you were male, God help you if you were female. Though the pain and joy of giving birth to a son or daughter was equal, their positions in life were not. *Mother will forgive you most every imperfection, my son; but you, my daughter, I expect to be perfect because I am not and I cannot forgive the imperfection in myself.*

The major chink in her armor was her obsession for Ben Randolph. She knew she'd pay for the privilege of loving him. Women like her always did.

The madam called her Eva. She selected the Hebrew name for its meaning—life, living. It was an appropriate choice. For it would happen that the wee babe of a "dime-a-dance-girl" turned pro would become a famous woman. But that would be many years ahead— in another place, another time. The madam sold her body; her daughter prostituted her soul, never realizing each crucifying word she wrote nailed her to a cathartic

cross. From an elite Las Vegas bordello to a prestigious New York publishing house—what was the difference? Once a whore, always a whore.
                                        —Fast Friends

CHAPTER TEN

The conversation was light, the champagne flowed, the candlelight was soft and the music mellow. Baroness Luedhof's guests were infected with a mad desire to live, to rejoice in the liberation of the city and to restore gaiety to Paris.

Silver was surprised. Fax's assessment of her reaction to the baroness had been correct: Anna was not only interesting but fascinating. She was like the candelabra suspended over the massive dining table—multifaceted and shimmering with a thousand colors. Silver had the feeling that Anna, like the glass prisms, would spin, twirl, and tinkle harmoniously with the wind, always brilliant, always pleasing to behold, but never predictable. The only difference was that Silver could see through the crystal. She could not see through the baroness. She doubted anyone could.

Anna looked down the length of her Louis XV table and the blurred faces of her guests to engage the passionate black eyes of Sasa Bailesti, thinking him to be the most exciting man in the room. Feeling her compelling stare, Sasa continued to carry on a conversation with the twittering ladyship on his left but raised his glass to his *libérateur*.

The exchange was subtle; the vivid memories it conjured were not. Both recalled the pivotal crossing of their paths.

Franz, the baroness's wine steward, was a fanatical member of the Resistance. Into his care was given one escaped and delirious Rom Gypsy, smuggled into France three months before De Gaulle's Free French troops marched through the Arc de Triomphe to the cheers of the crowd. Though Franz had tried to conceal the feverish stowaway in the wine cellar, Anna had suspected something and had pushed her way into the dank space to discover Sasa lying there . . . half dead and babbling nonsense. He moaned and called for Stephania, then thrashed and begged for a slice of bread or a drop of water.

Anna had been appalled that any human being, especially one under her own roof, could be so neglected. "Why do you ignore this man's agony? Help me strip these stinking rags from him. Get me broth and bread from the kitchen. Be quick and discreet."

Franz froze.

"Do you think I haven't known of your underground activities? Go, and go *now*. Every moment you waste, this man loses life."

For two nights and three days, Anna had gone to the cellar to sop the bread in broth and dribble the life-giving nourishment between Sasa's blistered lips. On the night before his fever broke, he had opened his glazed eyes and held out a trembling hand. As she gripped his bruised and scarred flesh, a mixture of compassion and possessiveness stole over her.

"I fear you are a dream, perhaps an angel who comes to guide me on a journey I long to travel," he whispered.

"I am not an angel, my friend. And the journey you will take is only to renewed strength and better days. I think you will survive whether you wish to or not. And I think you shall be glad, although you may not now believe so."

On the following day, the baroness and Franz transferred Sasa to her private suite. There she nursed him, rehearsed him, and secretly lusted for him. He was too vital a man to be wasted, too sensitive to be shared. He represented the cause she had longed to flaunt in the faces of the Nazi butchers. He also had the potential to be the consort she required: he was mystical, she was practical.

Most women would have found it difficult, if not impossible, to fabricate a background that even the most cynical of her peers would accept and believe. But not the baroness. She invented an imposing lineage, produced a title, and introduced the Gypsy as Duke Sasa Bailesti.

Anna returned her counterfeit duke's salute. The wine upon her tongue was rare and heady, the man at the opposite end of her table was rarer still and more intoxicating than the fine Chablis. He owed her his very life, and she intended to capitalize on his indebtedness: he would share not only her bed, but her life. The emaciated creature whom she had discovered in the wine cellar had mended handsomely, vintage beyond her expectations.

The baroness intended to marry the duke.

The baroness was not the only woman captivated by the dark Gypsy. From the duke's right, Silver witnessed the interchange between Sasa and Anna. She alone of all the guests saw the slight quiver of his glass as he silently toasted their hostess. She alone felt the faint movement of the tablecloth as his legs tensed. Something was not as it should be. She had heard Anna's tale of royal blood and dispossession, but there was a hint of suffering about him, a slightly haunted look, and though he seemed to be charged with energy there was something in his carriage that didn't speak of ease, but instead of anguish.

Anna leaned toward her guest of honor. "Fax, your wife

is beautiful—and, I suspect, fragile. Fragile things need to be protected, sheltered. Do you not agree?''

"And do you shelter the duke?''

"In more ways than one. He, too, needs protection.''

"I thought as much.''

"But he is a knowledgeable and charming escort. If you have no objections, perhaps he can entertain the lovely Silver while we pursue more serious matters.'' The pointed look she shot him was not misconstrued.

"An excellent idea.'' Fax adroitly extracted an escargot from its shell, and swirling it in the Madeira sauce, he studied his wife. Her pale cheeks were flushed, her eyes shining. For a moment he wished to trade places with the duke, to have known that spark of discovery upon meeting, that spontaneous combustion. Perhaps familiarity had neutered their response to one another. They had never experienced that magical chemistry. Fax assessed the other guests. How many ''perfect'' marriages were a travesty? How many imperfect affairs were a remedy?

Silver tilted her hat at a smart angle and slicked another coat of burnt sienna gloss across her lips, blotting them once more. Then she stood, fingered the soft wool cape that matched her cardinal red dress, and draped it across her bodice and over one shoulder. "Fax, darling, would you help with this pin?'' Silver extended the polished jet brooch. She hoped his touch might linger, that her arousal might be contagious, that he might say, ''I'd rather undress you''—that he might in fact do just that and take her then and there, wildly, repeatedly.

"There, will that do?''

His hands did not tarry and her high hopes did not materialize. Blinking, she rallied with a smile and a nod. No, that will not do. I want more, so much more, but you never notice. ''I'm concerned that I'm imposing on the duke.''

Fax leaned over the desk, redlining a contract. ''I hardly think he would find you an imposition, dear. Wasn't it his suggestion to picnic today?''

Yes, but I know perfectly well who orchestrated it. "Perhaps he wants a breath of fresh air more than my company. We've seen every museum, gallery, and cathedral in Paris. I think we have absorbed all the culture we care to." *And what have you been absorbing, my dear husband? What role are you playing in Paris? What have you gained from this war?*

"Haven't you been enjoying all the dinners and parties and dances, Silver? You looked to be having a grand time." He momentarily abandoned the contract and reached for his tobacco pouch.

When have you been there long enough to see how I looked? "Yes, Fax, it is fun, but I can't help but feel guilty."

For once, she managed to claim his attention.

"What on earth do you have to feel guilty about, Silver?" he asked.

She felt self-conscious. So seldom did she express an opinion; so rarely was he interested. "Do you ever give a thought to this war, Fax? Does it bother you? I had no idea what it was all about. I'm afraid my conception was a naive, romanticized version, the atrocities something sad I had read or heard about. Oh, yes, I helped roll bandages in the safety of my home while sipping sherry and gossiping, but I never pictured their destination, never visualized the wounds they would bind. I cannot condone all this frivolity when so many are suffering, Fax. It just isn't right. We are living in this luxurious suite while others are crammed into boxcars. We eat caviar while others starve to death. My clothes cost thousands of dollars while others are naked and freezing." She moved toward him willing a response. *I don't want my suspicions confirmed. I don't want to know that my extravagances are paid for with others' blood.* "Tell me, Fax, don't you believe there will be a day of reckoning for people like us?"

Though the unexpected appeal pricked his conscience, his expression remained placid. This wasn't the first time during the trip that she had shown curiosity about his associations and dealings, but she was becoming more insistent on answers, and it was bothersome. He had liked it better when her only concern was whether or not she would conceive each month. "Silver, dear, if a trio like Churchill, Roosevelt, and Stalin can't resolve this problem, what makes you think we can? Devastation is a result of war, but without war even more humanity is destroyed, through lost rights and forfeited countries. The price we pay is steep, I agree, but to relinquish all would be staggering. Some die, some profit, but ultimately the future is secured for the generations to come."

If you never come to my bed there will be no future generations to benefit from your righteous profit. Silver did not respond.

For a long moment, Fax focused on a point beyond her. "Do I believe there will be a day of reckoning? Yes, and it is then that those who now profit can do the most good, for it is they who will be responsible for rebuilding the ravaged countries, reestablishing the economy, and reshaping a better world for us all."

That isn't what I wished to hear. You have practically admitted your complicity and managed simultaneously to make it all sound so virtuous, the same as when you declare your love and yet neglect me.

"Profit is not totally devoid of honor, Silver."

And neither are you.

"A better world for us *all*, Fax?" she asked him. Her posture was rigid, her almond eyes accusing. "I must go. The duke is waiting." She brushed by him, retrieving her black kid gloves and bag from the desk. For the first time ever, she neglected to bestow her customary kiss upon his cheek.

For the first time ever, he noticed. He stood for a stunned second, staring after her. Perhaps she was actually pregnant. Why else would she be behaving so temperamentally? Dismissing the thought, he returned his attention to the munitions contract before him, again redlining, again trading with both the Germans and the Bolsheviks.

CHAPTER ELEVEN

The shrill factory whistle was music to Norma Mae's ears. Lord, but she would be glad to get off her feet and the hell out of here. A quick change of clothes and she could be down having a beer at Ed's Place, which oughta now be called Maureen's Place, because she was arunnin' it while Ed was off fighting Japs. Last Maureen had heard, Ed had the dysentery, which wasn't too surprising, considering how full of shit he'd always been. Maybe he'd come home cured. If he came home at all. She wished to God someone would come home. She was sick to death of dancing with women and 4-Fs.

"Hey, Grace, you going for a cool one?"

"Naw, this was my second shift. I've got to sleep, and the kids need me."

Norma Mae didn't think she'd ever have no whining, sassing kid. All they did was drain your spirit and your pocketbook. And Grace's figure didn't look so hot after three, neither. Matter of fact, she looked kind of like a pear. No, Norma Mae thought, she'd just keep her money and her pointed breasts and be the cat's meow the rest of her natural life.

"Norma Mae, wait up a sec, will ya?"

Oh, Lordy, it was Beanpole, with his little teeny tiny dick. She'd seen him round back sneaking a leak last week, and it had been all she could do not to laugh out loud. He was always following her about, slobbering, his eyes half wild. "What is it you want, Beanpole?"

"You wanna work an extra shift next week? I can put you on. All you got to do is jes be nice to me, *real* nice— know what I mean?"

"Yeah, you want me to hold your teeny tiny tally-whacker while you take a whiz. Go to hell, Beanpole. I don't got time for the likes of you. Lord, I wish there was somebody left 'round here besides the old and the infirm."

Norma Mae sashayed off, swinging her lunch pail and rotating her hips.

Beanpole hurried to catch up. "Why ya always be being so uppity, Norma Mae? You act like yours is the only piece of ass in town."

"Ain't nobody had it yet, Beanpole." Norma Mae struck a haughty pose. "I'm saving myself for a gentle-man."

"You think they fuck any better?"

"Maybe, maybe not." Norma Mae reached the factory gate. Beanpole's cackle didn't faze her in the least. She swiveled her behind suggestively. Let him go coop himself up in the john and drool all over his girlie magazines. She *was* going to get a gentleman. But right now she was going to get a beer.

CHAPTER TWELVE

The woodlands of the Bois de Boulogne had once been a dueling field where honor was redeemed, and a park where royalty cavorted, a place of trysts and treason, of minstrels and magic. It was all long past, but still the mood lingered, even to this sunny, breezy day.

The duke had a great need to redeem his honor, while Silver wanted for just one afternoon to foresake the image that bound her to Fairfax Bennett VI. Perhaps the Bois de Boulogne was still a place of trysts and treason; there were no longer any minstrels, but there was definitely magic.

As they lingered on the banks of the lake, Sasa wove a spell. It wasn't the first time. His dark eyes mesmerized, as they had that day at Montparnasse, the looks they exchanged potent, direct yet evasive, seeking yet denying, fleeting yet lingering, innocent yet guilty. His fingers laced with hers were warm and intimate, gentle yet possessive.

Both sought to escape the past and banish the future.

Silver's claim that she might be an imposition on the duke had been merely an excuse. A woman knew when a man was enchanted, knew when he was in need, knew when he was obsessed. But this man was different. *He* was the enchantment, the need, the obsession she wished to God she could deny. And yet he had said not one word that might substantiate her feelings. It was still an affair of the mind, sinless, yet the most dangerous sort of liaison. How had a practical woman such as she become so enraptured? Maybe it was all the product of an overactive imagination. After all, Sasa was European and by his very nature demonstrative, whereas she was a conservative American, by her nature, reserved.

He neatly sliced a wedge of Brie and held it to her lips. She hesitated. The offering was symbolic, and they both knew it.

"It is the finest. You will find it pleasing. Taste of it, Silver," he coaxed.

It was pleasing, and so was he. God help her, but as hard as she tried she could not deny that this man—this weaver of dreams, this poet, this utter temptation who had invaded her mind and troubled her conscience—was asking for admittance.

Daintily, she accepted his offering, smiling invitingly. She was totally out of character, but then so was the whole damn world.

"Who are you, Sasa Bailesti?" she heard herself saying. "I know you pretend."

He glanced away. "If I told you, would it matter?"

"Yes. I sense that you are not what you seem, and that Anna Luedhof protects you. You are playing a role, just as I am."

"Does your role suit you, Silver?"

"I don't know. It's the only part I've ever played." A wistful look crossed her face.

Sasa reached for her hand. "It is hard, is it not, to be another's marionette?"

In the intimacy of the Bois, free of the constraints that normally bound them, feelings were exposed, stripped of preense, polish, and amenities. Somewhere there was a common meeting ground, one they dared not explore but could not deny. It loomed between them, touched them, drew hem in.

Against the faint chirping of birds only the clink of their forks upon the Baroness's fine Limoges betrayed their houghts. Suddenly the act of eating became a sensuous enactment of the mating ritual, and it was then that Silver's poise failed her.

"Sasa, am I crazy, or do you not feel guilty that we, you and I, should have so much while all around us is this unbearable suffering?"

For a long moment he looked at her, unable to speak. Did he dare explain? Then suddenly, he had to. He wanted to tell this woman, for he believed she would understand. He longed to reveal his past without fear of censure or exposure.

"There hasn't been a day that I have not wished for my death, prayed for it even, yet clung to each hope, each drop of water, each crumb of bread, each offered hand. I feel guilty for surviving." At Silver's horrified look, he rushed on, his silence broken. "I was married. We lived in Romania. My wife had people in Vienna and she longed to see them. I did not refuse her—I never could. But there was a problem. We were both Roms, Gypsies, which meant there was no assurance of safe passage, but we went anyway. I did not know Stephania was pregnant. We managed to reach our destination, but then the pogroms started, and we were discovered hiding and sent to Dachau. They put us in the family camp. The barracks were long windowless buildings, with holes in the front and back for doors, and there were horses and the ground inside was ankle-deep with stable slime and rotting bodies stacked five and six high. Somehow Stephania survived to give birth, and our baby girl was immediately tattooed on her upper thigh. But there was no food and Stephania had no milk, and so our baby died."

Sasa stopped, unable to continue. Silver yearned to

touch him, hold him, soothe away his hurts, but she could not.

"At one end of the barrack there was a curtain," he began again. "They threw our baby on a pile of children's bodies and the rats crawled over her."

A gasp escaped Silver's lips.

"That very day they came and took Stephania to sterilize her, which they did by surgery, but they never sewed her up. After four days of agony poor Stephania died. I escaped sterilization. I cheated death by crawling out of a mass grave and made it out of Dachau on my belly. Why couldn't I save her? Why did she die? Why do I live?"

Silver looked into Sasa's eyes. Tears streamed from her own. She hadn't wanted Fax to fight in this war, but that he should have avoided it, even profited by it, while Sasa endured so much pain was intolerable. She had no answers for him, only compassion and forbidden love.

They were separated by a crust of bread, a slab of cheese, and two champagne glasses, far removed from Dachau but bound by it just the same. This was the moment for them; there would never be another. And they both knew it.

Tentatively, she reached for his hand. "Tomorrow Fax takes me back to Montauk Point and my sheltered life. I will never see you again."

"Silver." Her name was a groan upon his lips, but it came straight from his very essence. *He was condemned to love one woman and marry another.* "Though Anna is also a *gaje*—a non-Gypsy—she helped me survive. Without her, I would have perished. Honor dictates that I must marry her. But this one afternoon . . . this millisecond of eternity . . . belongs to us."

Silver drew his hand to her breast that he might feel the beating of her heart. Gently she kissed his fingertips, releasing them as they carefully brushed against the cardinal wool of her cape and unfastened the jet brooch Fax had secured hours before, removing her outer layers as he had stripped away his own masquerade.

In the grass of the Bois de Boulogne, beneath a lavender sky, Sasa wove a Gypsy spell around them, tales of happier times, legends of love and life and laughter. And Silver heard music—one moment a melancholy serenade, the next, a carefree tune—and understood his spirit, his need to be free, the passions that drove him.

As the setting sun cast long shadows on the red cape, Silver's ivory satin lingerie was crushed beneath their naked bodies. For this one golden moment they defied the future, but time was closing in on them.

In the Pacific, the Japanese resorted to kamikaze missions. Desperation it was called—a chance to regain one's pride.

Time wasn't just closing in on Sasa and Silver, the sun was setting on an era.

CHAPTER THIRTEEN

On April 28, 1945, Benito Mussolini and his blonde mistress, Clara Petacci, were captured by Italian partisans while trying to flee to Switzerland. Il Duce and his young *amore*, their bodies riddled with bullets and crusted with blood, were strung up by their ankles in Milan's main square.

Just minutes before the stroke of midnight on that same day, in a bunker below the burning city of Berlin, Adolf Hitler's loyal companion, Eva Braun, appropriately attired in a black silk dress, became his wife. The ring the defeated Führer slipped onto her third finger was too large, as had been his insane ambition for the Third Reich. The vows they exchanged were merely a formality, for a suicide pact had already been sealed between the Führer and Frau Hitler.

By April 30, 1945, all that remained of Mussolini and Hitler was an indelible stain upon history. The women who had shared their beds, booty, and triumphs also shared the brutal finale of their tyrannical reigns.

On that same date, Ben Randolph finally and without warning made a return visit to his mistress.

Though Moni had sworn she would shun him if and when he ever patronized her house again, she immediately fell victim to his apologetic smile and her undeniable desire.

Once in the privacy of her room, the months of need and anger fell away. All that mattered was fever, fusion, and the fuck of a lifetime.

In an instant they were sprawled on the bed, tearing at one another's clothes, their mouths searching, their tongues seeking, their bodies bucking. Grasping handfuls of her hair, Ben slammed her back upon the mattress, kissing her so savagely she tasted blood.

Wildly, she fought to free him from his trousers, working them down his grinding hips and over his muscled buttocks. His huge hard-on sprang free from his shorts and Moni's mouth closed hungrily around him, but he pushed her head away, rolled over, and lifted her so that her muff was at his lips, his cupped hands working her up and down upon his thrusting tongue.

Moni ground herself against his face, his five o'clock shadow chafing her inner thighs. This time there was no fear of losing control, there was only the desire for gratification and oblivion.

"That's it, Moni, ride me, ride me!" His voice was ragged. "You taste so good." Ben had never tasted anything as sweet as Moni. It was succor, it was nectar, it was life.

His fingers feathered her wet sheath, then slipped into her rectum. He was everywhere, his touch a lighted match, her need a tinderbox.

She, who had pleasured so many, who had given them what they wanted, what they needed, what they asked for, what they paid for, was taking. For the first time in her life, she was demanding something besides money, something beyond response. Then Ben was on top of her and

Moni writhed and panted, and sought release. As he pushed against her, she rose to meet him. She was the lock, he was the key. Turn, twist, thrust, shift. She opened herself entirely, drawing him in, begging him to take her, suck the breath from her, consume her. She wanted to be filled. For once an orgasm was all-important; his, hers—what did it matter? Heave, hold on, grind, withdraw, push, pull, contract, expand, brand, claim, claw, bite. Who cared? There were no lines, no rules; there was only a blur, a blues, a wail, a need that demanded release.

Moni turned and tongued his ass. *Surrender, surrender, surrender.*

On May 5, 1945, Wernher von Braun surrendered to the Americans, launching the U.S. space program, and Moni was maneuvered into introducing her child to Ben, setting into motion a charade of the most protective sort.

Vashon cradled Eve against her chest. As far as she was concerned Eve *was* part hers. It wasn't blood and it wasn't color that bound mother and child, it was love. Love for the mama, love for the babe, love for life. And Eve exuded spirit and sunshine—Nevada sunshine. Her cry said . . . "Feed me, keep me warm and safe, love me." And how Vashon did love her. But there was a man in the room upstairs who needed Evie even more, a man who never revealed his weakness for love, a man who came for release and was bound instead, a man who needed to know what a fine babe he had sired. And Vashon intended to show him. If he was fool enough to miss the likeness, then she wouldn't tell him.

She knocked on the door, closing her hand over Eve's Cupid's-bow mouth. "Shh! Sweet baby, you is gonna meet yo' daddy for the first time. He and Miss Moni jus' like that lullaby I always be asingin' you. *Yo' daddy's rich and yo' momma she's good-looking. So hush, little baby, don't you cry.*"

"Come in." Ben adjusted the sheet over his hips and doubled the pillow beneath his head.

"Afternoon, Mister Ben," Vashon said pertly. "Lordy, but this room is a mess." Her dark eyes surveyed the disheveled quarters. "Here, let me plump yo' pillow." Knowing Vashon's bent for tidiness, Ben clung to the crumpled sheet for dear life. Before he knew what was happening, she gently placed the sunsuited six-month-old upon his chest. Vashon yanked the pillow from beneath his head and pounded and pummeled it, then unceremoniously grabbed the nape of his neck and jammed it back under him. "Well, that's better, I'm sure," she prattled.

The babe upon his chest wriggled and cooed, tangling her tiny fist in his blond chest hair.

He started, wincing, and tried awkwardly to hold onto the squirming copper-haired infant. "Ah, ah . . . what is this, Vashon?" he cried.

"Why that's a baby, Mister Ben. You know. They wets, they cries, they eats, they sleeps. Then they grows up and breaks yo' heart." She shot a sly look in his direction as she busied herself collecting the clothes that were strewn about the room. "But don't worry none. She's fresh-diapered, just been fed—and I'll just bet yo' all out of ice. I'll get you some." She hurried toward the door.

"No—here, *wait*." He tried to pry the baby from his chest, but her chubby bare feet caught the sheet, exposing him. Fortunately, Vashon was already in the hall.

Easing onto his side, Ben cradled the baby in the crook of his arm and really looked at her for the first time. Her burnished curls nestled against his arm, and for a brief moment he allowed himself the luxury of sentimentality. He placed his forefinger within her grip and instantly the tiny fingers brought it to her gums. Kicking and gurgling, she gnawed her way into his heart. She was a born enchantress. But then, so was Moni. Only a fool wouldn't have seen the resemblance. She was a miniature replica of her mother.

"Ben, darling . . ." Moni's words trailed off at the sight

of Eve in the arms of her father. Suddenly, she detested Lincoln and his Emancipation Proclamation, for she'd like nothing better than to sell Vashon to the first unsuspecting bidder at auction.

"She's yours, isn't she?"

Ours. "That wasn't hard to guess. Yes, she's mine." Gathering every gram of strength within her, Moni determined to play this role to the final curtain. She had made it to Nevada, she had made it when Moni's Place only had three customers a week, and she by God could make it through this, the ultimate test. Yet she could not resist the one and only chance she might ever have to feel what it would be like if she were not the madam of a whorehouse and he were not a married man. Going to the bed, she let her gold lamé caftan fall to the floor and slipped beneath the sheet. Moni extended a forefinger to Eve, who clasped it with her free hand, and brought it to join Ben's. Perhaps, Moni thought, it would be the only time in Eve's life that she embraced her mother and father at once.

She could feel Ben watching her, feel him withdrawing, though he did not move. *He's going to ask, he's going to ask, and what will I say?*

He caught her arm, his grasp bruising her. "Who is the father, Moni? Who do you service besides me? I thought I paid for an exclusive arrangement."

The idyllic moment was shattered. Moni climbed out of bed and pulled the caftan on quickly. "What does it matter?" She poured a brandy and tossed it down. "I had no guarantee you would return." Wordlessly she opened the bureau drawer, extracted his gold wedding band, and threw it at him.

"I would have sent it, but women in my position aren't privy to addresses."

As Ben's hand snaked out to catch his ring, she inwardly cursed herself and her weakness. It had been dangerous to pretend she had a right to loving feelings, normal desires, a fickle flash of family bliss.

Eve's eyes followed the shiny object. She reached for Ben's hand, futilely trying to take it from him.

Ben put the baby down gently, then stood and replaced the ring on his finger. Naked, he strode to Moni, backhanding the glass and hurling it against the wall, sending shards of crystal flying and a spray of golden liqueur onto the pretty wallpaper. "She may not be mine, but you are. No one, nothing can change that." His mouth closed possessively over hers.

Moni broke free of his grip and raced for her daughter, rescuing Eve from a near spill onto the floor, which was scattered with broken glass. "Damn it, Ben, not now."

"Here's yo' ice, Mister Ben, and it looks to me like you sho' 'nuf be needin' some coolin' off." Vashon pranced into the room. "Ain't she a fine baby? Don't you worry none, Miss Moni, I be gettin' a dustpan and broom after dat glass. All the racket goin' on in here scarin' this chile to death." Vashon snatched Eve from Moni's arms and pranced out as purposely as she'd come in, soothing Eve with the lullaby's louder-than-usual lyrics: "*One of dese mornings you're gonna rise up singin', then you'll spread your wings and you'll take to the sky; until dat morning there ain't nothin' gonna harm you, so hush, little baby, don' you cry.*"

In the late afternoon heat, desperation turned to passion, carnal rituals brought release, and accusations gave way to apologies.

"He must be very special, Moni." Ben cradled her head against his neck, hiding his tormented face, muffling his words.

"As you are, Ben."

The madam's heart broke, but her will did not.

CHAPTER FOURTEEN

Two sets of glaring headlights came to a stop twenty feet from the New Jersey state line. Two doors slammed, two pairs of regulation black shoes sandwiched a pair of shiny red ones. The limp form of a Negro being dragged by a couple of Philadelphia beat cops was silhouetted in the harsh mustard light.

"You motherfuckers gonna pay for this." Then the black's head hit the ground, and he couldn't summon so much as a curse.

"Nobody holds out on us, especially nigger trash like you! We warned you, spade, but you're too damn greedy for your own good. You don't look so pretty anymore, asshole."

The regulation black shoes cracked his ribs. Pain splintered through his chest, knocking the breath from him.

"You dumb double-crossing cocksucking coon. Did you think we wouldn't catch you holding out? You think that piece of black meat between your legs is so good your whores wouldn't rat on you? You're a whore, prick. Our whore. And you know what happens to whores who renege? This, you son of a bitch.''

A nightstick whacked across his groin. He doubled up, vomiting. Another baton rammed his kidneys. A sickening moan echoed in the night as he lay face down in his own sour puke. He writhed in agony, then his bladder exploded and hot piss saturated his flashy clothes.

"You better kill me, cause I'll be back," he groaned.

"Yeah, when you're governor." They hauled him, half conscious now, across the state line. "You show up in Philadelphia again and you're dead. That's a promise."

The taller of the two officers turned the black man's pockets inside out, taking the roll of cash he'd fleeced from his stable of sluts. Their footsteps faded, their laughter grew fainter, and he began to believe he might survive.

Yellow headlights bore down on him. He tried to roll out of the way, but could not move. At the last second the tires screeched to a halt inches from his head.

"Just to show you how charitable we can be, we're gonna leave you the means to get the hell out of Pennsylvania. If you got any brains left, you'll drive south until you run out of road. So long, you stupid bastard."

The red convertible swerved across the center line and into the oncoming lane. Barely conscious, he jerked the wheel to the right, fighting double vision and narrowly escaping a head-on collision with a Pfeiffer's beer truck. The sweat that coursed down his body chilled him, and he pulled off onto the shoulder, shifted into neutral, and set the brake. He ran the back of his arm across his forehead, then wiped the perspiration and blood on his shirt. He felt his ribs, rubbed his kidneys and scratched at his piss-chapped legs, shaking his head. Those motherfuckers weren't going to get the best of him. He had *insurance*.

Unlatching the glove box, he retrieved an envelope-size leather folio and carefully untied its straps. In one side was his primary stash of cash; in the other, the ripped-out page from the orphanage records, to which had been pasted his birth certificate. The money would take him as far as he needed to travel; the papers would take him as high as he ever wanted to go. And that, he thought, just might be the exclusive old Bryn Mawr area outside Philadelphia, that stuck-up place where debutantes didn't dally with darkies.

His head lolled against the door. He licked his dry lips, cursing the crooked flatfoots for looting his liquor. He could almost taste the confiscated sloe gin. Seemed like all of his life he'd been thirsty, for booze, for women. For light skin and white power.

He'd always been caught between two worlds, never fitting in either. He wasn't white, he wasn't black, he wasn't legitimate. What he was was an enterprising bastard who had done his research. From the orphanage records he'd gleaned his parents' names; in the streets he'd found his father; and in the society columns he'd read about his mother.

His old man was a heroin addict—a main-liner—and his mother was mainline elite. Yeah, Booker T. Cooles wasn't going to be of much use to him on his rise up, but Buffy Chadds-Ford's connections would be.

CHAPTER FIFTEEN

On August 6, 1945, a United States Air Force plane called the *Enola Gay* dropped an atomic bomb on Hiroshima, leaving death and destruction in its fiery wake. The blast was tantamount to twenty thousand tons of TNT, and the frightful new weapon forever altered the dimensions of war. Silver Bennett, listening to the news as she endured labor in the canopied bed every Bennett had been born in since 1649, was afraid the birth of her child might very well demolish the carefully woven tapestry of their lives.

An ornate ceiling fan whirred ineffectively above the canopy as her well-intentioned but wholly incompetent mother-in-law mopped her brow. In addition to herself, there were thirteen people and the blaring radio in the easternmost wing of the mansion. All her friends had delivered their babies in a hospital, but it would never do for the next Bennett–De Ferrers heir to be born in such a place. So here she was, bereft of sterile surroundings and brisk efficiency—not to mention privacy—being subjected to the suffocating ministrations of two servants, one nurse, Mr. and Mrs. John De Ferrers IV, Mr. and Mrs. Fairfax Bennett V, her regular obstetrician, the family doctors of both the de Ferrerses and Bennetts, the Episcopalian priest—on the Bennett side—her dearest friend, Buffy Chadds-Ford, and Fax.

At the moment they were engaged in a lively discussion about the merits of the new bomb and the primary nationality of the next Bennett baby, who had the dubious privilege of becoming the first grandchild on either side. Having agreed to disagree on the bomb, they promptly compromised on the obvious English-French ancestral split and proceeded directly into a debate concerning the most suitable school for the unborn child. It was absolutely amazing, in retrospect, that she had been allowed to consummate her marriage without all of them present.

Had they known Silver's thoughts, they would have jumped one by horrified one into the Atlantic and let themselves be swept away. For Silver was fantasizing about escaping with her baby to a Gypsy encampment, bonfires blazing, tambourines tinkling, a fortune-teller pointing to the stars, saying, "The sun is in Leo. The laurel plant governs Leo. The child will be crowned with the wreath of fame."

For a brief space, Silver imagined she saw Sasa's dark eyes, filled with pride and unrestrained joy, laughing over her. She clutched the hand-embroidered linen sheet.

Always and forever Silver would see Sasa's flashing eyes, laughing, dancing. To the end of her days they would light her soul and damn her life. But she *could* hold the vision of his face before her now, she *could* remember his suffering, and he would inspire her to be brave. She would not scream or whimper, yell or shout, no matter how intense the pain. She would fight the doctors when they tried to give her a whiff of ether. She could afford the small price of holding him in her mind, but she dared not risk calling out his name.

Another contraction. Silver gasped. A hush fell over the observers. There was perspiration on Fax's brow. Irrationally Silver hated him for it; *he* wasn't having this baby. Detached, she inventoried the fair-haired, ivory-complexioned people, whose pale beauty matched her own finely chiseled features, and then suppressed an urge to laugh. For she, Anne "Silver" De Ferrers Bennett, of royal descent, who could trace her lineage back to the Emperor Charlemagne—on the legitimate side—was about to give birth to the child of a Romany Gypsy.

"Lauren. Lauren." Silver tested it softly, reverently, then louder, until the room rang with the sound of it and the inky-eyed infant girl stretched, yawned, and snuggled against her mother's breast, her tiny fist curling around the rattle Fax placed in her hand.

Born of a mother called Silver, recipient of a father's precious Paul de Lamerie heirloom, the Bennett heiress was launched on a sterling life.

Her maman called her Laura—derived from laurel— to be honored with a mark of distinction, excellence: a victor. It, too, was an appropriate choice. For it would happen that the aristocrats' daughter, who knew all the right moves, all the right words, all the right people and places, would exploit the jet-set life that others envied— but only after she paid the price, only after she survived a secret that should have been forever kept. She would challenge life to the fullest, soaring over its peaks and surviving the valleys of self-destruction.
—Fast Friends

CHAPTER SIXTEEN

Seven months after Lauren's birth, Sasa Bailesti looked at Anna's swollen stomach and wished for all the world he were back in Calarasi, Romania, sleeping under the stars.

He strolled out onto the balcony and breathed deeply of the night air. He might be royalty in the world's eyes, but he was a Gypsy in his soul.

He prayed that his son—for he knew it would be a boy—would know the joy of spending at least one night under the stars.

CHAPTER SEVENTEEN

Things sure had changed this year. First, President Roosevelt up and died and old Harry got himself sworn in, then the war ended and all the men came home, which normally would have thrilled her, but Beanpole had replaced Norma Mae with a returnee at the factory, and now she was just barely surviving on the pay from her new job at Allen's Drugstore outside of Memphis. Her meager wages barely kept a body in paint and powder, let alone nail polish.

She thought she'd be getting a raise 'cause old man Allen was getting a rise outta her. He was always touching her, one way or another, and when she bent over in the back room, he was arubbin' against her. She could feel his hard thing, and to tell the truth, it always gave her a rush. Yesterday she'd figured out there was a way to make more money and when she'd bent over and he started rubbin' against her, she turned around and touched him, real bold like. Didn't take him a flat second to unzip his pants and push his swollen thing into her mouth. Liked to have choked her to death those first few seconds, till she got the rhythm of it, and then she kinda liked it. It made her wet between her legs. Last night he'd come around to the shack in the middle of Dogtown, flaunting his fancy new car and asking if she'd come help with inventory. She'd been wanting to ride in that car anyway, so she went. But they hadn't done no inventory, whatever that meant. They'd gone straight out to the country and she'd sucked him off like he asked, and then he'd heaved and panted all over her, saying how her skin was like peaches 'n cream and her pussy was all tight and juicy. Yessiree, she felt pretty certain she'd be getting a raise today. He'd practically promised.

Lord, but it was hot. Just a burning day in Memphis. Even the flies was too hot to switch sugar jars, just sat there scraping their legs. Norma Mae stuck a cylindrical holder over the pointed stack of paper cups and fixed herself some ice water and drank it right there behind the soda fountain. She wasn't quite sure enough of her position yet to have a lemonade. Maybe tomorrow. As she chewed a piece of ice, she looked up.

Parked halfway on the sidewalk was the finest, shiniest red convertible that had ever hit Tennessee. It fairly shimmered in the sunlight. There was just a bunch of chrome on it and a big ornament up on the hood. Made Mister Allen's car look like nothing. Lord, she would give her eyeteeth to ride in such a fine car.

"Want to ride in it?"

Norma Mae looked up in surprise. She hadn't seen anyone come in, and here he was, sitting on a stool, looking for all the world like he had every right to be there. Now there was gonna be trouble for sure. He was light, real light, but still a nigger. Didn't sound like any nigger she'd ever heard, though. Sounded Yankee.

"How about a lemonade?" He put a twenty-dollar bill on the marble counter.

Her voice was barely audible. "Can't serve you."

He pushed the twenty closer. "You can keep the change."

Norma Mae looked at the twenty. It'd buy lots of nail polish, lots of movie magazines. She could get one of them new halter tops. He wasn't very dark, and no one was here. Just one lemonade wouldn't hurt.

He was nearly finished, the change from the twenty in her apron pocket. It was her lucky day. And if she got a raise, too . . .

"Git your black ass outta here, boy!"

Lord, it was *Mister Allen*. Now he was pointing his finger at her. "You! You git outta here too, and don't never come back. I don't need no nigger lovers mooning 'round here."

Norma Mae stood outside the drugstore. She was getting out of this town, going someplace—any place. She had nearly twenty dollars, plus the two dollars old man Allen had given her for wages. She'd take a bus, the first one out. Where it went was where she'd go. Weren't no sense going by the shack first, nothing there worth bothering with anyhow. She had makeup in her purse; that and the money was all she needed. Something would happen. It would work out. She knew about men now and what they liked.

She'd walked about six hot blocks when the red Buick pulled upside the curb. "Come on, I'll give you a ride."

Norma Mae didn't think twice. She jumped into the car. Lord, but it was pretty. She felt like Carole Lombard, and the man beside her was handsome enough to be Clark Gable—almost light enough, too. In the car, he didn't look like a nigger, he looked like a fine gentleman, just a little tanned from having the top down and not wearing no hat. She sneaked a look at his crotch. Guess it was true what they said 'bout niggers being hung like horses.

"Sorry I got you fired. Knew people were prejudiced in the South, but I didn't think they'd hurt their own. What's your name and where you going, babycakes?"

"Norma Mae and wherever the first bus takes me. I'm

just getting outta this place. Never liked Memphis much anyway. Nothing for me here. And what do folks call you?"

"My name is Aljolson Cooles, but my friends call me Red Shoes."

Norma Mae flapped the hem of her skirt, fanning her sweat-slick thighs. "Partial to red, huh, like your fine car?"

Intent on her shapely legs, Red Shoes almost missed the stop sign. "You got it, babycakes. Aren't you a smart one?"

And so it was that she'd ended up in Philadelphia with Red Shoes Cooles. It took her two months to get back to the South. By that time, she'd acquired a taste for black men and the feel of their cocks inside her. Oh yes, he'd been good to her on the trip, bought her pretty clothes and fancy meals, stockings, garter belts, and perfume. Took her to the beauty parlor and got a proper bleach job on her hair.

And made love to her. Lord, had he made love to her. Taught her how, that's what he'd done. And when she'd learned, he'd shown her how to keep from getting pregnant and started bringing men around. That's how he made his money, bought fine cars and clothes. And she was so crazy 'bout him, so itching for him, she didn't really mind. She would of done most anything to keep him happy. Then he'd asked her why she didn't have periods and when she said she did, he asked when was her last. " 'Bout two weeks before I met you," she'd told him. *Dumb hick!* he'd called her before throwing her out. Well, she was through with niggers, and nigger pimps, and the whole damn North. She was back in the South where she belonged, and she was gonna find a good man this time.

The ancient coupe jounced along the dusty Georgia road, causing beads of sweat to run into the valley between

Norma Mae's overripe breasts and around the broad swell of her stomach. She dabbed at it with a perfumed handkerchief. "God damn it, can't you be more careful? This baby's hitting every fuckin' bone in my body." She glared at the itinerant preacher man.

"Watch your language, Norma Mae. This is the Lord's car and I am a servant of the Lord."

She wiped her face and was furious to see the henna stains on the cloth. Preacher Man hadn't liked her hair blonde, wasn't good for business. Too flashy. "Couldn't be no hotter now, could it? This might be the Lord's car, but we sure as the devil must be driving through hell." She tried to straighten the seams on her stockings, but they clung to her damp legs. "Can't stand no more," she whined.

"Shut up." He'd be glad to be rid of her. She was good for saving a few souls, what with her acting and all, but since she'd gotten so big, all she'd done was complain and be a millstone around his neck. She was trying to say the baby was his, but he knew better. He'd first saved Norma Mae right at Christmastime, and it was now summer. Still and all, a baby might make the pockets open a little wider. Could be almost as big a draw as the mother. Maybe he'd dress them both in white; save the mother and baptize the child.

SAVANNAH 22 MILES. Norma Mae read the sign. She was sure as spit gonna dump this preacher man and find her a gentleman, once she got the lump of kid out of her belly, that was, and her figure back. She thought about dancing. Preacher Man didn't dance. All Preacher Man knew how to do was preach and screw. Seemed to her that preaching and screwing mostly went hand in hand, like one set off the other. She tapped her foot in time to the radio. She hoped to God the gentleman she was gonna latch up with knew how to dance; she dearly loved to dance, liked it almost as much as screwing.

"Shit! God damn it!"

"Shut up, Norma Mae, I won't have that language—Jesus Christ! What the fuck?!"

"My water broke."

"You're ruining my car." He swerved off the road. "Get out."

Norma Mae stood dripping in the dusty weeds alongside the road, wringing out the navy blue maternity dress, her reddish hair damp against her head. Preacher Man was wiping out the car. She couldn't resist goading him a little bit. "I thought it was the *Lord*'s car."

Preacher Man just looked at her. He intended to be a hundred miles down the road by the end of the day, or at least as far away from her as he could get.

Norma Mae stood in front of the boardinghouse, her brown cardboard suitcase in her hand. She would like to have freshened up before finding a place to have her baby, but Preacher Man just dumped her out here. There was only one way he practiced *Do Unto Others as Ye Would Have Them Do Unto You*, and *that way* wasn't going to do her any good for a while.

She didn't have any other choice; she walked up the cracked sidewalk. Least there were flowers in the yard.

"We don't take no children here."

"I don't have a child." A pain ripped through her.

"Well, honey, it sure looks like it ain't gonna be too long before you do."

" 'Nuther month, at least," Norma Mae lied, another pain impaling her. "Let me stay a week while I look for another room." She coaxed a tear out of her big brown eyes, digging in her pocketbook to get some money. Nothing persuaded like money. She was careful to open the bag far enough to show the Bible she'd taken to carrying. "Here, I'll pay you for two weeks in advance. When I find another place, you can give me back the second week's rent."

"Oh, all right, but I ain't having no kids here. You got that?"

"God bless you." She picked up the suitcase and waddled after the woman.

Norma Mae stuffed the pillow in her mouth, trying to stifle her screams. She'd moved to the worn linoleum floor when the pains worsened. It was gonna be bad enough without Boardinghouse Mama being mad about a ruined bed. She was so goddamn scared she thought she might die, next minute she was afraid she might not. No one ever told her it was gonna tear her apart. She didn't dare yell out, couldn't risk being turned out into the night. Hours she'd been like this, must be going on ten or eleven by now.

Her long nails clawed at the pillow and instinctively she bore down.

Oh, God, she wished she *would* die. The floor was hard, but not nearly as hard as it was gonna be on her if this baby was black. She had no way of knowing. Could be Mister Allen's. She prayed like she'd never prayed before. She'd been going to church, reading her Bible. Surely to God the baby would be white. Maybe she'd just leave the baby here and go off. She thought it might be getting close now; she could feel the head.

Another pain. She'd long ago bitten right through the pillow ticking. She drew up her knees, spread her legs, and pushed hard, willing this misery from her womb.

The baby came out bawling at the violence of its birth. Norma Mae passed out. When she came to, a man was kneeling beside her, wiping her off with towels. The baby was no longer attached to her but lay beside her on the pillow.

"Who are you?" she asked.

"I room next door. Heard your moans and then the baby cry. Figured you needed some help. You okay?"

Norma Mae glanced at the little girl. She looked white enough. She studied the man, noting his white shirt and loosened tie, his freshly shined shoes—new, too—and nice brown suit pants. His eyes were kind. She lowered her lashes and pouted her lips. "I'm a little wilted and parched. You surely did save my life and I thank you evah so much."

He puffed up, proud as punch. "Wasn't nothing."

The baby began to cry again, instinctively seeking warmth and comfort, but Norma Mae did not coo or smile at her daughter. Instead, she gave her attention to the man. Flirting was her specialty, not motherhood.

"Whatcha gonna name her?"

Norma Mae thought for a minute. She supposed he wouldn't think too highly of a body just walking off and leaving a newborn baby. He was waiting for a name. "Savannah," she said, remembering the road sign. "Savannah Lee Owen."

Her momma called her Savana. It meant "open," a peaceful meadow. It was not an appropriate choice. A city-limits sign inspired the name, but in reality Savana was never at peace. For it would happen that the southern magnolia was born into and wrote of the smouldering seamy side of life—her days and years a yellowed Tennessee Williams script, her existence a desperate struggle between good and evil; safe and exciting. The public would pay millions to buy her books and would wonder how a sweet Georgia peach could curdle their blood the way she did.

—Fast Friends

CHAPTER EIGHTEEN

The face of Vegas changed drastically after the war. Almost overnight the city matured from a brash and gaudy dot in the desert to a sophisticated piazza of sin. An influx of new faces, big money, and bad blood came to town. The once sacred ground of the Anasazi Indians was defiled by Glitter Gulch's neon lights, garish casinos, and underworld crime bosses like Bugsy Siegel. But perhaps the most notorious of them all was Marcus Anovese, who opened his Grand Flamingo Palace on Christmas Day, 1946. Among the attendees was Moni Leah Afton.

The slums of Chicago never boasted anything as original as the red-haired beauty who adorned the Mafia kingpin's establishment at its opening. The lady was not only popular at this gala affair but noticeably well connected. A connoisseur of connections himself, Anovese found the influential guard surrounding the redhead interesting.

As he mingled with his guests, the swarthy Anovese closely observed her, noting that she did not flirt like the dumb kewpie dolls he had known, but instead subtly enticed and expertly evaluated. He appreciated beauty, but even more he admired discretion and discrimination. In his business, such qualities were required if one hoped to experience longevity.

As was his style, he bided his time and made inquiries before arranging an introduction to the jade-eyed, jaded lady.

Moni surveyed the tuxedo-clad Italian, smiling coolly. "You're younger than I imagined."

His black eyes glinted as he replied, "Dagos never age. Few of us will live long enough to collect Social Security. Some deal, this New Deal of Roosevelt's."

"I seriously doubt, Mr. Anovese, that you and I ever will contribute to it."

He liked her candor. She'd researched his background and knew the score. They were two of a kind, a pair of sharks who fed on others' frenzies.

Moni liked what she saw. He stood not quite six feet tall, had black wavy hair, was good-looking in a brooding sort of way and immaculately groomed.

Their eyes locked in recognition, and the mistress of sin extended her hand to the master of vice. "Merry Christmas, Mr. Anovese."

A slow grin spread across his rugged face. "Yes, *Buon natale*, and let's hope it's a prosperous New Year for us both."

And so their association began. Yet when next they met, it was not such a civilized affair. Anovese had politely declined Moni's invitation to her New Year's Eve celebration. He never mixed business and pleasure, and he definitely had business to square with the madam. He commanded his bodyguard to bring the car around to the rear of the Flamingo Palace.

"Where to, Vese?"

"Same place you go on Saturday nights."

Josh Garr assessed Anovese in the rearview mirror

before casually asking, "Anything you don't know about me?"

Anovese sucked his teeth. "Know his weaknesses and you know the man."

The sleek black Pontiac sedan eased out of the drive and cruised down the boulevard. Intrigued by the capo's mood, Garr dared to pursue the subject. "You figger every joe's got a weakness?"

"Yeah, I do." The West Coast chieftain brushed invisible lint from his sharply creased trousers.

"Even you?" Garr kept his eyes on the road and wondered if he'd gone too far this time. During the interminable silence that followed, the Mafia soldier speculated on what made the kingpin tick. *Life is a crapshoot, but that don't interest you none. The silver in your pockets don't mean shit to you, and that thing in your pants is the only dick in the world that can think before it gets in deep trouble. You got beautiful babes galore, money to burn, you rub elbows with the powerful and mighty, rule your empire with a look, a nod, a one-syllable command—yet none of this controls you. You aren't really that far removed from the small-time thug who scrapped his way up through the ranks of the Luciano Family to become the capo di tutti capi's right-hand man. You still survive by an animal's instinct for danger and a whore's sense of timing. Your allegiances are yourself first, the Cosa Nostra second, and God third, and you see no conflict in any of this. You lose no sleep between bestowing the kiss of death upon a rival on Friday and kissing the widow's cheek after Sunday mass. Your perfectly manicured hands are washed of the blood spilled during the gangland wars, just as your perfectly laundered loot can't be traced to racketeering.*

Anovese's eyes narrowed as he scrutinized his bodyguard. "Every man has something he wants, something he would give anything for. Don't think so much. You tax your brain." He dismissed Josh with a flick of his hand and a flash of diamonds. He could have told the punk he wanted the one thing he'd never had, but it wasn't something a man admitted, especially one like him.

Josh pounded on the screen door of Moni's Place.

"*Shhh!* What you want? Everybody's napping." Vashon gave him a go-to-hell look.

"Well, wake 'em up! Mr. Anovese wants to speak with the madam." Garr jerked a thumb toward the sedan.

"Who da hell is Mr. Anovese?" The black woman looked down her nose at the errand boy before her, who apparently thought he was Jesus Christ reincarnated.

"You want to wear that smug smile facing backwards? Get the madam. Now."

It wasn't Josh Garr who convinced Vashon, it was the appearance of the stony-faced Italian in the car. He moved like a panther, a Simon Legree flexing, menacing beneath the European-cut silk suit. His jaw muscles tensed.

Since she'd been knee-high to a grasshopper and picking cotton in the fields, she could sense a storm brewing, be it in the sky or on an overseer's face. Instinctively, she knew this man was more dangerous than the Ku Klux Klan and a howling pack of wolves put together.

"Jes' a minute, I's be gettin' the madam." Vashon left them on the porch while she scurried up the stairs. "Miss Moni, Miss Moni, the Mob's after you. Best come downstairs real quick."

Moni, who had been amusing her daughter by playing patty-cake, roused herself. "Take Evie to her room, and no matter what happens, stay with her." There was no note of alarm in her voice. She camouflaged the sexy apricot teddy she wore beneath a chenille bathrobe, hid the small Remington pistol Ben had given her in the deep side pocket, and slowly descended the steps to the parlor.

Anovese had barged into her domain as though he had already taken over. He told Garr to get lost.

Alone in the parlor, Anovese gave the madam a penetrating look. He went to the bar. "Can I offer you a drink?"

"It's my liquor, you son of a bitch. What would you like?" Moni knew damn well she wasn't going to care for his answer.

"A piece of the action." He poured her a Scotch, neat.

She ignored his outstretched hand, forcing him to set the drink on the table beside her. Though Moni knew exactly what he meant, she feigned ignorance. "What kind of action did you have in mind? I'll fix you up."

"Ten percent of the gross." Anovese smiled, slowly, deliberately.

"Over my dead body. I run an independent house, and I have no intention of splitting with you or anybody else. I know who you are and I know your connections. But I don't scare easily. I built this business from scratch, and I'm not about to let you and the Mob move in on my action."

"Who in the hell do you think you are, dictating terms to *me*? I control Vegas, every dirty vice, every fucking dollar that changes hands in this town."

Moni sampled the Scotch and methodically smoothed a hand over the knickknacks on the library table, flicking dust from them in the way she would have liked to flick Anovese from her territory. "And I control my life, every dirty aspect, every hard-earned dollar from every fuck that takes place under this roof. What does one house mean to you? You take in ten times as much in one night as I do in a week. Why do you bother me?"

Anovese rubbed an index finger along his prominent cheekbone as was his custom when stalling for time. "There can be no exceptions. First there's one, then another. Then soon there is no order, no control. You still run your business. I just insure you can continue doing so."

"Go to hell. I'll burn this place to the ground before you extort one cent from me."

"Extortion is a nasty word."

"And you're a goon."

He eased his glass onto the bar. "I'm about out of patience." Anovese struck a match, watched it burn, then dropped it on the carpet. "No one can have too much insurance against unforeseen accidents. *Capishe*?"

Moni advanced to where the match had landed, just inches away from the tip of his polished shoes, and doused the small flicker with a splash of Scotch. She returned the icy look in his eyes. "Get out."

"No one talks to Marcus Anovese like that, especially a pussy that smells like sardines."

She slung the remainder of her drink in his face. "Come back when your greasy balls have dropped."

Moni turned her back on him and climbed the stairs. As she grasped the knob to her room, Anovese's hand clamped over hers. She jerked her hand away from his repulsive touch. "Get your dirty hands off me!" She backed into the room. Anovese closed the space between them, stalking, matching every step she took to the edge of the bed. He imprisoned her wrist and yanked her to him. "We're not playing a game. You want to stay in business; I can arrange it. You want to go back to where you came from; I can make that happen too."

Moni lurched free, somersaulting over the bed, withdrawing the over-under .41 from her pocket and aiming it at his chest. "Back where I came from? What the hell are you suggesting? I built this whorehouse. I do not intend to pay you for the privilege of keeping it. If I get fucked, it won't be by you."

Anovese stared down the barrel of the gun. *This crazy broad was packing a short-caliber rimfire weapon—a light powder charge and a heavy slug. She was fucking serious about blowing him away.*

Finesse. Finesse. All dames were suckers for finesse. As he cautiously inched his way around the end of the bed, her bead on him never wavered. "Eh, maybe we got off on the wrong track here. This is a business proposition—an arrangement."

"And this is a derringer, and loaded." She cocked the hammer.

He'd heard that sound before and it wasn't among his all-time favorites. "Okay, okay, a truce. I was perhaps unsympathetic, and you are perhaps *impetuoso*."

"I know exactly what I am doing and the vital spot I'm aiming at. You'll live, but you'll wish you'd died. *Castrato*, eh?" The glint in her green eyes left no doubt as to the intent of her improvised Italian.

As much as he admired her spunk, Anovese decided it was time to act. He lunged, catching her wrist and forcing her aim down between their legs. The barrel was strategically pointed at his balls. "I will. I'll do it. I'll castrate you," she hissed.

He bent her back over the bed, wrestled her for the gun, and pinned her to the mattress. "Ten percent. That's fair. Protection. You won't have no trouble."

"I never had trouble until now, God damn you! I made this house. It's mine, and not you, not the Mob, not Lucky Luciano himself, is going to take it away." She rammed her knee into his groin, gaining a momentary advantage, and pressed cold steel to his temple.

"Don't be an ass. If you singe a hair on my head, you are as good as dead."

The barrel bore deeper into his flesh.

"I hear you got a daughter."

His intimation was clear. Moni wasn't fool enough to think that he was making an idle threat—she knew better. If she killed him, there wouldn't be any place on God's green earth where the Mafia's vengeance wouldn't reach Evie. She slung the derringer onto the pillow and lay still beneath his crushing weight, staring in blank resignation at the ceiling.

"Now you're being sensible." Telltale traces of sweat marked the nickel-plated rod as Anovese eased off her and secured the gun in his massive palm. He straightened his tie, shoved the tail of his shirt back into his pants, raked a hand through his hair, and gazed down at her. At the moment, he was Caesar. He could give the sign: thumbs up, you live; thumbs down, you die. He offered his hand

and hauled her up from the bed, a deep, rich laugh of grudging respect and relief erupting from him. "You're tough, madam."

"If it were just you and me this would be finished." She looked away, disgusted by the sight of him.

He knew what she was thinking; you didn't get where he had without some losses. "You come have dinner with me. Tomorrow night. My hotel. We'll talk then. Bring the books."

"Do I have a choice?"

"No." He emptied the bullets into his pocket, tossed the derringer to her, and walked out.

Moni was purposely late for her meeting at the Flamingo Palace. She had taken particular pains with her appearance, wearing a severely tailored gray suit with the customary shoulder pads. A high-necked pink blouse glowed against her ivory skin and open-toed suede pumps graced her tiny feet. A double strand of pearls added a touch of class. The peacock plumes of her hat curved along one side of her face and the maroon veil obscured her sleep-deprived eyes. She carried a small felt handbag and a thick leather ledger.

Josh Garr met her at the door and promptly escorted her to Marcus Anovese's rooftop suite. His private quarters were tastefully decorated—a monument to pastels and understatement—the exact opposite of the man. Against such a backdrop he seemed even more dominant.

"You're late," he fumed. "I do you a favor, an honor, and this is how you repay me?"

Moni glanced offhandedly at the black-banded Elgin on her wrist. "Not by my watch." She went to the bar. "What would you like to drink?"

She might be an innocent in mobster maneuverings, but she damn sure was a pro at miming.

"Nothing, but if you've got the shakes, go ahead." Anovese made a mental note that this woman bore close watching.

Moni shrugged. "I'm not thirsty. Shall we get down to it?"

Anovese motioned to a game table. "The books."

Moni placed the journal before him and nonchalantly retreated to the windows, pretending to be absorbed in the panoramic view.

"Sit," he commanded, jerking his head toward one of the two chairs at the table.

Moni seated herself, crossing one seamed-stockinged leg over the other, folded her hands in her lap, and scrutinized Marcus Anovese for the entire hour and a half he scrutinized her accounts. By the time he finally closed the ledger, Moni's left leg had gone to sleep, her mouth was dry, and her stomach was cramping, yet she would not give him the satisfaction of even blinking. It was all she could do not to sigh with relief when he smiled at her.

"You keep good books. Very precise."

"Thank you." Moni relaxed slightly. "If you are finished . . ." She pointed a polished nail at the ledger.

"Of course." Anovese slid the journal across the table to her. He went to the telephone and notified the kitchen to bring up their dinner. "Now we'll share a drink."

Moni masked her awkwardness as one course followed another. Anovese was a generous and informative host. From the antipasto of *proscuitto e melone* to the main course of veal scaloppine *piccata*, the menu he had selected was outstanding. By the time Moni was served the Belgian endive *insalata* and, for dessert, a delicate *torta maddalena*, she had under Anovese's amused tutoring almost mastered the pronunciation of the Italian dishes and acquired an appreciation for what he called Old World cuisine, not to mention an addiction to the intoxicating sambuca liqueur, though she abstained from biting into the coffee beans the way Marcus did.

Anovese snapped the napkin free of his shirt collar and wiped the meringue from his lips. "You are satisfied?"

"That's a word I know something about, and the answer

is yes.'' Apprehensive as she had been about keeping this appointment, Moni now found herself enjoying the evening, though she took care not to forget the reason for this get-together. Anovese had two faces, just as she had two sets of books.

''You're a good-looking woman, Moni. There are two things a smart doll like you should never do.'' His expression grew solemn as he rested his elbows on the table and blew out the candles.

The sambuca gave her a sense of security. ''Really? Tell me, Marcus.'' She deliberately called him by his given name, looking at him from beneath the peek-a-boo veil. ''You've whetted my interest.'' She moistened her lips.

Anovese caught the opalescent strands about her throat and rolled the pearls between his forefinger and thumb.

Moni was ready. Sooner or later they all made a move, and considering Anovese's hot Italian blood, she was surprised it had taken him so long. *Who knew, a night in bed might change his mind about percentages and she might come out taking his money instead of the other way around.*

Exerting slight pressure on the leash of pearls, Anovese brought Moni's face to his until their lips were only a breath apart. She could see passion in his dark eyes.

Moni placed her hand on his knee. Expertly she raked long nails up his leg, then smoothly squeezed his balls and let her fingertips trail a natural course.

He was hers, and she knew it.

She was his, and he knew it.

He twisted the opera-length pearls once about his hand. The silk thread snapped and pearls shot in a thousand directions. ''A smart doll doesn't wear imitation pearls or try to con me with fake books.'' His fingers closed about her slim neck, exerting only a fraction of the power he possessed.

He didn't cut off her breath, he simply pressed the pulse of her confidence.

In the wake of his anger at being played for a sucker, she lost her hold on him. Her hand slipped from his firm erection and fumbled for another hold.

Anovese's fingers relaxed and withdrew, leaving red welts on her neck. "Twice you have gone for my balls—once to kill and once to cheat. You underestimate me. It is not a mistake you should make again. *Capishe*?"

"Would you give over what you had worked an entire lifetime for without fighting with everything in you to protect yourself from the hurt, the humiliation, the hunger that drove you to become what you are today?" It spilled from her lips unwittingly, and the tears came despite herself.

Anovese was not easily moved by tears and Moni's were no exception. What inexplicably touched him was this hard-assed woman expressing what he was: a cold-water flat, spaghetti with no sauce, stealing fruit from a vendor's cart, a knife in the ribs of a seven-year-old paperboy warming his hands over a trash-can blaze, a gang rape of his sister, the retaliation for which introduced him to butt fucks in the reformatory, the tines of a fork shoved under his foreskin and he submitting.

He looked into her small face, then, without knowing why he felt compelled to do so, tenderly traced the exotic plane of her cheek. Compassion was alien to him.

Confused by the emotions she saw playing across his face, Moni sat paralyzed, unable to ward off the spell he cast. The old Russian émigrés on the Row had told of such a man, a man who had taken possession of a czarina and caused the empire to fall. Was he as dangerous as the Siberian monk? Could Anovese's dark powers topple her kingdom? She did not flinch as he lifted the maroon veil, removed her hat, worked the pins from her hair, and slowly wove his splayed fingers through her silky tresses.

"Tears. It isn't you, Moni. You fight, you claw and scrap. You hold a gun at a man's head while kneeing him in the balls. You eat his food while swindling him. *But you do not cry.*'' He outlined her sultry lips with his thumb.

Moni felt his yearning, but before she could react, he withdrew. Standing, he turned his back and went to the bar, muttering gruffly. "Go on. Get outta here while I'm still in a charitable mood."

She recognized only too well the posture of alienation that shadows those who rule alone, sleep alone, cry alone, and usually die alone. She crossed the room, taking the bottle from his hand. "You really don't want to drink by yourself and I'm not in any hurry to go."

"Maybe you should be."

Moni shrugged. Catching the ends of his bow tie with the tips of her fingers, she plucked at them, playfully working the slippery material back and forth, slowly sliding it from beneath his collar, and flinging it away. "There are two things a dumb Wop like you should never do."

Anovese looked down at her with grudging respect. He cupped her breasts and arched a brow. "You wanna give me an education?"

"Two easy lessons; never question a woman's motives and never turn your back on someone unless you're sure they're a friend. *Capishe*?"

Her Italian was getting better. He poured two snifters of cognac and handed her the peace offering. "Most anything can be replaced—pearls, madams, and even a gangster's chieftain. But you can never replace trust once it has been betrayed."

"Enemies are expendable. Loyalty belongs to friends."

"If I made you a present of genuine pearls, could I expect a gift of your loyalty?"

"Forget the pearls, just don't demand ten percent."

Anovese did not commit. Not exactly. He merely saluted her with his glass.

A tenuous bargain was struck. He had little reason to trust her and yet somehow he did. She had small cause to befriend him and yet she recognized something that others did not: *Marcus Anovese was a lonesome man, made up of equal parts of violence and tenderness.* Both attracted her.

As the amber liquor blazed down her throat, the dangerous Marcus Anovese entered her life.

CHAPTER NINETEEN

Though the hot Nevada and Rub' al Khali deserts were thousands of miles apart, there were many parallels. Both were settled by polygamous nomads, the one by Anasazi Indians, the other by the Anizah tribe. Both wastelands had been flooded with the blood money of wars, secular and religious. Each had fallen victim to the tawdry opulence wrought by an abundance of easy riches. Each was home to a significant number of women whose only purpose was the pleasuring of men.

The differences were even greater.

In one, liquor was consumed with abandon; in the other, it was strictly prohibited.

In one, the women unveiled their bodies; in the other, the law of the land, the *Sharia*, required that even their faces be covered.

In one, the government regulated sex; in the other, sex dominated the government.

Twelve-year-old Prince Kenir Ashad studied the *Kamasutra*, which had been smuggled into the Shahdesh palace by a Hindu physician some centuries before and painstakingly translated by one of the concubines before it was discovered and its heretical message forever removed from the view of the women. Fortunately for Kenir it had been saved and passed down to the male members of his line.

He could hardly wait for his turgid *lingam* to enter a moist *yoni*. But wait he must, for before this ritual could take place they were going to make of him a man who could surpass all others, a lover of such rarity that the women would clamor and wail at the walls to be admitted into servitude.

In an hour the slaves, harem women, and the *tabeeb*'s assistants would come to take him to the chalcedonyx-walled chamber where he would submit to the sharp knife of the skilled palace surgeon.

He expected pain, yet he understood that it was necessary before pleasure. Into slits made in his penis they would insert precious pearls and small tinkling bells. When the incisions healed, he would be steeped in the passions of mind, body, and soul.

Schooled in patience and practice, postures and perversions, with women and men alike, he would know how to please and be pleased, dominate and be dominated, seduce and be seduced, borrow and give, cry and laugh, die and live again.

Kenir had no illusions about the unrest or sensual activity that fermented in the harem. Seldom were the women privileged to receive the king's favor in his private chamber; rarely were they permitted to exercise their expertise and slake their desire. It was unjust that self-possessed, cultured women, who had been trained since birth to pleasure men, were sentenced to abstinence.

They habitually risked death for the tabu touch of another concubine's fingers or tongue. They crept into each other's beds in the middle of the night seeking a caress, a release, or, as in *Kamasutra*, would position bulbs and roots between their *yoni*s for a *lingam*. The braver ones had their slaves dress men in women's clothing and smuggled them inside the compound walls.

He, too, had frequently been in disguise, though only as an observer. When he had mastered the mysteries of the flesh, he would rescue these women from the indignities he had witnessed. He would satisfy and possess them so surely and exquisitely that they would never seek alternatives. He knew he could do this, not because he was healthy and energetic, or because, as some might say, he was full of youthful fantasies, or that the genitalia concealed beneath his white and gold *thobe* was the envy of men twice his age, but because he understood the urgent, uncontrollable excitement of the *forbidden*.

The young prince, a member of the aristocratic Anizah tribe descended from Ishmael, son of Abraham, was at the threshold of manhood, and he intended to thoroughly avail himself of the skilled concubines for the remainder of what he hoped would be a long life, *Inshallah*. God willing. But unlike his father, the king, for him there would be one woman, one *yoni*, one love, that would obsess and be obsessed. *He knew.*

CHAPTER TWENTY
January 29, 1950

In the streets of Johannesburg, South Africa, a wild-eyed Zulu tribesman raised his machete and charged the Dutchman braced in the doorway of an apothecary shop. The Dutchman closed his eyes and squeezed the Luger's trigger. The acrid smell of gunpowder and the agonized scream of the Zulu turned his stomach. When the inhuman shriek subsided, he dared to open his eyes. Before him the black giant lay sprawled upon his back, a bloody, gaping hole where once his balls had hung.

The Dutchman clung to the doorjamb, his pallid face averted. He wretched repeatedly, until all that was left to drip from him was cold sweat. He had had no choice. It was them or him. It was self-preservation. He retreated into the shop, never taking his eyes off the street as he reloaded the Luger. Whatever measures he must employ to protect his interests against the black insurgents were justified.

On that same January day in an unheated pool hall in a Philadelphia ghetto, a cocky Red Shoes Cooles celebrated his twenty-fourth birthday.

Fat Eddie clicked the switchblade open, then shut, open, shut, open. "Hey, cat, we gon go clean out that drugstore across the street or not? I ain't in the mood for no mother-fucking birthday party." He squinted through a tiny hole where the red paint had been scratched from the window. "I need some shit, man." He clutched his stomach. "Bad."

"You're always strung out. Shut up now, you're ruining my concentration." Red Shoes ignored the junkie and sized up his shot. It would be tricky, but he was slick and smart. He was the best hustler around.

"Fuck you. Who needs you?" Fat Eddie left the door wide open behind him and crossed the street.

Red Shoes made the nine ball into the side pocket and chalked the tip of his ivory-inlaid cue. He went to the door and closed it. "Stupid nigger is going to get himself killed," he muttered, returning to the green felt table and analyzing his next shot.

By the time the drugstore's alarm went off, only the white cue ball and the black eight ball remained on the table.

By the time Red Shoes reached the sidewalk, Fat Eddie was blindly running up the middle of the street, slipping and falling in the dirty slush, picking himself up, and running again. He never saw the squad car that squealed around the corner, never heard the siren, never realized the cops had tried to brake before going into a spin. As far as Red Shoes could tell, Fat Eddie never saw nothing but visions of horse-filled needles dancing in his head. The impact of the patrol car sent his spindly body rolling downhill until he came to rest at the salted steps of the Lost Souls Mission.

Red Shoes snorted and two small clouds hung suspended in the frigid air. He turned up the collar of his full-length muskrat coat and strutted back inside the deserted pool hall. He squatted, eyeball to cue ball to eight ball, then moved around the table, lit a Chesterfield, and squatted again. The table slanted slightly to the left. He fanned ashes from the felt and chalked his cue again, rapping it against the bumper. Going to the window, he dropped the cigarette in Fat Eddie's half empty bottle of pop, spit out some loose tobacco that clung annoyingly to his tongue, and returned to the table. He slid the cue between his fingers and wiped them against his trousers. It was going to have to be an around-the-back shot. He placed the cue across the table and removed his coat, blew on his fingers, flexed them, and repositioned the cue.

Red Shoes moved to the opposite end of the table. He wasn't playing by the rules, but then he'd never intended to. His aim was perfect. The cue ball cracked into the corner pocket. He deliberately sank it just like he was going to deliberately sink his white mother. He put on his coat and took apart his cue, replacing it in the red satin-lined case, snapping shut the gold clasp. Before he left, he fished out the white cue ball, the souvenir of his outstanding game. If Buffy Chadds-Ford had balls they'd be white and they'd be his. She'd denied him all his life, but no more. A man had to do what he had to do. It was self-preservation. Whatever measures he must employ to protect his black interests against the white bigots were justified.

Buffy Chadds-Ford replaced the receiver in its cradle. It was no surprise Allister was staying over at his club again. His absences had become routine, so much so that she hadn't even bothered with a place card for him. She would preside alone over the evening, as usual. And as usual tomorrow he would bring home an appeasement, some eighteen-karat duplicate of the latest trinket he had besottedly bestowed upon his mistress. What poor Allister lacked in imagination he tried to make up in efficiency, but even here he occasionally slipped and presented her with a bracelet or cigarette case bearing the wrong initials. Since he tried to be so damn efficient, he could at least have chosen a mistress with the same initials. Little did he know that the jeweler regularly sent a courier by to redeem the merchandise and credit Buffy's private account. Actually, on reflection, she shouldn't be *too* upset with Allister. After all, he *was* financing tokens of her affection to a host of West Point cadets.

Even so, she would have liked for him to be here this evening. She had had the strangest feeling all day—nothing she could precisely define, yet a peculiarly strong sense of disquiet. She walked into the dining room and rearranged the already perfect glamelia centerpiece, then inspected the spotless crystal. Each ornate piece of flatware, every fold of every napkin was exactly as it should be. The tapers stood straight, the Chippendale chairs were evenly spaced. Satisfied with the dining room, she went into the kitchen, casting a critical eye over the staff and the bountiful spread. Everything seemed to be proceeding as well as usual, but she couldn't shake the vague uneasiness that was rapidly turning into a case of the jitters. She wished Silver and Fax weren't otherwise engaged. Silver always had a soothing effect on her, but she supposed Eleanor Roosevelt's invitation was tantamount to a command performance. She shrugged her bare shoulders, dismissing her disappointment, and tightened the screw on her diamond earrings. *Silver never refused Fax, and Fax—cool, cool Fax—never missed a chance to sift golden opportunities from snatches of bureaucratic gossip.*

Buffy poured a sherry. As she brought it to her lips, her hand trembled, spilling the dusky liquid upon her rose Mainbocher gown.

She stared at the wet blotch. A flash of another stain superimposed itself. Bloodstains on the cream upholstery of her Stutz-Bearcat. *Christ! How could she have forgotten? No wonder she had had the heebie-jeebies all day! It was the twenty-ninth of January. For twenty-four years she had loathed that date.* Despite the kitchen's warmth, Buffy shivered and gulped down the rest of her sherry.

Silver adjusted the folds of navy taffeta, spreading yards of lush fabric across the glove-soft leather seat of the limousine. The low neckline of her gown was clipped with diamonds, and her silken hair was caught up in a French twist, secured with diamond pins. She followed Fax's gaze to the panorama of Hyde Park.

The moon, a week shy of being full, illuminated the blanket of glistening snow. Ice-crusted shrubs and snow-laden trees stood sentinel before multichimneyed mansions. Windows spilled soft golden light upon the snowy lawns. Though her home at Montauk was as large if not larger, and certainly as magnificent, if not more so, she could not help but wonder if the occupants of these houses had lives that were more fulfilling than hers—like their hostess this evening, for instance.

She admired Eleanor Roosevelt, her accomplishments and her unwillingness to take a back seat to anyone, anywhere, but each encounter with the former First Lady left Silver more dissatisfied than ever. What would it feel like to be representing your country at the United Nations, to chair the Commission for Human Rights, to travel the world because of your own interests, to lecture and have someone—anyone—listen?

She didn't know if Eleanor Roosevelt was happy or not, but she was successful, and she was certainly a survivor. Silver supposed it was too late for her, but it was not too late for Lauren, and she was going to do everything in her power to rear her daughter to be independent.

Fax saw the look on Silver's face. If one could only control one's wife as easily as one could control nations, life would be simple. He was going to have to find something for her to do or he was going to suffer a disruption in the smooth tranquillity of his domestic routine. Women—all women—were changing, but Silver seemed more restless than most. Why couldn't she just have an affair like that Chadds-Ford woman? More discreetly, of course, but it would be a diversion.

They were easily the youngest couple in the room, Fax noted with satisfaction, and among the richest. There were more powerful people, but he was satisfied with his progress. For a time he had considered a political career—it seemed a natural progression—but that had been naive. Now he understood that power came not from the elected but from those who owned them. He planned his political strategies as meticulously as his corporate ones; indeed, they were virtually one and the same. But the world, as were the women, was changing since the war, and he needed to develop some new politicians and some fresh or revitalized ideologies. Any time sparks could be fanned into an inferno, money could be made, whether from the International Monetary Fund, profit taking on Wall Street, supplying munitions to warring factions, or merely grossing the extra advertising dollars when newsprint sold like hotcakes and retailers wanted on the bandwagon.

Eleanor characteristically had assembled an eclectic assortment of guests, but she would have been surprised to learn that she was aiding and abetting the flow of international funds with her well-intentioned United Nations and Commission for Human Rights activities, far more, in fact, than her late husband's Trading With the Enemy Act ever had. Gathered in the drawing room tonight in the name of international brotherhood were those who espoused great and abiding sympathy for the poor and underprivileged.

Fax knew that most used do-gooders of the world like Eleanor to salve their consciences, as did he, unstintingly giving of their time and dollars, but unlike some he had never deluded himself about his real purpose. And he knew, too, that by ten o'clock the next morning the World

Bank, which had carelessly been named the International Bank for Reconstruction and Development at its inception at Bretton Woods nearly six years before, would be tapped for hundreds of billions of floating dollars by the guests gathered here.

Yes, by no later than noon the next day, Eleanor would have financed understanding and brotherhood among international men, and the international brotherhood would have financed *understanding* men. It was a great system, Fax thought, a perfect system. It helped everyone and hurt no one.

Eleanor took his elbow. "I don't believe you know Ernst Papanek. He's in charge of the Wiltwyck School."

Fax found himself shaking hands with a balding, kind-faced gentleman who headed up Eleanor's pet project, and he knew at once this was the type of man who had never entertained a mercenary thought. "I hear you are doing some good work over there."

"We try." As Papanek's eyes bored through him, Fax made a mental note to increase his contribution to the school. "Excuse me, I must go speak to Sir Harry."

Papanek leaned forward, his hands behind his back. His eyes hadn't left Fax.

"He's from Johannesburg, into gold and diamonds. Also owns a chunk of Barclays South Africa, I believe." Fax allowed himself a faint smile. It always amused him that the Quakers, who promulgated peace and philanthropy, had pridefully rushed their bank in to hasten South Africa on its road to economic prosperity, and in so doing had competitively placed themselves in the hands of the Afrikaners and their apartheid doctrine. And the Afrikaners had done to Barclays just what Eleanor's guests were doing to her good deeds tonight, for the Afrikaners were skillful exploiters, using the bank's cash, competency, and contacts to further their interests. Sir Harry, on the board of Barclays, was the consummate multinational player. He faced east, west, north, and south simultaneously, and Fax suspected that Sir Harry probably had invoked both God and the devil to further his causes. Fax could learn much from him. "Excuse me," he said again, for Papenek had spoken, and he had missed the words, something he made a point never to do.

"I should very much like to meet him. Do you mind if I accompany you?"

"And so," Ernst Papanek expounded, elated by his rapid and successful elevation from headmaster to international sociological commentator, "what we are experiencing in New York is something I think, Sir Harry, that will have a significant impact not only on Johannesburg but on the whole of South Africa. In theory, your premise that an escalating economy will eliminate racial barriers is sound. In practice, however, the inverse is true."

Papanek glanced from Sir Harry to Fax. "Here, for instance," he continued, "we have a ghetto where the promised land was expected. What happens when a man cleaning out a barn in the fresh aroma of Georgia's gentle breezes finds himself crawling through the stinking sewers of a hellhole where there is no space, no quiet, no breath of God's great life? What happens to dreams of glory when escape from the cane, cotton, and tobacco fields means living on top of another, alternately sweating and freezing? Hope disappears. And when hope is gone, the song of the soul turns to fury and anger, and their children and their children's children are filled with frustration and hate and bitterness. And when those emotions are present, what do you have? You have trouble, big trouble, and you will have; mark my words, Sir Harry. Today's uprising in Johannesburg is merely a precursor of things to come." Papanek stopped. He had acquitted himself well, he thought, yet it shouldn't have been a revelation. It was axiomatic: throughout the history of mankind, the oppressed—if they survived—had become the oppressors.

But Fairfax Randolph Bennett was a million miles ahead of Ernst Papanek.

The blacks had gone to war, they had fought alongside their white brothers for the land they had tilled, and they had lost their lives for their country. They had seen and felt the world outside and they wanted their share. And Fax Bennett knew more than most that where there was desire, there was the potential for exploitation and profit.

He knew just how he was going to package this opportunity. He would call his concept Black Power. The implementation would be easy.

All he needed was an instrument.

CHAPTER TWENTY-ONE

Sleet drummed against the taxi and gathered on the sluggish wipers, slowing their progress uphill to Buffy's Bryn Mawr manor. The heater blew hot air and the smell of the driver's liniment into the back seat, where it commingled with wet muskrat, a whiff of mothballs, and Lucky Tiger cologne. The driver shifted into low gear as he attempted the icy incline. "You sure you got the right address?"

"What do I look like, a fucking illiterate? I know my numbers. Drive, man." Red Shoes sank back against the worn upholstery, fingering the fringe of the cabbie's discarded scarf. With an economy of movement, he slid it off the seat, and used it to wipe steam from the side window. Now he had a view, a view of the birthright he'd been deprived of, a view of the limitless horizon beyond the window, a view of the top of the hill. The rarefied air at this level was heady. Now he knew the addictive high that consumed Fat Eddie—white powder and white power were not all that different.

The tires spun, black smoke clouded his view, and the

cab slid back, rocked forward, slid backward and rocked again. Billowing more smoke they inched forward, then lost ground. "No way, fella. We ain't going up this hill tonight."

"The hell I'm not." Red Shoes flung open the door and stepped into the stinging sleet, draping the cabbie's muffler about his neck. *Nothing was going to stop him from reaching Buffy Chadds-Ford tonight.*

He crossed the street and began trudging up the slick, steep grade. Midway to the stately house, that same stately house he had cased so many times before, he was forced to hang on to the wrought iron fence and pull himself up hand over hand, his fingers sticking to the cold metal. By the time he reached his objective, his hair and coat were glazed with ice, his face and feet numb. But he had arrived. *Oh, yeah, he had arrived. He was at the Promised Land. No more slum rats, no more cockroaches, no more screaming babies, no more burning in the summer and freezing in the winter, no more hassles. He had been delivered.*

Red Shoes passed through the gate and swaggered up the winding brick walk. He stopped, gazing up at the brilliantly lit Palladian windows and watching the ever changing silhouettes beyond the draperies. Inside, his high-society mother was wining and dining guests, all of them warm and snug, full of shit and themselves. *Oh yeah, wasn't it sweet, wasn't it a fucking stroke of genius that he had chosen tonight to confront the bitch. Wouldn't she just be too, too, pleased to see him on her doorstep. He had been waiting a long time for this reunion.*

He whipped a handkerchief from his pocket and bent down, buffing the tops of his red shoes with the same flair with which he planned to polish off Buffy. Straightening to his full six feet three inches, Aljolson "Red Shoes" Cooles rapped the heavy brass knocker.

The summons was answered almost immediately by a towering Watusi, dressed in tails and white gloves, looking down his nose imperiously as he discreetly blocked Red

Shoes' entrance. "Yes?" The butler sounded like the ring that was missing from his nose was circling his tongue instead.

"I'm here to see *Miz* Chadds-Ford."

"Madame is occupied. If you would leave your calling card . . ."

He supposed he could ask for a pen and print *pimp extraordinaire* on the white cue ball. The butler looked like he had a cue stick shoved up his ass anyway. "Why don't you just tell her that Booker T. Coole's son wants to see her." His wide lips curled.

"Pardon?"

"Just do it, Jack, while I wait inside." He shoved past the black titan and strode into the library. He did not remove his wet coat before ensconcing himself on the settee in front of the fire, warming his feet on the andirons. It was only minutes until he heard the staccato click of heels across the oak floor. Without turning, he said, "You're looking fine, *Mama*."

The name, the name, the feeling, the feeling that had plagued her all day had come alive and had come to pay a call. Oh shit! She stood before him, examining his features closely.

"What do you think, Mama? Did you do good?"

"I didn't do anything. I don't know who you are and I'm sure as hell not your mother. What's your purpose in coming here? If you're cold or hungry, you can go to the kitchen."

"Oh, I'm cold, Mama, real cold. I've been cold since the day I was born. But no more." Red Shoes picked up the poker and stoked the fire. *Stir it up. Oh, it was warm, sweet, sweet warmth.* "Getting hot enough for you, Mama?"

It was stifling; she was smothering. He was pretty.

"You remember the day I was born, Mama? Was it as cold a day as today?"

"I haven't the vaguest notion what you're talking about or what you want from me."

"What I want from you? Oh, that's a loaded question, Mama. How do you ask for a life? How do you ask for a kind touch, for the lost years you owe me? Answer me that one, Mama, and I'll answer you."

For the first time, he engaged her eyes. Buffy put one hand behind her, reeling. . . . *She was fifteen years old. Booker T. was twenty-eight and wild and endowed with a prick that went to your jaw. He was so frigging good-looking, so frigging primitive, so frigging masculine. Thick. Thick lips, thick cock, thick cloying, gray delirium. Not white, not black—and surely to God—not the mistake that was sitting before her hearth. Fired and yet oh so cool.*

"What makes you think you can demand anything but my charity?"

"Your charity, bitch? I didn't come for charity. Oh, no, Mama, I don't want no more fucking charity. I want the real thing, Mama, and you are going to give it to me. I know all about you. I've been studying and following you for a long time. No, Mama, you don't even want to give me charity. You want to give me anything and everything I ever dreamed of wanting, 'cause if you don't, I'll smear your nigger-loving white ass from one end of Philadelphia to the other. You understand me, Mama? I think you do."

"You will smear my what from where to where? Who in the hell do you think would believe you?"

"I got a friend in the print room of the *Philadelphia Daily News*. I think he'd be glad to run this." Red Shoes pulled the leather pouch from his coat pocket. "It's all here, Mama, just like I tore it out of the orphanage records. It says Booker T. Cooles is my father and it says you are my mother—Margaret Elizabeth Holmes Reynolds. That is you, isn't it, Mama?"

"Quit calling me Mama and get your goddamn disgusting red shoes off my grate."

"That's my name, Mama, Red Shoes. Appropriate, don't you think? It has *color*."

"How much?"

Her blue eyes were frostier than the icy January winds.

"You wish I wanted money. It ain't that simple, though I know you have an *endless* supply. I could just keep coming back and coming back—bleed you dry, Mama."

"Then what?"

"Maybe I just want you to claim me." He smirked, flopping back upon the unyielding settee, carelessly throwing one hand across its carved back. "Oh, yeah, can't you just picture it? Buffy and her long-lost Red Shoes at the theater, the symphony? Or, perhaps, Mrs. Chadds-Ford and her mulatto baby tour Europe?"

"You are out of your mind."

"I've got it, Mama." He snapped his fingers. "I'll have some chocolate mousse with your friends. We could start there and see how it goes." He figured a couple more of these threats ought to set her up good. "By the way, Mama, you eat that with a spoon or a fork?"

"We've already had dessert. And if you have any hopes of my acknowledging you, forget it."

"Oo-*ee*, Mama. You sure are one hard-hearted slut. I wonder what Booker T. saw in you."

"He liked it." Buffy's face turned crimson at the inadvertent admission.

"What's your excuse? You get some kind of kick out of making it with black men? I can fix you up, Mama, no trouble at all. No charge, either."

"Just tell me what you want and get the hell out of here. I have guests."

"You got an illegitimate son, too." Red Shoes pocketed the leather folio.

Buffy had had enough. Her gown rustled as she made a move to leave.

Red Shoes leapt to his feet, barring her exit. "We're not

through, Mama. Or did you want to continue in front of your company?''

"For God's sake, just state your terms and leave me be.''

"I want power, Mama. I don't want to eat dirt the rest of my life because I'm half white and half black. I don't want to step off the street for nobody. I don't want to have to hustle day in and day out. I want to live in a big, fine house like this one. I want to wake up to fresh-squeezed orange juice served on a tray. I want to have people say, 'Yes, sir, Mr. Cooles, right away, sir,' and I want to give to the charities that fed me when you wouldn't. That's not too much to ask, now, is it, Mama?'' He crowded her face with his own. "Not that I give a fuck if it is. You owe me.''

She detected the foul odor of sloe gin on his breath and noted the nicotine stains on his even teeth. "And how do you propose that I get you this . . . this power?''

"I don't know, Mama. That's your problem. I'll be in touch.'' Before she could move, he bent and kissed her cheek. "You're looking whiter than usual, Mama. Better rouge up before you go back to your guests.''

Buffy stood paralyzed as Red Shoes opened the door and left. From the window she watched him, arms spread-eagled for balance, muskrat coat billowing as he skated down the gas-lamp-lined drive. Elation showed in his every movement.

It had gone pretty well, Red Shoes thought, coasting nearly twenty feet without a hitch. *It was a lot easier sliding downhill than it was crawling up.*

CHAPTER TWENTY-TWO

Norma Mae had taken stock of herself at New Year's, and the fact was that she was gonna be twenty-three years old this year, and while her breasts were still high and pointy, she still hadn't found herself a gentleman. She had just been adriftin' along, frittering away her days, wasting herself.

Yup. In the years following Savannah's birth she'd covered more territory than the traveling shoe salesman she'd ditched a month or so after the Great Inconvenience, laid more men than Red Shoes could have procured if he'd given discounts, and repented her wicked ways more times than a hellfire-brimstone-and-damnation preacher man could count in a month of Sundays. From Natchez to Mobile, from Tallahassee to New Orleans, she'd flitted from revival tent to beer joint, being saved and losing her soul, and she wasn't a bit pleased with herself. It was time to mend her ways.

One of her resolutions was to find a gentleman by Valentine's Day. She wouldn't mind having some roses instead of thorns. But there weren't many gentlemen in Hardaway, Alabama. The town simply didn't live up to its name, and she had just about exhausted all its potential, not to mention the male half of the population. No, she needed to go someplace else, but the truth was, she was so broke she'd been forced to do volunteer quilting at the local stitch-and-bitch group just for the refreshments. She didn't have enough money to go anywhere. She would like to get to Texas. There were big oil dollars in that state, and the word was the men there just bought their women anythin' their little ol' hearts desired. The men in Hardaway weren't real generous, but there was a revival in town, so she'd go see if the Lord could help her out of this mess.

"I got you a new dress." Norma Mae delivered this startling bit of news as she scrubbed Savannah's body half raw with Lava soap. "I want you to act real nice now. We're going to a revival and the preacher's a nice-lookin' man. You see that you mind your southern manners. You hear me, girl?"

"Ouch!" Savannah winced as Norma Mae drew a brush through the wet tangles of her straight blonde hair.

"What?" Sometimes the cold, arrogant expression on that child's face reminded her of something she was determined to forget. She yanked the brush through the snarls again, harder.

"Yes, Momma. I'll be good." Savannah was only three, but she had long since discovered the secret of staying on Norma Mae's good side. And yet tonight it seemed like maybe she was going to be a part of something. Momma was excited, and when Momma got excited, things changed.

Savannah picked at the ribbon sash of her dress. She much preferred playing paper dolls outside, which she was usually allowed to do so she didn't *distract* Momma, whatever that meant. This 'vangelist was thundering about the evils of sin and the salvation of God. She looked at Norma Mae and she recognized the signs. There was gonna be another uncle in her life. She hoped this one would be a good one, but he was shouting pretty loud, and the louder they shouted, the more they made Momma make those funny noises, and the more the bedsprings squeaked. She guessed God made some people just naturally noisier all over than others. But then again, he was big, and big men usually fed her better 'cause they liked to eat more and oftener, so maybe he wouldn't be *too* bad.

"And now, my brothers and my sisters, I tell you, I feel sin in this tent tonight, sin in this canvas house of God, and this sin grieves my heart and my soul and gives me great offense. . . ."

Savannah squirmed. She felt like she had done something bad, but she hadn't—she *hadn't*. She looked at Norma Mae, but Momma didn't even know she was there.

". . . And I am going into the field to pray, pray to God that he will remove the sin from this tent, wrench it from your very hearts, pray that he will mend your wicked ways and show you the path of righteousness, and while I am gone, I ask you to pray as Sister Grace sings her gospel songs for your salvation."

Savannah liked the music better. She liked the big fat lady singing. She hardly heard Norma Mae say, "You stay right here, I'm going to the bathroom."

But the singing stopped, the praying in tongues started, and Savannah Lee had to go to the bathroom too. She tip-toed out.

The moon was so bright it was almost like daylight, but she couldn't see an outhouse anywhere. She started into the field, then abruptly stopped. She knew those sounds, and sure enough, there was Momma and the preacher, leaned up against the big log pole that carried the yellow lights to the tent. Momma's skirt was over her shoulders and her legs were wrapped around the preacher's waist. She knew better than to interrupt, and so she ran to the side of the tent to squat, watching her urine trickle into the hole holding the spike the rope was wrapped around. She fidgeted with the rope, undid it, and nervously moved on to the next. She wished Momma would hurry. She wanted to go home. She undid another twist of rope. Oh, no, she had got her sash wet. Momma was gonna be mad. She took it off and tied it to the rope, making a bow on the spike. Sister Grace was singing again, and everyone was shouting, "Alleluia, brother," and then somehow the tent fell down and everyone came running out, and the next thing she knew she, Momma, and the preacher were on the move.

"Scum!" "Trash!" "Sinners!" "Whoremonger!" The shouts followed the car down the rutted road.

"We're being run out of town like common criminals," Norma Mae wailed, forgetting that she'd wanted to leave in the first place.

"Never you mind." The preacher patted Momma's knee and dried her tears. "Sometimes it's better to fight sin in a new town." Norma Mae stopped crying and scooted over next to the preacher, looping her arm about his neck, resting her cheek on his shoulder.

No one thought to comfort Savannah, so she comforted herself. *"Sometimes it's better to fight sin in a new town, sometimes it's better to fight sin in a new town, sometimes it's better to fight sin in a new town."*

When she woke up, they were in Mississippi. Norma Mae bought her some new paper dolls, and it was better. For a while.

CHAPTER TWENTY-THREE

Fax sat in his New York office. He had two matters to resolve this morning: first, there was the introduction of Black Power into the psyche of the niggers, and second, there was the illusion of woman power in Silver. One was for profit and power, the other for peace and privacy. He had been a fool to ignore the warnings.

Perhaps if Silver were more passionate . . . He had lust in his loins and a lady in his bedroom, but the age-old adage that what she needed was a good fuck wouldn't work with her. He respected her far too much for that.

What if he sent her into the ghetto to help the plight of the blacks? Eleanor Roosevelt could be counted on to help. Let Silver distribute a little of the wealth, salve the conscience that occasionally reared its inconvenient head, the way it had that day in Paris when she'd questioned his motives. She had a well-developed sense of compassion and sympathy; it would be easy to influence her with suggestions. She would play right into his hands. Handled properly, she could get elected to office by the blacks and serve as his power bloc. But that was risky. She possessed not only beauty and a sweet temperament but a keen intellect as well, keen enough to be dangerous, and if she started questioning she couldn't be led. No, that wouldn't do at all. She would have to be involved in something harmless—the arts, perhaps. He had no idea what her talents were, other than managing a household, but any fool could learn to take photographs. Yes, that was it. He would get her interested in photography. Should be easy.

He moved on to the issue of Black Power. Civil rights: second point on course. Black Power and civil rights. But what he needed was a smart and charismatic black. The problem was, he didn't know any. In fact, he knew few blacks. He started counting. Buffy Chadds-Ford's Watusi butler—he had his thoughts about that one. Poor Allister. Not that it was so unusual these days—he'd heard the Radcliffe girls were banned from helping Eleanor at Wiltwyck School now because they just couldn't keep their hands off the young studs. It said something about society, but he wasn't sure what, and he wasn't in the mood to address *that* problem at the moment. He would have to send his scouts out in search of a suitable black.

Buffy Chadds-Ford smoothed her hair back into a chignon and slipped into a sophisticated black crepe suit for her trip into the city. Fax hadn't sounded pleased about meeting with her this afternoon, but damn it, he was her only hope, and the only person she knew who wouldn't be shocked by her admission. He missed little. And he would care if her name was smeared from one end of Philadelphia to the other. He believed one lesion could produce a plague, and a scandal would jeopardize some profitable connections, not to mention the friendship between the Chadds-Fords and the Bennetts. Then, too, she was Lauren's godmother.

He would help.

". . . and so," Buffy concluded, her composure only slightly ruffled, "I couldn't shoot him, and I don't know anyone . . ." She let her voice trail off.

Fax wanted to praise the gods of fate, laugh at this turn of events that was only slightly less fortunate than his grandfather's timely legacy. But he forced himself to remain calm. Careful questioning had told him all he needed to know about Red Shoes. The black was handsome. He was smart. He was compelling. He was, in short, ripe for the picking.

"Amusement, Buffy, is one thing; murder is another. When Red Shoes reappears, as he will, send him to me. And now let's call Silver and I'll take the two of you to dinner."

Fax waited until the consommé had been served. "Buffy, you know a lot of women. Do they want careers?"

"Some do, some don't. Why?"

"It seems to me that a new movement is afoot, both here and abroad, since the war."

"Women have been rulers since Biblical times. Why should they be only ornaments here? Look at the baroness; she runs her affairs. And there is Mrs. Roosevelt."

Buffy was on the dangerous middle ground of what she instinctively perceived to be a marital tiff. She needed Fax's help, and Silver was her dearest friend, even if she didn't know Buffy's deepest, darkest secrets. "What do you want to do, Silver?"

"I don't know. I just know I am not fulfilled. What can I do? What have I been trained to do?"

There was no response. She was, as they all knew, what she had been reared to be: a wife and mother. How did one say that beneath one's polished surface there burned a fire that raged and blazed, that though the infrequent sex with one's husband was satisfying and occasionally fulfilling, he was consistently predictable and conservative; that he was generous with his money and stingy with his time; that what she wanted was to be the object of unrestrained desire. *The baroness had Sasa and her own interests.*

Fax noted Silver's look. "Perhaps I have been wrong, Silver. Women are entitled to the same civil rights as anyone who has proved him- or herself competent. And those civil rights include the right to work. When you decide what you want to do, let me know, and I will help. More wine, ladies?"

"And how is my goddaughter?" Buffy asked diplomatically.

"Beautiful. Smarter than any three people have a right to be. And of course I don't need to mention her overactive imagination, since we've all been more or less victimized by it on at least one occasion." Fax laughed. They all knew about Lauren's imagination. "She's almost mystical. If I believed in this sort of thing, I would say she can see and hear things others can't. Perhaps we should have tried harder to give her siblings."

Fax blotted his lips on the damask napkin. "I'm afraid she is a little wild. I do not understand her, I cannot control her, but I simply adore her." *There was only one other person who was as quick a study as Lauren, or strong enough to take his love and generosity and still remain her own person—a temptress with cat-green eyes and flame red hair, who was at once as hot as the desert dunes and as cool as the surrounding mountains.*

"You know," he said, as though he'd just had the thought, "I'd like Margaret Bourke-White to photograph Lauren. Perhaps she could catch both the whimsy and the determination." He paused, taking a bite of trout. "Other than Bourke-White, there are very few good women photographers. I've thought about it, and I think that women lack the insight, realism, and passion for making the craft an art form." He held up his hand as if to ward off the verbal barrage. "It's not their fault, of course, that they are too shallow to catch the subtle threads that hold the fabric of life together. It is the fault of men like me who wish only to spoil their wives and protect them.''

''I disagree, Fax. Entirely.'' It was not all his fault. She had sought to redeem her one indiscretion by being the perfect wife and mother, but it had not made her shallow.

''Nothing would please me more, Silver, than your proving me wrong.'' What Silver wanted most was attention, and like most women she would do almost anything to get it.

''Then I shall do so,'' she replied.

It had been easy. He would praise her to high heaven, and if she showed any talent whatsoever he would get her some assignments, arrange a showing, get anonymous patrons to inflate the price of her work. That should keep her satisfied. ''What do you think, Buffy? You think Silver can become a topflight photographer? As good as Margaret Bourke-White?''

''Without question,'' Buffy replied. Life was so wonderful she might even keep the latest trinket Allister had sent out this morning.

CHAPTER TWENTY-FOUR

Red Shoes dropped in on Buffy before breakfast. He might not know much about life on the hill, but he knew women, and they were more vulnerable before they got their paint on. He hadn't planned to come back quite this soon, but he missed Fat Eddie, his main hooker was having an abortion, and he was just flat bored. Needed someone to play off of. Life wasn't much fun alone; no one to fuck with.

"Morning, Mama."

Buffy wrapped her robe about her and pulled a cigarette from the crystal box. Red Shoes leapt to his feet, whipped out his gold lighter, and held the flame just beyond her reach.

Buffy's hand shook. She forced herself to look at the lighter, but her eyes met Red Shoes' above the flame as she leaned forward.

"Whatcha got for me, Mama? You get me what I asked for?" He snapped the lighter shut and rubbed it slowly.

"Yes. Take the train into New York. Go see Fairfax Bennett." She pulled a slip of paper from the pocket of her robe. "Here's the address."

"It better be good, Mama, you know what I mean? 'Cause if it ain't I'll be back, and I'll keep coming back until I get what I want. That's a promise, Mama." He put on his coat. "You can go back to bed now, Mama, get your rest. Isn't it about time for you to go up to West Point again?"

He was nearly out the door when he heard her voice. "Red Shoes, how is Booker T.?"

He whirled to face her. "He's a heroin addict, Mama. Ain't I just got fucking A-terrific parents? I ought to be the biggest goddamn cat on the seaboard."

And then he was gone.

When Red Shoes got to New York, he went immediately to the Madison Avenue address Buffy had given him, but he didn't make an appointment. Instead, for three weeks, wherever Fairfax went, Red Shoes followed. He'd never done so much traveling, nor learned so much. By the time Bennett had returned from his second trip west, Red Shoes knew his man—and knew the cream in Buffy's coffee-colored baby was going to rise to the top.

His insurance policy had turned out to have a double indemnity clause.

Now he sat in Bennett's private office, the entry to which was no longer a secret to him and the newly made key to which he had in his pocket. *This was gon be fun.*

The first thing Fax saw when he opened his door was the red shoes propped on his mahogany desk. The second thing he saw was the face of the best-looking black he'd ever seen. The third thing he saw was that whatever Aljolson "Red Shoes" Cooles wanted, he would have to give it to him, or else he would have to kill him.

"Do you mind telling me who you are and what you are doing here—and how you got in?" Fax placed his attaché case in the middle of his desk and sat on the corner, looking down at Red Shoes. The nigger's hands were exquisitely cared for, his nails perfectly manicured. His red shoes shone like mirrors, and the crease in his trousers was as sharp as Fax's, maybe sharper, since Fax had been on a plane for hours.

"Would you like a drink?" Red Shoes rose and went to Fax's bar. "A Manhattan, I believe." He pulled a lemon out of the pocket of his muskrat coat. "With a twist." He stirred the drink and placed it in Fax's hand. "I'm Aljolson Red Shoes Cooles. I'm here because my *mother*, Buffy Chadds-Ford, said I should come see you. Say, ain't she and your *wife* big muckety-mucks in that bitchy Daughters of the American Evolution? In answer to your second question, I got in because I got brains. Anything else you want to know?" Red Shoes mixed himself a drink.

"Yes. Mrs. Chadds-Ford said you wanted a job. What did you have in mind?"

"Well, sir, Mr. Bennett, *sir*, I didn't have in mind cooking, either in your kitchen or up at Sing-Sing, so if you thought you needed a chef or a henchman, let's just start over. I don't mind riding in limousines, but I sure as shit would mind driving one. I ain't into numbers and you ain't running no rackets. What I've been is a pimp, but the desert is just too fucking hot, if you know what I mean. My personality isn't suited to factory work. I kind of liked Washington—I was down there last week, you know. Now, working on this hydrogen bomb might not be bad, lots of power there, but I ain't a chemist. No, what I think would suit me just fine would be politics. I could do a service for my fellow man and my country."

"What makes you think you can become a politician?"

"Because I'm the Pied Piper."

"The red shoes are going to have to go."

"Gone."

"And the muskrat coat."

Red Shoes took it off and stuffed it into the mahogany wastebasket.

"Your name will have to be changed."

"How about Charles Chadds-Ford?"

"Clayton Robbins."

"Middle initial?"

"None." Fax picked up the telephone. "Bring swatches and two tailors. Fifteen minutes." He turned to Red Shoes. "You need a little polish."

Red Shoes affected an offended look and studied his immaculate nails. No point in making this too easy.

"I will hire an etiquette tutor for you. You will begin tomorrow. By then I will have located a suitable apartment for you. You will be moving to New York. Tonight." Fax turned to the phone again and requested a barber immediately.

This was going too smoothly. Red Shoes was beginning to suspect Fairfax Bennett had a more subtle sense of humor than he had believed. Clayton . . . Clay. Easily molded into whatever shape the sculptor desired. "How, exactly, are *we* going to go about this?"

"I will establish your credentials. I will plan your political strategy. In the meantime, you will serve as my assistant. I will pay your bills and you will do as I say."

"Sounds good, Ben—I mean, Mr. Bennett."

"You will also draw a very good salary."

"Shit, man, that's fucking A-terrific. I like mon-ey." Red Shoes drew out the word.

"If you've got something you want to say, say it, Red Shoes. I'm tired of your innuendos. If you hadn't done your homework, this extortion scheme of yours would have ended with your black prick rotting in a block of concrete in the Hudson River. Do we understand each other?" *This nigger hadn't hired a tail, he'd followed Fax himself. No small accomplishment—a big good-looking black who could make himself invisible. He was smarter than Fax had dared to hope. Maybe too smart.*

"Brothers under the skin and all that shit. We understand each other." Red Shoes could learn a great deal from a man like Fax. Power wasn't penny-ante blackmail. Power was lack of fear.

Fax watched the door close behind Red Shoes before he started laughing. He could hardly wait for the pimp-turned-politician to learn that one of his springboards up was going to be distinguished military service in the Korean conflict about to be staged along the Thirty-eighth Parallel. He was whistling as he left to go home for dinner and check on the progress of the darkroom he was having built for Silver. The battery of Hasselblads and tripods and lights should have been delivered today. He stopped at Brentano's and bought a book of Margaret Bourke-White's photographs.

As soon as Fax left the building, Red Shoes hotfooted it back across the street, rode up in the elevator, and let himself back into the office. He wanted his muskrat coat. It might get fucking A-cold in Washington.

CHAPTER TWENTY-FIVE

It was May 1, 1955, and the American-backed premier of Vietnam, Ngo Dinh Diem, was under siege by Ho Chi Minh guerillas. Civil war raged in Saigon's streets.

In New York Graham Greene's *The Quiet American* hit the shelves, received literary and political acclaim, and further drove home fifteen-year-old Michael Christian's ambition to invade and conquer the elite realm of publishing. He intended to be like the Buddhist monks who set themselves on fire for the cause. The only difference was the monks did it devoutly; Michael did it egotistically. He wanted to be a legend.

He walked from aisle to aisle in Brentano's, looking at books, studying bindings, papers, and typefaces. Last week he had seen an old man get out of a limousine in front of Stearns & Mendall. "Pick me up at eleven. I have a luncheon engagement."

"Yessir, Mr. Mendall."

Michael Christian could already hear it: *Yessir, Mr. Christian. At your service, Mr. Christian.*

Barbara Mendall, eleven-year-old daughter of Harry Mendall, publishing scion, was hiding from her mother, the former Della Stearns, publishing heiress.

"Barbara. *Barbara.* Come to Mother. Mother wants you."

Barbara shivered under her four-poster bed.

"Bar-BARA!" Her mother whisked the Belgian lace dust ruffle from the polished hardwood floor and grasped her arm, yanking it half out of the socket as she pulled Barbara from beneath the bed.

"Don't tell, don't tell. I will leave you and never come back."

Barbara didn't tell. She never had. She never would.

Eleven-year-old Evie Afton sobbed into her pillow.

"There, there, little angel, don't you cry." Vashon patted the curly head of her precious charge. "Nothing can be that bad."

"They won't play with me. They said my mother is a bad woman. Is she bad, Vashon? Is she?"

"No, sweetheart, your mother's not bad. Now, come on downstairs. Mister Ben has sent you a present."

Lauren Bennett's many guests gathered around the maypole erected near the Austrian carousel on the vast Montauk Point grounds. Silver's camera shutter went *click, click, click* at their antics, and Lauren, wearing a crown of lilies and lilacs, led the way by picking up the first ribbon and beginning the dance.

We could pick up any ribbon in life and the outcome would be different. The choice . . . the choice . . . that's what makes all the difference. Threaded in, threaded out. Knotted, twisted, looped, tangled, or tied. In a neat bow or an unraveled fringe. Silver missed the shot.

Lauren stopped suddenly, staring at the trees. Before her had appeared a boy about her age with dark hair and laughing eyes the color of lapis lazuli, and he was calling her name. She dropped the ribbon and ran toward him, but he vanished, as he did in her dreams. She returned to the maypole, retrieved her ribbon, and once more led the dance.

Buffy Chadds-Ford visited Booker T. Cooles in the exclusive Hennings Memorial Sanitarium. It wasn't an act of charity: should Clayton Robbins ever want to remind her she was his mother, he would be surprised to learn his father was alive and well and ready to be presented to the world. No, he wouldn't want that known. *Not now.*

Savannah Lee Owen whittled the pencil nub to a sharp point with her pocketknife and bent her head over the paper again. It was the third murder story she had written this weekend, and in all of them the preacher and Norma Mae got killed, but each time it was a different preacher and a different killer. . . . *And they found their bodies with their eyes gouged out and their legs severed.* She paused for a moment, then wrote *And their little girl just cried and cried and cried.*

Prince Kenir Ashad crossed the palace courtyard and entered the harem for the first time since his return from Saint Moritz. At twenty-one he was a favored international playboy. He possessed the Eastern propensity for male dominance in equal measure with Continental charm. It was seductive as hell, and he knew it. His endurance was legion and there wasn't a woman on five continents who had heard of him who didn't want him lock, stock, and cock.

Remni Bailesti motored along the coast with his parents and the Marquise DuBonnet. His father had that faraway look in his eyes, and the baroness and the marquise were deep in conversation. God, how he longed for a brother or a sister. He had too much of everything; he would have liked to have had someone to share it with. He was loved, but he was lonely. He closed his eyes and made contact with his imaginary sister.

Fax Bennett left the maypole dance early.

By midnight Ben Randolph was burrowing deep in Moni's warmth.

Evie slipped out to ride her new palomino naked through the silvery moonlight. She had named Ben's gift *Kemo Sabe*; it meant "faithful friend."

CHAPTER TWENTY-SIX

In one month she was going to be eleven, and she still had not found her prince. It was humiliating. *Snip, snip, snip.* The heavy scissors sliced the newsprint. She had nearly one hundred announcements by now, enough to master the wording. She had the stationer's name. She had worked out the invitation. It was really too bad Mommy and Daddy were going to be away on her birthday. They would have loved this party.

Lauren put the newspaper back in the garbage and went to her sitting room and rang for a servant.

"Yes, Mistress Lauren?"

"I'd like a Coke, James." She grinned at the butler. "Oh, and James, I'm going to become a reporter. Would you please have a typewriter moved into my room? Also, I would like to go to the hangar this afternoon and look around." She had to get the name and address.

"Certainly, Mistress Lauren."

Lauren crunched her ice, a no-no in any event and especially forbidden since the installation of her new braces, but it wasn't the greatest sin she intended to commit.

There. It was nearly perfect.

> ### BENNETT HEIRESS BETROTHED TO PRINCE ON ELEVENTH BIRTHDAY
>
> *Lauren Bennett, daughter of industrial magnate Fairfax Randolph Bennett VI and Mrs. Bennett, the former Anne De Ferrers, celebrated her eleventh birthday by accepting the proposal of Prince*

Oh, dear, Prince who?

> *by accepting the proposal of a prince who shall remain unnamed at the request of his father, the king, until*

Back to the garbage.

> *until the political unrest in their country has stabilized. The king, who said he couldn't be more delighted, has asked for the kindness of the press in re-establishing crucial governmental relations between his country and the U.S. Lauren, the prince, and a host of the Bennett heiress's friends met on the Caribbean island of Martinique to blow out the candles on her cake.*

She thought she would try *The New York Times* first. It would be easy. She had heard Daddy's assistant, Miss Andrews, do it for him a dozen times. She had Miss Andrews's accent down flawlessly, right to the little lisp when it was really big news. It was too bad she didn't have a photograph to courier over to the paper, but Silver would be furious if she took her favorite. Perhaps if she gave them her arrival time, the press would be waiting to photograph her triumphant return.

The invitation was easy. She would just have to watch the mail for the r.s.v.p.'s. She hadn't quite figured out how to get away from under the heavy security that constantly surrounded her, but she would, oh yes she would. Miss Andrews would also make the flight arrangements; she knew how to do that too. Daddy's crew and plane would fly them. Daddy's caterer would feed them. Her party would be in Martinique.

Her prince would be there. She knew he would, if she just thought about it long enough and hard enough.

CHAPTER TWENTY-SEVEN

Considering the headlines on August 6, 1956, Lauren could not have picked a more auspicious moment for her media debut. Speculation ran rampant as to the prince's identity. The Suez Canal was a sizzling hotbed after Nasser seized its control and revenues in retaliation for western withdrawal of financial support for the Aswan Dam, and the British, French, and U.S. were not exactly convivial bedfellows with the Egyptians. An unnamed prince smacked of a traitorous alliance. The Associated Press and UPI wasted no time in picking up the story.

Fax settled into his first-class seat and looked at his newspaper.

Silver dashed into the hotel lobby, slung her camera back over her shoulder and reached for a paper.

In Washington the president called Fairfax Bennett's office and tracked him down somewhere over Kansas.

By noon, James was in the hospital with a bleeding ulcer, the president was howling in the Oval Office, and Fax had two reporters and one editor fired, Miss Andrews in tears and hysterics, and his Martinique-bound plane slowly touching down on the runway of its home base.

Lauren looked out the window. It was not quite the triumphant return she had planned. The press, however, was there. She was first off the plane. Dark hair cascaded across her right cheek; on the left it was arranged behind her ear. She paused on the portable steps and in the best that Hollywood could offer, she said, "Caviar, dahlings? It's beluga," and proffered a crystal plate to the press. "Oh, hello, Daddy. You made it home for my birthday after all." She bent to kiss him.

"You will tell them this was a hoax and you will tell them now." Fax's fingers dug into her arm, pulling her off her throne and down the last two steps onto the tarmac. "You wanted to talk to the press—talk."

Lauren's eyes filled with crocodile tears. She sniffed bravely, courageously, and held out her arms to the crowd. "The prince was killed en route to Martinique. My heart is broken. I shall enter a convent tomorrow."

And Fax, watching this performance, thought it was one hell of an idea.

By morning Silver and Fax were laughing over their breakfast newspaper. Each account was more priceless than the last. "We really shouldn't let her have the satisfaction of reading these," Silver murmured between gasps.

"I know."

They didn't mention their guilt.

CHAPTER TWENTY-EIGHT

The Soviets put down the Hungarian Revolution in Budapest and shot Sputnik into space. In America the emphasis was on ethnic pride; Puerto Rican gangs rumbled on Broadway and integration galvanized the black population of Little Rock, Arkansas.

In Las Vegas gamblers put down their last silver dollars, and gangsters shot their enemies in Chicago, New York, Miami—anywhere but on the Gaming Commission's sacred golden turf. No one mentioned the host of victims already interred in the great desert; only the iguanas, gila monsters, and rattlesnakes slithering over their unmarked graves paid posthumous respect. Only those who survived the hits and the crime bosses' new edict remembered the desert ghosts and they weren't talking. They pulled the strings, puppeteers of vice, graft, and corruption, purveyors of greed, merchants of murder.

And this was Evie's world. It was all she knew. She learned it from Ben Randolph's lectures to Moni on legal loopholes and she learned it from Marcus Anovese and the *familia*. You took what you wanted, and if someone else wanted it too, you had to be quicker, slicker, and more ruthless. If you got caught, *then* you worried about the cost. But in her world you seldom paid the price, because you were smarter, smoother, and dirtier than the rest. What impressed Evie was people getting their way. Ben Randolph got munitions contracts and had style. Marcus Anovese got his Mafia minions to do his dirty work and had clout. Moni got both Ben and Marcus and had the advantage of their individual expertise.

Mother was smart.

Mother was smooth.

Mother was *dirtier than the rest*.

It was another command performance—Sunday brunch in the Flamingo Palace dining room. It was another Shirley Temple in a Manhattan glass, another maraschino cherry, another disgusting olive and anchovy omelet, another *bor*ing occasion with Anovese and her mother.

Excluded as usual from the conversation, she sat brooding, picking out the olives and lining them up around the gold-rimmed perimeter of her plate, then knocking them off one by one; spearing anchovies with her fork and burying them under the eggs. The gesture put her in mind of the rumors circulating about Anovese—the alleged scores of hits he had ordered and the stinking bodies left to rot under the sun-broiled sands.

At Anovese's annoyed look, she intentionally clanked her fork against the china. If he thought she was a minor irritation, she could turn into a major disruption by providing a little more stimulating brunch chitchat. "By the way, Marcus, did you know your Tampax dispenser is empty?"

Anovese's face turned as crimson as the red-flocked wallpaper. His index finger grazed his cheek; a telltale muscle flexed.

Moni kept her composure by swallowing half a muffin

whole. Since these deliberately shocking remarks from Evie were the norm these days, Moni wished Marcus would excuse her daughter from attending the Sunday brunches. But he was adamant about appearances. Curiously he seemed to require a facade of family. But they were not a family. She slept with him, she was his only friend, yet she would never belong to him, and her daughter wasted no opportunity to disillusion him. "Apologize immediately, then excuse yourself and wait in the lobby."

Moni heard the conversations of other diners, a cough or two, the clatter of busy busboys, but she did not hear an apology. She glanced at Marcus, saw his impatience. She looked at Evie, saw her defiance. "Now."

Evie stood, shoving in her chair and spilling their drinks. "So sorry. Excuse me, please." Her sugar-stiffened crinolines rustled as she flounced from the room, leaving a trail of white specks on the burgundy carpet.

"I'm going to kill Vashon if she doesn't quit petrifying one hundred yards of netting for that child to sugar-dust everything with," Moni said. "She thinks it makes her sweet and feminine. I think it makes her a nuisance."

"You worry over petticoats when your daughter disgraces you?" He snapped his fingers, drawing the attention of the maître d'. "I want every dispenser in every ladies' room in this hotel filled *immediatamente*."

Josh Garr watched the maid enter room 218. Soft, young, virginal. Pure, clean innocence he could bury himself in. He slipped in behind her, one hand already on his zipper.

Silver was alive as never before. Last month Chicago, the month before, New York. Exhibits, exhibits. Photographs sold, reviews ecstatic. Record prices. She was better than Bourke-White. Incisive, sensitive, a fresh eye, a genuine talent: those were the phrases used to describe her. In the West, they said she was hotter than a smoking gun. And she was in the West, her first real assignment, if you discounted the hula-hooping geometric perspective of the Duke and Duchess of Windsor. A *coup de maître* and now they called it art, and the entire nation was swiveling their hips to keep the flourescent plastic gyrating. Fax was still humoring her, pretending pride yet managing to imply he was responsible for her success. She didn't want to do trends, she wanted to make statements.

He wasn't responsible for this assignment. In fact, he didn't even know she or her 35-millimeter was in Vegas. It was a story. It would be the shot of a lifetime if she pulled it off. The Mob's West Coast kingpin was elusive; his bodyguard, Josh Garr, had smashed more cameras than anyone wanted to think about. The word was out: you photograph Marcus Anovese, you manage to develop the film, you die.

Josh's mouth closed hungrily, suckling the budding breast. He looked into the maid's eyes. Wide open, tiny sparks of pleasure that fanned him to flames.

The limousine slowed before the Flamingo Palace. Silver slid over and pressed the button, and the window went down. She removed the lens cover from her camera.

Josh Garr moved slowly, deliberately. He cupped the young buttocks in his hand, bringing them to meet him, driving himself into the honeyed, tight warmth of the child beneath him. Oh, Jesus, it was sweet.

Evie stuck another nickel in the slot machine, then wiped her hand on her tightly-belted skirt. *All money was dirty.* She jabbed another one in, then another. *Life was a gamble.* A buffalo: good luck. In it went. *Why couldn't she have a mother and father like other kids?* Two cherries and a banana. She heard the rush, the silver sluice, like water over the Hoover Dam. *If she couldn't escape, she would beat them at their game.*

She looked over at the roulette table. The croupier glanced around, then nodded at her. She plunked down her do-re-mi and bet. The wheel spun, the ball rolled, the checkerboard blurred. Thirteen black. She always bet the same sure number. The croupier grinned. *He always let her win. Men were such suckers.*

Josh looked at his watch. Time to bring the car around for the Sunday drive back to Moni's Place. But he just couldn't leave. Not now. This was more sanctifying than church, more holy than a host of angels. He bent his head to the young breast.

Silver unpacked her backup camera, slipping it into her lap. "Go when I tell you to go," she whispered to the driver. "It will be worth your while."

"I bet she's in the casino." Moni eased her arm through Marcus's.

"Like her mother, forever trying to make a buck."

"Look who's talking."

Anovese looked down at the small woman beside him. *A different time, a different place . . .*

"Go!"

Evie shot the croupier a conspiratorial look and dumped her dollars down the front of her boat-necked blouse. They wouldn't get past her belt—twenty-two inches cinched to eighteen. "Well, are *we* finally ready to leave?"

"You too good for us these days?"

The look she shot him was unmistakable.

He put one arm around Moni, the other forcefully about Eve, and propelled them through the lobby, intent on preserving the family image until he had her alone.

Silver's arm ached, but she didn't dare waver. His car wasn't there, but she wasn't taking a chance. If Bourke-White could hang off airplane wings, she could hold on a bit longer.

The doormen moved from their positions beside the potted palms, each extending one white-gloved hand to the heavy plate-glass doors. The doors swung wide, framing the Mafia kingpin, a beautiful redhead, and a girl about Lauren's age.

Click, click, click—Backup camera—snap, snap, snap. through the lens she saw him, no longer a loving husband and father figure, but a Brobdingnagian animal, salivating for the kill. "Go!"

The driver took off as Marcus lunged toward the car. *Snap, snap.* He turned back to the hotel. "Faster," she urged the driver. She turned and shot picture after picture through the rear window as he jumped into a car and gave chase.

The limo raced down Fremont Street, pulled into the new Tropicana, and parked alongside five other identical limousines. In an instant, Silver had switched cars, and the six-vehicle motorcade was back on the street, Silver crouched on the floor of one car. Then they split up, and Marcus Anovese was left chasing tail.

No one paid any attention to the aristocratic blonde as she boarded her private aircraft at McCarran. Just another discontented socialite. They came and they went; it didn't mean anything.

Silver ignored the crew's nervous looks and whispers as she settled herself for takeoff. Why did they think Fax would be furious about this trip? So she had virtually hijacked her own plane. She shrugged. They probably remembered all too vividly Lauren's escapade, but this was different.

She was elated. She not only had the shots, she had the contrast she'd wanted—black and white, good and evil, human and animal. She was still alive and she was on her way. Big time.

There was one hell of a commotion by the time Josh Garr raced through the lobby doors. Anovese fishtailed to a halt in the middle of Fremont Street and jumped out, leaving the motor running and blocking traffic. His fist dented the hood of the car and a string of Sicilian vulgarities filled the air.

"What's going on? Where's he been?" Garr looked dumbfounded.

"A better question is where the hell have *you* been?"

Holy shit! Garr knew he was asshole deep in it.

Anovese spied him. He charged, toppling palm trees and pottery as he one-handedly splattered Garr against brick. Vese's knuckles whitened as his fingers tightened on Garr's throat. "You set me up. You take a powder while they take my picture, you greedy motherfucker." He squeezed Garr's neck until the flesh accordioned between his fingers. "I should kill you. Here. Now. Personally."

Garr's head reeled. The sensation of choking was merely a figment of his disoriented mind, for Anovese's hold deprived his lungs of even a dram of oxygen. He could focus on nothing but the starbursts exploding in his head. The sound of crushed cartilage magnified in his brain, becoming deafening and terrifying. Garr knew the bastard intended to make good his threat. Here, in broad daylight and before witnesses; now, without mercy or a chance for a reprieve; personally, in cold blood and without any regard for the consequences. In vain, he clutched Anovese's wrist and tried to pry the man's fingers loose from his throat. "I was fucking a maid. You can't kill me for that," he wheezed.

The pressure eased slightly. "You were fucking the hired help? Banging some whore insteada running interference like I pay you to do?" Anovese's face twitched. Garr's knees buckled and he sucked a mouthful of air as Anovese's hand disengaged and fell from his throat. He was unprepared for the backhand crack that split his lip and slammed the side of his head into the rough mortar once more.

"I should cut off your prick, shove it down your throat, and send your lifeless ass back to wherever the hell you came from." Anovese looked at him, then spat upon him. The mucus dribbled down Garr's cheek and mixed with the blood trickling from his lacerated lip.

Vese had the power and not the slightest compunction about executing his threats. Many times he had issued vile decrees and often Josh Garr had been chosen to deliver his reprisals; Garr knew better than most the potential that lurked behind the hooded black eyes. Cautiously he wiped a shirt sleeve across his cheek, blotting the saliva and blood from his chin. "I'll take care of it, Vese, I swear. I'll locate the negatives, destroy 'em, and make the stupid SOB who snapped 'em wish he'd never been born."

Anovese's fingers tangled in Garr's tie, and he was yanked to his shaky knees. "A chance to rectify your mistake I'll give you, but one more foul-up—if you hump a cunt or screw off on my time, I'll break every fucking bone in your body, grind you into bait, and feed you to the fish. *Capishe?*"

Garr bobbed his head, and Anovese kicked him in the nuts and slung him aside like so much garbage. Then he turned and strode toward the limo, which a young, alert, and very ambitious attendant was guarding. The crime boss favored the flunky with a glance as he climbed in, grunting at Moni and Evie to get their asses in the car.

Deciding that this was not the moment to antagonize Marcus, Moni ignored his arrogance. She would debate his insulting remark about *"banging whores"* later. Her head held high, she nudged Evie, who stood gawking at the prostrate bodyguard.

The sight repulsed Eve. Never would she give Anovese the opportunity to bring her to her knees. Not now, not ever. She could *personally* guarantee it.

Marcus was brooding, nursing a bottle of Scotch instead of her tit, licking his lips and his wounds.

"You're not interested? A *whore* doesn't appeal to you tonight?" She rolled away from him and left the bed, covering her aroused body and feigning indifference.

She had his attention. He slammed the bottle down on the nightstand and cast her a disgusted look. "What's this? I want a blow job and you're giving me the cold shoulder?"

"You *want*! You always want. You tell me your troubles, tell me your pleasures, and you expect the *whore* to comply. Get a trained monkey, Vese. I'm sick of complying." Her magenta robe separated, revealing an alabaster thigh as she flounced into the bathroom and slammed the door.

Vese rolled his eyes as he slugged the Scotch. Redheads were too moody. *What the hell had he done? Who the fuck did she think she was talking to? An errand boy?* The booze numbed his brain. He needed it tonight. Today was the day for the dumps. First Garr and now Moni. He needed people he could trust. The East Coast gangland wars were closing in, and Luciano's territory was being squeezed. His allies were marked with the kiss of death. And Marcus, Little Caesar of Vegas, was high on the list; hence his paranoia. Now he had reason to suspect Josh Garr of setting him up. He was also wondering why Moni had chosen this particular time to defect.

He knew better than to drink himself into oblivion, but he was weary, tired of being strong, smart, and cynical. He wanted to be sucked off, snuggled close, and contented for just once in his turbulent life. He had had his fill of the cold side. No more. Just once he wanted to *feel*—not second-guess, not care, not give a damn if somebody put a slug in him tomorrow. It was all irrelevant. You played your aces and let the chips fall where they may, you bluffed, and if you failed to fake 'em out, well, so much for longevity and so much for an easy buck.

But it hadn't been easy. Every fucking dollar he'd pocketed had been tainted with somebody's misery or somebody's blood. Every fucking woman he'd balled had smelled of another man's cum and another man's money. Bought and paid for with the express intention of getting to him. Dupe Anovese. Go for his jugular. Get him. Wear chinchilla. Purr. Hide the shiv you were sworn to place between his ribs while beguiling the pigeon with soft fur and a softer clit. *They were going to get him.* The hit could come from any direction. From any paid-for assassin. How much was he worth? A thousand? Several? Perhaps six figures. It depended on whether the syndicate wanted expertise or a cheap amateur. He hoped their aim was accurate. One shot, one bullet, straight through the heart. He'd coveted Vegas. He'd set himself apart, he'd broken the code. The hit could come from foe or family. Luciano had warned him. *You presume too much, Vese. I appoint you* guardiano *of my vice-child but you disregard my rights. I am the godfather of Vegas. You were only my* strumento. *You stretch my* pazienza.

"Moni, come here. I need you." He hated the resignation in his voice. He sounded like the teenage thug who'd answered the judge's "Do you have anything to say for yourself before I pronounce sentence?" with a reconciled "Nothing." The next day he had been shipped off to the state reformatory.

She appeared in the doorway, hand on hip, her flaming hair tumbling over a hot cheek. "Need me, Marcus? Since when does Luciano's favorite need Vegas's madam?"

"Need, need. Why do you harp on a for-shit word? Soon I will fall from favor. I will no longer be the capo, able to shield you. Come to me. Hate me tomorrow but love me tonight."

She crawled into bed beside him, wrapping her arms about his hairy chest, nestling a silky thigh between his brawny ones. "It's not your nature to be resigned, Marcus. Can't you tell me what is going on? Do you think Garr is setting you up?"

He cuddled her head against the crook of his shoulder, so that he could avoid her eyes. "The thought crossed my mind," he hedged as he raked his fingers through her hair and let the strands slip through the web and fall to her shoulders. "Tell me, *cara mia*, this man with whom I share you, will he be around when I am gone?"

His tone frightened her. "I don't like this, Marcus. Please, let's not talk—"

"You make a habit of avoiding reality when it is inconvenient. I find it amusing, because you are normally so practical. Hard cash you readily accept, hard times you are no stranger to, yet you do your damnedest to dodge hard facts. I've known for years that he exists, that I am a necessary substitute, that he is the father of your child."

She stiffened. It was a giveaway. He was right. He had always suspected; now he knew for certain.

"I am not jealous," he went on. "You give what you can to me, I give what I can to you. It's a fair trade-off. I am a difficult man, a crude man. I know this. I complicate your life. I secure your business, I keep his place warm in his absences, and I know the side of you that you are afraid to reveal to him. Haven't I earned one exclusive night? I'm lonely, Moni. Touch me. Really, really, touch me. I want to feel you—the woman you are, not the man-pleaser you pretend to be. They're gonna take me out, Moni. I don't know when or where, but I know it. A hit comes when you least expect it."

His arms encircled her. His self-imposed alienation and vulnerability had pierced her. She cupped his head and turned her mouth to his. "You're not going to die, Marcus. We're survivors, you and I. You're scaring the hell out of me. I care about you. I do." She nipped his lips with her teeth. Her entire body trembled with desire. He had that effect. It was different with Ben Randolph, who had never been exposed to flea traps, rats the size of prairie dogs, chipped beef on toast or cramps in the gut when there was nothing but the aromas from next door to pacify the hunger. Marcus understood, and it was Marcus whose hunger she intended to pacify this night.

"I want you to have something." Anovese reached for his pants, fumbled in the pocket, and extracted a key. "This unlocks a Buddhist treasure. Remember the statue you admired on my mantel? Insert the key and it unlocks the andirons which, if you twist two revolutions to the right, will spring a trapdoor behind the fireplace in my apartment. I've stashed away nearly half a million of Luciano's leftovers throughout the years. The only other person who knew about the safe met a *sfortunato* accident. The money is yours, *cara mia*. Clean. No strings attached. Fuck the *familia*. I got no family left, only a sister in a convent who's taken a vow of poverty. Spend it well, Moni. Enjoy. And salute me now and then with the imported wine I supply. If you pass a cathedral, light a candle for my soul." He slipped the key beneath her pillow.

"It never was your money that appealed to me, Marcus." Her lips grazed his neck, then lingered at his nipples.

"The money will be a bonus, Moni." He twisted his fingers in her hair as he shoved her onto her back. His mouth descended on hers, his tongue thrusting and demanding. "What you like is primitive. And I am that."

Evie wished him dead as she lay in her room listening to the silence. She knew her mother was servicing the obnoxious Wop again. By now she had developed a sixth sense about rhythm and sensuality. Marcus dominated her mother like he dominated Vegas. But his downfall was coming, an Ides of March. She'd just studied Shakespeare's *Julius Caesar*. She was the soothsayer who spoke, who prophesied. *Beware Marcus . . . beware of Brutus . . .* And her middle name could have been Brutus.

She wished, she willed him . . . dead.

CHAPTER TWENTY-NINE

Michael Christian rushed out of City College, descended the subway stairs, and barreled through the turnstile. He was on his way to Stearns & Mendall to pick up his daily stack of manuscripts to be crammed in between studying, sleeping a couple of hours, and noshing a cold corned beef sandwich. He was lucky to have gotten the job and he would never fail to carry out his responsibilities, menial as they were. A reader, a lowly reader. But it was a start, it helped pay tuition, and it got him in the doors of the crème-de-la-crème literary house. Other readers picked up their assignments and left. Not Michael. They were invisible moles, tunneling through pulp, obscure. Not Michael: he *would* be noticed.

He shoved his way through the mass of people to the platform. He shifted the weight of his book satchel and carefully removed the fedora he hid during the day. He checked his watch. Perfect. He settled the hat on his head. It was an exact replica of the one worn by Harry Mendall. He untied his muffler and rearranged it around his neck, flipping one end over the other in the same fashion Mendall affected.

When he reached his stop, he bolted up the steps and into the teeming streets, fighting his way against the current of people going home, a salmon swimming upstream. No, this was not Michael Christian's destiny. He wanted to mold writers, to be a part of their impact—a man of distinction who would make no distinction between the intellectuals and the bourgeois. Of course, he would exploit them both in his ascent, although he would never forget that it was the poor, dumb masses that had ignited the spark within him. It was true that sovereign rule had to be mitigated with judiciousness, clear vision, and a broad scope, but he could not for one second allow sentimentality to cloud his purpose. He slowed to a walk at the sight of Mendall's driver leaning against the limo. Pausing at the corner to appraise his reflection in a tobacco shop window and adjust the brim of his hat a fraction of an inch lower over his brow, he eyed the display of Cuban cigars, thinking that if he ever got a promotion he'd splurge and buy a box for Mendall, kiss ass, do whatever he had to do. Out of the corner of his eye he glimpsed the driver moving into a position of readiness. Mendall's predictability was, at the moment, his strongest asset. He always left the S&M Building at precisely 4:45 and his devoted secretary of thirty-five years, Miss Birdie Threllquat, followed in the next elevator, arriving in the lobby at precisely 4:50. Michael paced himself perfectly to stride past the old man and tip his hat with a cordial "Good night, sir" midway between the S&M Building and the limo. He lingered in the lobby just long enough to usurp the doorman's duties and bedazzle Miss Threllquat with a smile, praying all the while he wouldn't end his promising career by saying, "Evening to you, Miss Thrilltwat."

Michael had detected some recognition in Mendall's face tonight, and Miss Birdie actually returned his smile. He hurried to collect his night's reading, making a point to greet everyone by name as he made his way to the editor's office and signed for the materials. One day his signature would mean something. In the meantime, he had thousands of words to read before the free period tomorrow when he would deliver his work, just in time to bid old Harry good morning.

CHAPTER THIRTY

Pat Boone crooned, Rock Hudson and Doris Day pillow-talked, and Eisenhower played golf while Mamie fluffed her bangs and nibbled on watercress sandwiches at garden parties. Except for Fidel and the beatniks, the trend was sickeningly wholesome.

This was not Savannah's world. She had learned about life the hard way—eating junk food out of paper sacks while staying on the move, dozing in the back booth of some honky-tonk while Norma Mae strutted her stuff, sitting outside of yet another tacky tent, playing with paper dolls by her lonesome while her mother was saved once more or listening on Saturday night to the country music greats—Kitty Wells, Patsy Cline, Jim Reeves, Hank Snow, and Eddie Arnold—belting out their songs and coming to her live from WSM at the Grand Ole Opry in Nashville, Tennessee.

Because of Norma Mae's religious itch, Savannah's elementary school years had included eighteen different schools in six states, but took her only six years to complete, partly because she was exceptionally bright but equally due to the accomplished fibbing with which Norma Mae had covered her truancy.

If the truth were known, the shy but pensive Savannah wasn't especially interested in school. It was boring. Her teachers weren't especially interested in her and she preferred it that way. Didn't have to answer any questions. The same went for prospective friends. She wouldn't make the effort because she knew she would probably be on the road again tomorrow. The contradictory cycles of Norma Mae's wicked ways and hallelujah benders confused her. The only thing she could count on for sure was the back of her momma's hand if she sassed or committed the unforgivable sin of being visible while Norma Mae was with a man. That was the gospel according to Norma Mae. As for herself, Savannah believed there was a God; she just didn't know where he kept himself and why he didn't answer her prayers.

By the end of the 1959 school term, Norma Mae had another attack of traveling fever. The suitcases were loaded into the secondhand maroon Studebaker, and she and the nearly thirteen-year-old Savannah headed west.

"Texas, maybe," Norma Mae said, gunning the oil-burning, gas-guzzling heap. "Yep. The hot Texas climate suits my mood just fine, 'cause I'm in heat myself. Maybe an oilman, or a big rancher. Whatever, he is gonna be a gentleman this time, Savannah. I promise."

"Hot" wasn't the word for Brownsville: it was sweltering. It didn't take Norma Mae long to meet up with her next beau. "Trashy" wasn't the word for him: he was scum. She hooked up with Skeeter at a roadhouse just outside of town. He was already drunk and it wasn't even noon. At first Norma Mae ignored him, but Savannah knew the pattern. He was rank-smelling, shabbily dressed, skinny as a rail, and double ugly—a far cry from the promised gentleman. But when he began to brag about a big gold strike in Mexico, Norma Mae started to take notice, and Savannah could see that for all his lack of refinement, Momma thought he was looking better and better. By the time he showed her a map of his treasure and gave her a little nugget, Norma Mae was convinced he was sent straight from the Lord.

Savannah was uneasy being in the house with Skeeter. She hadn't liked him from the first, and two days of his leering at her behind Momma's back hadn't changed her mind. She wished Momma would hurry back from town. Why'd she have to go after some crummy lipstick now, anyway? It was raining a river and dark as pitch outside. What with all that thunder and lightning going on, it was pure spooky being cooped up with Skeeter. She paced back and forth from the window to the screen door, looking for Momma, wishing to goodness she'd show up soon.

Skeeter belched. The sound was almost as disgusting as he was. "Bring me another beer, sugar. And then how's about you coming over here and sitting on old Skeeter's lap?"

Savannah ignored him, her attention riveted on the road.

"You hear me, gal? You deaf and dumb or what?"

His stale beer breath fanned the back of her neck. She hadn't heard him sneak up on her. "You're up. Get your own beer." Momma wasn't going to like her being sassy to her new beau. Maybe she'd get lucky and he wouldn't tell.

"Spunky, aren't ya?" he said, pressing closer and fiddling with her hair. Instinctively, she recoiled.

He jerked her around to face him. "Whatsa matter? Are you thinking you're too good for the likes of me?"

She turned her head from his mocking eyes. "Leave me be and I'll get you a beer."

"Changed my mind. I'd rather have you." He reached around to latch the screen door.

Terrified, Savannah broke free from his grip and bolted out the door.

Quick as greased lightning, he trapped her at the bottom of the porch steps, grabbing her by the hair and wrenching her back. "Stop it, you little bitch, or I'll break your fucking neck."

In the pouring rain, lightning flashing all about them, they struggled, Savannah writhing and kicking for dear life, Skeeter cursing and grunting for a piece of tail. Puny as he seemed, Skeeter was strong as an ox; meek as she looked, she resisted like a wildcat. One strategically delivered kick to his shin and she was off and running across the yard, trying to make it to the road, stumbling in the mud, panting, praying, almost away. Tackling her from behind, Skeeter drove her to the ground. They wallowed in the muck like pigs. Her skirt was up around her hips. "You want it the hard way, is that it?" He struck her across the face repeatedly, whipping her head from side to side.

She cried out desperately, "Momma's gonna kill you for this."

He sneered, tore open her blouse, brutally ground his mouth down on hers. The stench made her gag. "Your momma don't care 'bout nobody but herself." He fumbled to unzip his pants. She shoved him, but he was quicker, stronger. He pummeled her with his fist, bloodying her mouth, stunning her. She shivered.

"Those nipples hard for Skeeter? Kinda excited, are you?" Viciously he pinched her budding breasts.

She whimpered, her tears mingling with the rain on her face. Skeeter ripped off her panties, groping her private parts with dirty hands. "Good pussy, I'll bet. Probably better than your momma. You likin' it, gal? Feels good, don't it?"

She spit in his face. His body tensed, his hands went for her throat, squeezing, choking. When the pressure ebbed, she gasped for breath, half conscious. "Now you gonna do what Skeeter wants." He stuck his skinny cock in her mouth. "Wet it good . . ." He shoved it deeper. "Suck, or I'll . . ."

Savannah could not get her breath. Her eyes felt as though they would burst from their sockets. He jerked and gyrated. She tried to bite, but he snatched a handful of her hair and yanked. "Suck, bitch!"

Savannah flailed at him with her arms. He pinned her, one bony knee on her chest, the other alongside her pounding temple, forcing his cock to the deepest recesses of her mouth, shoving her tongue backward until she was gagging with each thrust.

"That's the way, you catch on quick. Suck, suck. Enough, you stupid cunt."

Mercifully, he withdrew. Savannah's jaw muscles ached. She vaguely distinguished the salty taste of blood. Then he was waving his engorged penis in front of her.

"Don't want to come yet, want to make it last, make it good." He squeezed his prick in his hand and rubbed it against her cheeks, slow and sickeningly. It felt like a cold snake slithering against her flesh, and she dug her backside deeper into the mud, praying for deliverance.

"Don't like that neither, do you? Well, girlie, I'm gonna bury it in you."

Like a cobra, he uncoiled from about her neck, reared, and plunged himself between her legs, shoving his cock inside, ripping her. He held her arms above her head, the mud oozing around them; his mouth muffled her screams. His frantic thrusting drove the air from her lungs, the fight from her body, and last shred of belief in a good and just God from her soul. How long could this go on? Is this what men did to Momma, what they did when she moaned and screamed and loved it so much she couldn't stay away from it? Savannah's mind went blank.

Skeeter felt submission in the body beneath him. The wildcat had become a kitten. Again he withdrew and flipped her over, ramming his throbbing pecker into her tight ass. "Jesus Christ, ain't no pussy in the world better 'n an asshole."

"God, no, don't."

Savannah's shriek was obscured by a crack of thunder, misunderstood by the maniac who took her. He slowed his movements, one hand cupped around her, fingering the bruised flesh between her legs, entering her vagina as he rhythmically slid in and out of her rectum.

For her it was searing pain. "Please, please," she begged.

Her soft pleas sounded like craving to him—just like her ma. His body tensed. This was all it took for him, just a little humble begging. He erupted and abruptly pulled out, smearing sticky sperm across her quivering buttocks.

His hands bit into her flesh and she was flipped over onto her back. He grinned demonically.

"Now lick it clean, cunt." He slapped her.

Savannah moaned, tears streaking her dirty face. Skeeter forced his slimy penis into her mouth a last time, a final degradation.

"You're a shit poor lay. No tits and a hairless pussy." He rolled off and stood. "Quit your sniveling and get up. Wash yourself before your momma comes home. She ain't gonna cotton to you trying to fill her shoes. Couldn't anyway," he sneered. He kicked her in the ribs, then left her on the wet, cold ground, vomiting, sobbing, shivering.

Savannah lay in the muck. Lightning struck nearby, and she cowered, drawing her knees to her chest, moaning, wondering, *Why . . . why me*, dear Lord? In the rain came whispers, quiet voices, like on the Mount, with fire striking the bush, a commandment coming down from on high. *Vengeance is mine. Whosoever defileth my temple shall also be defiled.* Savannah groped and clawed her way to her feet, stumbled and fell again. The voices urged her forward. *He is evil . . . he is evil.* She never, ever hurt like this—raw from mind to toe. Where, oh, where, was Momma? Blood ran down her leg. "Momma! Momma! Please help me!" Her momma wasn't there. She wasn't ever there when Savannah needed her.

Norma Mae checked the polish on her freshly manicured nails and then patted her golden hair. Was just about the color of real gold—would match the gold Skeeter was gonna cover her in. Sure was nice of him to pay her for getting all fixed up. Red Shoes was the only other man who'd done that. Sometimes she really missed Red Shoes. Skeeter wasn't anything to write home about in *that* department. She pulled out the new hot-pink lipstick and smeared it across her lips, pursing them at her reflection in the beauty parlor mirror. Sure was a stroke of genius to come in here and get a real good do on her hair. Should've been doing it all these years 'stead of giving herself second-rate bleach jobs. Lord, but she was a fine-looking woman, tits still as high and firm as when she was eighteen.

Norma Mae paid her bill, high heels clicking across the floor. Lord, but it was pouring. She looked outside again. An awning ran the length of the building. She could go next door to the drugstore. She was already late; a few more minutes and just one lemonade wouldn't hurt.

Savannah crawled through the mud to the porch steps and dragged herself to the screen door. Skeeter was swigging another bottle of beer, celebrating his conquest. She slunk in, unsure of her intent.

Skeeter cackled in the stillness. "Stupid cunt. Seen bigger mosquito bites than them tits."

Savannah listened, not to Skeeter but to the voices. *He is scum. No-good trash. It is your right, your duty, to kill him.*

Have strength—strength of will, strength of surprise. He doesn't think you'll rally. He doesn't believe you are human enough to hurt or care.

She cared. Oh, yes, she cared. Rivulets of blood dripped from her nose and vagina. She looked around, her gaze unfocused, until she spied an ice pick driven deep into the windowsill above the sink.

His back was to her, the ice pick handy. Only breathless seconds separated them. *Now . . . now! Move . . . move!* And she did, fast as lightning, quiet as a prayer.

Norma Mae turned the car into the rain-washed drive. It was still coming a flood. There wasn't any sense wasting a brand new hairdo. A few more minutes wouldn't matter. The lemonade was kinda upsetting her stomach. She pulled out the new frosted lipstick. Skeeter would think she was purely irresistible.

Skeeter turned, his eyes wide, the curse he would utter terminated at the instant Savannah plunged the ice pick into his unsuspecting heart. He doubled over. She stabbed him again and again. Then she jumped on him, riding him to the floor, lifting the pick, driving it home again and again. *It's all right*, the voices told her. *It's all right.* Blood gurgled from his purple lips. Skeeter convulsed, then went limp. *He is finished. It is over.*

Delicate spasms coursed through her bruised body, more euphoric than any sex act or abuse Skeeter could ever commit. She kicked Skeeter's body, rolling him over with her foot. Viciously she buried the ice pick in his scrotum, then crouched in the corner, her back to the peeling cabinets, her glazed eyes on the corpse.

When Norma Mae finally entered the run-down house and found Skeeter dead and Savannah Lee huddled in a corner, mindlessly humming a gospel song, she had no choice but to take charge. Slapping Savannah Lee across the face and roughly shaking her, Norma Mae ordered her to clean up quick.

"Come on," she yelled at Savannah. "Help me."

Savannah shook her head. Nothing, no one, could ever make her touch Skeeter again.

Seeing how perfectly useless the child was, Norma Mae grasped Skeeter's ankles and dragged his inert body out the door, bouncing him down the steps, through the mud, and to the gully behind the house. She remembered to remove the money from his wallet and the ice pick from his crotch before giving a mighty heave and sending his body rolling down the embankment to the rain-swollen gully below. She also remembered to say a few words on the departed's behalf as his corpse floated into a tangle of dead mesquite, including a short, but fervent prayer on her own behalf, asking that Skeeter's remains would rot quickly and they would escape being hunted down like common criminals.

Ice pick in hand, Norma Mae returned to the house and gathered up Savannah and their belongings. But there was one more thing she had to do before hightailing it across the country.

Hypnotically waving the ice pick before Savannah's eyes, she spoke softly. "I'm going to bury this pick so deep nobody's evah gonna find it, and you do the same with the memory of what happened here today." She continued waving the pick until Savannah's eyes began to follow it back and forth, back and forth. "Never tell. Pretend it never happened. You hear?"

As they crossed the rickety bridge, Savannah's gaze was drawn to the bloated creek below. She squeezed her eyes shut, but the image of Skeeter's corpse was indelible. She was unaware she was biting her finger until Norma Mae slapped at her arm. "Are you crazy, girl? Look what you've done. You've scarred your hand."

Savannah was fascinated by the tiny punctures welling with blood. Cold sweat broke out on her forehead, and relief flooded through her. Maybe she was crazy, but *she* was alive. Even if she didn't feel it, the blood confirmed it.

By dusk, they had made a clean getaway and had crossed the Louisiana border. Savannah slept now, lulled by the monotonous motion of the car and Norma Mae's rendition of "It Wasn't God Who Made Honky-Tonk Angels."

It was the only lullaby Norma Mae had ever sung to her.

CHAPTER THIRTY-ONE

Several months later, the night of the Halloween dance at Las Vegas High to be exact, Evie's festering contempt for Anovese erupted. Vashon had spent weeks sewing her sorceress costume—a creation cut from black silk and overlayed in tulle, with silver appliqués of stars and half moons and druid charms. Evie had pretended to be enthused about attending the silly affair, but in truth she had no intention of bopping or slow-dancing in the orange-and-black-crepe-papered gymnasium. High school dances were a drag. Chaperones, tutti-frutti punch, and letter sweaters were not her style. She'd long since given up trying to conform, to be part of the in crowd. Even if she'd worn her copper mane in a ponytail and sported penny loafers, even if she'd buttoned her sweater down the back and worn pert eyelet or snappy pop-beads or pom-pom ties, even if she'd hung out at Yummy Burger, sat in the cool booth reserved for the Sandra Dee types, sipped strawberry malts through candy pink lips, she still hadn't a prayer of penetrating the Gidget set at Vegas High. No,

Eve with her Rita Hayworth figure and Miss Sadie Thompson manner was not Sandra Dee material. She knew it. The Gidgets sensed it. And all the males at school smelled it. From the day of her registration, an undeclared war existed between her and the rest of the female student body.

Her one ally was Dustin Dade, a James Dean look-alike with all the trimmings—sideburns, studded black leather jacket, low-riding jeans, and a cigarette wedged between his even white teeth. He was the resident badass at Las Vegas High, a true rebel without a cause who headed a gang called the Diablos. He drove a raked, souped-up, moon-wheeled red and white '57 Chevy stenciled with the words EAT DUST AND DIE. Dusty had accrued more penalty hours and spent more time in the guidance center than any other student. In five years his sole achievement had been to make the faculty's most-wanted list. He'd been credited with initiating a fire in the auditorium, a rumble in the gym, and a food strike in the cafeteria. And once, after being cursed by a basketball coach for some minor infraction, he challenged the dribbling drip to a test of dexterity and guts along Dead Man's Stretch. The young and unseasoned coach kept the date, only to be blown off the road and end up in traction for the remainder of the semester. And still Dusty showed him no mercy; somehow he managed to sneak into the coach's private hospital room and recreate one of his idol's most notable scenes, hanging a plucked chicken from the pulley and weights that suspended the man's fractured legs. That's the kind of unoriginal guy Dusty was.

Yet when it came to Evie, the leader of the pack was a pussycat. The hot number wasn't any more acceptable than he, and he was a sucker for a husky voice and a great set of knockers. They were both defiant and in dutch all the time. He made his big move on her while they served a joint penalty hour for cheating on a chemistry exam. Though she didn't appear even mildly interested in his offer to buy her a beer at the gang's haunt on the outskirts of town, she stood waiting for him at his car after school.

"You like my wheels, good-lookin'?" He inspected his so fine reflection in the rearview mirror, then licked his fingers and slicked back the sides of his Dippity-Do'd pompadour.

She shrugged. "Why don't you show me what it can do? I got to be back at the whorehouse by five." She'd meant to shock him—to test him, the same as he had the basketball coach. She was a lot more dangerous than Dead Man's Stretch.

He slipped a cigarette from the pack he carried in his rolled-up shirt sleeve, flexed his tattooed bicep, and lit up. He took a deep drag and let the smoke curl across his upper lip. "I been to your old lady's establishment. Pretty plush. You selling or giving it away?"

"Neither—yet. And I'll decide when and with whom." She dropped her load of schoolbooks between them.

"Brace yourself, baby." A deafening blast of glass-packs, a roar of quad carbs, a pop of four-on-the-floor, a whine of Hurst linkage, and they peeled rubber out of the parking lot.

The '57 Chevy was fast, and Dusty was a kick. He never failed to give her a thrill, whether he was testing the speedometer and taking a sharp curve or burying himself in her soft curves and giving her enormous hickeys. For once Eve, not her mother, was desired, and for once Eve, not Anovese, was in charge. She convinced herself that she could out-Moni Moni and out-Anovese Anovese. Anything they could do, she could do better, double reckless, double often.

That's why she wasn't going to the Halloween dance tonight. That's why she had made plans to waltz through the jack-o'-lanterned front portal of the gym and out the back door. That's why Dusty would be waiting with his and the car's motor running and a change of clothes for her. They were throwing their own bash. No squares or Sandra Dees allowed. No virgin punch or bobbing for apples. They were too hip, too wild, too discontented to monster-mash their way through some Halloween hop. Besides, nobody was going to nominate them for king and queen of the dance.

Moni was easy to fool, absorbed as she was in overseeing the house, pleasing the johns, making a buck, turning a profit. Luckily a Shriners' convention had arrived in town, and Vashon was distracted by having to strip linens as fast as the girls could turn tricks. She hadn't time to be suspicious of Evie's vague answers to specific questions, like who was taking her to the dance and how come he hadn't the decency to pick her up at the house or send her a corsage.

"He works after school and can't get to the dance until later," she lied. "I'm going to meet him there to save time." That part was true. "Nobody wears a corsage at a Halloween dance, Vashon. Witches and Frankenstein's Brides would look dumb wearing tea roses."

Vashon seemed appeased. It was all set. Nobody would be the wiser. She just had to be sure to swallow plenty of Sen-Sens to camouflage the telltale booze-and-cigarette breath and to remember to wear something high-necked for a few days to hide the hickeys. Maybe tonight was as good a time as any to let Dusty unlatch her bra and cop a feel. He was hot and bothered and demanding more than French kisses and body clenches in the back seat.

"What time is the dance over?" Moni took time out from her ledgers to survey her daughter.

"About twelve thirty." Eve primped her costume, then spun about for her mother's review.

"You do look bewitching." Seeing her daughter attired in provocative black silk and makeup, Moni was suddenly struck by her maturity, her inherent seductiveness. *When had this transformation taken place?* "Was it necessary to line your eyes, Evie?"

"It's just for tonight. Don't gripe, okay? You don't have to send a car back for me. My date will bring me home." She scurried out the bedroom door and was half-way down the stairs when her mother's voice called after her.

"I forgot to ask—who's taking you to the dance?"

"Nobody special. Just a guy in my chem class. Bye."

At the emphatic slam of the front door, Moni dismissed her momentary unease and returned her attention to the ledgers.

No one was more surprised than Eve herself—except perhaps Dusty—to see Josh Garr saunter into the noisy juke joint and request Eve's presence in the limo parked outside. It had not occurred to her that Moni would mention her misgivings about her daughter's grown-up appearance and evasiveness to Anovese that night, or that he would act upon her motherly intuition.

"Buzz off." She turned her back on the bodyguard.

"I asked you nicely, Evie. Mr. Anovese doesn't like to be kept waiting. Let's go." Garr's tone grew more insistent.

Eve, who had changed into toreador pants, impudently swung one leg and chugged her spiked cider. "Tell the Wop that I'm not one of his stooges. I don't jump when he snaps his fingers. Unlike you, errand boy."

At that insult, Garr's fingers bit into her upper arm.

"You're blowing my concentration, faggot." The bang of Dusty's fist tilted the pinball machine. "Deliver the message and lay off my chick."

Cue sticks were set aside and an expectant hush fell over the Diablo gang. Only the jukebox dared to make a sound, the Fleetwoods wa-oo-waooing "Mr. Blue."

Garr's eyes slowly panned to Dusty. "Back off, punk—that is, unless you have no objections to wearing that shitty grin on the other side of your head."

Dusty flipped a cigarette butt at Garr. "Your threats don't mean shit around here, faggot. This is my turf."

Garr sprang at him, catching his wrist, spinning him around, wrenching one arm behind his back, and slamming him face first into the pinball machine, neon lights flashing, balls ricocheting, the scoreboard dinging. He pulled Dusty up by his greasy pompadour. "Any of the rest of you prettyboys want your face reconstructed?" He demonstrated his point like a Veg-O-Matic raconteur, shredding Dusty's face against the splintered glass.

Not one protest was uttered as he yanked Evie from the stool and dragged her biting, kicking, and cursing out the door to the blare of Toni Fisher's hot hit.

Garr shoved Evie into the back seat with Anovese, who locked the door and leaned back, a stony expression on his face.

Don't give him the satisfaction of thinking he can bully you like he does everyone else, she told herself. *You're Moni's daughter, don't forget.*

"You make your mother unhappy, Evie." His voice was gravelly. "This complicates *my* life."

"Well, that just breaks *my* heart. I hate you. I wish you were dead. You don't give a damn about my mother or me. You just like to play God."

"Your smart mouth will get you in big trouble someday. Shut up and listen. You bother me, Evie. And I don't like to be bothered. Your mother wants the best for you. Bad-ass punks and dumb little girls are a sorry combination. You either straighten up and be all that your mother wants, or I'll convince her to send you so far away that a postcard will take weeks to arrive."

"When are you going to convince her—during or in between humps? Or are you just going to eliminate me like anyone else who gets in your way?"

Anovese slapped her, and the force of it slammed her head into the window so hard her teeth rattled. "I'm out of patience, and your mother deserves better. You may talk to me like this once, but never again. Behave, or you'll find yourself living the life of a novice. *Capishe?*"

"Drop dead." She sulked in a corner of the back seat, her eyes blazing.

"Many share your wish. I don't intend to accommodate them or you." He addressed Garr. "Drop me off at the casino and take the brat home."

Eve sat transfixed before the parlor window. For over an hour she had been observing a small sparrow as it repeatedly flew against the glass. At first she'd thought the bird's attempts to pierce the invisible obstruction merely zany, but, after a while, its persistence and agitation began to intrigue her, its futile struggle to penetrate an alien environment acquiring some greater significance. Completely engrossed by the thumps and flutter of wings on the glass, she did not hear Vashon bustle into the room.

"What are you doin', chile, sittin' in here daydreamin? Dat old school bell done rang an hour ago, Evie. Yo' gonna be in a world a trouble again, sho' 'nuff." She punctuated her constant harping with plumps of the pillows and flapping of the draperies against the wall. "Yo' mopin' 'round here lately is gettin' on everybody's nerves. You better get off yo' fanny and on de move afore—"

"This dumb bird's been trying to get in the house for hours, Vashon. You'd think the silly thing would figure out it can't fly through glass, but it just keeps on beating its fool self against the window over and over again. It's giving me the creeps."

"I don like de sound of dat." She came to observe the eerie phenomenon for herself. "Dat's a bad sign, Evie. Mm-hm, de worst." Abruptly, she pulled down the shade. "Dat's what we call a supernatural suicide, it is. Dat bird's a soul tryin' to cross over from life to death. You get yo'self to school and forget dat bird, chile. It's an omen. A terrible, terrible omen."

"Oh, that's mumbo-jumbo nonsense, Vashon," Eve scoffed, and raised the shade. The sparrow dived for the window again, then dropped to the porch with a sickening thud.

Vashon shrieked and shrank from the window, her ebony eyes wide with alarm. "Gonna be a tragedy in dis house today. Some soul gonna depart dis good earth. De spirits never lie. Don touch dat bird, Evie. I means it. I got to warn Miss Moni. I got to convince her to close de' doors dis night. If she don listen to me, somethin' awful's gonna happen. Something evil—" Vashon broke off and raced upstairs to tell Moni.

Evie was not the least bit unnerved by the incident. In fact, she tingled with anticipation. She stepped closer to the window and stared at the lifeless bird lying on the porch. Usually Vashon's superstitious malarkey didn't faze her, but this time she found it stimulating. Her vision blurred, and the bird's carcass suddenly was transformed into a Sicilian corpse. Eve's lips twisted into a smile. Vashon could fret and wail and carry on all she wanted, but it wouldn't do a bit of good. Moni wouldn't close the doors tonight. It would be business as usual. Turkeys in the beds tonight and turkey on the table tomorrow. At least Anovese wasn't joining them for this holiday—she'd heard him tell Moni he'd come by *tonight*!

She blinked, smiled smugly, and waved adios to the broken bird. "Farewell, poor Sicilian sparrow. Mother will miss you. Too bad. So sad." She picked up her books and skipped out the door. Even the thought of receiving penalty hours for tardiness did not dampen her spirits. If Vashon's prophesy was accurate—and she chose to believe it was—it meant that tonight was the night Anovese would be erased from her life for good. But she wasn't going to take any chances. All day long and throughout her penalty hours, she would concentrate on summoning the dark spirits to fulfill the omen.

A toilet flushed. She heard his belt buckle hit the dresser as it did every time he started dressing. Shit, he was leaving, and he was still healthy as a horse. No gagging, choking spasms, no Moni shrieking for an ambulance, no fucking heart attack. No nothing but the sound of his footsteps following Moni's down the stairs.

A clank outside. She raced to the window and saw Josh Garr crouching by the jacked-up sedan, a tire iron in his hand.

The front screen whacked shut. Moni's voice. Then Marcus's. "What's the trouble?"

Garr banged another lug into the hubcap. "Sorry, Vese. It won't take but a few more minutes to change this. Must have picked up a nail or something. Tire's flatter than a pancake."

"Make it snappy."

Eve slumped her elbows on the upstairs sill, pinching her cheeks between her palms. *Damn Vashon! Getting her all excited, raising her hopes with all that mumbo-jumbo crap. Nothing awful was going to happen to the bastard tonight. Probably never, with her luck.*

A car swerved off the highway, its headlights blinding, speeding toward the house. Garr flattened himself against the ground. Anovese cursed in Italian and shoved Moni off the porch into the shrubbery. A flash. A machine gun burst. Another staccato barrage. Moni's scream. Taillights, then silence.

Moni scrambled to Marcus's side. Cradling his head in her lap, she tried to staunch the flow of blood with her ivory satin dressing gown. Garr vaulted the porch steps, shouting, "How bad's he hit?"

"Bad. Call an ambulance." *He wasn't going to make it. Blood was already seeping out his nose, his mouth.*

Garr dashed inside, shoving the quaking Vashon against the wall as he grabbed the hall phone.

"A setup," Anovese gurgled.

"Oh, God, Marcus, this isn't happening." Moni bent over him, tears trickling onto his cheek.

"Tears, Moni? It is not you. Don't cry for me." His mouth twitched. He tried to lift a hand. It fell. His pupils became fixed.

Marcus Anovese was dead, as dead as the sparrow that lay a few feet away from him. By her mother's sobs, Eve knew the prophesy had been fulfilled. She tiptoed back to bed, plumped her pillows Vashon-style, snuggled in, and pulled up the covers. The house was in chaos, everyone running, screaming, shouting, a siren wailing in the distance. *She better pull the covers over her head, at least appear as though the execution had upset her. So much for Thanksgiving dinner. Oh, well, what was missing a piece of pumpkin pie compared to never having to swallow another disgusting anchovy?*

CHAPTER THIRTY-TWO

"Guess what?"

By now, Fax thought, he should have been accustomed to Silver's enthusiasm, but it still rendered him dumb every time she responded passionately to a new assignment. By God, why couldn't she have responded to him like that?

"What, Silver?"

"*Life* wants an exclusive on the ruling royalty in Shahdesh."

"Oh, absolutely super, Mother." The nearly fifteen-year-old Lauren forgot her newly acquired sophistication as visions of gauzy veils, dark eyes, priceless jewels, and handsome sheiks commandeered her attention. "Please, may I go with you?" *She was going to meet the prince who had appeared in her dreams ever since she could remember.* She could feel it. She *knew*.

"The Middle East is boiling right now. I forbid either of you to go."

"I will be a palace guest of King Ashad. It is perfectly safe."

"Oh, please, Daddy." Lauren lifted her napkin and covered the lower part of her face, attempting a not too comic version of a come-hither look. If Grace Kelly could have Monaco, she would have a bigger kingdom, her very own Arabian nights. Her prince would whisk her away, hide her from the world and her parents, and she would emerge a queen above all others, her photograph on the front cover of every publication. She would write her memoirs. She would be famous.

Silver saw the look and remembered her secret cache of photographs. Lauren hauntingly posed along the shoreline at home, looking across the water, watching. Waiting. Or those where she was dancing with abandon, her long dark hair flying, her eyes bottomless pools of emotion, ever changing, drawing one in . . . into places one might not have the strength to go. Silver would love to show those photographs, but she could not. They were too private. They were her memories, her dreams. They were Sasa. "I'm sure I could arrange for Lauren to go."

"No." He would call the editor of *Life* tomorrow and put an end to this nonsense.

"Without Mrs. Bennett," the editor replied, "there will be no interview. King Ashad agreed to this exclusive only on the condition that Mrs. Bennett be the photographer. I've already scheduled an issue around it. Of course, I could use the file photos we have of the Saudis receiving the helicopters you sold them, but I hate to put out anything that appears so un-American. It's not popular with our readers."

"I'll sue."

"King Ashad has personally assured your wife's safety. I would suggest you assure King Ashad's, and all will be well. Is there any future feature you would like the magazine to do?"

"My daughter would like to accompany Mrs. Bennett. I will make those arrangements directly with King Ashad."

"Very good, Mr. Bennett. Thank you for your understanding."

Fax hung up, then dialed home.

"Oh, just marvy, Daddy. How super! Thanks."

Fax replaced the receiver and stared into space. He had a premonition of disaster.

Four armored Rolls-Royce limousines cruised through the Rub' al Khali Desert, hurtling mother and daughter toward the Arabian Sea and high adventure at one hundred forty-six miles an hour. Silver prayed and Lauren laughed. She couldn't get there fast enough.

In Riyadh there had been date palms and noisy bazaars, strains of rock and roll competing with the call of the muezzin reminding the faithful to face East in prayer, but here only she was alive in the lifeless desert, a flower blooming among withered shrubs, drifting sand, and goatskin tents. The sky and multihued Bedouin garments occasionally broke the tedium of camel-dotted dunes, but it meant nothing, for at the end of their drive, along the shore, there was a *palace*. And where there was a palace, there was usually a prince.

She saw it first, saw the sun glinting off the gold onion domes, saw the vast marble ogee arches, the turrets, the terraces, the balconies, the balustrades, the sculptured gardens, the indigo reflection pools, and the lone figure with the hooded falcon perched on his wrist.

The white-robed form ignored the caravan of cars. With a flick of his free hand, he removed the black hood from the head of the falcon perched on his wrist, and the bird soared into flight, relentlessly pursuing its prey. Only then did the sheik turn to look at the cars. Without changing expression, his eyes went back to the bird. He watched as it swooped down and deposited its quarry at his feet, resettled itself on his wrist, and waited for the hood to be dropped in place once more. Then and only then did the man throw back his head and laugh.

White teeth against a dark, sculpted face, hawkish black eyes above a hooked nose, a *risque-tout* mustache cresting a brooding mouth, long, strong fingers: these were her first impressions. She could see that he was possessive about that bird, and she knew instinctively that he was possessive about everything that belonged to him.

And just as surely, she knew he was Prince Kenir Ashad. She intended to be his.

She intended to be queen.

CHAPTER THIRTY-THREE

Vashon's caterwauling reached a crescendo as the taxi driver slung the last piece of ivory Samsonite into the trunk.

"Did you remember to pack the hat and muff Mister Ben sent you? Yo' gonna need 'em, chile. They get blue blizzards back East. And how about the quilted robe I made you? Yo' gonna freeze yo' tail off in 'dem babydoll pajamas. You got to be modest, too, not be flaunting yo'self all over de place. I figger 'dem girls at 'dat fancy school don' even strip to takes dere baths." Vashon paused, pulling a handkerchief from the sleeve of her best Sunday-go-to-church dress and blowing her nose until her ears popped. "I put the Vicks Vaporub in myself," she muttered. "First sign of d' sniffles, swab your chest good with the salve, 'n be sure to wear an undershirt afterwards 'n stay outta drafts. Do like I tell yo, chile, or you'll be takin' fever 'n chills 'n tuberculosis 'n end up in one of those sanitary wards, croupin' 'n spittin' blood till a band of angels comes to carry you away. Serve yo' mama right if she had to drape herself in mourning black the rest of her natural days. Serve her right if I quit her service 'n go to that fancy school wit' my baby 'n takes care of her.'' Vashon wailed again, bear-hugging Eve to her flat bosom, squishing her charge's nose and bouffant hairdo as she rocked her to and fro. *''Dere, dere. Hush, little baby, don' you cry.''*

For Vashon's sake Eve mustered a sniff, but the truth was that not so much as a solitary tear glistened in her eyes. She was too angry to cry, too angry to feel anything but contempt for her mother. Even from the grave, Anovese had influence over Moni. No matter how adamantly her mother denied it, Eve knew that he'd planted the seed of her exile. She'd pray for him—pray that the buzzards banqueted on his greasy remains, pray that he burned in hell for eternity.

''I don't mean to intrude, but the meter's running, *ladies*.''

''Shut yo' mouth. You rush my good-byein' again 'n more than dat meter gonna be tickin'.''

Evie glanced back up the walk to the figure silhouetted behind the screen door of Moni's Place, then squeezed the black hand that had nurtured and paddled her since the day she was born. Without another look, she jumped into the back seat of the cab.

''Yo' be as hardheaded as yo' mama.'' Vashon sighed. As usual, she was caught smack-dab in the middle, dodging the crossfire. ''Blow her a kiss, Evie. She's hurtin' inside.''

''She doesn't need my kisses. There's no profit in them. I'll write you, Vashon.'' Eve tapped the driver on the shoulder and the taxi pulled out onto the highway.

Through the silver mesh, Moni watched her daughter disappear from her life. Though she was a pro at partings, this time—this heartbreaking once—she could not hide the tears or deny the emptiness she felt. Her green eyes strained against the fuschia sunset, trying to keep the taxi in sight until it was a speck on the barren horizon.

The years rushed forward and sucked her back in time. Once again she was the Cannery Row émigré chasing after a Packard that was carrying away her dreams. For an instant, she had the urge to run screaming after Evie's taxi, as she had charged after Smoky so many years before. She hadn't relinquished her dream then and she wouldn't now. She would grab her daughter back into her arms and bind her to her forever.

Her fingers froze on the doorframe. No. *This time it could not be, this time she could not tamper with fate. She had no choice but to remain behind with her past, for this time it was Evie's future at stake*—her *dreams*, her *chance at life*. Moni's hand fell to her side.

She neither responded to Vashon's injured air nor flinched when the screen door whacked shut in her face. How could she, when the only emotional constant in her lonely life was gone? Evie would never understand her sacrifice, never know how much Moni would miss her, never know that she alone had succeeded in breaking her mother's heart.

Moni turned from the door and slowly climbed the stairs to her room. This afternoon she would grieve in private; tonight she would greet the customers with a smile. That was what they paid for; that was her first priority.

That was why she was the best.

The school station wagon came to a halt outside the ivy-covered stone walls of Bulwer-Lytton. Eve's first emotion at the sight of the Tudor-style academy was grudging awe. Here, embosomed in winter's crystal splendor, steeped in tradition, its aura of permanence etched against a pearl sky, was Respectability. Neatly shoveled walks flanked by hillocks of snow beckoned like Oz's Yellow Brick Road. Where would they lead?

Where the main walk led was through the front doors, their leaded red and white diamond panes playing a last game of twilight checkers on the foyer floor, and into the office of Miss Prudence Broadbeck, headmistress. Her domain was formal, stuffy, and intimidating. Every leather-bound book was precisely one inch from the edge of each varnished shelf, each picture and plaque was exactly centered and aligned on the paneled walls, and each fold of the brocade draperies fanned in perfectly measured pleats from the stiff tie-backs. Evie instantly had the sensation of having trespassed upon hallowed ground and felt that if she dared to disturb so much as one speck of nonexistent dust or foul the air by breathing one small breath, Miss Broadbeck would accuse her of sacrilege. She was unlike any woman Evie had ever encountered.

"Have you finished your inspection, Miss Afton? I trust everything meets with your approval."

At the crack of the pointer on the desk, Evie snapped from her reverie and insolently appraised the headmistress. She was corsetted from armpits to snatch, a tank in tweeds and sensible Red Cross shoes. Unrouged, albino lashes fringing bulging eyes, nondescript blonde hair ossified by setting gel into rigid finger waves and pulled into a chignon, this paragon of perfection was marred only by the click of her dentures at the climax of every flawless sentence.

"Are you chewing gum, Miss Afton?"

No answer.

"Have you not read the student handbook that was sent to you?"

No answer.

"Chewing gum is a definite infraction of *our* rules." A booklet was thrust into her hands.

At a crack of the offensive gum from Evie, Miss Broadbeck's standard welcome speech went out the window. "You will memorize all one hundred thirty rules and be prepared to recite them before me *and* the student body before breakfast tomorrow morning. Failure to comply will result in your immediate expulsion. That would be most regrettable, Miss Afton. To my knowledge we have never had such an incident at Bulwer-Lytton, but perhaps, considering your nonconformist behavior, you choose to distinguish yourself thus?"

She had no choice. She couldn't—wouldn't—go back to Vegas, wouldn't admit she couldn't hack the respectability she had spent hundreds of hours yearning for, had resented her mother for not possessing or providing. She had no intention of forfeiting her chance at it on the first day; she swallowed her gum and her pride. "No. I don't want to be dismissed, I want to fit in."

"No what? Rule Number Two."

Evie guessed. "No, Miss Broadbeck."

"Very well, you may go to your room. Suite eight. Your luggage will be delivered promptly. Breakfast is at six thirty A.M., sharp."

Evie didn't unpack her bags and didn't turn down her bed. She just lay down and studied the handbook throughout the night, not even covering herself when the radiators whistled their last blast of steam. Not only had her luggage been delivered, but five custom-made navy blazers and five pleated skirts, three navy, two gray, hung in wardrobe bags in her closet. *Shit!* Why hadn't she bothered to read the handbook before this? She had red socks, green socks, white socks, striped socks, diamond socks, bobby socks. No navy or gray.

She had never had a friend, a roomie, a cohort. She had never traded secrets or clothes, so borrowing socks did not occur to her.

Eve was barely settled at the end of a table when Miss Broadbeck motioned for her to come to the front of the room. "Our new student, Miss Eve Afton, has a recitation to make this morning. You will not touch your eggs, bacon, biscuits, juice, or sip so much as one drop of milk until she is finished.''

Two hundred fifty freshly-scrubbed and well-rested faces turned in her direction as she got to her feet, cleared her throat, and pulled at her sagging bobby socks. A twitter of giggles rippled across the dining hall at her improper attire and quivering delivery of Rule Number One: *"You shall at all times comport yourself in a manner such as to render yourself worthy of the Bulwer-Lytton tradition of graciousness and gentility, mindful always that our demeanor is dignified, pleasant, and our minds engaged in the highest pursuits of which we are capable."*

At the recitation of Rule Number Thirty, an inkling that there might be one hundred more to go while their oatmeal turned to glue caused a general infraction of Rule Number One: graciousness and gentility were abandoned as the students leaned on their elbows—in itself an infraction of Rule Number Twenty-Seven: *Slouching and elbows on the table are considered gauche and unacceptable.* The young ladies began to trade eye-rolling glances and yawn broadly.

At the delivery of Rule Number Eighty-two, the hostility in the dining hall was colder than the eggs and bacon on the plates. Evie Afton would not win any popularity contest. She was a troublemaker, a misfit. The unspoken intent to ostracize her swept through the room like a typhoid epidemic.

By Rule Number One Hundred Fourteen, Eve's cheeks flamed, the unaccustomed wool scratched her legs, and she thought about Vashon, Vegas, her horse Kemo Sabe, and riding bareback through the bone-warming blaze of the desert sun, concentrating on anything but the chilly reception she was getting from her peers. The prostitutes were downright saintly compared to these bitches.

Eve finished Rule Number One Hundred Thirty and faintly heard Miss Broadbeck tell her to be seated and everyone to begin eating. Just as she reached her place, her plate was knocked to the floor. Every girl in the hall glared at her, daring her to complain.

Eve was miserable at Bulwer-Lytton. She was regarded as a maverick, an outsider, and she, in turn, considered her schoolmates a bunch of paper-doll snobs. She had dreamed of a respectable environment, but in truth Bulwer-Lytton was a mortuary where everyone was embalmed with blue blood and prejudice. Late at night when the other girls giggled, shared secrets, and broke every other rule they could, Eve moped in her room. She'd come nearly three thousand miles to be scorned. Would there ever be any place she truly belonged or anyone who would fully accept her?

At night she grieved, but each day she bluffed her way through. They expected her to be tough. Well, being tough was what she did best.

CHAPTER THIRTY-FOUR

For all of her short life, her looks, her imagination, or her father's name had been enough to command attention, but this week she had been ignored, except for the afternoon with the women, who dressed her in gowns and jewels and lined her eyes with kohl. It was difficult to seduce a prince when the only time you were allowed in his presence was while your mother photographed him. He seemed not to notice even then. Yet gold bangles appeared nightly on her service plate, costly orchids and jasmine petals were strewn across her bed, and ropes of pearls were miraculously found about her neck when she awoke in the morning. Still, he would not acknowledge her presence. She might as well be dead.

It was the best idea she'd had in days. The back of her right hand flew to her forehead—one must always remember not to offend with the left hand, though the explanation of the weird custom was disgusting—her lips parted, and she sank to the floor, managing to topple Silver's tripod in the process. Scarlett O'Hara could not have done it better. Immediately there was a flurry of activity, water was called for, she was being fanned, her head elevated, and a glass pressed to her lips. She risked a faint flutter of her thickly lashed eyelids. He was the only member of the royal family who remained seated, regally posed for posterity—and then he winked at her.

Lauren spluttered and coughed. He held his formal pose and didn't look in her direction again, even as the litter bearers bore her out of the grand hall to her room in the guest palace.

She hadn't fooled her mother and she most assuredly had not fooled the prince. It was the degradation of degradations. She would not leave her bed for the remainder of their visit.

She refused dinner. Hunger wasn't even a close second to her humiliation. She allowed herself to be bathed and rubbed with almond oil but once back in bed dismissed the attendant, suffered Silver's tender good-night kiss and knowing amusement, flung herself back upon a stack of silk pillows, and pouted.

The guest palace, built in the days when Suleiman the Magnificent and his barbaric Turks marauded Shahdesh, was cleverly devised to protect against the ever present threat of insurgents. A torchlit labyrinth spoked from an octagonal courtyard and ribboned between marble walls. The ancient path had once been tread by scimitar-bearing aides as they combed the palace, spying through peepholes disguised behind elaborate friezes. Throughout the centuries, hidden eyes had routed out treachery as unaware guests conspired and cavorted. Royal whim decreed the occupants' fate: those who offended the king received a bloody slash across their conniving throats; those who aroused the royal prurience wore blood red rubies about their ivory or ebony necks.

Tonight, as he had every night since the young American's arrival, Prince Kenir Ashad moved purposely along the torchlit secret passage to Lauren's suite. Expressionlessly, he watched her, the only sound was the ragged catch of his breath and the faint tinkling of the embedded bells, rumored to have pleasured legions of women around the world.

Tonight his beloved infidel had succumbed to the heat and removed her thin gown. She slept now, the sheet bunched between her long legs, one hand innocently cupping her breast. As a girl, she was intoxicating; as a woman, she would be devastating. He wanted her with every fiber of his being, but she was too young.

He would have to wait.

Lauren's hand crept up her smooth stomach, across her pink-tipped breast, felt about her throat. Her eyes flew open. There were no pearls this morning.

And then she saw it.

A doll. Her cheeks flamed and she covered her nakedness. *She was but a child to him.*

She clutched the exquisite bisque-headed French doll to her, rubbing its white ermine muff against her skin. Stiff parchment scratched her cheek. She extracted the gold-embossed note and eagerly read the message: *For now, a toy to cuddle, saghir wahid.* Young one, indeed! She would show His Royal Highness Prince Kenir Ashad who was what.

Behind the Moorish tapestry, Kenir threw back his head and laughed as she hurled the doll against the wall just as he had known she would. In his experience, women who engaged in dramatic displays were women who had no other vent for the dark passions that drove them. This nymphet was more dramatic than most.

His eyes narrowed in appreciation at the sway of her buttocks as she crossed the room to retrieve the glittering enticement he had concealed within the doll. He watched as she read his second note: *For later, a bauble whose luster will fade next to the flawless brilliance of your beauty.*

She stood before the mirror, the teardrop titan pearl teasing the flesh beneath her navel, the topaz and diamonds encircling her slender waist as her leonine black tresses tumbled down her back. She smoothed her palms against her pelvis, pressed them in a V under the pearl, and arched her swan neck. Then slowly, so slowly it seemed an eternity, her fingers found the forbidden spot and Prince Kenir Ashad, watching her watch herself, knew that no matter what the cost nor how long his wait, he had to *possess* her.

When next she saw Kenir, instead of looking at her with the promise of his note he seemed to assess her with a mixture of possessiveness and uninterest. It was an irresistible combination, and Lauren responded in kind.

At midnight of her last day in Shahdesh, she awoke to find him standing at the foot of her bed, his eyes amused. His generous gift and her budding womanhood were revealed beneath the gossamer Grecian gown. "What? No gasps, no protests? Do Western women expect a prince to come calling in the middle of the night?"

"I can only speak for myself." She unconsciously bolstered her faltering confidence by running her fingertips across the lacy web of diamonds and topaz. The gift evidenced his interest even when his attitude belied it. "Yes, I knew you would come. And there is nothing yet to make me gasp." She smiled at him. "Nor is there going to be." She rolled over.

"One day you will be mine, all mine, every luscious inch of you, and I *will* make you gasp."

"I don't want to be a mistress. I want to be queen." Languorously she turned onto her back, stretched, and looked at him seductively. "And can you promise me that, Your Royal Highness?"

Kenir melted across the bed, stretching sinewy muscle

over the length of her yielding flesh, his mouth gravitating to hers. His masterful kiss sucked the breath from her, his swirling tongue probed until she was dizzy, his Arabian heat branded her into bondage, and the hardness of his manhood foretold her destiny.

Lauren's left hand raked through his raven hair, her right, her strongest hand, grasped his gold-braided sash as she planted a sleek leg in the slit of his flowing *thobe*, grinding their bodies closer, closer, closer.

With a groan and all the willpower he could call upon, Kenir pushed her from him and denied what might have been. "When next we meet, princess, the promise will be fulfilled."

He vanished into the shadows and for the second time in as many days, the frustrated Lauren resorted to masturbation.

And for the second time in as many hours, Prince Ashad positioned himself behind the walls, watching every minute move, every undulation of her hips, every dip of her finger, every fondle of her nipples, listening to every moan, every sigh, every staccato breath, taking his pleasure as Lauren did hers, he in a damp stone abyss, she in a canopied cocoon, until simultaneous spasms engulfed them both.

Oh, yes, the promise would be fulfilled. But he had promised one thing and Lauren had heard another.

Silver paced the library, the jeweled girdle dangling from her clenched fist. "And then, when we were going through customs, having already declared the numerous pearl and gold trinkets Lauren acquired on this trip, she denied having anything else to declare, but *someone*"—she glared at Fax—"*someone* forgot to take care of our processing and they *strip*-searched her to find *this* . . . this indecent harem relic hugging *your* daughter's bikini-clad hips. All she needs is Sally Rand's fans and she could be a burlesque queen. Really, Fax, don't look at me like that. She refused to return it and would not forfeit it to the customs officials or to me. She then proceeded to throw a fit and created such a ruckus that I was forced not only to pay the duty and an enormous fine but to give in and let her wear this monstrosity the rest of the way home." She dropped the offensive belly belt in a Yongle relic. *That vulgar pearl was so huge it nearly stoppered the elegant blue and white dragon flask.*

"She's just a girl. Her head is full of grandiose ideas. This infatuation is temporary, Silver." His mind was on an Indo-Chinese civil war. Rumor had it that Eisenhower had pledged U.S. support of the Diem regime to forestall the Communist domino effect in Southeast Asia. Fax needed plenty of time to prepare for the expected demands of another drawn-out holocaust, and he had little time to dwell on domestic issues. "Silver, it was at your insistence that Lauren accompanied you on this trip. I knew it was going to be a fiasco, but neither one of you would listen to me. Your glorious assignment was all that was important, so you take care of it."

His pet project, Magnesium of Nevada, was in full swing, operating on around-the-clock shifts, and he was functioning under nearly the same pressure. This upcoming war in Vietnam was only one of his commitments—he had his own private KKK to worry about. Martin Luther King, the Kennedys, and Khrushchev all had dreams; Fairfax Bennett VI had his. And, regrettably, Clayton Robbins had quite a few, too. He still had to keep tabs on the popular Southern congressman while working to imbue national black pride and underwrite the mushrooming civil rights movement. Reining in such an unpredictable man as an ex-pimp turned statesman, who was more ambitious than scrupulous, was no easy task. Schooling him on issues and tempering his natural aggressiveness was costly, in terms of time and funds. Fax simply hadn't the energy or desire to concern himself with this domestic Middle East crisis.

It was on the tip of Silver's tongue to say "She is your daughter, too," but the words stuck to the roof of her mouth. *Liar!* Fax's daughter would never do anything so gauche as to accept a heathen bribe. It was Sasa's offspring who would be drawn to the mysticism and romance. "This is serious, Fax. Lauren has always had a definite penchant for the *outré ordinaire* and this is not a girlish infatuation."

Jesus Christ! First Moni sought and received his counsel when she could no longer contain Evie. Now Silver was demanding that he provide an instant solution to Lauren's insurrection. Why hadn't he heeded his instinct? He couldn't call King Ashad and jeopardize sensitive negotiations. This was what was delicately referred to as a stalemate. "What would you have us do, Silver? Put her in solitary confinement? Novice her to Our Sisters of the Immaculate Conception? Marry her off to this shah of Shahdesh before her virtue is compromised?"

"Don't be sarcastic. I don't think we need resort to such extreme measures, Fax, but perhaps the time has arrived for her to go away to school."

"Whatever you think is best." He scanned the latest stock quotes. "Metals are up. I think perhaps a British school."

"She has already broadened her horizons more than sufficiently. That is the crux of our problem."

Bulwer-Lytton. She was going to suggest it any moment now. His Adam's apple bobbed against his Windsor-knotted tie.

"It has to be an all-girl academy, of course. I think she should remain close to home, but in a highly structured and rigidly supervised environment. My alma mater seems as suitable a choice as any."

"Bulwer-Lytton? I don't think that is a good idea."

"Why not, Fax?"

"Do you want them to warp any natural instincts she might have, turn her into one of the proper prim?"

Silver blanched. "Am I to assume that you assign this neutered characteristic to me as well?" For the first time ever, she considered assigning some blame of her own, neutralizing him as he had so subtly rejected, so smoothly undermined her throughout the years.

"Not at all, Silver. I just think Lauren is at a tender age and I don't think we have the right to arbitrarily consign her to an asexual sisterhood. I have no sons, and Lauren may someday wish to take over my business affairs." The possibility had never occurred to him until that moment, but the concept certainly added credibility to his excuse. "In that eventuality, she must be groomed to deal with men as equals, or better, learn to manipulate them. She needs to understand the male species and what motivates them, needs to know their deficiencies, defenses, and desires."

My, but hadn't he come a long way from the time when he thought women lacked the insight, realism, and passion to photograph the subtle threads that held the fabric of life together? "And may I presume you are looking forward to becoming a grandfather in the near future? Fax, I don't think you understand the intensity of Lauren's hormones. They're running amok, I'm telling you, amok. We are running a great risk. She has the imagination and she has the derring-do and she most certainly has the determination to follow through on anything she sets her mind to. The only alternative is for you to offer her an immediate partnership in the business—or offer her hand to that Arabian Merlin. What is your preference? And while we're on the subject of this newfound appreciation for equality, is your crusade discriminatory? I mean, one never knows, you could drop dead tomorrow, and I might have to reign as regent until Lauren can take over. Or perhaps she will renounce your kingdom to become queen of Shahdesh. Tell me, Fax, does your ideology apply only to your daughter, or would you like me to expand my knowledge of the male species so I, too, can 'manipulate' them?"

He recognized blackmail when he heard it. His only recourse was a fervent prayer. After all, it was a big school. What were the chances of Lauren meeting Evie? What was his risk of being exposed? "I'll make a sizeable contribution to assure Lauren's entrance and arrange for her enrollment tomorrow, Silver. I'll make the contribution to the De Ferrers Endowment, if that meets with your approval."

It did. Although she hated to be separated from her daughter, considering their hectic schedules and Lauren's newly acquired interest in the Moslem culture, the private boarding school was the only sensible course of action. She kissed his cheek, proper prim.

Holy moly! Lauren beat a hasty retreat from her eavesdropping. So her mother was a cold fish and she was to be confined in a dungeon of dullards, dropped on the doorstep of conformity, banished to the clutches of men-hating dragon ladies.

But before she was consigned to contrition city, before Silver or Fax remembered the evidence of Kenir's promise and her promiscuity, she had to rescue her prized possession from the Ming artifact.

She would accept her fate with dignity, go to the gallows with courage, face her dismal future fearlessly. After all, New York City—by turnpike and limousine—was less than an hour away.

The ingenious wild Gypsy arrived at Bulwer-Lytton to meet her next challenge—the worldly, defiant, but unchanneled Eva.

—Fast Friends

CHAPTER THIRTY-FIVE

The syndicate's snuff of Anovese had made a believer out of Josh Garr. Sin was the way of the past, salvation the way of the future. In the Bible Belt a thousand miles from Vegas several months later, he emerged a new man, with a new name and a renewed appreciation for religion and Swiss bank accounts. There was profit in the Word and man blessed with the power to convey it could gain a kingdom on earth. That was heaven according to Joshua Garland.

He'd learned Scripture under the heavy hand of a stern father and a ready belt. A man had a way of remembering verse, chapter, and book when it meant deliverance in the truest sense of the word. Twenty dollars and the lick of a stamp got him a doctorate of divinity. He took care of the rest with a voice like Gabriel, the onyx eyes of John the Baptist, ivory linen suits, white buck shoes, miracle cures, and the sincerity of Jesus Christ himself.

At first he preached to his flock of devoted followers in a leaky tent, then a rented tin-roofed hall, until finally—compliments of many generous troubled, saved, and *satisfied* benefactresses—he gained the lands and funds to erect his very own gold-domed True Gospel Tabernacle.

CHAPTER THIRTY-SIX

The first time Michael Christian saw Barbara Mendall she was standing on the sidewalk in front of the S&M Building, holding a cello case and peering at street signs as if she had no idea where she was. Her glasses were too thick, her hair too thin, her clothes too baggy, too drab, too brown. She blended into the colorless pavement, hardly noticeable between the spittle and bird droppings, and he had the sensation that at any moment she would disappear into a crack between the concrete slabs, never to be seen again. Then suddenly she thrust the cello case into old Harry's driver's hands and in a desperate frenzy stomped the very same insignificant crack he had imagined would swallow her.

Step on a crack, break your mother's back.

He heard the words, saw her actions with a clear understanding. He felt certain she would have gone on forever had not the driver gently taken her arm and halted her pantomine seconds before Mendall emerged from the S&M sanctum.

An impervious Harry strolled through the double doors, kissed the mouse's cheek, and inquired, "So how did the audition go? Will my daughter be playing at Carnegie Hall on her sixteenth birthday?"

"Not this season, Daddy. I need more practice."

Practice made perfect, and Michael Christian was not only practiced, but perfect. Reading would give way to wooing. Mendall's daughter might not play the cello worth a shit, but she would be worth millions playing second fiddle to him. She would be his own private express to the top.

For once Michael did not intrude. It didn't matter if Old Harry recognized him today. He would have to embrace him when he gave the bride away.

CHAPTER THIRTY-SEVEN

In the months following Skeeter's untimely death, a pressing need to be saved consumed Norma Mae. She was, even if she did say so herself, nearly a model of motherhood, having settled Savannah down in Florida, as far away from Brownsville, Texas, as she could get without leaving the South. She worked in a family restaurant and saw to it that Savannah attended school regularly. On Sundays they went to church. Murder broke a major commandment: it required a major redemption, and this time an itinerant preacher man would not do. Not at all. Atonement for an ice-picking called for a big-time evangelist, and she had one in mind.

The sound of the Reverend Joshua Garland's radio broadcasts was her only caress during these long, lonely, and horny months. She'd seen his picture on the cover of *Newsweek*. She thought him sexy as hell, and she was biding her time until the True Gospel Tabernacle was completed. She believed the gold-domed monument would be a worthy stage for the expiation of their transgression,

Joshua Garland the tailor-made instrument to drive the demons from her body and the devil from Savannah's soul. The child hadn't been right since Brownsville, but Norma Mae had a plan, complete down to the last fine details of mother-and-daughter white dresses, platinum hair, and holy expressions. She devoted her evenings to coaching Savannah rather than humping another hillbilly. Hicks were consigned to the past; the future held a handsome prophet. All she needed was a little more money, and she figured the good Lord would provide for her the same way he was providing for Joshua Garland and the True Gospel Tabernacle.

CHAPTER THIRTY-EIGHT

Lauren, followed by James, Silver, and their driver, traipsed into her assigned room at Bulwer-Lytton wearing a Persian lamb jacket, a strand of Kenir's pearls, and a little black traveling suit, and trailing eight Louis Vuitton trunks, fourteen suitcases, and seven hatboxes. It was an impressive entrance.

Evie Afton took one look at her new roommate and the entourage, casually pulled out a cigarette, lit up, and sent great rings of smoke billowing up from the bed, where she was sitting in leopard-skin print underpants and bra. She made no move to cover herself or to speak.

Holy moly! What a dynamite figure! Even the unperturbable James was gawking. Lauren bet this bombshell wore a D cup, and here she was with a double A. "Hello, I'm Lauren Bennett, your new suitemate."

Who gives a shit who you are? Evie exhaled another whiff of smoke, then expertly French-inhaled it. *Who was this prissy Miss Congeniality of 1961? No doubt the pampered darling had memorized all one hundred thirty rules before she learned "Mary Had a Little Lamb", would be class president by next week, and valedictorian in short order.* Eve wanted to puke.

"Which is my dresser? Where's my closet?" Lauren tossed her fur and handbag onto the empty bed.

Evie crushed out her cigarette, pulled on a quilted housecoat, and padded into the bathroom, locking the door.

Silver drew a deep breath. The girl's manners were deplorable, but there was more. She looked familiar, very familiar, but where could Silver have seen her?

Undaunted, Lauren opened drawers and doors until she discovered space and began unpacking, leaving empty trunks for James and the driver to carry to the attic. This room was really too cramped for anything.

Evie pressed her ear to the door. God! Her ladyship's cortege had finally left. She had read the Classic Comics version of *Pride and Prejudice* twice in preparation for tomorrow's lit class, plucked her brows, given herself a manicure, done a double set of bust exercises, and was getting more than a little claustrophobic in the green-tiled crapper.

As soon as she had kissed her mother good-bye and the Montauk Point contingent departed, Lauren stripped to her imported lace bikinis and matching French-cut bra, retrieved the monogrammed flask that Auntie Buffy had secretly given her from the inside pocket of the lamb jacket, readjusted Kenir's jeweled girdle so that the pearl nestled in her navel, placed his picture—which she'd stolen from her mother—on her nightstand, and propped herself up on her pillows, slowly stroking her tummy and swigging confiscated Grand Marnier straight from Godmother's gift and Daddy's private stock.

"That's an infraction of Rule Number Ten."

"Drinking, or touching myself?"

"Drink— . . ." *Holy Shit!* Eve's gaze came to rest on the glittering diamonds and mammoth pearl. "*Where* did you get *that*?"

Lauren crossed one leg over the other, pointed her toes with their polished nails, and swept her midnight tresses behind her ear. "From a prince."

Eve snapped her fingers. "That's it! I've got it now. You're Anastasia, the long-lost Romanov princess and that little trinket is part of the imperial loot smuggled out of Russia in the hem of your dress." Evie curtsyed and pitched herself back on the bed, laughing hysterically. "Pray tell, Your Highness, what must one do to earn such royal favor? A royal fuck?"

"A royal what?"

"Fuck. You know, just fuck." At Lauren's bewildered expression, it dawned on Evie that Her Highness's reading material had not included *Lady Chatterley's Lover* or *The Tropic of Cancer.* "Are you from this planet? I mean, *everyone* knows about sex."

"Sex? Why didn't you say so? I know about *sex.* I almost had it with the prince. And had we consummated our love, I really would be a princess and have a kingdom of my own by now. I will someday, you know. I am going to be queen. He promised."

Dingbat! Tutti-frutti. Her Highness must be sipping crushed peyote from that silver flask. "Oh yeah." Evie propped her chin in her hand. "And I think you're queen of bullshit, that's what I think."

"And I think you're common, not to mention jealous." Lauren took another swallow. "Queen of bullshit? Oh, no. Queen of Shahdesh."

"I've never heard of it. Where *is* this mythical kingdom?"

"On the Arabian Sea, where priceless gems like these wash up on the sand with the incoming tide and it rains gold on Tuesdays and Thursdays between nine and half past four." *She'd give the plebe a sampling of bullshit.*

"An Arab? Get serious."

"I am. There's his picture." She pointed to the night-stand.

Evie bounded off the bed and grabbed the tortoise shell frame. *Jumping Jehoshaphat!* He was enough to make anyone cream in their jeans. She sank down on the bed next to Lauren, mesmerized by the white-robed sheik. He was magnificent. She'd grown up in the company of dangerous men, and they all had a look through the eyes. Her Highness would be royally fucked, all right, in more ways than one.

"Isn't he just marvy?"

"He's okay, but I've seen the type before. They come and go at Moni's Place."

"Who is Moni?"

"My mother. She's the hottest madam in Vegas. Men pay her a king's ransom all the time. She has this one john from back East who brings her jewels and she had a Mafia chieftain that left her half a mil of Mob blood money before he was wasted by a hitman on our doorstep." *She'd give her ladyship a sampling of the cold, hard facts of life.*

Holy moly! This girl had a wealth of information at her disposal. "I'm sorry I called you common. You're not at all. I bet you know things *nobody* here knows. Important things, like what men really like and what really, really, happens when men and women fuck." *She hoped she sounded crude.* "I know they get hard in their private place, I felt Kenir when he was on top of me and I think I know what *it* feels like because I did *it* to myself, but I don't know what to do to a man. I'd give anything to know, so I can please Kenir when our moment comes."

It? What in the hell was the doing-it-to-yourself she was talking about? Eve's experience had been limited to heavy petting in the back seat of Dusty's '57 Chevy, and though she had a broad general knowledge of sex, she hadn't gotten around to *it* yet. This was the first time since her arrival at the dungeon that anyone had bothered to have a conversation with her, let alone show any interest. She examined her manicure and said slowly, "Listen, you'll soon learn I'm an outcast around here. I don't fit in. I'm not like these tight-assed twerps."

"You're unusual, but I like the unusual."

"From the first day I got here, I've been in trouble. The headmistress hates my guts, and if she catches me with booze in my room, I'll be expelled on the spot. She's just looking for an excuse to get rid of me. But I don't want to go home—not ever."

Lauren passed the flask. "Have some Grand Marnier. Daddy made a huge endowment to the school and my mother is an alumna. They wouldn't dare do anything to me. If there's a problem, yours or mine, I'll handle it. I always do."

"I've had some experience with protection rackets. What do you want in return?"

"For openers, teach me how to use that Tampax I saw in your drawer."

"Only if you'll let me try on your belly belt."

It was a great sacrifice, but ultimately for Kenir's own good. She fastened the girdle about Eve's tiny waist.

Eve reached for the flask. After her first sip, the heady liquor appealed to her more than the dazzling jewels.

By bed check, Lauren had spent an interminable amount of time practicing inserting tampons and fainting while Evie had polished off the Grand Marnier and passed out.

By morning, Evie was suffering the chills of her premiere hangover, and Lauren, raw but triumphant, threw away her sanitary napkins. By vespers, Evie had introduced Lauren to Classic Comics and Lauren had ghost-written a Dear John letter to Dusty.

It was the unlikeliest friendship that ever existed. It took Her Highness and the Vegas Pagan exactly three days, six hours, eighteen minutes, and forty-two seconds to get themselves transferred to the huge dormer suite on the third floor and less than a week to establish themselves as the leaders of the pack. If you were allowed into Laura and Eva's circle of intimates, you were in—in so far that your most coveted possession was an engraved invitation to Creative Masturbation 101; if you were out, you were so far out you begged to be shipped to a school in Siberia.

—Fast Friends

CHAPTER THIRTY-NINE

The evangelist took the South by storm, the sinners by their hands, and their soul-saving tithes to his safety deposit box.

They came in droves to hear Reverend Joshua speak. The believers received the laying on of hands in public; the privileged in private. But once established, discretion demanded that Joshua Garland sow seeds of salvation instead of wild oats. Only a few select women continued to experience Joshua's true calling—a more intimate and expert lay. Paradise for these ladies was Joshua between their legs. Contributions poured in as his mesmerizing words flowed out. All who heard him hailed him a modern-day messiah, blessed by the Lord with the divine power to heal and forgive in his name.

Yet his life was far from perfect, for the infatuated tribe was becoming bothersome, not to mention embarrassing.

The answer came to him in the stillness of the night as he was on his knees, once more serving another of his demanding disciples. It was time to take a wife. He prayed God would create a mate in Joshua's own image: a saint by day and a sinner by night, one who looked like a madonna but had the morals of an alley cat.

CHAPTER FORTY

Norma Mae poured the last of the diluted peroxide over Savannah's head as J.F.K. took his oath of office. She'd never forget his inaugural address for as long as she lived: "*We observe today . . . a celebration of freedom, symbolizing an end as well as a beginning, signifying renewal as well as change . . .*" The Lord had sent her a sign. She paid no attention to the immortal words, "*Ask not what your country can do for you—ask what you can do for your country.*" She had her own New Frontier to forge.

Two days later, for the first time in her life, Norma Mae Owen's timing was absolutely perfect.

On the fine Sabbath morning that Joshua Garland threw open the front doors, welcoming one and all to the glorious christening of his True Gospel Tabernacle, Norma Mae and Savannah sashayed down the center aisle and received the salvation that was long overdue. As the tambourines incited fervor and the organ simulated the sweet sound of angels' harps, Norma Mae's eyes were fixed on the man beneath the cloth while Savannah's thoughts were imprisoned by the corpse they'd left in a rain-washed gully along the Tex-Mex border. In a performance that left not a dry eye in the house and touched the hardest of hearts, Norma Mae confessed to every sin but the one they could never admit. Alleluia, brothers and amens rang out, and the frenzied flock rose to its feet and swayed in unison, invoking God's love. The good, handsome, and hot-blooded Reverend gave himself over to the Lord's will and embraced the wretched, golden madonna who would become his wife and cleave only to his con.

He looked at Savannah Lee and promptly decided he would have to wean that sniveling kid—ship her far, far away. A school back East perhaps.

It was all Norma Mae could do not to turn around and stare at the guests attending her wedding. There were senators and governors, movie stars and Broadway playwrights, four-star generals and sports greats, astronauts and country music legends, and four cousins from Fayette County she'd wanted to impress. Every last one of them was either famous or rich or both, excepting her kin, who had accepted her gracious invitation only to escape the Tennessee revenue men nipping at their heels.

Joshua had arranged for people to come in and do her up right. She was a sight to behold in a Paris creation—looked almost like an angel standing right next to God's holy instrument. She was a far cry from the ragtag dreamer making mudcakes on the banks of the Loosahatchie River. Pretty soon she'd be sipping champagne 'stead of Kickapoo Joy Juice, wearing gold instead of peeling beads, fucking with the Lord's blessing 'stead of tempting his wrath by dallying with the devil. Joshua was a religious man, better than a gentleman or a Texas oil baron, and she was thrilled to death she was coming to him with her virtue, for once, intact. He'd wanted her in the worst way, but she'd made him wait, and it had been real hard. *Blessed are they which do hunger and thirst after righteousness, for they shall be filled.* It was her bargain with God. And *seeing* as how Joshua'd had a near permanent erection since their betrothal she knew her cup was gonna runneth over. She pushed aside the momentary thought of Red Shoes. God might read her mind and send a lightning bolt to strike her dead on the finest day of her life. She was going to be a faithful wife and do the Lord's work for the remainder of her days.

The wedding was a grand and glorious affair, not like some others she'd had, and she could hardly wait for Joshua to carry her over the threshold, deposit her on the nuptial bed, strip the gown from her body, whisper his undying, unending devotion, and then fuck her like she was a *sirène fatale.* Maybe she ought to tone herself down a bit at first, or he'd be just like all the rest, not ever wanting to stop and not able to even if he wanted to. She couldn't have him thinking she'd had *too* much experience or neglecting his profitable pulpit for her divine pussy.

Norma Mae emerged from the bathroom, a vestal vision in a fluffy float of white nylon and lace. There were angora pompoms on her satin slippers. Her hair had been brushed to a golden sheen, her cheeks and lips lightly rouged. She admired her five-carat diamond, then smiled at her husband. She'd never had either before, and it was difficult to divide her attention so.

"Take it off."

He liked to have scared her to death. For a minute there, she'd thought he meant the ring. Her gown whooshed over her head and dropped to the floor. "Anxious, are you, sugar? Me, too." She had only advanced a step when he startled her again.

"Scrub that evidence of harlotry off your face, plait your hair, and put this on." He thrust a stiffly starched and heavily ruffled pinafore into her hands. "Tie these ribbons in your hair."

"I gave up wearing aprons when I quit phosphating sodas behind the counter at Allen's Drugstore."

"This has nothing to do with the past, Norma Mae, and everything to do with your future. 'Wives, submit yourselves unto your own husbands, as unto the Lord, for the husband is the head of the wife, even as Christ is the head of the church.' Ephesians, chapter five, verses twenty-two and twenty-three."

"But, Joshua, I look so pretty in this."

" 'Likewise, ye wives, be in subjection to your own husbands; that, if any obey not the word, they also may be without the husband, for whom they should adorn themselves by the plaiting of hair, and wearing of gold . . .' "

Norma Mae's eyes followed the tantalizing gold cross swinging from his fingertips, the pinafore and ribbons falling from her hand as she reached out for it.

" '. . . and putting on apparel. For after this manner in the old time the holy women also, who trusted in God, adorned themselves, being in subjection unto their own husbands.' First Epistle of Peter, chapter three, verses one through five."

Norma Mae snatched the frippery from the floor and ran into the bathroom. This wasn't part of her bargain with God, but she'd do her best. She glanced at her ring and put the cross around her neck, then scoured her face, braided her hair, and put on the pinafore with no underwear. She removed the slippers and tied the ribbons in bows around her braids. She'd expected all the folderol of a fancy wedding to give her the hives, but she'd never anticipated being jittery in the sack.

Norma Mae's arm ached from flailing the cat-o'-nine-tails across Joshua's taut buttocks. He'd white-hot fucked her, sure enough, but he hadn't let her move and insisted she not make a sound. She felt like a ragdoll just lying there. And to think she'd been worried about appearing too knowledgeable. Then, for his awful sins, his unspeakable lust, he demanded she beat him until she drew blood.

"Harder, Norma Mae. *Harder*."

The cat-o'-nine-tails cracked through the air, slashing his flesh. She brought it down again and again, and then Joshua screamed, doubling into a ball as he clutched the sheet to his groin and spilled his seed once more.

Joshua knelt in anguish by the window, moonlight gleaming across his sinewy back, his blood-crusted buttocks obscured by the shadows, his normally commanding voice ragged with repentant quivering.

" 'But if ye bite and devour one another, take heed that ye be not consumed one of another. This I say then, Walk in the Spirit, and ye shall not fulfil the lust of the flesh. For the flesh lusteth against the Spirit, and the Spirit against the flesh: and these are contrary the one to the other: so that ye cannot do the things that ye would. Now the works of the flesh are manifest, which are these; adultery, fornication, uncleanness, lasciviousness. And they that are Christ's have crucified the flesh with the affections and lusts. For he that soweth to his flesh shall of the flesh reap corruption; but he that soweth to the Spirit shall of the Spirit reap life everlasting.' Galatians, chapter five, verses fifteen through twenty-four; chapter six, verse eight."

Judas Priest! He'd been going on for hours like this. *Well, she had one for him.* " '*Ye shall not make any cuttings in your flesh'. Leviticus, nineteen, twenty-eight.*" Norma Mae buried her head under the pillow, the heavy gold cross snuggling between her breasts. This bleating lost lamb of God was apparently gonna go right on recitin' the livelong night. If she couldn't screw she wanted to sleep.

CHAPTER FORTY-ONE

The pill went on the market and the girls went on the pill.

Most of the students at Bulwer-Lytton went home for the summer break of 1961, while Lauren and Eve struck out in search of extra credits and high adventure in the Adirondacks.

And following that summer, which would never again be spoken of, the two fast friends stood at attention before Miss Prudence Broadbeck, once again answering for insubordination and staunchly refusing to break up the demonstration they'd so successfully staged outside the administration building, protesting Kennedy's increased commitment of military personnel in Vietnam.

"My dear Lauren and Eve, we cannot have and we will not tolerate our girls participating in, let alone instigating, anti-American rallies on Bulwer-Lytton soil. Your parents and the board of trustees would find such behavior most unbecoming."

Eve smirked. The thought of Anovese being blown away on Moni's doorstep flashed before her. Only with the greatest restraint did she refrain from enlightening the headmistress, less affectionately known as Prudie Broadbutt. Instead, she nudged Lauren in the ribs.

"Do you find this conversation amusing, Miss Afton?"

"No, she doesn't. However, I do, and somewhat tedious besides," Lauren replied haughtily.

Miss Broadbeck stiffened in her chair. "Would you find expulsion amusing and somewhat tedious, Miss Bennett? And do not think for a moment that your latest editorial has escaped my attention, or that your father's most generous contributions to the de Ferrers Endowment will deter me should you persist in pursuing this dissident course you are set upon."

Eve rushed to Lauren's rescue. "To which editorial are you referring, Miss Broadbeck? 'Rampant Campus Pregnancies' or 'Flagrant Drinking on the Hallowed Grounds of Bulwer-Lytton'?"

Prudence Broadbeck forgot herself and nervously fingered the lace jabot of her otherwise severe blouse. It was difficult with these two to tell exactly where creativity left off and their journalistic noses sniffed out truths. "I'll be lenient *this* time. . . . There is a small matter in regard to which your talents could benefit Bulwer-Lytton, and you might redeem yourselves."

"And, pray tell, Miss Broadbeck, what might that be?" Lauren mocked her. The girls exchanged smug looks.

Driven to the point of apoplexy, Miss Broadbeck lost all control. "Don't be impertinent. I still have the option of expelling your refined asses from this recherché institution."

"Institution is right; sanitarium would be more like it," Lauren muttered.

"Did you say something, Miss Bennett, that you would care to share with us?"

"Yes, madam, I did. I do not feel your foul language is in keeping with the dignity of Bulwer-Lytton."

"She has a point," Eve chimed in. "My mother would

be appalled. After all, we have certain standards, and you're supposed to be our role model."

Lauren choked.

Miss Broadbeck's face went crimson. "Go to hell, you little twerps. You do what I say, or . . ."

"Or what, Miss Broadbeck?" Lauren asked sweetly.

"I will tell your parents about the anonymous ad and the dial-a-dirty-message service you two initiated."

So Prudie knew. The old bitch must need that endowment worse than they thought. God! Their license was as limitless as their imaginations.

"Do I make myself clear, girls?"

"Perfectly, Miss Broadbeck," they said in unison.

Eve rallied. "And how is it that Bulwer-Lytton can use our considerable talents, Miss Broadbeck?"

"We have the daughter of a renowned evangelist enrolling as a new student. Because I have the utmost confidence that she will have a stabilizing effect on you two, I have assigned her to your suite. I expect total cooperation and a smooth introduction of her into the student body. No tricks. Furthermore, you will immediately disconnect the direct phone line into your quarters."

"And when might we expect this paragon of virtue, Miss Broadbeck?"

It was Prudie's turn to smirk. "Why I believe she is unpacking at this very moment. You may go now." The headmistress busied herself with her schedules. The girls rolled their eyes, pivoted, and exited her austere office.

"Bitch!" Evie muttered. "What can you expect from a broad-butted bore?"

"An evangelist's daughter, that's what." Lauren laughed. "Do you think she can be tempted to talk dirty?"

"Are you kidding? What would a preacher's daughter know about smut?"

"You never know, Evie. Did you ever see *Elmer Gantry*?"

Savannah Lee looked around the suite. She belonged in this fancy school about as much as Norma Mae belonged on the stage of the True Gospel Tabernacle performing miracles. Fuck. The only miracle Momma could do was make a limp prick stiff—she'd heard her say so. She began to unpack. There was no room for her belongings in the closet nor in the bathroom; there wasn't even room under her bed. Who were these messy, absent roommates? Her only clue was a layout sheet for an upcoming edition of the *Bulwer-Lytton Bulletin*. Perhaps they had something in common, after all—a desire to write.

The telephone jangled. Savannah listened to it ring, then decided maybe she should answer it and take a message.

"Hello."

"Talk to me, baby. Say something soft and nasty," a husky voice requested.

"Fuck you." Savannah slammed down the receiver.

In the doorway, mouths agape, Lauren and Evie applauded their new roomie. "Welcome to Bulwer-Lytton. Next time, get a number."

CHAPTER FORTY-TWO

It was the war hero, the human rights champion, the Pied
Piper congressman Clayton Robbins who spoke so earnestly at Coretta King's table, but it was the showman, the
black bastard formerly of Philadelphia, Red Shoes Cooles,
who with a flick of his wrist and a flip of Coretta's china
smashed the cherry-covered cheescake upon her white
tablecloth. "I'm telling you, we have to turn America upside down in order for it to turn right-side up."

The representative from Bobby Kennedy's Justice
Department choked on a cherry pit.

Coretta King watched the red glaze ooze across the
snowy cloth—to her it represented a sign of blood yet to be
spilled across the land.

Martin Luther made a mental note to paraphrase Representative Robbins's profound words in a forthcoming
sermon.

"My apologies, Coretta. Sometimes I just get so in-
flamed with the cause that I forget where I am or what I'm
doing. Dr. King is inspiring. Our mission not only requires

brave men, it demands freethinking individuals with the courage of their convictions, men who dare, who will sacrifice their very souls for the benefit of mankind. Your husband is all of these things, and we are here to serve him.'' *Yeah, yeah, yeah. Bro King is a dedicated cat, all right, Coretta. He loves all God's chillun', it's just that he loves some a little more 'n others. That ol' black magic that he weaves has everybody in a spell, Coretta. Now, I'm into black myself: black-mail. And what I can't prove, the Bureau's fat man will verify with phone taps.* ''I'll have a new tablecloth sent over tomorrow.''

''That's not necessary, Clayton. We all must sacrifice, and a tablecloth can be bleached. People cannot. And even if they could, more than just color separates us now.''

Bobby Kennedy's emissary added another dollop of cream to his coffee, stirring it with true Kennedy vigor.

''And what impact has the latest sit-in had in Washington?'' Martin Luther King addressed Bobby's delegate.

''Congressman Robbins's assessment is probably more valid than my own. What's your opinion, Clayton?''

''The White House is fully behind our efforts, even if J. Edgar Hoover isn't. We are guaranteed protection.'' *His name had changed, his way of life had changed, he'd gone from the ghetto to the government, from muskrat to cashmere, but he was still selling and still covering one thing: his ass.*

Martin Luther King pondered Clayton Robbins's assurance. ''I wonder,'' he said, ''if the day will come when we will no longer have to concern ourselves with protection but can go forward productively, with no thought as to whether we are black, white, red, or yellow. That is the day I live for, but it is foolish to think we can walk through a fire without being burned, be bludgeoned without bleeding, attain the slave's dream of freedom and break the two-hundred-year-old shackles without severing our members, without sacrificing our bartered peace. As you so dramatically put it, Congressman Robbins, we must turn America

upside down to turn it right-side up. And we shall do so."
He stood. "I'm sorry to make this an early evening,
gentlemen. The Freedom Rides begin tomorrow in Mont-
gomery. Will you be riding with us, Clayton?"

*You bet your sweet ass, Luther. I got blisters on my butt
and bunions on my feet from sit-ins and marches. These
bus rides are gonna be a piece of cake.* "When have I not
been at your side? Good-night, Coretta. The dinner was
superb as usual. My only regret is that I missed your
famous cheescake."

"Dr. King always enjoys your company, Congressman." *He was too glib, too patronizing, too much a political animal. The question was, did he stand by her husband's side or scheme behind his back?*

Red Shoes stretched out on the hotel bed, delaying calling
Fairfax Randolph Bennett. He was entitled to a moment's
gloating. He'd integrated the troops in Korea and distinguished himself as ordered by his mentor. He'd acquired
the requisite college degree. He'd given up pimpin', had
kissed babies, shaken a million hands, made more speeches
and appearances at veterans' posts, ladies' auxiliaries, and
church socials than any six stumpers, and eaten more
chicken than any ten niggers could ever devour. He'd
greased the palms of poll watchers to make sure his opponents' votes didn't exceed his. He'd worked his way up
through the political ranks, kissed ass, licked boots, and
sucked bipartisan tit whenever Fax Bennett told him to.
Now he was the right man in the right place at the right
time. All he had to do was orchestrate King's footsteps,
keep fueling the civil rights movement, report to Bennett,
and he was practically assured of being appointed to the
Appropriations Committee, and from there he intended to
secure the lucrative chair seat. He had connections, he had
power, he had nothing but open doors to welcome him.
He'd even sat at Buffy's table as an invited guest. He'd
come a long way from the day he'd delivered his demands

to her. Then he'd wanted power most, but times had changed. Power was fickle; people were disposable. He needed more, he wanted more—he would have more.

Money.

CHAPTER FORTY-THREE

The unlikely combination of roommates became an unholy alliance. Eva had longed for respectability and been exposed to decadence; Laura had longed for a taste of the worldly, and Eva was a tantalizing sip. When Savana arrived on the scene with her magnolia ways, a hint of smoldering sadness, and handled her first Dial-A-Dirty-Phone-Call caller with magnificent presence, Her Highness and the Vegas Pagan welcomed her into their private sorority. During all-night gab fests, Laura and Eva shared confidences and Savana entertained them with gruesome homespun yarns. Impressed with her obvious creativity, they invited her to join them on the staff of the Bulwer-Lytton Bulletin.

Throughout the fall and winter term, they helped each other through the crunch of finals, sneaking in after curfew; they counseled and consoled over trifling romances gone sour and sex education in general; they pulled each other through bad drunks and horrible hangovers, squabbles with their parents, menstrual

cramps, bouts of the flu, and one major, wildly extrava-
gant shopping spree in New York City, complete with
limo, hotel suite, clothes, plays, and nightlife, all
financed with Laura's unlimited funds. By the spring
term, they were, through thick, thin, and sin, three fast
friends.

And so it was that the three misfits—three bright,
rich, misfits—brought to press the most sensationalistic
exposé that had ever been or would ever be published
about a conservative East Coast prep school. Their sub-
ject: the art of fucking your way to an A, making the
dean's list via the hot line, and Prudie Broadbutt's closet
lesbianism.

—*Fast Friends*

Before the lurid article went to press, there was a discussion as to the ultimate wisdom of exercising journalistic freedom. The threesome sat around a dimly lit desk,
sipping contraband Grand Marnier from the case the SAE
fraternity had so thoughtfully substituted in lieu of pay-
ment on their last month's outstanding account to Dial-A-
Dirty-Phone-Call. Casually, they debated the pros and
cons of recounting the numerous incidences of the Bulwer-
Lytton staff's immorality. Immorality was a subject
Savannah and Evie knew firsthand, and one which Lauren
loved to exploit.

"We know the consequences. Should we do it or should
we not?" Lauren steepled her fingers, assuming her
editorial role.

"Doesn't matter to me. What are they going to do,
bounce me out two months before graduation? I doubt
it." Eve drained the Baccarat snifter.

"You have the most to lose, Savannah." Lauren shot
her a compassionate look. "How do you vote?"

Savannah thought for a poignant moment. She realized
if she agreed her fate would once again be determined by
Norma Mae's whim, yet she felt it was imperative to de-

nounce the abuse of innocent young girls. "Remember the quote on the masthead of the *Bulletin*? *'Beneath the rule of men entirely great, the pen is mightier than the sword.'* Fuck 'em. Let's do it."

Lauren looked at Evie. "Agreed?"

"All for one and one for all, no matter what." Three Baccarat glasses clinked.

"Screw Prudie and to hell with the dignity of Bulwer-Lytton." Evie quaffed the amber liquid in one smooth gulp.

"Do you suppose Europe is nice this time of year? I have the distinct feeling I am going to be exiled shortly." Lauren propped her long legs on the desk and leaned back nonchalantly.

"Pretend you're Mary Queen of Scots, captive in the Tower of London."

"Not funny, Evie, considering Mary was beheaded. I'd rather be famous for giving head than losing it."

"The Tower of London is a luxury hotel compared to where I'll probably end up," Savannah sighed. "Praise the Lord and pass the Grand Marnier."

In the shadow of the Eiffel Tower, far across the Channel from London, where Lauren contemplated imprisonment, Sasa Bailesti handed his son Remni keys to a new red Ferrari convertible, a gift for his sixteenth birthday. "Enjoy, my son."

Remni roared out of the driveway, a picnic basket and a giggling mademoiselle beside him, and Sasa's heart constricted with longing. Ah, yes, he remembered Silver. How could he not? She was unforgettable.

"Are you coming, Sasa?" The baroness still retained a heavy Austrian accent, even after all her years in Paris.

Sasa watched the Ferrari wind along the estate's cobblestone drive. "In a minute, my sweet." God, how he yearned for a little respite from Anna and his memories. Just last week someone had mentioned Silver's name again. An exhibit in New York, they had said. She was becoming renowned for her unique photographs. Still lovely as ever. But, of course, like vintage wine, Silver would only improve with age.

Remni's car was out of sight. Sasa turned and followed Anna into the chateau.

Remni raced the smooth-handling machine along the coastal road at a reckless clip. Francine's gay chatter bored him. His mind was miles ahead, plotting their romantic interlude at the villa. Fast cars, fast girls, and fine champagne constituted his idea of a grand time, and he intended to avail himself of all three. Anna, Sasa, and Francine's parents had thought the servants adequate chaperones, but Remni thought the villa's faithful staff deserved a long weekend off. In his pocket rested a painstakingly accurate forgery of Anna's quaint hand, serving as insurance of an undisturbed weekend. Francine had promised to make him a gift of her virginity; he anticipated losing his own. He felt it in his own best interests not to let her know he was seducing her on the enthusiastic recommendations of a dozen or so of his closest friends.

They arrived at the villa overlooking the blue Mediterranean. After magnanimously offering the staff a brief holiday, Remni was forced to produce the corroborating note. Still skeptical but charmed by his sunny disposition, the servants departed.

The hour of Remni's graduation into manhood was at hand. The picnic basket remained unopened at the bottom of the winding staircase, and now his and Francine's hastily discarded clothes adorned the ornate bannister. The tawny-skinned young count was inexhaustible and sensual, Francine an endless orgasmic delight. Afternoon turned to dusk, dusk to night. The two champagne glasses sat empty. Francine cuddled close, satiated, and though Remni's virile body was momentarily gratified, his heart was not.

As he lay with his hands locked under his dark head and his lapis blue eyes focused upon the glittering European sky beyond the balcony's open doors, he felt beckoned by mystical forces. He knew the stars foretold a future, but the destiny they portended was just beyond his reach.

CHAPTER FORTY-FOUR

The campus was atwitter with scandal, with everyone placing bets on how quickly the senior editor and her contributing staff would be kicked out of Bulwer-Lytton. Miss Broadbeck remained behind closed doors, unavailable for comment.

When news of his daughter's imminent dismissal from Bulwer-Lytton reached Fax during a strategy conference with Clayton Robbins at Lutece in New York, he was struck by chest pains. He asked the congressman to drive him to the school, saying it would give them a chance to continue their discussion.

They gathered in the visitors' lounge, awaiting the appointed hour—the preacher, the prostitute, the photographer, the international power, the ex-pimp, and Norma Mae. They studied one another surreptitiously, assessing reactions and praying the secrets would be kept.

With studied insouciance, the three fast friends walked in to greet their parents.

Fax's color and expression frightened Lauren.

Savannah wished Norma Mae looked as elegant as the other two women. *Why did Momma always feel it was necessary to drape herself in gold from head to toe? Joshua Garland's eyes reminded her of Skeeter.* Suddenly she was cold.

Evie stared at Ben Randolph. *Why would Moni bring him?* At that moment, to her amazement, Lauren greeted Ben with a kiss on the cheek and a most contrite "You don't look well, Daddy. I'm really sorry about this misunderstanding." Bewildered, Eve looked at Moni, who sat statue still, her green cat eyes on Silver.

Silver's attention focused on Eve. *What was it about the girl that had bothered her from the moment they met and at every meeting thereafter?* She watched Evie cross the room, sit beside the attractive redhead clad in blue fox, and touch the pearls at her mother's throat, saying, "Those are new. A gift from Ben?" The sight of the two together triggered Silver's memory, taking her back to that early assignment, and Vegas . . . and Anovese . . . and a photograph on her studio wall. But there was something more, something that hovered on the fringe of her consciousness.

Moni refused to be baited by her daughter. Neither could she bear to look at Fax's direction, for she knew he more than she was sweating beneath that cool exterior. Her gaze swept to Josh Garr, who apparently had seen the light and traded his gun for a cross, a Mafia kingpin for a pulpit. Deliberately, she gave him an enigmatic smile. "Excuse me, Reverend Garland, but haven't we met before?"

Joshua Garland favored her with a broad smile. "Not that I recall, *madam.*"

Norma Mae paid no attention to the exchange between her husband and Moni. Her mind was on the Yankee nigger. She fingered her gold chains, wondering what in the hell had brought *him* to Bulwer-Lytton. *Sweet Jesus!*

Did he recognize her? Was this her private Armageddon? Had he come to claim his black blood?

Clayton Robbins smelled Norma Mae's fear from across the room. He recognized her in spite of all the glitter. His ebony eyes slid to Savannah, his mind taking inventory of her features while tallying the years. They added up correctly, but her color didn't. *But then again . . .*

The bands about Fax's chest tightened. He discreetly rubbed his left arm. *Dear God! What was Moni thinking?* It had to be as difficult for her as it was for him, perhaps more so. At least Silver was spared the ache Moni must be suffering. How could he—a man who had spent years pitting political power against political power and nation against nation—have been so inept as to have allowed Moni's and Silver's daughters to attend the same school? *Damn! What he wouldn't give to have that monumentally disastrous decision to make again.*

Lauren touched Fax's arm. "You haven't met my roommates, Daddy. That's Savannah and this is Evie."

Savannah nodded and smiled shyly. Evie lifted her head, mockery in her hazel eyes. "Nice to meet you at long last, Mr. Bennett."

The meeting with the trustees, the dean, and Miss Broadbeck was a very civilized affair. Concessions were made on both sides. The girls were spared expulsion but agreed to voluntarily withdraw. Eve, with only two months left to graduation, would be awarded her diploma, though not at the ceremony. Lauren and Savannah would be given recommendations so pristine they might have written them themselves. The board of trustees, in the interest of protecting the school from further scandal, agreed to let the dean and Miss Broadbeck continue until they could find suitable positions elsewhere, their good image restored by the girls' contrite apology and complete retraction in the *Bulwer-Lytton Bulletin*.

Clayton Robbins found himself in the humbling position of being pressed into service as a porter, as the girl's caravan of luggage was transported from the third floor to the waiting cars, and it was during one of these numerous trips that Norma Mae managed to brush against him on the narrow stairs. He was still hung and she was still hooked. She leaned back against the wall, her breasts jutting out, her lips pouting.

"Why don't you visit the True Gospel Tabernacle sometime, Congressman?" Her eyes traveled his length, lingering suggestively upon his crotch. "Perhaps after the services, we could share a lemonade."

In spite of himself, Clayton Robbins felt a familiar hardening in his loins. "Still have a taste for lemonade, do you, Norma Mae? How about black men? Still got a taste for them, too?"

"Maybe, maybe not."

"That kid mine?"

"Maybe, maybe not." Norma Mae ran her fingers lightly along his arm and thrust her pelvis forward as she began descending the steps once again. At the bottom, she turned to look at him. "Come see me, Red Shoes."

As Evie brought another load to the car, Fax took advantage of the moment to speak privately with her. "Thanks, Eve. I appreciate what you did in there."

"You mean what I didn't do. I kept quiet for Lauren's sake, not yours. And maybe I felt just a little bit sorry for Mom."

"We need to talk. I'll make a point to be in Vegas Monday, if you're agreeable."

"It's a little late for explanations, don't you think?"

"I hope not. Believe me, Evie, I do care about your mother and you."

"The same as you care about your wife and Lauren?"

"No, Eve, but just as much. I cannot live without your mother."

Joshua Garland had carried the last ton of baggage he intended to. He looked impatiently at his watch. Where in the hell was Norma Mae?

Fax's chest pains intensified when Silver invited Moni and Evie to Montauk Point for the weekend. His tension eased only minimally when Moni declined on the grounds that business required her to return home immediately.

Lauren watched Silver and Moni, wondering what Silver would say if she knew Moni was madam of the classiest whorehouse in the West.

The time for parting was at hand. Many tears, kisses, and hugs later, Savannah, Eve, and Lauren were forced to begin their separate sojourns, but vowed they would come together time and again.

CHAPTER FORTY-FIVE

Fax and Silver were having a rare argument behind the closed library doors. A blazing fire removed the damp chill of the nippy spring day but did nothing to warm the air between the two. Outside the closed doors, Lauren listened intently, peering through the crack. Not only was it high drama, her future was at stake.

Fax was defensive. Had Silver remembered the photograph of Moni, Eve, and Anovese? Had she made the connection? "I should never have acceded to your wishes. I was opposed to Lauren attending Bulwer-Lytton, as you will recall. The school is not the same as when you attended, Silver; the caliber of students has dropped. As it now stands, anyone with new money and a little determination can enroll their daughter—as Mrs. Garland did, for instance. No class whatsoever." Fax tapped his pipe on the faceted crystal ashtray. "What do you expect when she associates with girls like that?" He methodically refilled his briarwood Dunhill, tamping down the aromatic tobacco.

"Do not blame Bulwer-Lytton or the girls. Had your presence been more visible while Lauren was growing up, this wouldn't have happened. Don't you feel the slightest accountability for the years of neglect? Why would a young girl start something so disgusting as a dirty-phone-call service for men to call? That was a cry for masculine attention, a cry to ensure that her father, who is always halfway around the world, would hear. Tell me how you can excuse yourself from that." *But would it have made any difference? Would it have subdued Lauren's passionate heritage? She didn't know.*

"And I presume that you are faultless, Silver. Look at your friends. Are they off shooting pictures God only knows where? Are their egos so fragile they must seek an identity outside their homes? Are they compelled to look for external approval? No! They are content with being wives and mothers."

Silver paused, her voice lowering dangerously. "I seem to recall, Fax, that it was your idea I have a hobby, your idea for the first exhibit, you who encouraged me at every turn. Why? I'll tell you why: because it kept me out of your hair and allowed you to live your life without really including me. It freed you from having to concern yourself with giving me attention when it was inconvenient, and it was usually damn inconvenient."

Lauren cringed. Only once before had she heard Fax and Silver exchange a disagreeable word, and never had they raised their voices at each other. Part of it was exciting—there was sensuality there—but something told her her life would never again be the same; while she was the focus of their discussion their dissatisfaction with each other was the real issue.

Fax looked contrite. Perhaps for the first time ever, Silver had his undivided attention. She seized the moment. "Did it ever occur to you, Fax, to sweep me into your arms. Did you ever once feel a consuming passion for me? That's what I wanted—not the chance to photograph insects, war-torn countries, or Mafia men and their molls. Do you have an idea how it feels to be empty, so that no matter what you do or achieve, there is still an ache inside that says, 'This is not enough, there has to be more'? Do you, Fax? Or are you so cold, so power hungry, that there is nothing more for you to feel?''

Good God, how much did she know? The picture of Moni and Eve was from a long time ago. She could not suspect, but it didn't stop the painful constrictions around his heart. By sheer willpower, he forced himself to ignore the warnings.

Silver saw the agony in Fax's eyes and felt guilt. Had he cared more than he had revealed? She reached toward him. "Fax, I love you. I haven't always been the best wife." *But only once was I unfaithful.* "Please forgive me. We will work this out."

Fax turned away, his voice curiously bitter. "There is nothing to forgive. You have been a perfect wife. You are bright, beautiful, and talented. You have given me a lovely daughter, a fine home, and a peaceful life. Your accomplishments are legion. What more could a man ask?" *Silver had wanted to be loved the way he had loved Moni!* "What are we going to do about Lauren?"

Lauren took this as her cue to blithely breeze onto center stage. Past experience had taught her the wisdom of referring to herself in the third person during discussions affecting her. She positioned herself between them, in front of the fire, looking her most imposing and loving best. "Do you think Lauren would benefit from a stint in Europe? I understand they maintain the strictest of standards. Perhaps that would tame her wild streak."

Both Fax and Silver laughed. Lauren, by assuming responsibility for her problems, had freed them from much of the blame. As usual, they were charmed. As usual, she succeeded. They agreed to begin the search for the proper English school.

By the end of the day, the peaceful surface of the Bennett home was restored. Lauren was plotting weekend escapades in the South of France, Fax made airline reservations to Las Vegas, and Silver accepted a new assignment. She would have much preferred a second honeymoon, but Fax had not heard what she said, and so, like so many other women caught between the memory of a consuming love and the reality of a dishonest marriage, she would immerse herself in her work.

CHAPTER FORTY-SIX

"Afternoon, Mister Ben. She's upstairs, wearing out dat floor. Won't leave her room, won't eat, won't talk. I guess she's pretty upset about Evie getting kicked out of that fancy school she paid all her hard-earned money for."

"Where is Evie?"

"Out. Don't know where. Nobody knows nothing 'round here today. Never saw a day like this. Never want to see one again."

Fax retraced the worn path he had traveled so many times before to Moni's bedroom and arms. He entered without knocking.

Moni stood before an open window, a small figure staring into space. She looked vulnerable beneath the emerald silk dressing gown. Her hair was piled in loose curls atop her head. She had never looked more beautiful or desirable than she did at that moment. He went to her, caressing her arms as he lightly kissed the nape of her neck.

She made no response.

"Vashon told me you've been in seclusion since Eve was expelled."

Shrugging off his embrace, Moni finally spoke. "Why are you here, Ben? Or is it Fairfax, or Fax, or Randolph, or some other alias you fabricated to protect your other life? I should think you have more urgent responsibilities that require your attention at home."

"Moni, give me a chance to explain."

Pivoting, she allowed him to see the depth of her fury. "I was humiliated. For the first time in my life I felt like a common whore—the private, sleazy fuck of the respectable Fairfax Bennett. How dare you subject me to that?"

"Calm down, Moni. You're hysterical. You can't believe that sticky situation at Bulwer-Lytton was my fault, or that I was indifferent to your embarrassment. I never thought we'd meet there. I didn't know what had happened until the last minute. I am guilty of not thinking to call here first to warn you. For God's sake, Moni, be reasonable."

"I'm a redhead, I don't have to be reasonable. Trading social amenities with your wife while you sit between us is not only degrading, but absurd." She marched past him, her back rigid, her chin high. "Just tell me one thing, Ben, one thing. Whatever possessed you to suggest Bulwer-Lytton for Eve, knowing full well that Lauren would be attending?"

"But I didn't know. It was Silver's wish that Lauren follow tradition and go to her alma mater."

"And whatever your wife wishes, you grant."

"Unfair, Moni. You had your relationship with Anovese, and you have known for a long time that I'm married."

"But until that disastrous encounter, I never realized how very married you are. I played it straight with you and for over twenty years you've been deceiving me, making me believe I was special in your life, when in fact I was only a convenient layover for a busy tycoon." Moni ignored the pain in Ben's eyes and went on, "I've been a fool. I should have been charging exorbitant rates over the years for the services rendered. I could've retired a decade ago."

Fax pulled her trembling body to his. "Stop it, Moni. Don't say these things. My God, don't you know by now how desperately I love you? Perhaps I was selfish, but you are the one obsession I couldn't deny myself. You have always been and will forever be absolutely essential to me." He held her tight, tighter, tighter still.

Her mind told her not to give in, but she loved him, and she could not resist the tears in his eyes. Right or wrong, heaven or hell, they were meant to be together, if only now and then, if only within the confines of her bordello, if only in fleeting ecstasy. Her arms encircled his neck, her forgiving lips conveyed the ultimate surrender she had suppressed throughout their years together. "I've tried so hard not to make demands," she said, kissing his cheeks, his throat, "tried so hard not to complicate your life or compromise my own." She molded him to her, running her tapered nails through his silvery hair. "But no more, Ben. Loving you is worth the painful risk. I couldn't stand losing you . . . even knowing you can never really be mine."

Fax swung Moni into his arms and carried her to the bed. "I have never truly belonged to anyone else. Only death can separate us, and if there is any possible way, I will defy even that to lie with you one last time."

Later that evening, with Moni's permission, Fax spoke to Evie. She was sullen and contrary, but he was determined to safeguard her future.

"I want to know your plans, Evie. Have you some particular vocation in mind?"

She wore shorts. Indolently swinging her bare legs over the arm of her chair, "Oh, I don't know," she drawled.

"Given my background and natural flair, I could go into competition with Mother Moni."

"I think it's time you quit blaming your mother for loving and supporting you in the only way she knows how. Given a few years and mistakes of your own, you may come to realize just how much she sacrificed in your behalf."

"Is this where you tell me the bedtime story about how awful things were for the little waif from the docks and how hard times make for bad ladies? I've heard it before, thank you. The truth is, Moni could have gotten out of the business years ago, but she didn't. She's rich as Croesus, but she'll never have enough—money or men. You aren't enough for her either."

With a swift and unexpected motion, Fax yanked Evie to her feet, shaking her roughly. "If you have no respect for me, at least have some for yourself and your mother. I asked what you intend to do with your life. Your options are unlimited. Now let's talk." He slammed her back into her chair, folded his arms, and waited.

Except for Josh Garr's yanking her out of the juke joint when she was thirteen, this masculine attention was a new experience for Evie. It hadn't been easy having johns as her only male standard. She had never cared about pleasing them. They were only heard through the paper-thin walls. But Ben was angry. "I don't know what really interests me, Ben—I mean, Fax. What would you suggest?"

Fax felt himself mellowing. Lauren had never seemed to need a father, and after Silver's accusations, he wanted to be needed, to make up for his absences. "Actually, I do have a thought about your future—one that might serve both of us well. How does politics strike you?"

"Stuffy and dull."

"You are naive, my dear. Politics are for the shrewd and daring. They require a quick mind, a glib tongue, and a killer instinct. I think you qualify."

Eve grinned, but she was instinctively suspicious. "You

have a purpose, Fax. What is the reason for my sudden political ambition?''

"You're an observer, Evie, and I want someone watched."

"Who?"

"You remember Congressman Robbins?"

"Yeah. Slick and black."

"It's the slick that bothers me. I need someone in his camp to keep an eye on him."

Eve decided to flaunt the full extent of her political knowledge. "Is he Democrat or Republican?"

"Does it matter?"

"No, just asking."

"Then it's settled? You'll join Robbins as a public relations staffer and periodically report to me about his activities."

Eve nodded.

Fax couldn't resist a final comment. "Public relations ought to provide a suitable vent for your creative flair. I presume you won't get kicked out of Washington." He turned to leave.

"Fax?"

He looked back at her. "Yes?"

"You're okay, you know. When I was little I used to wish for a father. Now that I'm older, I don't care so much, but I know now who I had in mind."

He covered his sudden surge of emotions with a wink. "You're all right too, Evie. Keep in touch."

CHAPTER FORTY-SEVEN

Norma Mae, both upset and titillated by her chance encounter with Red Shoes, couldn't get herself together. It had all been entirely too trying. Everything, just everything, was falling apart.

Savannah saw it coming. Every time Norma Mae got upset and couldn't sort something out, Savannah paid the price not only for her own sins but for Norma Mae's as well. Some things just never changed.

"How could you disgrace your father like that?"

"He isn't my father. I don't even know who my father is. Do you?"

Norma Mae's hand cracked across Savannah's face. "The Lord says honor thy Mother."

"The Lord *says* a lot of things, but I haven't found many of them to be true, except maybe you reap what you sow." For the second time in her life, Savannah defied Norma Mae.

"Now, honey," Joshua Garland put his arm around Savannah. Her skin crawled.

Oh, God! For the first time, Norma Mae allowed herself to see Savannah's developing body. She knew, knew better than anyone, the depth of Joshua's abnormal cravings, the hundreds of nights she had been taken in every position, pretending to be a young girl or boy to please him. Now she saw Savannah's revulsion, saw Skeeter's ice-pick-stabbed body. *No!* She wouldn't give up the gold twice in a lifetime. It was more than a body could take.

"Norma Mae, why don't we keep Savannah home with us? Send her to school here. Let's be a real family. Close and loving." Why he'd ever thought to be rid of the girl was now beyond him. She was a pretty one, with those big, sad eyes. She could get the faith real quick. He could see it, smell it, taste it.

Savannah and Norma Mae spoke simultaneously, their motives different, their reasons the same. "No!"

By the end of the day, Norma Mae had wheedled, bargained, and seduced Joshua into allowing Savannah to spend the summer working as a counselor for the True Gospel Tabernacle's youth camp. Come fall, she would be enrolled in Miracle Mountain Bible College, a strict Christian school where she could not fall from grace, even with all her wicked ways. But Norma Mae's trying day also had had its reward. She had managed to find time to accept the private phone call from Congressman Clayton Robbins.

It was going to be a long, hot summer.

And she didn't believe just plain old lemonade was gonna quench her thirst.

CHAPTER FORTY-EIGHT

The search for a proper British school was successful, and Lauren was quickly enrolled. Her last school year passed in a flurry of excitement and perfect grades. From the polo fields to Ascot, from the Emerald Isle to the Eiffel Tower, from noblemen to princes, Lauren's style, skills, comprehension, and contacts were polished to a dazzling sheen. By the time she completed her final form, she was no longer willing to enroll at Radcliffe, the college intended for her since birth. Like the formal family dinners, it reeked of monotony.

In an attempt to be close to her daughter and determine what direction Lauren's future should take, Silver wangled a European photographic mission and an accompanying writing assignment for Lauren. As the summer progressed, the ache of old wounds gripped Silver, and she struggled with a jealous desire to force Lauren home to Radcliffe and predictability. Her daughter was leading the life she had longed for, and she resented that it was Lauren's contacts who abetted their work. But they worked well together, the shots and copy were candid and unique, and the American public would be treated to a taste of European nobility that otherwise would have been inaccessible to them. Their joint effort earned both American and European press awards.

Silver began to think of future projects but did not acknowledge her primary motivation—to become part of Lauren's exciting world. Lauren rebelled, wanting to join a friend in Paris for a year, supposedly using the time to find herself. Silver acceded, Fax concurred, and Lauren took up residence on the Champs-Élysées, ensconced in a charming *grande pièce* filled with French antiques, Impressionist paintings, the freshest of flowers, and the best of old wines.

She was barely eighteen years old and her entire life stretched before her, rich with promise. Her days were filled with illuminating chats at sidewalk cafés and quaint bistros, and companions both young and fresh, old and wise. While the remainder of the world turned to electronic entertainment, Lauren absorbed people. Her curiosity made her a formidable conversationalist. After all, she was in training to be a queen. She wanted to know everything about everyone, and they, her subjects, were flattered and confided in her. Though her nights were filled with dates, she had no need for the pill she regularly swallowed. Her innumerable beaus found more in her than they ever dreamed of discovering, but Lauren did not meet one who stirred her imagination. There was in her mind a vision of one heart to be conquered. She spent a great many hours ruminating on her ideal lover. And she most certainly desired a lover. Unfortunately, Lauren was a person of absolutes. Her life was perfect and so must be her love, total and consuming. He, this mythical lover, must meet her expectations, and her expectations were beyond the pale.

CHAPTER FORTY-NINE

Within months of her arrival on the Washington scene, Eve's ability to promote Robbins while keeping tabs on his private activities surpassed even Fax's expectations. An integral part of the congressman's retinue, she did not miss a trick when it came to ferreting out favorable press coverage for the recently appointed junior member of the Appropriations Committee and the Defense Subcommittee. Nor did she overlook an opportunity to rifle through his personal files or eavesdrop on late night caucuses that smelled of stale cigar smoke and reeked of secret trade-offs.

She sat in the deserted office, scrutinizing Robbins's appointment book. There were several suspicious entries—brunch with known lobbyists from opposing camps; an outing at the theater scheduled for next Friday night, the tickets a token of appreciation for his support of Duvalier's intent to spill Dominican blood and sell Haitian plasma to American blood banks. God only knew how many Washington Perle Mestas would be recipients of

voodooed transfusions and what rare strain of island viru-
lence the sterile plastic sacks contained. She flipped the
page, focusing on incriminating notations rather than
trivia. *Now, here was an interesting item. So the illustrious
bastard had plans to attend the Cohen bar mitzvah. Why
would he be cozying up to the space program's leading
high-tech supplier? What was in it for Clayton? She was
sure he'd be dragging the sack for more than gefilte fish,
matzo balls, and red horseradish. This little gem ought to
be worth a big bonus.*

Eve started at the jangle of the phone. It shouldn't have
caught her off guard. Fax called at precisely nine o'clock
every other Monday.

"Congressman Robbins's offices. Eve Afton speaking."

"Hello, Evie. I'm between flights and haven't much
time."

"And I'm reading between the lines of Robbins's
appointment book. When I tell you what I've stumbled
onto, I don't think you'll mind missing connections,
because believe me, your congressman isn't."

Eve switched off the desk lamp, slipped off her pumps,
and propped her stocking feet on the windowsill. It had
been a long and draining day. Playing Mata Hari took
more energy than fucking the slavish coterie of admirers
she'd acquired since storming the Hill. She sighed, gazing
out upon the lighted rotunda and cherry-blossomed
avenues. She'd had an instant affinity with D.C. It was the
ideal roost for a sharp go-getter like herself who could
party with the best and yet never forget to be slicker,
quicker, smoother, smarter, dirtier. And in this Olympic
orgy of bipartisan, bisexual bedfellows, that was saying
something.

She leaned forward, wriggled out of her linen jacket,
flung it over the bronze bust of George Washington Carver
by the window, and settled back to take in the view.

Oh, yes, Moni's daughter had at long last found her ele-

ment. She was one-on-one with her peers and fast distinguishing herself as a ruthless and innovative PR person. She reveled in a multitude of lovers, from pages to ambassadors. Her days were busy; her nights erotic. *So why did she feel apart from it all?*

Was it because she had struggled throughout her formative years with the stigma of being Moni Leah Afton's mistake? Because she'd constantly fought the cliché, like mother, like daughter? Had daily wrestled the devils that drove her? Would there ever be any respite? Why was there no sense of fulfillment in accomplishment or men moaning her name in the wee small hours? Why did she always have to outwardly deny, then inwardly crave, that Camelot world from which she felt forever barred?

Fuck! Washington was nothing more than a glorified version of Bulwer-Lytton.

She'd exploited and exposed those aristocrats, and these bureaucrats wouldn't be exempted either.

Eva's motto: give only as good as you get. Her approach: make them want what you project to the point that they'll forfeit their self-esteem, their wives, their millions, their children, their futures, perhaps even their lives for the privilege of lying with you. She had that certain knowledge, certain detachment, certain and most elusive ingredient that made the strong beg, the great tumble, the cynical believe. Her appeal, whether real or illusion in the minds of men, was a mystery. The men she'd conquered hadn't a clue to the secret of Eva. So smooth, so expert was she that they fell victim before they realized there had been a silk-sheet skirmish—that was, until the ace navy pilot entered her life.

—Fast Friends

CHAPTER FIFTY

Christmas, 1964. The slopes of Saint Moritz beckoned.
Switzerland was new territory. Lauren and her roommate,
Chloe, laden with gaily wrapped gifts and high hopes,
boarded the plane. They were part of the rich and
beautiful. Puff the Magic Dragon was making his rounds,
but Lauren was drinking champagne, wearing designer
clothes, and flirting outrageously. Life was one big beautiful picnic and Switzerland was just another course.

Saint Moritz, the playground of the world's aristocracy,
was, as usual, teeming this Yuletide with lords, ladies, film
stars, and scions of industry. Swathed in furs and jewel-
bedecked, they gathered from the four corners to celebrate
the holiday in a blaze of daredevil sporting events, mountains of caviar, and cases of champagne.

By the time Lauren and Chloe reached the snow-covered
Engadine Valley and checked into the Palace Hotel, they
were on an incredible high. Lauren was convinced that
somewhere in Saint Moritz destiny awaited her. She had a
feeling. *She knew.*

Count Remni Bailesti was young, handsome, rich, and titled. He made love with French finesse and Rom passion. Christmas 1964 had come and gone, and every day there had been a new beauty, every night a new conquest, sometimes two, and once, on Christmas Eve, there were three. All were meaningless.

He moved through the throngs of revelers with effortless grace, looking for the goddess he'd seen defying the slopes. She hadn't even favored him with a glance. Her concentration was focused entirely on her skiing. She swooped down through lightly crusted snow, a graceful ballerina. He'd followed her for a long time, then lost her. Now he imagined her perfume, her personal scent, the wild taste of her lips, and the feel of her supple body against his. He could not explain it, yet *he knew*.

Count Remni Bailesti was not the only young, handsome, rich, and titled man looking for the raven-haired beauty this New Year's Eve. In his brand new palatial villa high on Suvretta Mountain, Prince Kenir Ashad donned his tuxedo and onyx studs in preparation for the New Year's Eve midnight schuss down the mountainside. Earlier in the day, leafing through a houseguest's magazine, he'd stumbled upon Lauren and Silver's work and learned Lauren lived in Paris but was spending the holidays in Saint Moritz. He'd made her a promise long ago. He wondered if she remembered. If not, she would. *He knew.*

Lauren was busily pinning up her hair—not in a coiffure designed to display her luxuriant tresses, but to camouflage her femininity. She intended to compete in the traditional late-night event, but as a man. Her hastily purchased and altered tux was on a hanger. Her breasts presented no problem, but her well-shaped derriere had been another matter. Substantial padding broadened her narrow shoulders and hid her seductive curves. A debonair mustache and stage glue waited on the back of the lavatory.

The new year drew nigh, but Remni was no closer to finding the elusive goddess. He tossed down two bullshots and gathered his poles and skis.

A quarter of the way down the mountain, a skier veered from the safest route, daring the night and the moguls. Remni couldn't help himself; he had to follow. For a while he was content to follow the intrepid skier, but when the opportunity presented itself, he dispensed with caution, took a dangerous jump and assumed the lead.

Lauren's sharp intake of breath cut the stillness. Even she didn't have the courage for such a jump. Determinedly, she pushed forward, more reckless by the second, regaining her lead, only to lose it minutes later. Their descent was magnificently orchestrated, a choreography of guts and glamor and synchronization. They soared, they glided, they flew. There was only the two of them, the night, and the magic. Far away, torchlight glistened on the snow, but Remni and Lauren were lost in the silence with only the *whooshes* and the cutting edges of their skis on pristine snow. Midway through the treacherous run, truth rammed itself into Remni's awareness. The daredevil was his goddess. A smile curved his lips.

They finished the run together, simultaneously removing their goggles. "Well done, Sir . . .?" Remni congratulated his companion.

For the second time, Lauren's intake of breath was sharp. She could not speak. Before her was the man who had always hovered on the fringe of her knowledge, the nameless, unknown vision who had been in her dreams since childhood. As she stared, Remni stepped forward and removed her hat. Her hair tumbled down, framing her oval face. His eyes adored her, his arms embraced her, his lips came down on hers. The world spun, the mountain moved, the celestial bodies realigned themselves around Venus, the planet of love.

From his vantage point at the congested finish line, Kenir's smoldering eyes surveyed the touching scene. Once he was too early. Now he was too late. When next they met, the temptress who would be queen would be his. *He knew.*

CHAPTER FIFTY-ONE

If Savannah's summer at Joshua Garland's True Gospel Tabernacle's youth camp was a nightmare, Miracle Mountain Bible College was torture. At Norma Mae's insistence, Savannah had been tested for early admission, deemed gifted, and incarcerated. Joshua Garland's focus was on money, pedophilia, and bamboozling parents; Miracle Mountain Bible College's emphasis was on mandatory academics, theological brainwashing, and terminal boredom. As usual, Savannah was without alternatives. Her quick mind and the years of Holy Roller preaching she'd been subjected to aided her Bible study, but she was not even remotely challenged—not, that was, until literature class provided a vent for her pent-up frustrations. When she wrote a particularly gruesome short story based on a newspaper account of a local murder, she horrified her classmates and was put on probation for doing the devil's work. While Garland seduced prepubescent bodies, Savannah plotted her third and final defiance of Norma Mae. Like Lauren, she hoarded her monthly allowance, saving to make a fast getaway. For once, God glanced with favor on Savannah, having imbued Joshua with a need to ensure her silence about the not so wholesome activities at his youth camp. Unbeknownst to Norma Mae, Savannah received a new '64 Starfire convertible. Knowing full well it would not be allowed on campus, Savannah kept the car in a garage outside school property, an hour's walk and a lifetime of freedom away.

CHAPTER FIFTY-TWO

From the first moment of moonlight madness, Lauren and Remni were inseparable, often secluded in his villa in the south of France, but sometimes racing at Monte Carlo, joining a yachting party, or participating in a polo match. One inhaled, the other exhaled. They had it all and all they wanted was each other.

Lauren periodically talked to Fax and Silver, but told them nothing of what she was doing. Her allowance checks were duly deposited; she paid her share of the rent to Chloe. No one was the wiser. If Fax and Silver applied pressure, she made outrageous excuses and bought time. She thought of Evie and Savannah. Savannah wrote, but Lauren was too busy to read the voluminous stacks of correspondence. Later, she told herself. From time to time she dashed off careless notes with incomplete sentences about fairy-tale love and smartly phrased observations on life.

CHAPTER FIFTY-THREE

From the moment she spotted Lieutenant Mac Ames at the fund-raising gala February first, Eve was drawn to him. Nineteen sixty-five might not be such a bad year after all. His cool blue eyes followed her as she mingled and maneuvered in the congested room.

"Nice ass on the redhead. I sure wouldn't mind knocking off a piece of that."

"Take a number. At the rate she's going, she'll make the *Guinness Book of World Records* by Tuesday. And enjoy it while you can, because from what I hear nobody gets seconds." The CBS correspondent gave a short laugh.

"What's her name?"

"Evie Afton."

"Besides starring in wet dreams, what else does she do?" The cleft in his chin deepened when the correspondent winced. "Say, you wouldn't happen, by chance, to know her address?"

"She's a staffer for Representative Robbins—you know, the one who got jailed today in Selma with Martin

Luther King on the voter registration issue." The correspondent made a mental note to check out the serious parley between L.B.J. and Tip O'Neill. "Believe me, pal, I wouldn't be doing you any favor by passing along her address. Maybe you'll get lucky and the urge will pass before your number comes up."

"Why does the gentleman in dress blues look familiar?" Ophelia's deafness made it impossible for Evie to be discreet, but the old bag knew *everyone*. "I can't place him."

"I'm sure you'll find a way, dear."

The witch hadn't lost any of her acerbity along with her hearing. "Tacky, tacky, Ophelia."

"You've probably seen his picture in the paper. He's almost a national hero, a veteran test pilot. He's broken all kinds of records—and all kinds of hearts, too, from what I hear."

Spying Norma Mae and the Evangelist coming toward her, Eve quickly kissed the dowager's pasty cheek and excused herself. *What in the hell were those two doing here?* Probably some fund-raising of their own, as if they needed it. Good God! The woman was a walking, talking Babble-on of gold bullion.

"Well, isn't it a teensy tiny world, Joshua? Looky who's here." Norma Mae's rotatin' motatin' all but invited a dislocated hip as she zeroed in on Evie. "You settin' Washington on its ear like you did Bulcorn-Lyceum?"

"Leopards don't change their spots, Mrs. Garland. You know that." Eve shot a look at Josh Garr. "Isn't that true, Reverend?"

His hand grazed her bare back on the pretext of offering solace. "Even a harlot found redemption in our Lord. Souls are never lost, they just sometimes go astray."

"My soul isn't astray, but your hand certainly is."

Before Norma Mae suffered a case of the vapors, Eve latched on to the convenient arm of the passing Henry Kissinger. *Where was the Lieutenant?* Her eyes scanned the room. *Ah, yes, there he was, cornered by gossip columnist Maxine Cheshire*. She caught his eye, then coyly looked away. The suggestive glances they exchanged amounted to good sport. Sipping her third martini, she plucked the olive from the plastic sword's tip and rolled it on her tongue as she grinned at the fly-boy, then abruptly gave the Secretary of State her undivided attention.

For the first time in his life, Mac Ames experienced a stab of jealousy. Usually it was he who was envied, he who inspired pangs of inadequacy in other men. At thirty-seven, he was a legend. He had gone further than any man alive—to the brink of space itself. But tonight he didn't want to glimpse infinity, he just wanted to explore a particular heavenly body. His sun-baked face was a study in concentration as he watched Eve. It wasn't that her wiles were original or subtle but that her intensity was singular.

He would have preferred to explain away her effect as nothing more than a gin-induced hallucination, but he could not. He engaged her eyes again, saluting her magnificent conceit with a wink.

She arched a brow and traded her empty glass for a full one. She had no intention of making this easy. If he could navigate his way to the edge of space, he should have no problem ascertaining the location of her digs in a city where any tidbit of information was available for the right price.

He made inquiries, then he made an exit. Since he was not the sort to walk away from a challenge and she was not the kind to issue an idle dare, he would be on her doorstep when she arrived home. He had no doubt that she expected him.

Modesty was not one of Eve's stronger traits, so she hadn't the slightest compunction about assessing the wear and tear of a three-hour fuck and an inordinate consumption of gin on her face. "Shit. Toots Berber probably looks better.'' She leaned closer to the mirror, and applied a cover-up to the dark circles under her eyes as dawn crept over the capital.

Mac laced his fingers behind his tawny head and admired the perfect symmetry of her heart-shaped ass. ''Who's Toots Berber?''

''A shriveled-up bag lady who hangs around on the Hill.'' She snatched up a brush and raked the bristles through her snarled hair. ''So, Lieutenant, am I the fantastic lay you imagined I was?''

She turned, bending at the waist so her thick mane tumbled forward, and whipped the brush through the tangles.

His gaze traveled from her bouncing tits to her Valentine bottom. *She looked terrific from any angle.* ''Yeah, you're about what I expected.'' *All this and a butt-fuck too. She was something.*

Eve's head snapped up and she peered at him through a veil of copper wisps. Usually they at least had the grace to heap accolades at her feet. ''Good. I'd hate to be a disappointment.'' She swept the hair from her eyes and strutted to the dresser. ''Although, personally, I like a quicker fuck than you, the change of pace *was* refreshing.''

''Why do I get the idea that you derive some kind of perverse kick out of emasculating men?'' *Oh, yeah, babe, I had you pegged from the first. All the good it did me; I'm no less a sucker than all the other poor bastards you've reputedly reduced to so much spermatozoa. Maybe I do wish my number hadn't come up.*

''What are you? Some kind of amateur shrink? Show me your credentials.''

He experienced a split second of perpendicular flight, soaring through her blanketing cloud cover, climbing higher, accelerating faster, penetrating deeper—to the very brink of the secret of Eve.

He eased back the covers. ''You don't want to be analyzed. And believe me, babe, this hard-on is authentic, and I give great therapy.''

Eve howled with laughter. "You really are an egotistical asshole." She went to the nightstand and wound her clock. "I have to get up in a couple of hours and, besides, I never go back for seconds."

His brawny arm coiled about her waist and forced her onto the bed. "I do. You don't mind if I help myself? This is a smorgasbord, isn't it?"

CHAPTER FIFTY-FOUR

The impeccably dressed Michael Christian stood before his new father-in-law, Harrison Mendall, masking the smugness he felt. It had taken him half a decade of perseverance and plotting, but he had finally wedded and bedded—in that order—old Harry's rich-bitch daughter. He had emulated his idol to a tee. It was true that Harry was a legend, having overseen the growth of publishing from a literary endeavor to a multimillion dollar enterprise, but only after marrying founding father Stearns's daughter. Everyone, including old Harry himself, had forgotten that fact. But not Michael. He harbored no delusions about his own premeditated choice of marrying the coldest, most indifferent woman any man ever mounted. The only thing that bothered him was that he suffered pangs of conscience less and less, and with each passing day he felt more and more justified. He had tried to be patient, tried to be sensitive to her hang-ups, he *really* had.

"You're looking fit and fine. How was the honeymoon, Michael? I trust Barbara enjoyed the cruise."

"The Greek Isles were lovely and we're grateful for your generosity, sir." *It was scary how good he was getting at manipulation.* "Such a trip would be beyond my means for quite some time."

"Not so long as you may think, my son. Congratulations. You are now a senior editor."

Michael allowed his dimples to deepen, but he had no control over his racing blood. The thrill of power exhilarated him as nothing ever had. Yes, he had made the right decision. His rage to achieve burned so intensely he would fuck a block of ice if it meant getting what he wanted. And what he wanted more than anything in the world was to be the reigning golden boy of Publishers Row.

His rise to the top would be meteoric, his unanticipated descent faster, for Micah never counted on the variable of love or a passion that redefined hell. He never counted on Eva.

                                        —Fast Friends

CHAPTER FIFTY-FIVE

Silver and Buffy Chadds-Ford lingered at the front door of Bookbinder's. The strong summer breeze off the Delaware River whipped at their hats.

"If you're determined to photograph the Marrish myth, Silver, then please be careful. Everyone knows the man is *paranoid* about his privacy." Buffy kissed her cheek. "Call me as soon as you get back. I'll be dying to know if you succeeded."

The stowaway crouched between the Victorian seats, photographing the bizarre contents of the boxes thrown about the unoccupied coach. She balanced herself against the steady vibration of the train and snapped picture after picture, roll after roll, recording and rerecording every shred of filthy evidence documenting Marrish's psychasthenia. This was more than she'd hoped for, a pictorial exposé on the decay of a genius: the addiction, the obsession, the dementia of a tormented visionary.

For the first time, Silver had reservations about the

wisdom of accepting this assignment. Had she suspected the extent of the recluse's eccentricities, she would have declined *Fortune*'s freelancer's dream. But no one had known.

She used the remaining twilight to inch her way to the rear where her gear was stashed, carefully capping the lenses of her cameras and reloading and recasing. Then she huddled on the floor, not daring to concentrate on anything but her purpose—to photograph Noel Marrish.

He was going to accomplish the impossible, obtain the unobtainable. When he and Marrish concluded their deal in the desert this night, the term *defense contractor* would take on new meaning. If just one nation could become so impregnable, every other would be forced to follow suit. Who could resist the one thing that would end the possibility of nuclear war? The sophisticated laser technology would set in motion a galaxy of power and profit. Billions would become trillions; trillions, zillions. And this time it would be profit with honor. Fax stared at the stars he would soon control.

The private train streaked through the desert, then slowed, brakes squealing, gears grinding, metal wheels screeching along the rails until it came to a halt among the cacti and iguanas. A door slammed, two cars were uncoupled, and then the engine went on down the deserted track, leaving two cars silhouetted against the sand dunes. Another door opened. Two men stepped out and approached Fax. He allowed himself to be searched, then led into the darkened car.

Silver shoved her gear, her canteen, and her coat out the window, and quietly dropped to the ground beside them. She readied her camera. This had to be it. If she was ever going to get a shot of Marrish it had to be now. She edged around the car, spied the men inside, and began her infrared invasion, praying that it was Marrish she was capturing.

As lights approached, she ran to the opposite side, climbed onto the iron wheels and shot through the windows, dropping back to the ground as the lights came closer. She could hear muffled voices, boxes being shuffled, a van pulling away, an automobile departing. Quickly she shot again and caught taillights disappearing, and then it was only the two empty cars and her, alone in the desert.

At the first flush of dawn, she abandoned her coat, picked up her gear, slung her canteen around her neck, and started walking. She had pulled the photographic coup of a lifetime and she'd be damned if she wasn't going to make it to a darkroom.

Moni sat in the darkened room awaiting Marrish's arrival. The only predictable thing about him was that every time he walked out on a wife, he'd show up in Vegas and send for her. Once he'd been young and handsome and a ladies' man, but the last time they had met . . .

Moni remembered when he had liked light, lots of it, spotlighting his iron-man physique. Perhaps this new darkness fetish was only vanity, prompted by the ravages of age. With Noel, you never knew.

Her long hike was followed by a ride which was followed by a smooth flight. Home! In the warm, familiar safety of her darkroom, Silver ran her prints. *Mother of God!* She sank against the wall. *What in the hell did her husband have in common with Noel Marrish? And how, by all that was holy, could she release these pictures that were supposed to be the crowning glory of her career?*

CHAPTER FIFTY-SIX

Lost weekends and steamy sex became a hard habit to break. Mac knew full well that to disclose his growing affection for Eve would be like volunteering for a suicidal test flight. But she represented the ultimate impetus, a seduction more exhilarating than breaking the sound barrier, more challenging than his death-defying missions.

Beyond the window panes of her brownstone, lacy snowflakes fluttered down, ethereal crystals exquisitely unique. Fleeting. Like her.

Christmastime was supposed to be the jolly season, but this was ridiculous. What the fuck was wrong with him? He swallowed hard, eased his arm from beneath her, and shakily lit a smoke. Eve opened her eyes, reached up and guided the cigarette wedged between his fingertips to her lips.

"What time is it, Mac?"

"Anxious to get rid of me?"

"They're predicting a blizzard tonight, and if you miss your flight, you may not be able to get another one."

She was uncharacteristically preoccupied with the mundane aspects of his life. He usually had the feeling that after he had served his purpose her interest waned drastically. "Yeah, I suppose a missed flight would screw up your roster, baby." *Great. Swell. Expose your insecurities, Ace Ames.*

"What's with you, Mac? What I do while you're away has never been an issue with us."

"Yeah, well maybe it's becoming one." He ground out the cigarette in the ashtray perched on his stomach. "Ouch, God damn it! You chap my butt and I burn my stomach." He clunked the thin glass ashtray onto the nightstand. "Why can't you buy some decent ashtrays instead of stealing them from every goddamn hotel on the East Coast?"

"Don't get so tetchy, Mac. I don't keep the men, just the souvenirs."

Mac flung back the sheet and sat on the edge of the bed, his palms pressing his forehead and his fingers in his hair. "I can't handle this open relationship crap anymore, Evie. Your fucking other men is fucking with my mind. It's worse than—"

"I thought crackerjacks like you got their kicks testing the limits." She brushed a kiss across his shoulders.

"Stop it. You're always doing that, distracting me. You get me hot, we screw some more, and never settle anything." He shrugged. "All I can think about is you. No matter how high or fast I go, I can't get you out of my head. Jesus! I'm humping you in my sleep, during briefings, in the goddamn cockpit. It's no good."

Eve retreated from the bed, pulled on her robe, and knelt before him. "I thought we were two of a kind, Mac, a couple of thrill-seekers with everything to gain and nothing to lose." Positioning herself between his thighs, she slipped her arms about his waist and rubbed her cheek across his midsection.

He stiffened, clutched a handful of her hair, and tilted

her head back, forcing her to look into his eyes. "You're right about one thing, baby. I am an all-or-nothing guy. And I want all of you. Marry me or set me free, Evie. Like I said, I can't handle this crap anymore."

The ultimatum stunned Eve. His wasn't the first proposal she'd received, but it was by far the most sincere. The earthy pilot aroused her conscience as well as her passion. She tried to hide her sensitivity behind a nervous laugh. "You're no more the marrying kind than I am, Mac. We'd hate each other an hour after the 'I do's.'"

"So, your answer is no." His fingertips memorized the silk of her hair.

"I can't be exiled to some godforsaken desert. I'd go mad. Try to understand." She put her hands around his neck and drew his mouth to hers.

He pried her from him, yanked on his pants, grabbed his shirt and tie, and walked to the door. "I understand you better than you do yourself, sweetheart. I'll get over you. I'm going to fly you right out of my system." He paused at the threshold to light a smoke.

"Fly high, baby. You're better at it than me."

After leaving Evie, Mac took his regrets to the first bar he came to. After that he took her up with him each and every time he flew—and took her to his fiery death when he lost control of his plane and plunged into the desert on Christmas morning.

Eve refused to assume responsibility for Mac's death. Yet she could not perform the simplest of daily functions, such as getting dressed or going to work. Instead, for New Year's 1966, she ordered a case of Ballantine's thirty-year-old Scotch and moped about the brownstone for two weeks. "Damn reckless fool. I wouldn't have made the difference. We couldn't have made it work. I *won't* feel guilty." She flopped on the bed, fighting the memories and wallowing in stale linens, Scotch, and remorse. "You would have pressed it to the limit anyway, you stupid son of a bitch. Did you think I'd look good in black? I can walk away from any man whenever I please. I never owed you or anybody else a damn thing.''

But there remained that nagging *what if*. What if she had accepted Mac's proposal? What if she was wrong? What if Camelot did exist? What if she could rewrite the ending?

And eventually she did just that, sitting down at her dusty typewriter and letting the yearning flow onto the paper.

The clatter of the keys was the only sound she acknowledged. The phone rang and rang late into the night, but Eve never answered.

Weeks later, their bittersweet romance, its ending revised and heartwarming, was in the mail to New York, and she was back at work after a nearly terminal bout with alcoholic toxicosis, which she reported to Representative Robbins as a severe case of the flu.

Eve. Something bothered Lauren about Eve. She tried to call to wish her Happy New Year from the Luedhof coffee plantation nestled at the base of Kilimanjaro, but there was no answer. Ever. Finally she gave up; she hadn't time nor the inclination to concern herself with Eve's lack of response, for Lauren had Remni. He was all she needed, all she would ever need. . . .

It wasn't until Evie received another of Lauren's exuberant letters that she realized the power and potential profit of love. The power was Lauren's; the profit could be Eve's. She was happy for her dear friend, but more important, she saw an endless reservoir of story material. Having always been on the outside looking in, Eve did not mean to plagiarize but only to recount the *what if*s that never seemed to materialize in her own life.

She hadn't heard from New York. They probably weren't interested in another love story. God knew, even

Eve found them trite. But her own affairs weren't enough and certainly spying and reporting on Robbins wasn't enough. What did give her satisfaction were these imaginary excursions into the Camelot world she transferred from her mind onto the page.

> And well it paid. New York, like Washington, was seduced by the siren who wrote about the glory of love like an angel and wrote the sex scenes like a pro.
> —Fast Friends

CHAPTER FIFTY-SEVEN

Savannah made it as far as New Orleans before her savings ran out. She was nineteen years old and flat broke. She had two options, both precedents set by Norma Mae: either hustle tables or hustle men.

First she applied at the better establishments. No openings. She was too young and lacked experience. After a week of being turned down, she heard about a place down by the docks, an oyster bar where the clientele was coarse but the tips were good. Savannah became the night girl at Wooly-Bullies.

Her Dial-A-Dirty-Phone-Call days at Bulwer-Lytton had been good training for sexy talk and no action, and she now had a crock full of silver dollars to prove it. She moved into a room above a dry cleaner, where she slept till noon and wrote until four, chronicling the sights, sounds, smells, and sickos of New Orleans. At four she scrubbed herself clean, symbolically washing away the putridness of life before having to again endure it at Wooly-Bullies.

Daily she told herself it would not be much longer until

she had enough money to quit and be on her way to sunny California, just as she deceived herself that soon she would sell one of her short stories to *Harper's* or *The New Yorker*.

It was just another humid night, with the same old gropes and the same old lines, when an especially drunk and obnoxious roustabout made an especially crude remark and pinched Savannah's nipple.

Suddenly Skeeter's face was before her. Savannah slammed the tray into the roustabout's face. Glasses, ice, and liquor spewed and splintered across three tables.

The roustabout jumped to his feet, cursing, and went after her. Savannah grabbed an oyster shucker's knife from the bar, her eyes as deadly as the weapon. No man would ever again violate her. She aimed for his groin, her breasts heaving.

"Crazy cunt! Point that at me and I'll shove it elbow-deep up your ass." He stepped toward her.

Savannah went for him. A blur flashed between them, someone grabbed her wrist, whipped her about, and held her at bay while kicking the roustabout in the gut and sending him sprawling upon the floor.

"Give me the knife," a soothing voice urged. Beau Boudreaux held out his hand.

Disoriented and shaken, Savannah reluctantly did as he asked, staring at him wide-eyed. Beau Boudreaux was the first person ever to champion her. He was a newcomer to Wooly-Bullies, but a welcome one. His features—ice blue eyes, jet black hair, and a heartbreaker of a smile—were as distinct as his style.

That's all it took—a timely rescue, one understanding smile, and a leisurely drive out by Lake Pontchartrain after closing time, and she became Beau's girl. A tool pusher on an offshore oil rig, working fourteen-day shifts, Beau had no roots, but once involved with Savannah Lee he wanted to put some down. He moved her out of the dingy room above the dry cleaner into a three-room bungalow with a magnolia tree in the back yard. It wasn't a lavish villa or a fancy uptown house, but it didn't matter to them. For here they shared a deep and abiding love, and Beau replaced her nightmares with dreams of the future.

After weeks of chastely holding her in his strong arms and shielding her when she awakened, moaning and fretful from the nameless demons that stalked her nights, he heard her screams cut through the night.

"Skeeter . . . No!"

Roughly shaking her awake, he demanded, "Who's Skeeter? What's he doing to you?"

Savannah shook the cobwebs from her mind and froze. *Never tell, never tell.* "One of Momma's men. He's dead. It doesn't matter."

With a Cajun's sixth sense, he had known from the start that she was not a virgin, but he'd restrained himself from making love to her until Savannah reached out to him. Now he stoically accepted what he believed to be the only justifiable reason for her bad dreams and erratic mood swings—rape. He would hold her close and wait for her to heal.

And on that pivotal night when she entrusted herself into his care, he unselfishly assumed the burden. Extraordinarily patient and giving, Beau was that rare and special kind of man who thrived on being needed. Hot-natured and fiercely protective of the things he held dear, he was the parent she never had, the love she had never known, the best friend who would never forsake her in stormy weather. On the eve of Mardi Gras, Savannah became Beau's lawfully wedded wife.

It was far easier to love Savannah Lee than to understand her, and Beau Boudreaux did. When she confided to him that her childhood fantasy was to become a writer, his response was supportive and slightly awed.

"If that's what you want, sugar, then I want it for you. I only ask two things—that you love me the same no matter how famous you get and that you take time out to have my babies."

The following day Beau brought home a new electric typewriter, a ream of paper, and Savannah's favorite, peach ice cream. She rewarded him with an ecstatic kiss and his first night of sleeping alone while she wrote until dawn. Before retiring at daybreak, she composed another letter to Evie, filled with the news of her marriage to darlin' Beau, questions about Lauren's recent whereabouts, and a subtle reminder of the all-for-one-and-one-for-all pact they'd made at Bulwer-Lytton.

Then she stumbled into the kitchen, rummaging through the junk drawer in search of her grass and papers. Knowing that Beau wouldn't approve, she cautiously hid her habit. She tiptoed to the bedroom, making certain he was fast asleep before adroitly rolling a joint and stepping out onto the back porch to smoke it.

She relaxed on the steps, toking on the reefer, inhaling the scent of sweet magnolia blossoms and longing for the day when the name Lee Boudreaux, the pseudonym she'd selected, would be revered in literary circles.

Yes, ma'am, the song of the South had changed for Savana Lee—from blues, blues, blues to jazz, jazz, jazz.
   —Fast Friends

CHAPTER FIFTY-EIGHT

The newly formed National Organization of Women was holding meetings across the country. Nationwide, women had decided to speak out, to take affirmative action, to fight masculine oppression. The time had come to realize the dream of the suffragettes: to carry their votes out of the bedrooms and into the boardrooms of America.

Moni's mind searched for something to focus on other than the imperious summons from Marrish. Why in the name of Christ hadn't she declined this time? Ever since that morning two years ago when he'd returned to Vegas, she'd promised herself each time that it would be the last. But then the call would come and she would go, out of pity and remembrance for the man he had been. There weren't many people left from the old days, and she felt sort of obligated. Poor old thing was mad as a hatter. She thought of Evie. Fax had said Evie was fine, but some verification would be nice. God, she missed them—Fax almost as much as Evie.

Marrish's sentinels admitted her to the penthouse suite, escorted her to the dressing room, and informed her that Marrish awaited her in the sauna. She stripped, wrapping her flame-colored hair in a Turkish towel, and stepped into the redwood sauna. It reminded her of a coffin.

"Join me," a voice commanded.

Her eyes could not adjust to the dimly lit interior. She felt like she was being smothered.

"You're very punctual, an attribute I admire."

"And you're invisible, Noel."

"Am I, Moni? Who is it you wish to see?"

"You, only you." *Anyone but you.*

"Are we going to extend ourselves today, Moni? Is there something so deliciously depraved that it whets your jaded appetite merely to think of it?"

This was part of his ritual, this pretending that he was still a man. She always humored him. All he ever wanted now was for her to sit nude while he talked, and sometimes his incoherent ravings went on for hours. "It's your money, Noel, your depravity. What is your fantasy, your pleasure?"

"Eager, Moni, too eager. It doesn't become you. Patience, my dear."

Marrish materialized out of the darkness, one clammy hand fondling her breasts, the other slipping into the silky wetness between her legs. Shocked, she writhed about, uttering an accomplished moan. He pushed her mouth to the erection rising from his needle-marked groin.

Then he withdrew. "First you must pleasure my friend. I want to watch. It excites me."

He frequently talked to invisible people. This should be interesting. "Your desire, my time."

"Your time, my Jurgen—my trusted friend and constant companion."

"Tell me about Jurgen."

"He's hung, he's horny, and he's primitive."

So, the Noel of old was back in form. "Do you speak from experience?" Her tapered nails grazed his scrotum.

"Observation only, my dear."

Moni left the suffocating sauna and stepped into the frigid air of the plush master suite. One look at Marrish's unusually bright eyes alarmed her. He was assessing her, a twisted smile distorting his face.

Wordlessly, he placed her upon his bed, spread her legs, and inspected her for defects like a slave at auction. His fingers parted her. Then, as if judging her unworthy of his touch, he placed her hands between her legs, instructing her to masturbate. He inserted his half limp cock into her mouth, his breath coming faster. "Get ready, Moni. Jurgen is impatient."

Moni looked at the ceiling. She was an expert on ceilings and headboards and floors. She hoped Jurgen was a quicker trick and more of a man than the repulsive billionaire.

Marrish cackled wildly as he pressed the intercom. "Send Jurgen in."

Out of the corner of her eye, Moni saw a huge Rottweiler come into the room. She shoved at Marrish, twisting her head away. "No. No. No!"

Marrish backed off the bed, laughing maniacally. "Come, Jurgen." The Rottweiler obeyed and stood at his side. "Isn't Moni lovely? Doesn't she excite you?"

Jurgen panted, his tongue out, primal lust in his eerie eyes. He sniffed the sex-charged air, his agitation barely contained.

"Enough. Get that damn dog out of here. Even Chihuahuas terrify me. I can't stand it. Quit laughing. This isn't fucking funny, Noel. How would you like to be trapped in a snake pit?"

Snakes were his private nemesis. For a moment, Marrish hesitated. But only for a moment. "She's yours, Jurgen. Make friends."

Moni cowered. Marrish was serious. Jurgen *was* aroused.

The dog jumped on the bed and then on Moni, his nose nuzzling the vee of her tightly clenched thighs. Frantically, she kicked and pushed at Jurgen. "Call him off, call him off! I'll kill you for this."

Jurgen growled and bared his teeth. He nipped Moni's forearms and his giant paws scratched her breasts. Marrish's insane laughter mingled with Jurgen's growls and Moni's cries. "I'll do anything. Please, please, make him stop."

"But this excites me, love. You see?" Marrish held his fully erect penis for Moni to admire.

Distracted by his master's move, Jurgen bounded from the bed, whining, his red tongue flicking Marrish's cock.

Marrish swatted Jurgen's nose. He went to the quaking Moni, straddled her ashen face, and plunged himself deep into her throat.

Moni construed Noel's rejection of the dog and his interest in her as a reprieve. If she could just hang on, complete this act, and get the hell out of his clutches, she would retire from the business and forget about compassion for old times' sake. She of all people should know better than to get sentimental. Maybe *she* was getting senile. She willed herself to relax, perform the service for which she'd been paid an exorbitant sum.

God! If he'd only come. Perhaps if she tried the finger trick. She inserted her forefinger into his asshole, massaging the sensitive walnut-size gland that always drove men into sheer rapture.

It didn't work.

Jurgen joined the orgy, suddenly ramming his nose between her legs. Moni's heart stopped. Before she could react, he licked her. Hysterical now, she clawed at Marrish's back. The savage motion again diverted Jurgen. He raised his head. Moni's legs locked together. Jurgen climbed her body, preparing to mount her. He hunched against her tensed thighs, frenziedly burrowing his nose and tongue in Marrish's heaving ass. Marrish shot his cum into Moni's raw throat.

For the first time ever, Moni called Fax on his private line. She was sobbing, making no sense. Finally, after long moments of patient and soothing talk, Fax got the story out of her. He was livid with Marrish, disgusted with Moni, and furious with himself. He promised to be with her as soon as possible, but first he had an urgent matter to attend to.

He did a great deal of soul-searching during the evening flight to Vegas. The conclusions he reached would have a major impact, both personally and nationally. His alliance with Marrish had been unholy from the start. Better to be done with him. Demigods such as he and Marrish had mortal weaknesses. Fax fully acknowledged his: Moni. He also knew Marrish's: an aversion to snakes and a fetish for chocolate.

The terminating scene between Fax and Marrish was reminiscent of the power clash between Zeus and Cronus, the outcome changing forever the course of the future. Once more, their meeting took place in the desert in the middle of the night. Before exiting Marrish's car and heading for his own, Fax deposited a boot-box-size silver casket on the seat.

"What's that?"

"A bonbon bon voyage." Fax closed the door on the deal of the century and started toward a new life.

The desert moon gleamed on the silver box, beckoning to Marrish. He could not resist. No woman ever satisfied him, but chocolates always did. The lid was obstinate; his desire escalated. Fiendishly his fingers clawed at the lid. The casket cracked open, the contents slithered into his lap, hissing. He thrashed wildly, groping for the door, trying to escape the diamondback rattler coiling to strike.

Only his blood-curdling screams and the deadly shake of rattles disturbed the stillness of the desert graveyard.

Moni's Place would be no more. She was retiring to the mountain retreat outside of Aspen, Colorado, that Fax had deeded to her, and he would join her as soon as he had confessed to Silver. His wife had always been reasonable. Her blessing and a divorce were too much to hope for, but her understanding and a permanent separation were realistic expectations.

There were things even more important than staggering wealth and stifling codes of behavior. Moni was the love of his life, and he was a wiser man.

Late in the night, wrapped in one another's arms, they tenderly kissed and stroked, talking of things never before possible and things that should have been said long ago.

"There's one more thing I must tell you." Moni sat up in bed, drawing her knees to her chest. "I've practiced it in my mind a million times. It was so easy. I knew the words. I knew exactly how you'd react. But now . . ." Moni shook her head. *They were finally going to be together. She could keep quiet. Nothing would change. But if she told* . . . "It's just that after concealing this secret from you for so long, I don't know where to begin, and I'm scared to death of how it will end." She reached back, not daring to look at him. "Give me the strength to do this. Give me your hand."

Fax's fingers intertwined with hers.

"I loved you so much, wanted you so much, missed you so terribly whenever you were gone that I did the only thing I could. I got pregnant." She held her breath, sensed him holding his. His grip on her hand intensified. "I kept a part of you. Eve is yours, Fax. Yours and mine. I did it deliberately, and I'd do it again."

What a fool he had been. The years wasted on guessing, on jealousy. "Oh, Moni." He crushed her to him. "I know why you did this, why you kept silent. How can I ever make up for my absences, your sacrifices?"

"In all these years, I have never asked anything beyond what you freely gave, my darling. But I am asking now." Moni pulled back and gazed into his blue eyes. "Claim her, Fax. It would mean so much." Her chin quivered. "She doesn't need your money, but she desperately needs a father's love. It was the one thing I could never provide for her."

His hands tangled in the mass of red curls, drawing her head down and cradling her soft cheek against his strong one. "Oh, Moni. How hard it has been for you both. It's unnecessary for you even to ask. She's part of us. How could I not acknowledge her?" His arms clutched her fast, as though to let go would be to deny life itself.

He was oblivious to the pains in his chest.

CHAPTER FIFTY-NINE

After all this time, it suddenly became convenient for
Norma Mae to develop overwhelming concern for Savannah Lee's whereabouts. There hadn't been any word or
attempt to locate the girl since her flight from Miracle
Mountain Bible College.

More significantly, all attempts to meet with Clayton
Robbins for the past few months had failed. He was avoiding her. She refused to be brushed off like some pesky fly.

"Joshua, I'm worried 'bout Savannah."

"I'm sure she's fine, Norma Mae. Probably living in a
commune somewhere."

"No. It's a mother's duty to know where her daughter
is. You remember Savannah's Bulcorn-Lyceum roommate, Evie Afton? Well, she works in Washington. Maybe
she's got some notion what that girl's up to now. I think,
Joshua, that I must go to the capital and see what I can
find out."

*She missed her Mandingo, as she affectionately called
him. She really ought to thank Joshua for that name. If he*

hadn't been doing his bleatin' lamb of God routine every other night, she might have gone all her days without ever reading 'bout Mandingo. Maybe in a previous life she'd been a plantation belle, and Red Shoes had been her slave. He certainly wasn't acting like that now and she had to get up there and remind him just which race was superior.

Joshua was not overjoyed about the possibility of her locating Savannah, especially if she discovered that he had provided the means for her daughter to fly the coop, although a few days' relief from Norma Mae would be a blessing. *Amen.* "Do what you must, Norma Mae. I'll try to get along without you."

Neither was Clayton Robbins overjoyed by Norma Mae's sudden and unannounced appearance in his Washington office, but he quickly changed his mind when she sat on his desk, hiked her skirt, and crossed her legs, revealing that she wore no underpants. Her interference might be inconvenient, but her let's-get-it-on attitude never was. And the danger of Norma Mae was that she made him forget all else except making it with her just one more positively, absolutely, final, last time.

The call came from one of Evie's snitches over on Pennsylvania Avenue. House Minority Leader Bartwell had unexpectedly announced his decision to step down as head of the Appropriations Committee and named Robbins as a probable successor. She was so eager to share the good news that she entered Robbins's private office without knocking.

There, on top of the desk, amidst important legislation, overturned lamp and spilled pencils, open blinds and blaring music, Evie discovered the esteemed congressman copulating with the revered Reverend Garland's wife—she flat on her back, her ankles linked about his neck, and he with his trousers and Fruit of the Looms bunched about his knees, bumping and grinding, pumping and humping, moaning and crooning like nothing she'd ever seen.

Evie was about to make a discreet retreat when she overheard Mrs. Garland beg Robbins, "More, oh, yes, deeper, harder, faster, Mandingo." Evie slowed her exit, unable to resist.

"I'll give you more when you answer one question, Norma Mae. I've been banging you off and on for twenty years and I want to know. Is that daughter of yours mine?"

Evie was really interested now. She eased the door to, so that she might hear the answer.

Norma Mae was wild with wanting. She'd tell Robbins anything—hot was cold, day was night, white was black—to get him to resume. "Oh, probably, Clay. Why's it so important anyway? And, damn it, why now?"

"It's important, Norma Mae. The first black presidential candidate can't have some quadroon kid suddenly calling him Daddy."

"Way things stand between us, that kinda makes me First Lady, don't it, Red Shoes?"

Evie nearly choked.

Robbins shuddered. "On second thought, forget the whole damn thing, Norma Mae. It's not that important. Let's just screw."

Evie shut the door. Some rascal impulse made her knock and them scramble. While she waited for permission to enter, an unthinkable prospect struck her. Jesus! Wouldn't it just throw Savannah for a loop to find out she might be part black? It made Eve wonder about her own bloodlines. She immediately discounted the possibility. Moni, for all her faults, was selective.

This had certainly been a productive and enlightening day.

Red Shoes got rid of Norma Mae and collapsed in his chair. Bartwell's resignation was great news. He was as good as in as head of the Appropriations Committee. The only hitch might be that damn Saturn rocket burning up on the launch pad at Cape Kennedy this morning. He picked up the newspaper. There would be an investigation. How far could it be traced? This had to be stopped, and stopped fast.

By nine that night, Red Shoes had called in his markers and covered his ass. Neither his nor his cohort Cohen's name would be scorched by the fire. The widows would not break the NASA-God-Country-apple-pie tradition of infallibility. They would not talk. He wished he hadn't been so premature in shipping Norma Mae back to True Gospel Tabernacle.

CHAPTER SIXTY

TWA's New York-Paris flight approached Orly. It had been a long trip—Las Vegas to New York, New York to Paris. Yet he felt compelled to have his talk with Silver at the earliest opportunity. Perhaps having their confrontation in Europe wouldn't be so bad—she could stay on with Lauren for a bit and recover from the shock, if indeed she was shocked. He had no feel for Silver's reaction. Hadn't in years.

Silver was attending an exhibit of masterpieces confiscated by Hitler as spoils of war and only recently recovered. Again she thought of Sasa. That she had never encountered him in her travels nor made any effort to do so was almost unbelievable. She was growing older. Life was getting shorter. Perhaps she should ask him to lunch, maybe even show him a picture of Lauren.

As they were climbing the marble steps to the exhibit, Anna grew faint, clutching Sasa's arm for support. The

Marquise DuBonnet was coyly fondling Madame Chardes's breast. "I know how much it means to you to see these works, Sasa, but I am suddenly so very ill," she said shakily.

One look at Anna's wan face and Sasa relinquished all hope of attending the exhibit. He glanced wistfully up the stairs and then back to his wife. "Another time, Anna." He shrugged.

Fax checked with the concierge of the Hotel de Crillon and was directed to the exhibit. Entering the grand foyer, he crossed paths with the baroness and Sasa and exchanged pleasantries. "Have you seen Silver?" he asked.

Masking his surprise, Sasa answered with a tense smile. "Regrettably, we have not seen her. Anna became ill as we arrived and we dare not linger. Please remember us to Silver and give her our love."

"She'll be sorry to have missed you. Anna, I hope your indisposition is fleeting." Fax bid them farewell and went on to look for Silver. He found her shortly, deep in reverie before a painting of gypsies. When he touched her arm, Silver turned. She was stunned to see Fax beside her. He didn't look well, and her astonishment quickly turned to concern. "Fax, are you ill?"

"Only tired, Silver. I have come a long way. We must talk."

A million thoughts went through Silver's mind. Had something happened to Lauren, whom she had been surprised not to find in Paris? Did Fax suddenly miss her? Before she could pursue it, he took her arm, led her from the exhibit, and helped her into his limousine, instructing the driver to return to the hotel.

Alone in the *appartement*, Fax blurted out his story to Silver. He told her that for over twenty years he had given Moni Afton the passionate love that Silver longed for, and that out of that passion was born Eve. He asked her understanding and forgiveness. Again she thought about the red-head in blue fox, the haunting photograph of Anovese accompanied by a woman and small child, the time when she'd deliberately blurred Fax's face in the photograph with Marrish and never asked questions, his long absences over the years, the irony of Eve's attending Bulwer-Lytton. It had all become crystal clear.

"For the sake of everyone, can we reach some amicable solution?"

The wasted years, living with her own guilt, the unrequited longing, crashed down on her. Her oh so civilized world had just collapsed and she was not angry, not hurt—just numb. "Haven't I always been amicable?"

"Yes, Silver, you have. I am sorry, truly sorry."

"So am I—sorry for us all. When will you be leaving Montauk Point?"

"Is this a divorce or a separation, Silver?"

"Whatever you wish."

"There is something else. I am going to acknowledge Eve as my daughter. Lauren will have to be told she has a half sister, but I want to tell Evie first. I would appreciate it if you wouldn't discuss this with Lauren until I return. I fly to D.C. in the morning."

Silver knew she should be truthful as well, but she could not. "Lauren isn't in Paris and I have no idea of her whereabouts. I will leave her enlightenment to you."

"Yes, of course." Fax came to Silver, resting a hand on her shoulder as he looked into her eyes. "You are a beautiful woman. Most men would have loved you to distraction. The fault is mine. You deserved better." With a swift kiss to her cheek, he ended twenty-nine years of marriage and bid her a fond adieu.

Back in his room, he called Eve, informed her he would be arriving in Washington, and asked her to dinner. She eagerly accepted, anxious to share her latest findings about Robbins and Reverend Garland's wife.

Thirty-five thousand feet above the Atlantic, on his way to claim his daughter, Fairfax Randolph Bennett VI suffered a fatal coronary.

The loving message from Sasa to Silver was never delivered.

CHAPTER SIXTY-ONE

On a bleak February day in 1967, they gathered again—the bereaved wife, the grieving mistress, the heartbroken daughters, a tearful Savannah, darling Beau, the preacher, one ex-pimp, and Norma Mae—this time to bury Fax. The coffin was borne along the rugged coastline, drawn by six black horses, their harnesses jingling as the Episcopalian priest delivered a short and poignant tribute to one of the nation's leading industrialists.

Among the mourners present were many dignitaries and a handful of men who stood to gain from administering the trusts established to run the Bennett empire.

The cold mourners filed into the mansion to warm themselves by the fire and trade memories. The reception would have done honor to a king. Gradually the guests took their leave, including Clayton Robbins, who had nervously watched Norma Mae consume a decanter of sherry and feared her giddiness might become an embarrassment. Joshua Garland was none too comfortable either, standing with Norma Mae, Savannah, and Beau, especially when

Norma Mae was oohing and cooing over her new son-in-law. "Well, now I know why Savannah has kept you all hush-hush. Aren't you something?"

Lauren and Evie sat before the roaring fire in the library. The shock of Fax's death and of learning they were half sisters had, for once, left them speechless. Savannah joined them. "I'm sorry, I really am sorry about your daddy, Lauren. He seemed like a nice man."

"Thanks, Savannah. Tell Evie. He was her father too."

"I don't understand."

"That makes three of us," Evie choked.

Lauren looked at Eve, then at Savannah. "What we are trying to say is that Fax and Moni were lovers for years. We're half sisters."

For some inexplicable reason, Savannah felt excluded. "Isn't life a bitch?"

"How would you know? You have Beau," Evie muttered.

"And he is a prince, Savannah." Lauren softened the edge of Evie's remark. "Where'd you find him?"

"New Orleans. He's the best thing that ever happened to me. No one else ever loved me."

"We do, Savannah." Lauren's eyes were bright.

Suddenly ashamed, Eve went to Savannah and hugged her close. "All for one and one for all, wasn't that the pact? I'm a little out of sync and bitchy as hell. Forgive me."

"Forgive what?" Savannah bottled and corked this hurt as she had every other and was grateful when Beau called to her from the door.

"Your momma wants to go home, sugar."

Amid hugs, tears, and kisses, the friends parted once more, with promises of happier reunions and more frequent letters.

With Evie and Lauren upstairs and all the other guests having departed, Silver and Moni retired to the library to talk.

"You were wife to a man named Fax. I was mistress to a man called Ben. Yet I truly believe that he never sacrificed the happiness of one for the other. In a sense, we are both better women for having loved and been loved by him." Moni stood and hesitantly extended her hand to Silver. "You've been most fair about Eve, perhaps more so than I would have been were our roles reversed."

Manners and a philosophical attitude could get one through anything. Silver accepted Moni's gesture of gratitude. "Don't give me too much credit. Acknowledging Eve was Fax's last wish."

"You could have refused or disregarded it," Moni pointed out.

"You should know better than anyone that Fax wasn't the sort of man one refused." For a moment, they studied one another, understanding the pain they saw reflected in the other's eyes.

Moni picked up her gloves.

Silver turned her back, tracing her fingertips along the edge of Fax's desk. "I envy you your passionate memories."

Moni paused at the doorway, glancing at Fax's picture over the mantel. "As I will always be jealous of the fierce devotion he felt only for you."

James delivered yet another silver wine bucket and two fresh glasses to the young women upstairs. They were sprawled across the bed as in the old days at Bulwer-Lytton. He was invisible to them as he disposed of his duty and withdrew.

Evie surveyed the elegant room that smelled of old money and a pampered existence. She remembered the paper-thin walls of Moni's Place and the nights she spent hearing the noises that made her an unacceptable playmate for those with whom she would have been friends. This could have been her room. It *should* have been *her* room. A couple more gulps, a hundred more secret resentments, and she erupted into tears.

"Oh, Christ, Evie, don't do this."

"I can't help it. I'm coming apart at the seams. It's not fair, it's just not goddamn fair."

"So where the hell is it written that life is fair?"

"How can you say that? Your life has been a snap. You've always had everything—a father, an acceptable mother, respectability. You don't know how I feel."

"I lost a father, too, Evie. Have you forgotten that?"

"But you had him for most of your life. I never had the luxury of a father. I don't know why the fuck it suddenly makes a difference, but it does."

"But you have me, and Savannah."

"But you and Savannah have Remni and Beau. What do I have? I'll tell you what I have—just another fuck-over. Moni could have told this secret long ago. How different our lives might have been."

"Evie, look at me." Lauren grabbed her by the shoulders. "What's past is past. We can't change it. Our parents made mistakes. We'll make mistakes too. But one of them shouldn't be living on *what ifs*."

Evie's eyes bored into Lauren's. "*What ifs* make money, Lauren. And I'm going to make a gang. You have your Remni, Savannah has her Beau, and I've got my angle and a New York editor interested."

"Interested in what?"

"Romance, Lauren. Romance."

"Don't tell me you're balling an editor?"

"Hardly. I wrote a fucking book." A satisfied smile lit Evie's face. "It's going to be published next month."

"Well I'll be damned."

CHAPTER SIXTY-TWO

Another boring party with editors, agents, writers, and publicists was in full swing at the Christian penthouse. Barbara was in her glory; Michael was in his private study. Ordinarily he would be mingling, his antennae fully extended for tidbits of industry news. But he had a secret obsession, one that got him through the long, cold nights with Barbara.

A stickler for perfection with uncanny intuition about the marketplace, Michael studied the Washington author's galleys. He had a gut feeling that the country was ready for romance, and this lady just might be Stearns & Mendall's ticket into the new direction. There was more; in Eve Afton's novel he'd sensed such yearning, such warmth, such passion, that it ignited more than Michael Christian's intellect.

CHAPTER SIXTY-THREE

Remni met Lauren's flight at Orly and immediately whisked her off to Champagne.

Lauren was propped up in bed, her dark hair fanned out against the Belgian lace pillow slip, the sheet draped about her breasts. Remni sat on the edge of the bed, his eyes adoring as he leaned over to kiss her. "Don't ever go away from me again, Lauren. I could not bear it."

"Never, Remni, never." Her fingers caught in his hair, drawing him closer, her mouth savoring his. "The weeks without you were an eternity. Nothing can take me from you again."

She stretched her arms high above her head, her laughter filling every crevice of the room and every corner of his heart.

"I love this morning, I love this holiday, but most of all, I love you." Tears of joy glistened in her eyes as she flung her arms about Remni's neck and pulled him down upon the feather bed, smothering him in sweet, carefree kisses.

Their young bodies rolled over and over, a swirl of apricot and bronzed flesh. With a fierce motion, Remni cradled her in his arms, tenderly gazing down upon her radiant face. His fingertips smoothed wisps of hair from her temple. *"Bien-aimée."*

"Yes, as you are my beloved. Oh, Remni, what did we ever do to deserve all this happiness? Do you think it's too good to last?"

"If it ended tomorrow, we have had more than most. But it won't, my love. My purpose in life is to make each of your days and nights better than the one before."

"You couldn't possibly make me any happier than I am at this moment."

"A wager, my angel: I'll wager I can make you happier before breakfast is served."

Lauren tilted her head. "Really, monsieur? And how does Count Bailesti intend to do that?"

"By proposing that you become my countess."

She had never thought about it. Incredibly, it had seemed a mere formality of the certainty in their hearts. Before she could close her mouth, Remni had reached into his silk robe hanging on the bedpost and extracted a jewel-encrusted Fabergé egg from the pocket. "Here, love."

"Oh, how beautiful. It is exquisite, Remni." Her fingers tugged at the tiny gold clasp and the egg opened, revealing a magnificent ring—a huge square-cut ruby surrounded by dazzling diamonds set in white gold.

Remni removed the heirloom from the egg, slipping it onto Lauren's hand, bringing her fingertips to his lips, and branding her palm with a searing kiss. "You are my world, Lauren, my reason for living. In my spring, you are my meadow of clover to romp in; in my summer, you will be my sunny warmth to languish in; ah, but in the autumn, you will be my vibrant colors that I wear with pride; and in the winter, when others grow cold, you will melt my heart with your touch as surely as you do now. And when my lips are a breath away from being stilled, your name will be upon them.''

They were married in a vineyard amid a profusion of lilacs. It was springtime; summer descended quickly, and Remni basked in Lauren's effervescent love. The season was heady, and theirs. There was no reason to believe his prophesy of a lifetime of bliss would not come true.

CHAPTER SIXTY-FOUR

Savannah rubbed her aching back as she looked down at the cribs. God, she couldn't believe it. Her newborn twins were both asleep. Finally. If she could just lie down and die. But she could not. Beau was out on a rig again. A storm was brewing in the Gulf, and offshore the wind and sea would be lashing insanely. She could not tell from the sketchy radio reports whether Beau was being evacuated or not, and the drilling company's phone was busy. The radio now said gale-force winds.

Gotta have something to calm me down. No, can't. She ran to locate her private stash, and rolled a joint. *Shouldn't do, shouldn't do.* But how much did God expect her to take? The grass made it all easier, obliterated the tension, the routine, the disappointments that came regularly in the mail. One rejection after another: *We are sorry, but we cannot be encouraging with regard to publication here. While the writing is unique and has much to offer, I regret to inform you that it does not meet our needs at the current time. Please consider us again.*

She looked at the week's rejections for the hundredth time. If only Beau were here to hold her, comfort her, tell her she was a good writer, that she would sell a book, a short story, anything. Her heart pounded. The grass wasn't working. Faces were everywhere, ghosts standing behind her, twisting, tearing at her. The wind drove branches against the windowpanes, echoing the clash in her mind of mother and wife versus writer and achiever.

How did a woman do both? How did she keep on believing in herself when the world rejected her? How could she keep changing diapers and revising manuscripts with only two hours' sleep? How could she keep up with a hot-blooded, horny Cajun from off the rigs, and keep mixing formulas with hash?

How could she keep on hiding her habit and being the perfect wife and mother? So far, so good. If you wanted something badly enough, sheer will and God's grace would grant it.

Write some more. It was three A.M. Did she dare risk the hum of the typewriter?

No.

Best to reread Evie's latest letter. God, things were easy for her. She'd read her book, knew there was another in the works, and knew that Evie secretly scoffed at the whole concept of love while receiving acceptances and advances in amazing succession. It made Savannah sick. For all of Eve's marketability, she really wasn't that good a writer. God knew, she loved Evie, but the truth was the truth, and the printed page was the printed page. Eve wrote tripe. No depth, no difference, no dedication. Just big bucks for big books.

Once again she retrieved Lauren's letter from beneath the stack of *Publishers Weekly* magazines, a short note reeking of French perfume, now stained with coffee and pabulum, which blithely announced that Lauren had become the Countess Bailesti with all that the title conveyed, which, to Savannah's mind, was considerable. *Her fucking ring would support us for a year at least.* But that was okay. When she made it, she was going to have it all, including a rock that would put Lauren's to shame. Not that she cared about such things, just about being the best goddamn writer the world had ever read.

Yeah. Evie could keep her fictitious love, Lauren her count. Savannah had the real thing—talent, and Beau and the twins.

CHAPTER SIXTY-FIVE

"A cable, madame."

Silver hung up her negatives to dry. "I can't open the door. Please read it to me."

" 'OCTOBER SEVENTEEN, 1967. MARRIED JULY SIXTEEN. NOT KING, BUT CLOSE. NOW ON EXTENDED SAFARI IN WILDS OF NAIROBI. RECEPTION FOUR P.M. NOVEMBER TWENTY-FIRST AT HOTEL DE CRILLON IN PARIS. EXPECT YOU. LOVE AND KISSES, LAUREN.' "

At her request, James reread the cable. Nothing changed, yet everything became different. She slumped against the wall in her red-lighted room, the recent development more earth-shattering than her shots of the famine, which negatives now dripped solution into the tray. "Oh, Fax," she cried aloud, "we should have heard this together, should have shared it. But we never really shared anything, did we? Lauren's married and I am widowed, and as always, I'll cope."

Evie offered to pay Savannah's way to Paris. She pridefully declined.

Silver traveled first class, which was exactly how the reception was planned.

Anna and Sasa were resplendent and beaming beside the enchanted newlyweds, greeting guests and wondering where Lauren's mother was.

The plane was delayed and Silver was late, much too late, for her own daughter's reception.

Evie was well into the champagne and kissing her half-sister's cheek when Silver entered the candlelit salon, attired in a gown that had kept seamstresses up around the clock ever since she received the cable. The dress of silver bugle beads with its handkerchief hem flattered her curves, set off her hair and turned every head in the room.

Silver didn't know what was going on. There was Sasa before her, Anna at his side. Automatically she did what was expected and put her hand in his.

Sasa beamed as he had not in years. He knew his place, knew what he could and could not do, but by God, she was as devastatingly beautiful as ever, and he could not hide his longing as she extended her hand. He bent and kissed her cheek. "My dear Silver, it has been so long."

"Too long, Sasa."

Anna smiled coolly. She felt the current flowing between her husband and their old friend. "Yes, yes, too long, much too long. I understand we missed you at the exhibit several months ago. And where is your charming husband?"

Dead. Buried. "Fax passed away at the end of January."

Involuntarily, Sasa's eyes closed. My God, she is free.

"But we saw him then, at the exhibit. We asked him to remember us to you."

"Mother, I am so glad you made it. Meet my husband, Remni Bailesti."

Silver looked at Sasa. She looked at Remni. Bailesti. *Bailesti. My God! It isn't so, dear God, please, not so.*

Never. It can't be. Reflexively she let Remni kiss her cheek as she reached to Sasa for support.

Sasa felt her trembling hand, squeezed it in his own, trying to say with a touch, *"We may not have made it, but our children did, and isn't it time that destiny took its course?"*

Silver backed away. Away from her daughter, away from her son-in-law, away from Sasa.

It was time for confession. Time to tell the secret she had hoped to take to her grave.

"Are you not happy our children have wed, my darling Silver? Are you not thinking back and wishing it was what we should have known? Are we not one, have we not always been the lovers who should have known the sweet, wondrous joy of being free to choose? I love you, Silver. I have loved you since the moment I first saw you. I dream of the afternoon we shared, of the hopes, the despair, the desperation, we knew. Why do you look so sad? Why do you gaze into my eyes as though you search for the future?"

"There is no future in this madness. Listen to me. You are my only ally, Sasa. You say you remember the picnic. Do you remember all of it?"

"How could I forget? It is in my dreams with the dawning sun and the midnight moon."

"Lauren is your daughter . . . *married to your son!* Help me, Sasa, help me. What are we to do?"

Stunned, he looked across the room at Lauren and cursed himself. Yes, he could see it clearly now, should have seen it before, should have seen it the first moment he laid eyes on Lauren. *Dear God, his son wed to his daughter!* "Silver. I did not know. And you cannot tell. Ever. Leave them, leave them be. They are so happy, so perfect together."

"It's wrong, Sasa. Do you realize we're talking about incest? That's unthinkable. It cannot happen. You have to help me."

Sasa took her hands, looking deep into her eyes, into her heart. "Promise me. Promise me you will say nothing. Incest is the worst sin a Gypsy can commit. Let it die on our lips here. Don't do this to my son."

"What about my daughter?"

"She is my daughter, too. She has Gypsy blood. She is alive and happy. So is Remni. Why destroy them? Are we—you, me, Remni, Lauren, Anna—to pay now for something that should have been settled years ago? Why didn't you come to me, tell me?"

Silver shook free of his grip. "You owed a debt to Anna. I made no demands on you. Don't you dare condemn me now."

She did not heed Sasa's warning, failed to comprehend the Gypsy code of honor. She had spent a soul-searching night, and guilt won. It was time to rectify the mistakes of the past. The day following the reception, Silver requested a private audience with Remni. Against Sasa's wishes, she told Remni Lauren was his half sister.

The knowledge was too much for Remni, the sin too great. He had made love to his sister. He loved her as he could never love another; he had mated with her in every way there was to join with another spirit. To have to accept that he could never again hold his beloved wife in his arms, never again shower her cherished body with kisses, never again ease his limbs atop hers in a surrender that was sweeter than honey, wilder than a raging sea, was unthinkable, unbearable. For in his heart he knew that though they were two separate bodies, they shared the same soul. And now he knew why. Alone he cried, choosing to protect Lauren from the truth.

"I love you, Lauren, I loved you through every season, whether we lived it or not. Somewhere, someone should have told me not to love you, but they did not and I can't stop, for I hear your laughter, I see the zest of living in your sparkling eyes, and I want to live, so desperately want to live, but I cannot dishonor everything we ever believed—springtime, summer, autumn, and, my darling, this, our winter of destiny. With the last breath I take, I beg you, forgive me, my *bien-aimée*, for no one will ever love you as I do. Remember me, Lauren. . . .''

He locked the bathroom door. He put the barrel of the gun into his mouth. Slowly he squeezed the trigger; determinedly he ignored the natural resistance of the hammer cocking a split second before firing, the instinctive opposition of life to death. A deafening blast, a last flash of Lauren, and Remni's torment was over—the top of his skull blown away, driblets of bloody tissue and gray brain matter splattered against the silk moiré walls.

Silver was barely in the front door of the house at Montauk Point when Sasa's call came to tell her of Remni's death.

Another suitcase was packed and Silver returned to Paris for the funeral.

Savannah left her babies with Beau's mother and picked up the ticket Evie had wired.

Another tragedy, another reunion. The two friends could not comfort the inconsolable Lauren. Remni's suicide was unfathomable.

Sasa's arms tightened protectively about his daughter. He loved her twice as much, felt her anguish doubly. His own burden was unbearable, his only son so needlessly sacrificed by Silver's rash and futile obsession with propriety. Gypsy codes be damned, this was his son and his daughter, his children. Where he had always loved Silver, idolized her, he now just as intensely hated her.

Consoled by her longtime friend the Marquise DuBonnet, Anna wept uncontrollably throughout the service and entombment.

Silver stood paralyzed, unable to come to terms with her guilt or give solace to Lauren. The revulsion in Sasa's eyes marked another death. For years she had sustained herself on the passionate memory of Sasa and now he, too, forsook her. She hadn't meant for this to happen. . . . Dear God! If only she could amend her mistake, resurrect Remni. But there were no redeeming miracles for Silver.

Eve and Savannah secluded themselves with Lauren in an upstairs suite of the Bailesti chateau. She lay on a bed, knees drawn to her chest, her body racked with sobs, her eyes as bleak as the barren landscape outside the frosted windowpanes. "I want to die, too. I want to be with Remni."

There was nothing Eve and Savannah could say. When she cried, Eve and Savannah cried, when she wrapped her arms around herself and rocked, they wrapped their arms around her and rocked too. They took turns stoking the fire and administering sedatives.

The friends stayed close, keeping vigil throughout the days and long nights.

CHAPTER SIXTY-SIX

During the late sixties, Savannah's output of manuscripts equaled her intake of speed. Beau was still unaware of her hype-it-up, type-it-up routine, since she mellowed out with downers and managed to maintain the model mother–ideal wife illusion. Neither the twins nor Beau were ever neglected. Mostly she wrote late at night and into the dawn, and went through the day as if she had had twelve hours of rest. The fact that Beau spent weeks at a time offshore made it easier for her to continue the up-down cycles.

Beau was truly concerned about Savannah's continuing failure to get published. He'd read her work and believed she was exceptional, but those dumb Yankee bastards in New York hadn't the sense to recognize her specialness. At odd moments he had difficulty correlating the raw violence of her writing with the soft-spoken, fawnlike creature he married. He told himself it was only literary license, but her battle to overcome the rape of which she had never spoken was most probably a factor. Her private struggle to reconcile the past only made him that much more protective of his bruised Georgia peach.

Beau and Savannah Lee and the twins were the typical young family, their weekends enlivened by trips to the zoo, Sunday picnics, frolicking in the back-yard wading pool, Beau barbecuing while Savannah kissed scraped knees, found missing Barbies and Kens, and mediated the frequent spats between the flaxen-haired girls.

Norma Mae's visits were infrequent and traumatic; the girls were especially unruly, like forest animals smelling fire. Beau was cautious and withdrawn, as though he considered his mother-in-law's mere presence a threat. Savannah refused to leave her daughters alone for one second with Joshua and tried her damnedest not to get cornered herself. After each and every confrontation with her mother, she was in a grand funk, finding herself almost wishing that Norma Mae and her disgusting "evangelist" would fall off the face of the earth.

She wrote with a vengeance once they departed, pages and pages of gruesome attacks and bloody horror. She felt those pieces were some of her finest and was devastated when the senior editor of one of New York's most prominent houses told her he found her work offensive.

Beau was unavailable when the letter came. The twins were visiting his mother in Baton Rouge. Her spirit shattered, Savannah popped pills, then wandered aimlessly along Bourbon Street. She was dazed, depressed, lonesome. She sat on a park bench in Jackson Square, sipping chicory coffee purchased from a street vendor, and stared at the cathedral across the street.

Tears streamed down her gaunt face. Passersby were oblivious, making no contact, not even offering a simple "Good evening." Beau, gone . . . the twins, gone . . . dreams . . . gone . . . She removed the small vial of Valium from her shoulder bag and washed down yet another pill with lukewarm coffee. How many was that now—pills, or rejections? Who the fuck cared? And what did a queer-ball editor know about life? Pansies and princes and ivory towers were bullshit. White collars and leather briefcases and athletic clubs were crap. She didn't intend to ever write to please New York. They could go straight to hell.

Savana got to her unsteady feet, staggering into the throng of locals and tourists. The night closed in. The city came alive. The humidity and sensuality steamily rose; mournful blues wailed through the Quarter. The smells of crawfish and gumbo intermixed with the stench of puke and piss in the gutter, a blend of spice and decadence. The lady that was New Orleans was not unlike the lady who was Savana.

—*Fast Friends*

She awoke in the red, white, and blue honeymoon suite of the Royal Orleans Hotel, a stranger sprawled on either side of her, both male, both good-looking, both dead to the world. From the way her body ached, she had no doubt that she had satisfied the pair. *Ménage à trois.* Jesus H. Christ! She couldn't remember a fucking thing.

What day was it? What time was it? Where were her clothes? *Out . . . have to get out. Beau comes home today.* She eased between the bodies to the foot of the bed, then tiptoed about the suite collecting her scattered belongings. Holy shit! She was raw from top to bottom, front to back. Hurriedly, she dressed. Gulping down two more Valium, she snuck from the room and jabbed the elevator button. *God! Let me pull this off and I swear I'll never, ever, do it again. I can't risk losing Beau.*

Beau never knew. He assumed her skittish state and flushed face were due to the acceptance letter from a major publisher for the very same work that had triggered her first bout with severe depression. She convinced Beau that they should use her advance money to move on, fooling herself that leaving New Orleans would put a swift end to her Norma Mae–like tendencies. Houston had plenty of rig work. The change would do them all good. Things were looking up. More money, a bigger house, and a start on the road she had always yearned to travel: the road to recognition.

The book was not an instant success. Insufficient publicity, a bad jacket, and inadequate distribution thwarted her desire to skyrocket. But the book did sell, and it was followed by another, and another. Slowly and surely she was building a readership and a reputation as one of America's leading gory storytellers. But just as slowly and surely, the downward-spiraling pattern of depression, drugs, nymphomania, and nomadic flights became standard behavior. Savannah basked in the sunshine of achievement, but the darkness was always there, closing in on her. Beau worried about the depressions and shielded her more than ever.

CHAPTER SIXTY-SEVEN

Others might have been saved by work, but Lauren had never worked and so had nothing to distract her. She could have gone back to Montauk Point and Silver, but she elected to remain in France, closer to the memory of Remni. Anna was more and more engrossed with her friend, the Marquise DuBonnet, Sasa more and more reclusive. He did rally himself sufficiently to propel Lauren out into the world. She was young and she must survive. All gentle hints and suggestions failed until, as a last resort, Sasa told her he had sold the villa and that she must reestablish herself elsewhere. It took the dispirited Sasa's last shred of courage to oust her from her home.

For Lauren there would be no more hurt, no more pain, no more anything. Feeling wasn't emotion but sensory, like touch; like hot and cold, it was external, it didn't occur in your mind or in your heart. You might have a small burn, a minor cut or frostbite, but you healed, you were okay, and all that remained was a caution to watch it next time. She'd go one further; she'd throw away caution, add a fine edge to life, draw the last dram of adrenaline through her pores and expel it into everything she did.

The months of self-pity and exile came to an abrupt halt. Chloe had married. Lauren's apartment was subleased, her belongings in storage. Her jewelry went into the vault, save for her ruby ring and the jeweled girdle Kenir had given her.

She joined the first Greek yachting party she could find on the Riviera. It had no port of destination, just the blue Mediterranean. The booze flowed, and there was an unending supply of cocaine and studs. At first, she was uninterested in everything but sunbathing and memories, but the opiate effect of snow and the natural response of one passionate young body to another took over. As she would later write Savannah, sanity was riding the prevailing wind, but it was blowing into another port. She didn't have to think or analyze, just experience one high and one hard body after another.

The postmarks on the letters Evie and Savannah received told the glitzy story—yacht to yacht, resort to resort, man to man. Lauren was the darling of the jet set. She was at the forefront of the world, discoing in Monaco, tobogganing in Austria, diving in the Caribbean, boating in Venice, on safari in Africa, lighting up in opium dens in Thailand, meditating in Nepal. And on it went.

Kenir Ashad adjusted the binoculars, the roll of the sloop's deck making his observation of the tanned playgirl more difficult than usual. He had followed Lauren around the globe, biding his time. He didn't want the memory of another man shadowing his reentrance into her life. She had much to get out of her system before he introduced her to Persian rapture.

CHAPTER SIXTY-EIGHT

Michael Christian desperately wanted a child. Not only for the obvious reason—insurance against Mendall's defection—but also as an antidote to Barbara's intolerable coldness. In order to gain his heir, he knew his only alternative was an exercising of his husbandly rights. He plotted, patiently waiting. But even more, he longed for a woman who lurked in the recesses of his mind. She was an enigma, exaggerated out of proportion, he was sure. Yet somehow he discounted the stereotype of a romance author—a dog with no class and even less allure. The longer the elusive Eve Afton refused his offers to visit Stearns & Mendall, the stronger was his obsession.

The golden boy, his wife, his unborn child, his mistress would rue the day their paths collided.
—Fast Friends

CHAPTER SIXTY-NINE

Eve was bored with Washington, sick to death of one lousy fuck after another, and with Fax dead there was no need to ride herd over Clayton Robbins. She was ready for a change. Savannah's letters were full of favorable reviews, pictures of the twins and darlin' Beau, while Lauren's went on about escapades and the highs of life. Eve wrote about heartbreak, in-the-nick-of-time reconciliations, and happy-ever-after endings. Trash. But the *what if*s still intrigued her, and the royalty checks kept her in style.

There were letters from Moni too, arriving without fail every Tuesday. Evie hated Tuesdays, for then she was required to come up with another excuse as to why she could not visit her mother this month or next. It was hard to concoct feasible excuses, especially when Eve herself did not understand why she resisted Moni's pleas for absolution. Eve knew she had no right to condemn; her own morals were hardly above reproach. But still she could not forgive Moni for keeping the secret of Fax and depriving her of a father. The madam had gotten what she wanted: a benefactor, a lover, and her one, true desire. Eve had never gotten what she wanted, ever: a man to love her no matter how awful she was, a man to hold her no matter how much she pretended not to need him. But men did not do that ever, and she did not do that—ever.

On her neat desk lay the latest invitation from Michael Christian to visit the house that wished to promote her. Why not New York? And why not Michael Christian? His letters drove her to distraction. Did he think he was Maxwell Perkins reincarnated? The man needed a lesson in apples—Eve picking the Big Apple and tempting Adam with the forbidden fruit. Perhaps he believed himself to be her savior. Promo he had demanded, and promo he would get.

Neither was prepared for the other. Contrary to his earlier belief, Michael had come to expect a troll; he hoped for the best—and was stunned when Eve sauntered into his office. Dressed in black and smelling of seduction, Evie arched an eyebrow, smiled beguilingly, and assumed the offensive as she took her chair.

Michael wished to God his original concept of Eve Afton had been accurate. This gorgeous redhead was a hot number. A feeling—a delicious and petrifying feeling—gripped him. He hungered, and she was delectable. He *yearned*. And there sat Eve Afton, a touch away, awaiting his move, awaiting her publisher to commit.

Promo he willingly delivered, compliments he piled on, but commitment he withheld. And it was commitment she wanted because it was her weapon.

From the moment of their meeting and throughout the next few years, the power play between Eve and Michael intensified. He asked for concessions, such as background for publicity, megabucks publicity. She was fiercely protective of her shady history; a madam for a mother did not good copy make. Had Michael known the truth Eve with-

held, he would have disagreed adamantly. Lust, refined
and sold wholesale, would put Stearns & Mendall at the
summit of love's furious pinnacle.

And so it went, back and forth, publisher versus the
house's leading author. Sales soared, and Eve and Michael
parried with each other.

I don't like you, was the message she sent him.

You're a commodity, that's all, he telegraphed back.

You're frustrated and horny and putty in my hands, she
flashed during marketing sessions.

You're a tease and a fake and sexy as hell, he signaled in
between cover approvals.

*You want me, but I'll be damned if we're going to end
up in the sack*, she challenged.

*Do you think I'd jeopardize years of groveling to ball
you, sweetheart? Forget it! You aren't worth the risk. I'll
bet you sizzle, but I've no doubt you'd burn me in the end.*

The tension became too much for Eve. Quite unexpectedly
she boarded a plane for Colorado and Mama Moni. The
retreat Fax had left his mistress was serene, almost paradise. Vashon now suffered from sickle-cell anemia, so the
roles had been reversed; Moni was taking care of her.

As Evie straightened Vashon's afghan and gave her a
snort of Scotch from a flask, Vashon grunted, "You're a
little bitch, Evie. I powdered yo' butt and beat yo' ass but
you never, ever learned a damn thing. You been givin' yo'
mama a hard time since you could spell it. You been
whorin' and hurtin' and thinkin' dere be some excuse for
yo' ways. Well, plain truth is, dere ain't. You is Moni Leah
Afton's daughter, a mixture of de greatest kind of love and
de worst kind of ache a woman's been born to know. I can
only tell you one thing, sweet chile. Yo' mama loves you
like nothin', 'cept'n Mister Ben maybe, dat ever walked
this green earth. I saw her when you was born, saw de pain
'n de joy, saw de misery 'n de once-in-a-lifetime smile. You
was her angel. You still is, no strings, no demands. You is

loved 'cause you is special. You is his and dat makes you yo' mama's love chile.''

Eve buried her head against Vashon's bosom. "I've been so mean, Vashon. Tell me, oh, please, tell me, how do I say the four little words? How do I say, 'I love you, Mama?' ''

Vashon cradled Eve's head, crooning wisdom while bestowing little love-pats. "It's simple, chile. First say, 'I love myself.' Then say, 'Mama, I'm sorry. Mama, I love you. Mama, I'm the fool and you is the sensible one.' ''

"Is she, Vashon? I wonder. She waited so long. She gave up what might've been.''

"Oh, honey, it *was*. You gotta live it to know. She did. You is still asking, so you ain't discovered what she knew in 1941.''

"You're a crazy old woman." Evie hugged her neck.

"And you is a mess, chile, doing what you accuse yo' mama of doing—waitin' too long. But when you let go, God help us all.''

"Mama . . .'' Not since she was a little girl had Evie called her mother Mama.

"You're troubled," Moni observed.

"Are love and trouble synonymous? I'm confused. There is this man who disturbs me, who antagonizes me, who drifts in and out of my dreams.''

"Is he real?''

"Yes, very.''

"Then you must make a choice, Evie. Weigh it. Decide if he is worth it.''

"And what if he is? What do I do then? He's married, Mama.''

"So was your father, Evie.''

"I hated you.''

"I know.''

"Was it worth it?''

"Yes. Every minute, every hour, every year. I have you, baby. Need I say more?"

"Yes. Do you think of Fax? Do you have regrets? How did you handle the love when you knew he was committed and you were Madam Moni?"

"I was always Madam Moni. He knew that. And I loved him from the first and I will love him to the last. Eve, my darling, in many ways you are so much like him. If I could protect you, I would. You will suffer if you don't accept feelings—feelings that are not paid for, or asked for in one way or another. Stop it, Eve. Stop it before it swallows you and you can't finagle, can't scheme, can't squirm your way out. Either banish this man from your life or take a risk and let him in. Only you know what is right for you."

"I don't know, Mama. If I make the wrong choice, if it hurts, can I come home?"

"Always, Evie, always."

Eve ignored her survival instincts, falling for Michael Christian like she didn't have good sense. For several years they played a high-stakes poker game, at conferences, book fairs, speaking engagements. Still, they kept to their separate rooms and separate lives, engaging in a dangerous standoff.

Eve was there to celebrate the birth of Michael's son, there to lead the ecstatic father to his room and leave him to his dreams.

Once in her own room, she tossed, she turned, she moaned, she yearned, she refuted and reconsidered. Michael was more intoxicating than the ever present Scotch. Drink enough of anything and you can build up an immunity, she thought. Drink up, get high, lie down, take Michael to bed and he would lose his appeal. After all, what could it hurt? He was just another lay, just another man, and he, like all the others, would mean nothing in the

end. When she had had her fill, she would walk away as
always.

At a writers conference in Atlanta, Michael and Eve were
thrown together once again. His room was down the hall,
ten paces and a million miles from her. She invited him in
for a nightcap. Why not? A little Scotch was good for the
soul.

A record heat wave had hit Atlanta. The temperature
was soaring, and the air fairly crackled.

"Now that you're a father, Michael, will you be a good
one? Will you always be there?"

He sensed the hurt. "Was your father always there,
Evie?"

She resorted to old tactics, shrugging and tossing him a
provocative smile. "Why do you call me that? Only my
closest friends call me Evie."

"Who are your friends?"

"Have you heard of Countess Bailesti and Lee Boudreaux?"

"Are you trying to impress me?"

"Aren't you impressed with me just as I am?" She
linked her arms about his neck, recklessly drawing his
mouth to hers.

"Don't kiss me, Evie. For both our sakes, don't."

She disregarded his plea, slowly guiding his lips to hers,
firmly making contact, fully aware that it was a Pandora's
box she was opening, and to hell with the consequences.
No one had ever kissed her like that, no one had ever
aroused such feeling. She drew away. "If you're as smart
as I have come to believe you are, you'll tell me good night
and good riddance."

He heard the warning, but misunderstood. "Not
tonight. No more polite good nights. Let's call a truce,
Evie. Let's not think about morning. For once let's not be
adversaries." His lips smothered hers. "I want you . . . I
always have." He was all over her, guiding her to the bed,

then falling on top of her, stripping away her sedate clothing. "My God!" he breathed. "You're beautiful, Evie. So soft, so sleek, so sweet."

She grasped his neck, pulling his face, his lips against hers. "You say you want me, Michael. Then show me . . . touch me . . . take me! Live the moment we've imagined a thousand times."

She guided his hands, moved them expertly over her breasts, abdomen, and down, down, lower, lower still, where her warmth welcomed him.

He was mad for her, kissing her, igniting her. She writhed, gasping his name and uttering all the classic lines he remembered from her books. He recoiled. "I thought you'd be the lady in between the lines. Jesus, Evie, you're not! I imagined you were what you write—sensitive and seductive, not mechanical sex and practiced phrases. You make love like a *whore*."

Eve bolted upright. "What the hell are you talking about?"

"You're experienced and calculating—technically perfect—but what I want to know is, where is the *real* woman? I don't see or feel or sense her. You are like a lovely seashell: you whisper of fathomless depths, but you are empty." Michael lurched from the bed, his face contorted with pain. "Quick fucks are easy, Eve. If you decide you want to make love, you know where my room is."

She was stunned, unable to comprehend his walking out. No man had ever rejected her. *You make love like a whore.* His words stung. She had never really put herself in the same league with Moni, hadn't realized she'd become a professional. The only difference was she hadn't bothered to charge for it.

What she had spent her entire life denying was what she had become. It was a rude awakening, a bitter truth—and it was time to decide whether to continue or risk knocking on the door of Camelot. What if she didn't know *how* to make love? What if there was no love in her at all? What if

Michael rejected her again? What if her dream world *was* merely a dream, and what she had always known was reality? What if, what if, what if? This time there was no book to write, but something to live through.

Eva's what ifs did not materialize. Her timid knock on Micah's door opened the sluice of desperate love. The toll of his infidelity and her admission to Camelot was staggering, but Eva, like her mother, would lovingly pay the price.

—Fast Friends

CHAPTER SEVENTY

Lauren flipped through a couple of pages of Evie's latest romance. Leaning over, she dipped the small silver spoon in the crystal caddy of cocaine, then snorted daintily. Jesus Christ! One would never suspect that the author of these hokey-ass fairy tales grew up in a brothel or had lived in the political sauna of Washington. She certainly hadn't learned a damn thing. It was all too unbelievable. Eve hadn't the faintest idea what life was about, or sugar-coated fairy tales either, for that matter. She didn't know the difference between love and sex. Lauren did. Savannah didn't sugarcoat anything; raw sewage tumbled out of her like she had backed-up plumbing for brains. She spouted gore, murder, and violence. For all her twisted plots and brutality, she was simply writing about the seamy side of life, and anyone could tell you that was awful to begin with. It was sordidness in the fast lane that was *très* exciting.

Lauren Bennett, author. She ought to write a book. After all, *she* had written news releases, *she* had been the editor of the Bulwer-Lytton paper, and Evie was regularly collecting royalty checks for romances chock-full of excerpts lifted from her letters about Remni. She had lived, she knew the score.

Another snort.

Yes, she could write better than God himself. With half the effort.

CHAPTER SEVENTY-ONE

"Look this way, Countess." "A smile, Countess?" Lauren's agent tried to rush her through the crowd of reporters, but the Countess of Glitz always paused to deliver a quotable quip.

Lauren checked into her suite at the Beverly Hills Hotel and flung her lynx coat across a chair. Congratulatory vases of flowers filled the rooms, and even the bath was full of bright blooms. She counted at least fourteen bottles of champagne before getting bored. A schedule lay on the bed. Idly, she picked it up. Tomorrow it would begin, the adaptation of her best seller for the screen. It had been easy, so easy. When her boat had docked at Lisbon she had bought a Bottega Veneta notebook and a Montblanc pen and had begun the outline of her exposé—names changed to protect the guilty, of course. She'd never had to hope the book would be accepted, never had to worry about a rejection letter, never had to struggle to write or fight off depression. Word had gone out all the way to New York cocktail parties, and offers to read her work had poured in before the typists could turn her gilt-edged pages into a manuscript. She'd been on every talk show in England, France, and the U.S. Being the Bennett heiress and a countess hadn't hurt, as Eve and Savannah had not failed to point out to her. Evie couldn't relate to what she wrote and Savannah said she didn't pay her dues. They didn't think she could write for shit, but none of their books had been made into a movie, so screw them.

She picked up the phone.

CHAPTER SEVENTY-TWO

Leasing the beach house at Malibu had been a great idea. Not that the Beverly Hills Hotel wasn't home sweet home, but she missed the sea. The film was in the can, the premiere days away. In two hours her dear friends would arrive for a long-awaited reunion, the first exclusively frivolous one since Bulwer-Lytton.

It was as though the years had not intervened or the bond weakened, as though their innocent mischief had not been replaced by new and perilous habits, as though Evie wasn't a lush, Lauren a coke freak, and Savannah a tripper. The three Bulwer-Lytton outcasts didn't feel threatened in the least.

"We haven't done so badly." Evie kicked into the surf, flipping her auburn hair. "I'm becoming popular, so they say. Savannah is getting good reviews, and you've got Hollywood at your feet. Who would ever have believed that we would write anything other than that silly editorial?"

"I thought it was an exceptionally good editorial." Savannah winced at the sting of her sunburn, chilled now by the breeze. "What's more, I *always* intended to be a writer."

"And I once intended to be queen." *What had become of Kenir Ashad?*

"I'm serious," Savannah persisted.

"So am I."

Evie sank to the sand, hugging her legs, her chin upon her knees. "Actually, after three days of being deprived of male company, a king or a grocery sacker would do for me." She glanced at Lauren. "Is that gorgeous houseboy of yours private property?"

"Certainly not. All for one and one for all."

Savannah ignored them and concentrated on the waves.

"Are you missing darlin' Beau?" Eve teased.

"Not really. I have something else on my mind."

"Don't be mysterious. We share almost everything, don't we?" Eve flicked sand over Savannah's feet.

"I want to ask a favor, Lauren."

"Of course I'll take Beau off your hands for a month or two, but you've positively got to make other arrangements for the twins."

Eve rolled over, laughing uproariously. "If he's too much for you, Lauren, I *am* the queen of romance, remember."

"Oh, fuck! Savannah and I know you're just a pretender to the throne."

Savannah twisted her hair. "Will you two stop! I'm being serious."

"So are we."

"Oh, for Christ's sake. Spit it out, Savannah. Then, Lauren, you say, 'Sure, fine, whatever you want.' Then I'll suggest we have a drink on it."

"Okay, here goes. Beau wanted me to ask you if you'd mind paving the way for an introduction to your producer. He thinks my last book is movie material, too." Beau had never said any such thing.

"Good as done." Of course, she'd have to meet him first herself, but it would be no problem after the premiere. "Evie, how about you? You want an introduction, too?"

"I just want a goddamn drink and maybe the houseboy later."

"That's the trouble with you, Evie. You're not serious about your writing. No dedication whatsoever."

"Savannah has a point, Evie. You ought to get off the sauce and quit wasting your talent. With all your escapades you could write a blockbuster. Washington smut sells as well as any other."

She might just do that. Someday.

Moonlight rippled across the water. It was somewhere between three and four in the morning, and Lauren and Evie coordinated the swing of their hammocks to the passing of the Grand Marnier bottle, the civility of glasses having been dispensed with hours before.

"Do you suppose she's popping pills again? I think she's got a problem." Eve almost fell out of the hammock.

"She, who?" The countess hiccupped indelicately.

"Savannah Lee, dummy. She's been missing for hours."

"Oh, she's probably humping the houseboy."

Like bullets, they shot from the hammocks, colliding at the door in their haste, not believing for an instant their nasty suspicion was true. They tiptoed unsteadily down the hall, shushing one another.

"Ohhhhh!" Savannah's moans drifted into the hall.

"Watch this." Lauren eased open the door and reached for the light. "Bed check!" She flicked the switch, spotlighting the startled pair.

"Oops—Wrong bed, gorgeous," Evie slurred at the houseboy. "My room's across the hall." She addressed herself to a bare butt. "Tacky, tacky, Savannah."

It was now eight o'clock in the morning, the sun was already hot, and they had been on the beach for hours, listening to Savannah's sorrowful confessions. Eve was trying to stay awake. This was probably important.

Lauren was truly shocked, but her raging headache impaired her patience. They had sympathized, hugged, cajoled, but she could see Evie was as disgusted as she. For years Savannah had been conning them with her wedded bliss, setting herself up as a shining example of motherhood, wifeliness, and near martyrdom.

"Savannah, I hate to cut this short, but all of us look like hell, and I, for one, feel even worse."

"But, but—"

"We won't tell, we won't ever tell, will we, Lauren? Not a living soul. All for one and one for all. Come on, we need a quick pick-me-up and a major repair job."

Eve had a Bloody Mary, Lauren ran a rail, Savannah downed two Valiums, and they all traipsed into Elizabeth Arden's Beverly Hills salon, emerging rejuvenated several hours later to lunch at Ma Maison.

Eve's surprise of gold Cartier lighters engraved *All for one and one for all, Love, Evie* seemed to temporarily abate Savannah's gloom.

For Lauren's debut, Kenir Ashad purchased a diamond bracelet in lieu of a crown. He was glad she had had her silly weekend. It was the last she would ever have. Her life was about to change.

Silver swept regally into the premiere. She felt excluded from the pageantry and naked without her camera. It was so easy to hide behind it, but covering her own daughter's momentous success would be gauche.

She took a glass of champagne and found herself looking into the eyes of a healthily tanned gentleman, and for a heartbeat her breath caught in her throat. She almost missed his words.

"Whatever happened to classics like *Gone With the Wind*? I'm a friend of the director. What's your excuse?"

"I gave birth to the celebrated author."

He silently toasted her and quaffed his champagne.

Silver spared him further embarrassment. "I'm Anne De Ferrers Bennett."

"Paul Hunter. Bar Harbor and Palm Beach."

"Montauk Point. My friends call me Silver."

He wasn't as distinguished as Fax nor as Continental as Sasa, but there was something kinetic about him—something she liked very much.

Flashbulbs popped, microphones were shoved in her face, and questions and requests assaulted her from all directions.

"Will you deny or confirm rumors that you have been intimate with heads of state, rock stars, and the Italian soccer team, Countess?"

"If they say so, I'm sure I have, though I really can't recall them, individually or collectively."

"Is it true, Countess, that your potboiler is autobiographical?"

"Don't be silly, darling. I've led a much wilder life."

"Why didn't you marry Pierre Trudeau?"

"Because half of his cabinet threatened to commit suicide. Pierre was very narrow-minded about monogamy. And, besides, when I agree to sleep with one man exclusively, he'll be a king, not a prime minister."

The press relished every minute of her outrageousness. In the crush of this unprecedented success, Lauren forgot her promise to introduce Savannah Lee to her producer.

At the moment of her greatest triumph Lauren's eyes met Kenir's across the room. *O Hamlet, speak no more: Thou turn'st mine eyes into my very soul; and there I see such black and grained spots as will not leave their tinct.* She was no longer a child, but a woman, and he was no longer the prince of her romantic youth, but the master of her darkest secrets. Where Remni had been her other half, so that they had reflected each other's sunny warmth and tenderness, Kenir Ashad was her mirror image. The loving, laughing, kind, benevolent, and judicious side was balanced by a kind of depravity and obsession. In him were the seeds of her salvation or her destruction, and she watched, fascinated. It was more seductive than cocaine, more fulfilling than any sex she had known. Theirs was the oldest struggle; and the serpent danced between them in the Garden of Eden, while the kundalini force crawled up their spines. She stood, unable to move as he crossed the space between them.

He had waited years for the black hood to be removed, and now he closed in as his hypnotized quarry waited.

"We meet again, Countess."

"What are you doing here?"

He dropped the diamond bracelet in her hand. "Don't you know? I am Kass Productions."

She understood immediately: he owned her. He had bought her option, he had made her movie, he had engineered her moment of glory. And inside her the tiny fear grew a little more. Maybe she hadn't done it on her own, maybe she didn't deserve it, maybe her talent wasn't so formiddable. *Maybe she had nothing without him.*

She ignored the bracelet. "Why did no one tell me?"

"Remember my promise?" *When next we meet, you will be mine.*

He cupped her chin, turning her head from side to side, then took her hand and slowly twirled her about, appraising her. He studied the white and black evening gown, the way it hugged her body, complemented her dark beauty. "The dress does not become you."

"It is perfect and you know it."

"No. It is not worthy of you." He bent and kissed her hand. Next week he would have the dresses he had already ordered sent over. The week following, it would be a new hairdresser. The third week, a diction coach. One, two, three. Correct perfection, create insecurity. By the first of the following month, she would be pliable, her confidence shattered. But he would tell her he thought she was beautiful, that she never looked better, that she had far exceeded the great beauty promised in her youth.

"Coke?" he asked.

"No, thanks. I no longer have need of it." Lauren glared at him, remembering her pre-Elizabeth Arden snort.

But you do and you will, my dear. Your success isn't going to last forever. You will need it and you will need me. I know you better than anyone on earth, I have studied you for years. I know exactly what you want. You are driven by a passion that won't release you. In your efforts to forget and not feel pain, you think you have partaken of life, but there are avenues of pleasure even you have never traveled. You have used in order to erase your memories, but you have existed years without feeling, and I will make you feel. You will be mine, Lauren. Mine.

And she would. He knew.

Lauren understood exactly what he was going to do, but in possessing her, he would become the obsessed. Throughout history, the conqueror always became the conquered, and he of all people should know that. He underestimated her. She smiled, at once revealing the depths of her innocence and the intensity of her worldliness, but she did it quickly, so quickly he could not be certain what he saw, and she felt, more than saw, his response. She linked her arm through his.

It was her mistake. She did not remember that the men in her life had deserted her, that Fax lay buried along the Atlantic shore, Remni was entombed by the Mediterranean, and Sasa, in Paris, had thrown her to the wolves.

She was so independent she never counted on being vulnerable.

CHAPTER SEVENTY-THREE

Momma was driving her nuts about that goddamn tent. Every ten minutes the phone rang and Norma Mae would deluge her with another divine inspiration. One would think this was the greatest crusade ever held. Savannah glanced at the clock. Thirty . . . twenty-nine . . . twenty-eight. The only calling Moma missed was that she should have been a circus director.

"Savannah?" *Who else, Momma?* "I got them to put it on a metal frame so no one could pull it down." *Yeah, Momma, my girls might do what I did to you and you'd get run outta town again.* "It's gonna be in white, like God's clean canvas for his greatest masterpiece." Norma Mae paused, pleased with herself. Savannah must have gotten her writin' talents from her. Weren't no sense in neither one of them hiding their God-given gifts under a bushel.

"Sounds nice, Momma." *Why are you suddenly wanting to talk to me, Momma? I don't understand. I needed you years ago.*

"It's gonna have scalloped edges around the top trimmed in gold, with True Gospel Tabernacle lettered on the awning in twenty-two-karat gilt."

"Perfect, Momma."

Six . . . five . . . four. She was three seconds early.

"Savannah, it's gonna be flame retardant. I thought with the candlelight service—"

"Good idea, Momma."

"And I've got a surprise for Joshua." *And he probably has one for you, Momma.* "I've ordered him a brand new pulpit. It's gold, Savannah, all gold."

"You did good, Momma."

Norma Mae hung up, pleased. Joshua was going to look like God descended to earth behind that pulpit, and she'd be standing right there beside him, diamonded, diademed, and diaphragmed, 'cause she didn't want any more *diapers*, even if Savannah wasn't quite so much trouble these days.

CHAPTER SEVENTY-FOUR

Norma Mae watched the bronzed skin of the shirtless workers. There was something purely thrilling 'bout watching a man pound a piece of steel into the ground. Sort of gave her the shivers all over just to think about it. They were gonna save a lot of souls tonight, give them over to God. She could just feel it in her bones. Maybe she'd do a miracle, too, give someone back their sight, make a cripple get out of a dinky old wheelchair and walk again, ease their sorrows, soothe their fears, save them from the clutches of hell.

It was a real shame Savannah had had to cancel out at the last minute. She'd have been proud of her mother. Norma Mae was proud of herself. Next to her wedding, this was the finest day of her life. She was doing something important for a change, and it was going to be first class all the way. She was gonna match the tent, all white and gold—her lucky colors.

It was all too excitin'. Why, they were already settin' up TV cameras and running cords all over the place. She'd have to be careful not to trip, and she had to remember how she was supposed to look at the camera. All Joshua's people had told her there couldn't be any more of those embarrassing moments, like the time they filmed her looking right at the ambassador's fly while his wife was talking to her. No, there wasn't gonna be one screwup tonight.

He was the strangest-lookin' man. Been going around all day while they were setting up the tent, holding his Bible, spouting Scripture worse 'n Joshua after one of his fuckin' and flailin' sprees. It wasn't that he was ugly. In fact, there'd been a time . . . but he was certainly peculiar. Hadn't even looked at her, and she knew she looked fine in that sundress. Men'd been pretending to wipe the sweat off their brows all day just so they could shade their eyes and look at her. There was something wrong with him. He just wasn't natural. She hadn't specifically heard him talking about Sodom and Gomorrah, but then, again . . .

Joshua'd gone off with his tube of Q.T. tannin' lotion to sun hisself. He never felt right wearin' all that dark makeup and he did look so much better in white when he was dark. He was gonna look purely Christ-like coming down from the top of the tent, held by guy wires, only they weren't really wires, they were spun filament, so fine, so clear they could hardly be seen, and then she'd clip them and the boys on the platform above the tent would pull them up while heads were bowed in prayer.

The faithful and the not so faithful filed into the enormous tent, receiving candles as they entered. They paused to light the tallowed wicks at True Gospel Tabernacle's Eternal Flame of Salvation before taking a seat on one of the hundreds of white folding chairs.

As the lights dimmed, Norma Mae picked up the microphone and stepped into the spotlight. She silently bowed her head and let the spirit of the Lord sweep through her, trembling from head to toe. Then, when the expected hush came over the audience, she raised her head and gave her viewers a radiant smile. *She'd done it right, just like they'd coached her, but then, they had no way of knowing she'd been getting the Holy Spirit off and on for all these years, and she hadn't seen any reason to enlighten 'em.*

"Brothers and sisters, we are gathered here tonight to seek and receive God's blessing, to confess our sins, to deliver our wretched souls from damnation, and I ask, I beg, that you put your hearts and souls and minds into callin' forth the full strength Our Lord Christ Jesus has given you that miracles might be wrought here tonight." Norma Mae raised her arms to God. *Lord, but she would have loved to have seen that on the monitor, her breasts must be pointing right at it, higher than they'd ever been before.*

The cymbals clanged, the timbrels jingled, the harp beckoned hosts of angels.

"If there are any weak or infirm of body or spirit, follow the oxcart, come forward that we might touch you, that you be healed, that you be spared the flames of hell."

The trumpets sounded.

And down the white-runnered center aisle there came a crudely built oxcart, pulled by two white oxen. Walking beside the oxcart were four of the tent workers Norma Mae had persuaded to dress in shepherd's clothing, flowing white wigs, and beards, like Uzzah and Ahio coming out of the house of Abinadab at Gibeah.

" 'And they brought in the ark of the Lord, and set it in his place, in the midst of the tabernacle that had been pitched for it, and they offered burnt offerings and peace offerings before the Lord.' " Norma Mae switched the microphone to her other hand. "Let us sing. *'Hail, to the Lord's anointed, great David's greater Son! Hail, in the time appointed, His reign on earth begun! He comes to break oppression, to set the captive free; to take away transgression, and rule in equity . . . He shall come down . . . He shall come down . . . '* "

The crowd gasped as the golden pulpit was put in place

and the Reverend Joshua Garland descended from the heavens.

It was worthy of Louis B. Mayer, if she did say so herself. Even Joshua was half speechless 'bout that pulpit and half the congregation was right behind the cart, either wantin' to be healed and saved, or just gettin' a better look. This would teach them to tell her how to act. She hadn't gotten where she was and all this gold without having a lick o' sense herself.

She moved to Joshua's side. Sometimes she gave him just a little squeeze when he wasn't emotional enough. Seemed to help get him fired up. Camera people knew about that. It was just her they didn't want lookin' at nothin' but people's faces. *Lord! It was that weird man again, coming down the center aisle, but now he was a lookin' at her, his eyes glowing.*

She wanted to look down, see what he was fiddling with, but she couldn't. They'd catch her sure as the world. True Gospel Tabernacle had had a couple of this kind before, exposin' their ramrod selves just when she was fixin' to do a miracle. 'Course some said that was a miracle in itself. She kept her eyes on his face, remembering to smile devoutly, murmuring, "Yes, oh, yes, come unto me, all ye who are lost and heavy-laden."

She reached over and gave Joshua a little good-luck squeeze.

Norma Mae and Joshua never saw the Molotov cocktail that landed at their feet.

Norma Mae died with one hand on her Bible and the other on Joshua Garland's crotch. She didn't have to give up the gold twice in a lifetime, for her charred body was covered with it.

Clayton Robbin's funeral wreath was as extravagant as it was unusual. Only Eve Afton had an inkling about the symbolism of the white lilies and black orchids, but she didn't have time to dwell on it, for her attention was on

Lauren, the handsome Arab at her side, and the ever-present photojournalists who captured the countess's every move.

She wasn't surprised by Savannah's unnatural composure, but she was a little amazed at Lauren. It seemed that the wilder her lifestyle, the better she looked.

CHAPTER SEVENTY-FIVE

Savannah slammed down the phone. Her hands trembled. It was the third call she had had in the past hour. Since Norma Mae's death, everything had been going wrong. Now her latest novel had stirred the homicidal instincts of a maniac. Her mailbox had been filled with threats against the twins, against Beau, against her. She was terrified to leave the house, terrified for the girls to go to school, terrified to breathe. The police were watching all of them, but it wasn't enough. Beau didn't want her to have a gun, but she insisted. She held it now, telling herself she was practicing. *Visualize, visualize. You can do it.* The memory of Skeeter mingled with her relief of being rid of Norma Mae. Recollections of faceless men and countless hotel rooms bombarded her. A new town, another fresh start, another therapeutic book. Yes, this was what they needed—she, Beau, and the girls.

But at the moment, what she really needed was another refill of her Valium prescription.

CHAPTER SEVENTY-SIX

The chairman of the Appropriations Committee, with his finger in the subcommittee pies of defense and military construction, held a profitable and powerful position and could afford most anything he wanted, but there were few things that really gave Red Shoes any satisfaction these days, not even the fresh-squeezed orange juice his butler served him every morning.

He bent over the copy machine. Now *this* was fun, his one true enjoyment. Six fresh copies of his completed but never submitted application for membership in the National Society of Sons of the American Revolution. Every few months he mailed a set to Mama and once in a while, for good measure, he leaked a rumor to the press about the society's discriminatory policies. And in return, Mama never failed to contribute generously to his campaigns or causes. Of course, this new largesse of hers came after Booker T. got rehooked on the big H and cancelled out *her* insurance policy.

Yeah, Mama was as easy a touch as she had been a lay. His daddy might have liked the latter characteristic, but Red Shoes was fond of the former.

CHAPTER SEVENTY-SEVEN

Silver and Paul Hunter spent a great deal of time together, traveling between their various homes—Palm Beach in the winter, the Northeast in the summer, and cruises in the spring and fall. Neither mentioned marriage. They were content. Paul was a sensitive and passionate lover and Silver, at last, knew how it felt to be the center of a man's world.

Yet she was never without the guilt of Remni's death and all that it had wrought. Lauren's behavior was increasingly wild, and Silver could no longer disregard the danger signals. She had hoped never to have to tell Lauren why Remni killed himself, but she could not stand by and watch her daughter destroy herself as well. The truth could not be more destructive than Lauren's life-style, and perhaps if she was told, she would finally stop searching for the answer only Silver could give her. Her daughter's association with the Shahdesh prince was also a worry. He was obsessive, and his domination of Lauren was going to drive her over the brink. She appeared to have given control of her life to him. Silver knew that when he deserted Lauren to return to Shahdesh, as he surely would when

King Ashad died, her daughter would not survive this second loss.

She summoned Lauren to Montauk Point, sans Prince Kenir Ashad. Silver began where she should have begun long ago, hoping for understanding, praying for forgiveness.

When Silver had confessed, Lauren turned her back on her mother.

Silver rose and approached her daughter. "I beg you, Lauren, for your sake as well as for mine, to find it in your heart to forgive me."

Lauren whirled to face her. "Forgive you? *Forgive you?* Never! I wish it was you who were dead and that you'd taken this awful truth to the grave with you."

"Lauren, please . . ." Silver gripped the back of a chair for support. "Lauren . . ." Suddenly Silver could not talk or even think. Her arm was paralyzed. She tried to move but fell to the floor.

Lauren glared at Silver, watched her lips trying to form words. She had no pity, only anger, no forgiveness, only rage, and a blinding need to hurt as badly as she had been hurt. "If you're having a stroke, it's too goddamn bad it didn't hit you at the reception, before you ruined all our lives."

Lauren ran out of the house. She didn't look back.

CHAPTER SEVENTY-EIGHT

Michael was not selfish with his love or his son. Against Barbara's wishes, he included Justin in his and Eve's weekend excursions—skiing in Vermont, sailing at Cape Cod, carriage rides in Central Park, ferry rides to Staten Island, and trips to Aspen to ski and visit Moni. Barbara was no better a mother than she was a wife. Like Michael, Justin was starved for a woman's affection. Eve was drawn to the boy. He was the child within herself that she could never love, but she did love Justin, and she was beginning to like herself. And she absolutely adored Michael. The publishing world was civil but felt the liaison an affront to the memory of Harrison Mendall, no matter that his daughter was a cold snob who refused to give Michael his freedom. After all, she was New York society and she was ill, a severe diabetic.

No longer was Eve dependent on Scotch. No longer did she need to see life through a haze in order to tolerate it. No longer did she steal the love from Lauren's letters and rearrange it on paper for vicarious gratification and substantial advances. As a matter of fact, she wasn't even writing these days. Her what ifs were devoted to making up outlandish bedtime stories for Justin, making love with Michael, and dreaming of a country house where the three were free to be a family. Life was good for Evie, and she gradually gave over her cynicism to believing in fairy-tale endings and happy-ever-afters. Surely Barbara would eventually consent to a divorce.

CHAPTER SEVENTY-NINE

Savannah Lee sent her latest manuscript Federal Express to her agent. Another depression, another round of men, another move was coming on. It didn't take long. Soon she was unpacking in still another house, another town, another state.

She bent over a packing crate. What goodies would she uncover this time? It was always exciting to move, sort of like Christmas. You saw things you looked at without seeing most of the time. Good Lord—she'd forgotten about the gun. She unwrapped it from the piece of blue felt, examined it, then carefully rewrapped it and locked it in the bottom drawer of her desk. She should get rid of that thing. Later. First she needed to jot down the idea for a new book that was germinating in her mind.

CHAPTER EIGHTY

Prince Ashad had made no secret of his invasion of Beverly Hills, acquiring one prime piece of real estate after another, and he made no secret of his possession of Lauren.

Estranged from Silver, ensnared in the cycle of writing one blockbuster after another and adapting them for the screen, and entrapped in the Hollywood maze of parties, drugs, and superficiality, Lauren was easy prey for Kenir. Subtly and surely, he dictated what she wore, what she ate, what she thought, what she dreamed. Slowly but surely, he undermined her identity.

Lauren turned the Lamborghini sharply into the drive of her leased estate and left the motor running as she rushed inside. Moving vans filled with her belongings lined the curb.

"Come with me, Countess. You don't live here anymore." She was strong-armed into a limousine and whisked away, the Lamborghini's motor still running. She was smoothly transferred to Kenir's mansion, a monarch butterfly trapped in a silken web of opulence and depravity.

> *He had studied and followed her for years. He financed and supplied her increasingly expensive cocaine habit. He fed her romantic streak, exploited her fascination with danger, channeling her eroticism and fueling her escapist urges until she became nothing but a slave to her primitive desires.*
>
> *—Fast Friends*

Nights of scented oil massages, silk pillows on marble floors, shadows of torches held aloft, skillful fingers tantalizing her while he watched passively, postponing her ultimate fulfillment, were interspersed with nights of strategically inserted French-knotted silk scarves or ropes of South Sea pearls, which Kenir expertly extracted from her, driving her to the region of senselessness where there was no comprehension, no reason, no reality but her craving. He had thought of everything: contraptions that lowered her onto him, raised her, turned her, until she cried out for completion. And when those games became too routine, too tame, too boring, they played deadly ones, driving in the mountains, Kenir instructing her to masturbate and climax before he drove them off a cliff.

Eve's voice sounded funny, tinny and distant. Kenir's fingers tightened around Lauren's throat. The imported eunuch thrust the dildo inside her, slid it back and forth, around, then inserted another in her rectum. She could hardly concentrate on Evie's words. Kenir yanked the phone from the wall, bent and kissed her nose. His breath fanned her nostrils. She tried to inhale it, to breathe. The receiver slid from her hand and she took the dildo from the eunuch. At the last possible moment, Kenir released his grip and popped an amyl nitrate capsule under her nose. Blood and oxygen rushed through her, she spasmed uncontrollably, and he held her in his arms, gently wiping the perspiration from her brow. "I love you," he whispered. "I have always loved you."

And he did. He could never make her queen, but neither could he give her up. Any day now his father would die and Kenir would be King of Shahdesh. If she wouldn't accompany him under his terms, he would abduct her and keep her with him. But he would never make her his wife, never make her his queen. His Islamic religion forbade it.

Eve dialed again. There was no answer . . . no answer . . . no answer. She paced, smoking furiously, clutching her silk robe about her, then strode back across the room. She snatched Lauren's book off the sofa and flipped to the disturbing pages. This wasn't gratuitous sex to sell more copies; Lauren didn't need to do that. This was a desperate plea for help. She picked up the phone. "Savannah? Have you read Lauren's last book? . . . Yeah, I know you just moved again and you're writing too. . . . I know you meant to—Listen, Savannah, it doesn't matter. Are you okay? I mean, I want to read you something. It's important. Page one twenty-eight.

" 'Tatiana sat in the middle of the floor, staring at the silk taffeta draperies and the tassled cord, waiting for Serge to unveil whatever lay behind them. His black military boots gleamed in the soft yellow light. "You have suffered much, my dear, but there is no need for you to suffer more." He pulled the cord, revealing a life-size painting of Tatiana, nude. "I will make you want to live and not join your dead lover. Tell me, Tatiana, do you want to live? Do you? Or do you want to go Ziven?" He spat on the floor. "Ziven! The name means 'vigorous, alive,' Tatiana. And Ziven is dead. Dead!" He approached her, his steps echoing across the travertine floor until he knelt beside her.

" 'Tatiana did not answer.

" 'Well, then." He pulled the gun from his belt, clicked it open and spun the cartridge for her to see. Five chambers: four empty, one lead bullet.

" 'Tatiana dipped her silver spoon into the caddy of cocaine.

" 'Put the *arúzhiye* to your head, Tatiana.'' He tongued her almost to release, once, twice, again and again until she screamed, then denied her, forcing her to whirl the cartridge, pull the trigger at her temple. If she fired three times and lived, he would fuck her into oblivion. It was as simple as that. And when he finished, he made her watch while he emptied the remaining chambers and the bullet into her painting. Tatiana did not care. She was dead inside. Orgasms, one after another. Highs, one after another. Without Ziven, there was nothing left that mattered.'

"Lauren *is* Tatiana, Savannah. Don't you understand? Tatiana means 'fairy queen' in Russian. That's what Kenir's doing to her. They're playing fucking Russian roulette while she's snowed out of her mind and all you can say is, 'Where does she come up with these ideas?' Savannah, get smart. We've got to do something, and we've got to do it now.''

CHAPTER EIGHTY-ONE

Evie and Savannah jerked up and down the hilly street in the rented Volkswagen. "Shit, Savannah, I thought you knew how to drive. Let me." They switched places. "I used to drive Dusty's souped-up Chevy. I can shift." The sound of gears stripping alerted two gardeners and one UPS man. Savannah sniffed, and Evie glared at her. "You're right. The limo would have been less conspicuous. Should we go back and get it?"

"Not now, he's leaving." Savannah pointed to Kenir getting into his white Rolls-Royce. "Back down the street and wait."

As soon as the Rolls was out of sight, the VW buzzed into the drive of the Beverly Hills estate.

"Jesus, Lauren. You eating sugar out of the bowl?"

"It ain't sugar, Savannah." Evie yanked the spoon out of Lauren's hand. "Good God, Lauren, how much do you weigh?"

Lauren looked down at her body as if it belonged to someone else.

Evie rolled her eyes at Savannah. "Come on, we're going to go to lunch and fatten you up." They marched Lauren upstairs. Savannah helped her dress and distracted her while Evie packed some of her belongings.

"Where are we going?" Lauren's eyes glittered as she picked up her handbag.

"It's a surprise. Come on." *Oh Jesus*, Evie prayed, *don't let it be the surprise I'm afraid it has to be.*

They ditched the Volkswagen at the L.A. airport and were at Scoma's in San Francisco in time for lunch.

By twelve thirty Evie's worst suspicions were confirmed. By two o'clock, the scheduled limo had picked them up and was cruising north along Highway One toward the Big Sur area.

Lauren, irrational, paranoid, and convinced Kenir was following them, was unaware of their destination until the wrought iron gates clanged shut behind the limo and the manicured grounds and ivy-covered buildings of the private sanitarium loomed before her.

"This is a fucking loony bin. What the hell do you think you are doing?"

"We're going to get you some help." Eve placed a hand on Lauren's arm.

Trapped between Evie and Savannah Lee, Lauren went berserk. Her arms flailed at them and she began shouting obscenities as the driver brought the car to a stop. "You aren't sticking me in that goddamn place—that's for crazies. I'm not some fucking nut. If anyone needs help, it's the two of you. Evie, you're a fucking drunk and Savannah, you're a frigging nympho, hooked on speed and Valium." Lauren tried to crawl over Eve. Eve grabbed her wrists, struggling to hold her while trying to avoid being bitten and scratched.

"We're going to straighten your ass up whether you like it or not, so make it easy on yourself and on us."

Savannah snapped to and tried to assist Evie. "I knew this wasn't going to work."

"Just shut up and get some attendants out here."

"No!" Lauren's scream reverberated through the car. "I'll never forgive either of you for this."

"Get going, Savannah. Now!" Eve winced at the latest kick to her shins.

"I can't leave you, Evie. She's out of her mind and dangerous."

"I can handle her, God damn it. She's my sister. The driver is here if I need him."

Savannah sprang from the car. Taking the steps two at a time, she disappeared inside.

Lauren pitched herself out of Eve's grasp, retreating into a corner of the back seat, where she huddled, her eyes wild, her mind momentarily clear. "Leave me alone. You aren't my half sister. Fax wasn't my father. You don't understand—Remni was my half brother! Incest, damn you, Evie, incest! That's why he killed himself. That's why I fucking don't care anymore, about anything or anyone. I survive the best way I can. Savannah better be bringing a goddamn army if you think you are going to lock me away in that hellhole."

Eve gawked at her, unable to speak or move. Lauren seized the opportunity and bolted from the car, running across the lawn like a madwoman. Eve vaulted from the car in hot pursuit, shouting for help.

Lauren made it to the gate, frantically trying to scale the ornate metalwork. It required four attendants to pry her hands and body free, five to put her in the straightjacket, but only one to carry her inside.

It took a great deal of love for Eve and Savannah to leave Lauren. Her pitiful cries echoed in their ears as Evie signed the admission papers, prepaid from her own funds the thousands needed for Lauren's care. Eve knew that but for the grace of Michael's love, she might be in the same condition. Savannah dealt with it by banishing from her mind the frightening prospect that her problems were as severe as Lauren's.

Savannah watched Eve's shaking hand and pale face. For some reason she felt excluded again. Evie was withdrawn. "You did the right thing, Evie. I was against it at first, but after seeing Lauren I know it had to be done."

Eve burst into tears, shocking Savannah. Evie rarely cried, not even at Fax's funeral. "Is there something you're not telling me, Evie?"

"No, nothing, Savannah." *She's not my sister. I had no right to commit her, but there are times when a lie is necessary, times when you must say or do whatever it takes, times you have no choice but to be slicker, quicker, smoother, smarter, dirtier.*

In the weeks and months of Lauren's slow convalescence, Eve regularly jetted west to visit, sometimes bringing Michael, sometimes alone. Sometimes Lauren recognized them, sometimes she did not.

Savannah sent flowers, notes, and peach nighties, but could not bear to see her friend. The murders in her new book were more brutal than ever.

Kenir's abduction of Lauren had been thwarted by Evie and Savannah, and now his search was halted by his father's death and his own ascension to the throne. He was forced to leave for Shahdesh without her, but she would be his again someday. *He knew.*

CHAPTER EIGHTY-TWO

Barbara Mendall Christian had been going to her analyst's plush office twice weekly for the past ten years in an attempt to discover why she could not feel or express love. He'd long ago given up hope there would ever be a break-through or that she would go to another doctor. He sus-pected her visits were inspired by the voguishness of being in therapy rather than by any deep-rooted desire to find the source of her problems. But since she had manipulated him into continuing therapy, he felt obligated to keep trying alternative methods of treatment. Today he planned to regress her under hypnosis.

To his amazement, he uncovered Barbara's early sexual abuse by her austere mother. It was a classic case of block-ing and would probably take another decade to satisfactor-ily resolve. And Barbara was apparently unaware she had revealed anything of her awful history.

As they chatted at the end of their session, Barbara men-tioned that Michael had again asked her for a divorce.

"And what did you say?"

"I told him I would never give him a divorce and reminded him I control Stearns & Mendall."

"Do you think it wise to perpetuate your marriage with threats?"

"I'm not threatening Michael, I'm stating facts: his career, his son, his money, are gone if he leaves me. I put up with the embarrassment of his mistress; he can put up with this marriage of convenience."

"I understand Michael's motivation for staying. What is yours for keeping him?"

"I'll be damned if I know. That's why I pay you."

"Perhaps you want to punish Michael. Sometimes we inflict our pain on others."

"That's absurd. I'll see you Thursday."

And every other day hereafter for a very long time, Mrs. Christian.

Barbara strolled along Fifth Avenue, noticing no one, seeing nothing. *Maybe you want to punish Michael, . . . punish Michael . . . punish Michael.* Yes, she wanted to punish Michael. He was going to live. She was going to die. More and more he flaunted his mistress. More and more she was forced to hide her deteriorating condition. She resented how much he loved Justin. All she'd ever known was abuse and unrealistic expectations. Oh, yes, she'd been an utter failure—as a daughter, a concert cellist, a wife, a mother, a human being. But there was one thing she was going to do well. She was going to die and let Michael marry his mistress. She wasn't going to give him the satisfaction of a divorce, of knowing that he wouldn't have to endure her much longer. *Punish him, punish him, punish him.*

She hailed a taxi, directing the driver to the law offices of O'Toole Tate. Her forty-nine-percent interest in Stearns & Mendall would go to the Juvenile Diabetes Foundation. Michael would be devastated. All of the years, all of his plotting, all of his sacrifices would be for naught. *Renal failure and dialysis, codicils and disinheritance. She was going to suffer, but Michael would suffer more.*

CHAPTER EIGHTY-THREE

Beau burst into the hotel room and caught Savannah with another man. He exploded in a rage of jealousy, his fingers tangling in her hair, wrenching her off her latest pickup, slinging her across the room, then charging the cowering man like a wounded bull. Within minutes, the hotel room was a shambles. Beau gripped Savannah's slender throat, and dragged her to her feet while her lover groaned on the floor, his once handsome face reduced to a bloody pulp.

"I ought to put us both out of our misery and strangle you here and now! Tell me why." He threw her on the bed and banged her head against the wall. "Why? Why? *Why?*" His fingers bruised her flesh, but it didn't hurt nearly as much as his tormented eyes piercing her heart.

"I didn't mean to, Beau. It's just that when you're away and the books are done, I'm so empty. I can't explain it. Won't you forgive me? It hasn't happened much, Beau, I swear it."

"You bitch." He backed away. "No more. Wallow in it

if you want, Savannah, but I'm through. Do you hear me? I'm through!''

"I can't make it without you, Beau. Please, oh, God, please, you gotta stand by me now!"

The revulsion on his face knocked the breath from her. He stormed from the room and walked out of her life, taking the twins with him.

Unable to sleep for days, a very distraught Savannah removed the gun from her desk drawer. A vial of Valiums had spilled across the desktop and come to rest against an ashtray full of roaches. The house was in total disarray, but was nothing compared to Savannah Lee. Her hair was stringy and uncombed, her old nightgown pocked by burns, and her eyes swollen. Slowly she unwrapped the blue felt and stared at the .38.

Eve tossed, turned, snuggled closer to Michael, then sat up straight. Her skin was clammy, her breath rapid. She eased herself out of bed, grabbed Michael's robe, and slipped from the room. As she put the glass of milk in the microwave, she spied Lee Boudreaux's latest book on the counter. She hadn't even congratulated Savannah on the great reviews and on finally making it to the number-one slot on the *New York Times* best seller list. It really was a hell of a book. She checked the clock as the buzzer went off. It was late, but not too late. Savannah Lee wrote all night anyway. She dialed Savannah's private number at her plantation just outside Macon, Georgia.

Savannah started at the shrill ring. It might be Beau. Oh God, let it be Beau. At the sound of Evie's voice, she burst into sobs.

Oh shit! First Lauren and now Savannah. When were they ever going to get their lives straight and just let her lead hers? The first time she'd ever had any happiness, and they had to screw it up with their problems.

For hours Eve talked to her, assuring Savannah she was not forsaken, promising she and Lauren would be on the first available flight. Savannah muttered something and the line went dead. Eve immediately redialed, but Savannah didn't answer. She prayed Savannah wouldn't be foolish, but she could not dispel her fear. Panicking, she called Lauren. During a brief discussion Lauren agreed that they could not risk the adverse publicity that notifying the sheriff of Bibb County would create. They would have to see to Savannah themselves.

They found Savannah in her office, goofy on pills and high on grass. Eve made coffee while Lauren held Savannah under the shower. They called the maid back to work on the house and they went to work on Savannah.

"God, you look pathetic. No wonder Beau walked out on you."

"He caught me with another man. He's never gonna forgive me. I've lost my darlin' Beau forever."

"If he put up with you this long, he'll be back," Eve stated positively. "Quit sniveling and get your shit together."

"But what if he won't? What will I do? I don't have a life without Beau. I don't want one without him."

Lauren and Eve looked at each other. "Then you go to him. Tell him you love him, how much you need him. Promise him you'll never do it again. And *don't*. My God, Savannah, you have each other. He is still alive. Don't throw it away when it can be salvaged." Lauren's voice was ragged as she made her plea.

"You didn't see the hate in his eyes when he told me he was through with me. I can't go to him."

"Then Evie and I will."

Eve and Lauren were sequestered in a modest motel room with a heartsick Beau.

"There's something inside her . . . something that eats at her, makes her this way. I've tried love, I've tried patience, I've tried everything, I've swallowed my pride when her writing supports us, but I can't tolerate her looking for answers in the arms of another man. Damn it! I won't."

"What do you think causes her to do this, Beau?" Lauren asked.

"I think it goes way back . . . before me. When we first married, she'd wake up in a cold sweat, reliving something so terrible she couldn't even talk about it. She'd let me hold and kiss her, but we were together months before we made love. I sensed she had to resolve a fear of me before she could accept me. We never talked about it, and gradually she got some better." Beau shrugged. "Now it appears she'll sleep with anyone." He buried his face in his hands. "Why, damn it, *why* did she do this to me?"

"I don't know, Beau," Lauren said, "but I don't think she'll do it again. She loves you desperately." She took his hand, forced his eyes to read hers. "She won't make it without you."

"The two of you have so much going. She's a name now, the money is rolling in, it could be so good for you. Go home, Beau, go home," Evie urged. "You're miserable, too, without her."

Beau's voice broke. "I don't know. I have to think it over. Nothing makes much sense anymore."

"Sure, Beau, take your time." Lauren glanced around the dingy room. "We'll look after her until you decide one way or the other."

Savannah had never spent a more miserable two weeks. No pills, no dope, no Beau, no twins, just Lauren and Evie constantly hovering over her. She'd never tell them her secrets, just as she had never told Beau. Better to play their game and pretend she was recovering.

After much torment, Beau agreed to forgive and try to

start anew. He and the girls came back to the magnolias of Moss Marle. Savannah regained her will to live.

Lauren and Evie departed with the customary hugs, tears, and kisses.

They had confiscated all of her drugs, but unfortunately they forgot to dispose of her gun.
                                        —Fast Friends

CHAPTER EIGHTY-FOUR

Lauren went from Macon to Montauk. She hadn't seen Silver in several years. Since her mother's confession, she'd edited her out of her life like so much bad prose. She'd gotten very good at forgetting those who had deserted her, the ultimate protection—or was it revenge? She didn't know, but the result was the same. They did not exist, therefore they could not hurt her. But she had been hurt. By blaming them, by denying them, by burying them, she lost herself.

Even knowing this, she might not have considered going home had it not been for Evie's insistent speech: "Don't you remember your own words, what you told me after Fax's funeral? You said, 'What's past is past. We can't change it. Our parents made mistakes. We'll make mistakes too.' And, Jesus, Lauren, you've fucked up royally. If Savannah and I hadn't intervened, your brain—if you'd lived—would be jelly. You survived, you pulled through, and don't you think it's time to use the brain we risked the wrath of Kenir to save and see how your mother fared? Trot your screwed-up ass home and get it over with.''

Twice before, Silver had loved, and twice she had been deserted for other women. But not so with Paul. His constant devotion had wrought miracles, helping her overcome her handicaps, those brought on by the stroke and those instilled by Fax's indifference and Sasa's rejection. A month earlier, Anne De Ferrers Bennett had become Silver Hunter. There was only one emotional scar Paul could not heal, one area of her life that was not reconciled.

Silver saw the limo cruise up the drive. It wasn't an infrequent occurrence, for the men administering her empire came and went with regularity, but this time inexplicable tears welled in her eyes. At once Paul was at her side. "What is it, Silver? What's wrong?"

"Nothing's wrong. Lauren has come home."

"Silver, don't do this to yourself." He was aware of the hours his wife spent blaming herself and the many times she secluded herself in her office, reviewing the framed memories and detective's reports, all the while silently praying that one day her daughter would return.

"No, Paul, it's her. I know it's her."

The house, the grounds, the trees, the wind-tossed Atlantic looked the same. How did one go home? She hadn't gone home when there was no place else to go, she hadn't gone home when life was more than she could handle. Hadn't gone home, hadn't called, hadn't written. How could she go now?

She stood for a moment, watching the sea, trying to sense what she would find inside. Then she looked at the familiar windows to her past, afraid. That Silver had lived she knew, or the lawyers would have notified her, but was she bedridden? Was she able to speak, to hear, to comprehend? How did she live? And how did one forgive one's mother? Silver's actions had been wrong, but had she,

Lauren, not been so headstrong and secretive, her mother would have had an earlier opportunity to reveal the past, to have saved Remni. How to forgive? She lifted the knocker.

The heavy door opened wide. "Welcome home, Miss Lauren."

"Oh, James." She threw her arms around the beloved butler. "Where's Mother?"

And then she saw Silver coming toward her, elegant, her posture perfect as ever, despite her slightly jerky gait and the walking stick. She knew from Silver's smile that everything was okay, that her mother had forgiven her and forgiven herself, and in an instant, Lauren did the same.

"I have read all of your books. But you haven't had one out in a long time."

"I've given up writing."

"You have an empire, if you want to run it, Lauren."

"Maybe later, Mother. I am not ready yet."

"Are you sure you are all right? Sure you are sufficiently recovered to cope? What would you do if Prince Ashad tried to reassert himself? He's a dangerous man. And my sources in Shahdesh tell me he has not given up his quest to possess you. His fanaticism grows worse daily. You should keep a low profile. If you choose to do it here, Paul and I would be delighted."

"I intend to keep a low profile, Mother. I'm no longer dependent on drugs, no longer susceptible to Kenir. I'm going out of the country again, but this time I know exactly where and why I need some solitude to put myself back together."

She squeezed her mother's hand reassuringly.

For years she had been on the run, a Gypsy girl without roots. One of her first acts upon arriving on Grand Cayman was to buy a house on the beach—not a mansion or a villa, but a breezy, sunny house, open to the wind and the sea. It wasn't on Seven Mile Beach, but on Old Man

Bay, away from the throngs of tourists and away from the limelight.

She had had her fill.

Nothing short of murder would ever induce her to return.

CHAPTER EIGHTY-FIVE

Clayton Robbins was indicted for bribery and shamed before the nation. Though he was never convicted, he lost his powerful status in Congress and his bid for reelection.

He returned to Philadelphia and did little but watch video reruns of *The Postman Always Rings Twice*, rock on his front porch, sip lemonade, and reminisce about the hot summers of yesteryear.

Red Shoes never thought he'd miss Norma Mae so much.

CHAPTER EIGHTY-SIX

Sasa and Anna's marriage deteriorated as surely as her health. After Remni's death she no longer made an attempt to hide her lesbian relationship with the Marquise DuBonnet. They traveled together extensively, but Sasa no longer cared where Anna went or with whom she spent her time. When she died in the Spring of 1982, he felt free to contact Lauren, although it took him a while to locate her on Grand Cayman.

Lauren's housekeeper directed him to her private beach. For a long moment, he savored the sight of her, keeping his distance and summoning the courage to reenter her life. Suddenly she stood up and ran into the water. So many years it had been, and she still had the buoyancy of youth. She looked almost the same as the first day he'd seen her.

Sensing an intruder, Lauren slowly turned back to the beach. Her first reaction was joy, her second dismay. She tensed.

Sasa read her thoughts. "I had to do it, Lauren. I could find no other way to save you. And I did not sell the villa. I kept it for you, should you ever want it." Lauren ran to him. His Rom eyes, so like hers, returned her sparkling smile, his arms her embrace. "You look well, my daughter," he said.

"I am well . . . at last, Papa." It was easy to revert to the familiar endearment, though it now meant more than "father-in-law." "Mother told me everything. I've made my peace with her and I am happy you are here."

"How is your mother?" Sasa's heart constricted.

Lauren told him the truth. "But she is recovering. She has remarried."

"Is she happy?"

"Very."

"Then I am glad." *She was so beautiful that day, Lauren, you have no idea, in her red wool, her innocence, her trust. It was a terrible joke life played on her, played on all of us. And what pain we caused in the name of honor.* "Lauren, I want you to make me a promise."

"Anything, Papa."

"If ever there is anything you want—anything that is good for you, that makes you happy beyond all else—then go after it. What appears to be the right action often is not. Do not waste yourself."

Lauren did not answer.

"You have made millions from your books and movies. I know you inherited more from Fax, and I presume you will receive the rest of his money someday."

"Billions."

"Remni's estate has been held in trust for you, Lauren. I inherited all of Anna's, and you are my sole heir. You have or will have properties around the globe, monstrous sums of cash, art beyond value. In short, you will be the world's richest woman."

"I don't want or need any of it."

"You can't stay here forever," he protested.

"Can't I?"

"No." His voice was soft. "Nor will you want to."

"Why do you say that?"

"God has tested you, forced you to confront every aspect of yourself, and he does not do that to amuse himself, Lauren. No, my daughter, you will not be allowed to rest. There are other things for you to do."

Again, Lauren did not answer.

Before Sasa departed for Paris, he extracted a promise from her that she'd spend Christmas at the villa. He knew what her future held. He had consulted the stars. But she would have to discover it for herself.

Ah, Silver, I hope we both live long enough to see it. It will make everything worthwhile—our passions, our tragedies, our lives.

CHAPTER EIGHTY-SEVEN

"Walk away from me, Evie. Jesus Christ! If you love me, then do as I ask because I can't . . . God help me, I can't give you up." Michael's strength crumbled. "Barbara's never going to consent to a divorce. I'll never be free of her." He turned his back, hiding his tears.

Eve's arms encircled his waist, and she rubbed her cheek along his bare shoulder. "It doesn't matter, Michael. I love you so much that I'll accept whatever arrangement fate dictates. I once bragged that I could walk away from any man, but not this time, darling. It'd be easier to cut out my heart. You and Justin mean too much."

He pivoted, clutching her to him. "What are we to do? How long can we go on like this? We have no future, not even a glimmer of hope. I can't bear leaving you and going home to her. My life is five days of hell and two of heaven. It's not fair, Evie. We were meant to be together. I hate her. I wish she were—."

"Don't say it, Michael. Don't even think it. It's bound to work out. It has to."

"Oh, Evie," he groaned, wishing to God her blind faith was justified. But he knew better.

He knew Barbara.

He knew only a miracle could bring him, Evie, and Justin together as a family. "How I have paid for my ambition. I never counted on truly loving anyone or anything but my work. And now that I do, I can't have you, not completely—unless I give up my son. I can't do that, either. I'm damned. Damned." He began to cry, disintegrating in front of her eyes.

CHAPTER EIGHTY-EIGHT

Rurik Valenchka gulped his peppered Stolichnaya, waiting for a moment to reinsert himself into the conversation. As virtuoso guest violinist of the Philharmonic, he was accustomed to being feted, not made privy to his host's domestic dramas. The Christians had been sniping at each other for thirty minutes, barely aware of his presence. He was reminded of Eduard Hanslick's words on Tchaikovsky's Violin Concerto in D. *The violin is no longer played; it is yanked about, it is torn asunder, it is beaten black and blue.* And perhaps it was appropriate, for had not Tchaikovsky composed it during the period immediately following his disastrous marriage to a half-wit conservatory student? Barbara and Michael didn't sound like a couple orchestrating a conflagration for diversion. They did not appear to share the passion that usually inspired such intense emotional displays. Rather, he suspected, they were genuinely engaged in a contretemps of major significance. He accepted the maid's offer and exchanged his empty glass for a full one.

"I'm sorry that I won't be able to attend your performance tomorrow evening," Michael Christian said.

"He has to take his mistress to dinner. He, too, will turn in a classical performance, I'm sure." Barbara sampled Rurik's vodka. "Won't you, Michael?"

"Put that down." He glared at her.

"Why should I? Wouldn't you be happy if I died?" She looked at Rurik. "I have diabetes, but I do so love a drink now and then." She sipped again.

Michael snatched the drink from her hand. "Stop it, Barbara."

"Oh, come on, admit it. Tell Rurik you'd like nothing better than to be rid of me. Right, darling?"

"If he really wished you dead, Babs, he'd encourage you to drink."

"Tell him, Michael, tell him you'd like me dead. That you'd like my share of Stearns & Mendall. That you would like my son to live with you and your slut."

"I don't think Rurik is interested."

Au contraire. It was getting interesting. Slut? He would have the most fascinating gossip for tomorrow evening.

"Oh, but he will be, because let me tell you something, my clever coward of a husband. I will never, ever give you a divorce, and should you be praying ever so earnestly for my death, do not waste your few chances with God. And while I am on the topic, if you don't cease your badgering about a divorce, you will live to regret it, because I can fix it so that neither you nor Justin inherit my interest in Stearns & Mendall. And where would you be then? Back to reading the slush pile." *She was getting to him, she could see it. The Mighty Michael was on the verge of losing his composure for once.*

"What do you mean, you can fix it?"

Rurik quaffed another shot and looked at his watch. No one noticed.

"Remember your refusal to seriously entertain the German consortium's offer to buy Stearns & Mendall? Well, they approached *me* and *I* might sell. What would happen to your dreams of captaining the publishing industry then, darling? That's what you've coveted most, isn't it? Shall we put it to the test? Would you trade a lifelong ambition for your whore? With a stroke of the pen, I could sell you out, past, present, and future."

The bitch. Michael had never known such rage. *She wouldn't do it—she couldn't.* "Your mother would never sell, and she owns controlling interest."

"Wrong, darling." Barbara calmly went to the secretary, removed a photocopied document, and thrust it into their guest's hand. "Read this to him, Rurik."

Rurik's eyes swiftly skimmed the page. He needed another vodka. He needed to have accepted Mayor Koch's invitation. He needed to phrase this as pianissimo as possible.

"Go on. Read, Rurik."

"It is a power of attorney from one Della Stearns Mendall appointing Barbara Mendall Christian to act on her behalf and to vote her shares on any proposition placed before the board."

Michael grabbed the paper and read it, then crumpled it and threw it across the room, his eyes ablaze with hatred. "You wouldn't dare."

"Oh, but I would, Michael. I have nothing to lose. You have everything. You *and* Justin."

He lunged at her, furiously shaking her. "You bitch! You coldhearted bitch! I'll see you dead before I let you deprive Justin of his birthright." The back of his hand cracked across her face.

Rurik jumped to his feet. "Michael, don't do this." He placed himself between the Christians.

For a pregnant moment, Michael's rage bored straight through Rurik; then Rurik was shoved aside and Michael confronted Barbara. "If you so much as mention that German option ever again, I'll kill you. Do you hear me? With God as my witness, I swear I'll kill you.'' Michael grabbed his jacket and strode out of the penthouse.

The analogy had been correct, for Tchaikovsky, that most Russian of composers, had definitively expressed what he, Rurik, had just witnessed: life's music was, indeed, most intense in the finale.

CHAPTER EIGHTY-NINE

"Go home, Michael, try to talk to her again." Evie wound her arms around his neck and brought his lips to hers. "I love you. Maybe you should just let her sell everything. You can get another job."

"But Justin can't get another inheritance."

"Then you're going to have to come to some kind of terms with Barbara. You can't go on like this. It's destroying you."

Michael returned her kiss, but did not answer.

"She's taken to her bed again, Mr. Christian. She won't let me in, even to bring a breakfast tray. What should I do?"

"Take the weekend off, Mrs. Brighton. I'll cope with her."

She hoped she wouldn't live to regret this. She wouldn't blame him if he made good on his threat, but she didn't want to be an accessory. She prayed he would insist. She needed a reprieve. Mrs. Christian was getting loonier by the day. Just like Cousin Mary, whose brain calcified in the latter stages of her diabetes. Of course, she hadn't been loony, just dense. Something more was wrong with her employer—much more. "Are you sure, Mr. Christian?"

"Yes. Justin's camping out with his troop, so I can manage." He flashed her a dazzling smile, but his eyes looked haggard. "I've a ton of galleys to review, and the Chinese restaurant delivers."

"Don't forget to see that she takes her insulin. It's in the refrigerator." Mrs. Brighton turned to leave. "Oh, and don't forget to see that she eats. Remember her last hunger strike?"

"I'll take care of it. Enjoy your weekend, Mrs. Brighton."

CHAPTER NINETY

A vial of insulin was taken from the refrigerator. A needle pierced the sterile seal. The insulin was syphoned into a syringe, then expelled down the kitchen drain. The process was reversed. Saline solution was substituted in the vial. The refrigerator light went out. Footsteps retreated. A toilet flushed.

Scoops of potting soil lightly pattered against the society section of the newspaper. Rubber gloves and a syringe were planted among the ficus roots, then camouflaged with potting soil.

Hands smoothed the dirt, and a newspaper rustled as it was collected and discarded in the trash.

Wordlessly, Michael picked up Barbara's untouched breakfast tray, carefully setting the vase and unopened rosebud on her nightstand.

"I can read your thoughts, Michael. You're thinking maybe this time the crazy bitch will sign her own death warrant. If I lapse into another coma, how long are you going to wait this time to call an ambulance? Until I'm dead?"

He didn't respond.

"You don't have the courage to do it yourself. No, coward that you are, your only hope is that the more irrational I become, the more my self-destructive tendencies will work to your advantage. How encouraged you must be when I fast. I'm sure your every moment is consumed with conjecture about my delicate and tenuous condition, with praying that I'll lose track and miss an injection."

He set the insulin vial down next to the bud vase.

"Poor taxed Michael. It must be frustrating as hell each and every time I dangle hope before you, then spite you by living. Go on now, get out."

"We'll be bitter enemies until the bitter end, won't we, Barbara? You could have made it work, if you'd given it half a chance." Michael sighed and closed the door behind him.

Barbara picked up the syringe, stuck it into the vial, suctioning out the first of her two daily fifty-unit doses of NPH before injecting herself. She never let anyone watch her and she never forgot to stash the used syringes in a plastic bag in the decorative box in her makeup drawer. She glanced over at the coral rosebud, twitched her numb feet, and smiled. *Yes, Michael, bitter enemies to the bitter end. And beyond. How I'd love to see you at the O'Toole Tate offices the day after my funeral.*

Michael rubbed his hand across the stubble on his face, then braced his palms against the mantel, knocking an empty gin bottle to the floor. As the early light of dawn seeped into the room, he stared into the dying embers, visualizing the life ebbing from Barbara. He heard the Sunday morning church bells chime.

An annoying scratching impinged upon his consciousness, the sound of sand being whisked to the hardwood floor. He turned. *Damn cat. If Barbara had paid half as much attention to Justin as she had to that damn Siamese, he wouldn't have asked for more.* He jerked the cat away from the ficus, brushed the soil into his hand, and replaced it in the pot, tamping it down, collecting a few dead leaves that had fallen during the night and disposing of them.

Mrs. Brighton let herself into the penthouse. She paused briefly outside Mrs. Christian's bedroom door, then glanced at her watch. Midnight. Tomorrow was soon enough to deal with *that one*. She yawned and proceeded down the hall to her own quarters.

Michael rang Mrs. Brighton's room. "I'm leaving for the office now. See if you can get her to eat. She hasn't touched a bite from her tray, but I heard the refrigerator door close in the middle of the night. I'll check back around noon."

As the medics wheeled the stretcher into the Park Avenue penthouse, Mrs. Brighton frantically dialed Michael's private number.

"Mr. Christian's office."

"Where is he?"

"He hasn't arrived yet, Mrs. Brighton. Is there a problem?"

"Yes. Mrs. Christian has lapsed into a coma. Tell him to come to Cabrini Medical Center immediately."

Barbara was pronounced DOA, the initial cause of death, pending autopsy, listed as cardiac arrest, exacerbated by advanced insulin-dependent diabetes mellitus.

Mrs. Brighton pulled the covers over her head, then threw them back and crawled out of bed, her feet searching for her slippers. She knotted the sash on her robe and opened the door to find the Siamese meowing at Mrs. Christian's bedroom door.

"Hush, Sultan." She scooped the cat into her arms, stroking its back. Sultan refused to be consoled. "Let's both go have some warm milk." She padded toward the kitchen, carrying the cat.

Michael bent over the trash compactor, feverishly sifting through the debris.

"What are you doing, Mr. Christian?"

Startled, he bumped his head on the edge of the counter. "You didn't happen to pick up a piece of paper off my desk, did you? I've lost the notes about Mrs. Christian's burial arrangements. I've got to find them."

"I didn't touch anything, but I just saw them there this evening. Just a minute." She let Sultan leap from her arms and left, returning in a second. "Here are your notes." Poor man. He was just so distraught.

Michael snatched the sheet from her hand.

"Sultan and I were going to have some warm milk. Would you like some, too?"

"That would be nice."

Mrs. Brighton went down the hall, then hesitated a moment. *Mr. Christian was rummaging in the garbage again. What did it all mean?* She stepped inside her room, closed the door, and leaned against it, her heart pounding. The sound of Michael's footsteps came down the hall. He went into Mrs. Christian's room and shut the door. Drawers and doors opened and closed. He was searching for something. He wasn't grief-stricken, he was in a tizzy. *Blimey, he had killed the bloody missus!*

"My name is Emma Brighton. I am housekeeper to the Christians and I need to talk to a detective." She plunked her tapestry bag on the counter, folded her arms across her bosom, and bullied the young desk sergeant with her most imposing scowl.

Shortly thereafter she was relaying her suspicions to Detective Gus Lamonte. "I gathered these syringes." The plastic bag was placed before him. "I am sure these are the last ones she used. You see, Mrs. Christian had this habit of accumulating several days' worth of syringes before she would let me throw them out." She shook her head. "She was a weird one. I believe this might be what Mr. Christian was searching for in her room last night."

Gus Lamonte examined Mrs. Sherlock Holmes's exhibit A. The British always loved a good mystery. "Don't you think that's a pretty big assumption?"

"By itself, yes. But considering all the facts, no." Yanks were always so cheeky.

"Okay." He would humor her. "Besides the syringes, the rummaging in the trash compactor, and ransacking the deceased's room, what makes you think Christian iced his old lady?"

"I am just giving you the information I feel a moral obligation to divulge. For years, they have been at each other's throats. Then there was this latest commotion. There's no mistaking the threat Mr. Christian made. If you doubt me, there was another witness, a Mr. Valenchka, who was the Christians' dinner guest that particular night. He also heard the vow Mr. Christian made. Mh-mm. Said as God was his witness, he'd kill her, he would. Intent. Isn't that what you call intent?"

"I threaten to kill my old lady every other day. It don't mean I intend to follow through with it."

"Yes, but then Mr. Christian told me to take a holiday. He was most insistent." She sat up even straighter, leaned forward, and placed her hand on his desk. "Opportunity. Isn't that what you call opportunity?" She snapped her fingers. "Oh, and when I came to tell him I was leaving, he was standing in the kitchen with the refrigerator door open and a bottle of Mrs. Christian's insulin in his hand. I asked if he needed help—we rotate the supply, using the older first—and he said no, he was just checking to make certain he didn't need to reorder before I returned."

The biddy was building a half credible case. Lamonte sheared the cellophane off the Hoyo de Monterrey cigar and ran it under his nose, savoring the aroma. "Didn't you mention a kid? Was he there that weekend?"

"No, he was camping with his scout troop. Mr. and Mrs. Christian were alone. In fact, Justin hasn't been back to the house since . . ."

"Oh yeah? Where is he?"

"With Mr. Christian's mistress. It's no secret, everyone knows about her. And I do believe Eve Afton is what you might call motive."

As much as he hated to admit it, the limey busybody's theory held water; it was beginning to smell like there'd been foul play. "Okay, okay. Tell you what. I'm gonna run your *evidence* through the lab. Why don't you keep this under your hat, go on about your business as usual, until we see what turns up." He stood, ushering her out of his cubicle. *Gus Lamonte was going to do a little checking on his own.*

He called for the department's preliminary report on the DOA. The next morning, lab results in hand, he notified the coroner's office to look carefully for an insulin link.

And with that, State of New York v. Michael Christian was set into motion.

Michael punched the button for the ground floor. It was going to be ground floor for him at Stearns & Mendall as well. He laughed ruefully. Barbara had been his express to the top and his chute to the bottom. Her codicil had damn sure seen to that. She hadn't even provided for Justin. He felt sick to his stomach. For years he had worked, sweated, groveled, placated, and Barbara had demolished a lifetime of toil in one fatal blow. If Della had her way, he would soon no longer be the golden boy of Publishers Row; he would be just another editor without a job.

Gus Lamonte chewed on his unlit cigar, unblinkingly watching the elevators come and go. He always liked this part of an investigation. It gave him some kind of perverse satisfaction to catalogue people's reactions when he was about to do them in. He figured this Christian character was gonna be unflappable, a tough nut to crack. Geez! The guy almost pulled off the perfect crime. Probably happened a dozen times a day with no one ever the wiser. Even though his case against Christian was purely circumstantial at this point, maybe if he kept leaning on him, Christian would eventually break down and confess. Didn't matter, he would nail him anyway.

Spying his man in the swarm of people exiting the elevator, Gus flashed his badge and identified himself. "I'm Detective Lamonte, Mr. Christian. I know the timing is probably bad, but I need you to accompany me back to the precinct house and answer a few questions."

"Yes, this is a bad time, Detective. I'd prefer to do it later."

"Well, I'd prefer that we did it now. In fact, I insist." He took Michael Christian's arm.

Lamonte's intuition had been right. Christian was not intimidated. He had a plausible explanation for every question. And he was admitting nothing. Gus had no choice but to let him go.

The boys in the newsroom met the boys from the coroner's office for suds at Clancy's Tavern and were told off the record that Barbara Mendall Christian's death wasn't as cut-and-dried as they had reported.

"Extra, extra! Read all about it! 'Foul Play Suspected in Mendall Heiress's Death.' Buy your paper here."

PUBLISHER PRIME SUSPECT.

BEREAVED HUSBAND CUT FROM BABS'S WILL.

HE LOST THE MILLIONS; WILL HE KEEP THE MISTRESS?

HUSBAND AND MISTRESS QUESTIONED AND RELEASED read the caption above the picture of Michael and Eve ducking into a taxi outside of the precinct house, their faces shielded.

NEW JERSEY PHARMACIST IDENTIFIES CHRISTIAN AS PURCHASER OF SALINE SOLUTION.

CHRISTIAN CHARGED WITH MURDER IN THE FIRST
DEGREE.
MISTRESS MAKES MICHAEL'S BOND AND RETAINS
DEFENSE COUNSEL RALPH DENNARD.

Eve and Michael pushed their way through the throng of
reporters and into Eve's limo. "Dennard is waiting for us
at his office. Christ! There are probably more reporters
there. Vultures. Are you up to it?" Michael leaned back
and closed his eyes.

Eve brushed the hair from his forehead. "Justin is doing
all right. I protect him from this as much as I can."
Michael groaned. *She didn't want to ask him, but she'd
avoided it as long as she could and she had to know, had to
hear him say it.* "Michael, did you do it?" A quiver passed
along his jaw. He did not open his eyes nor did he answer.
Her fingers froze. "Michael, please tell me you didn't do
it." He opened his eyes, staring at her, through her, but
still did not answer.

The pain in his eyes shriveled her insides. "Forgive me,
Michael. I shouldn't have asked."

Again the crucial question was posed to Michael. "Did you
murder your wife, Mr. Christian?" Ralph Dennard tugged
on an earlobe and assessed his client.

"No."

"What about the pharmacist who identified you as the
purchaser of saline solution in Jersey?"

"I didn't buy it."

"All right, then we proceed from a position of innocence. Now, I want you to be perfectly candid with me
about your marriage, and specifically, be clear on the
events that occurred in the days immediately prior to your
wife's death."

After Michael had recounted the facts, Dennard stared
at his collection of Navajo pottery. "Suicide. We will take
the position that Barbara, in her unstable state and realiz-

ing her condition was fast deteriorating, chose to end her own life. And in some twisted, sick way, she planned to inculpate you from beyond the grave. Otherwise she would merely have stopped taking her medication. We will immediately contest the will on the grounds that she was mentally incompetent."

Eve expelled the breath she had been holding. Dennard was every bit as good as his acquittal record attested. She relaxed in the deep leather chair.

"About your relationship with Miss Afton. I think it would be to our advantage not to deny the situation. After all, it has been going on for years, and Barbara, as well as the rest of the city, knew of it. We must convince a jury that this may have been Barbara's motivation in incriminating you. She had repeatedly refused to give you your freedom to marry Miss Afton and willfully and selfishly elected to deny it even with her death."

Eve thought Michael's stony face softened a bit.

"We still have a major problem. The prosecution will contend that you somehow had prior knowledge of this latest codicil and in revenge, you coldly and calculatingly plotted and executed her death."

"That's ridiculous. It doesn't make sense. Justin and I stood to benefit only if she was alive. Only a fool would shut off the golden spigot."

"The state will say you intended to do just what we have to do to keep you from frying—contest Barbara's will."

There was no end to his hypothesizing. It was worse than plotting a novel. Eve's head swam and she rubbed her throbbing temples.

Michael sprang to his feet and slammed his fist on Dennard's desk. "The woman was crazy. And mean. And vicious. For what she did to Justin, she deserved to die, but by God, I didn't kill her!"

"One outburst such as this in the courtroom and you'll only give credence to the state's contention that you have a violent and explosive temper, and once a jury's convinced of that, even I can't save you. Sit down, Mr. Christian. We have work to do."

Evie studied Michael as he moaned and tossed fretfully, his arm flung across his forehead. Earlier, his lovemaking had a sense of desperation, a fatalism she couldn't shake off. But she, too, was tired, her perception distorted. She dismissed her disquiet and smoothed the sheet around his chest.

CHAPTER NINETY-ONE

CHRISTIAN MURDER TRIAL BEGINS.

MAID AND HOUSEGUEST TESTIFY MICHAEL MADE DEATH THREAT.

CORONER TAKES STAND TODAY.

INSULIN DEPRIVATION CONFIRMED.

MICHAEL SAYS BABS KILLED SELF.

NEW JERSEY DRUGGIST SAYS HE'S POSITIVE PUBLISHER BOUGHT SALINE SOLUTION IN HACKENSACK.

"Your witness, counselor." The smug DA bowed to Dennard.

"You previously stated for the record that you have no doubt that the defendant was the man who purchased saline solution at your pharmacy on the night of October twenty-fourth? May I ask you, was it an especially busy night?"

"No, sir. He came in just before closing. It was only the two of us. I remember thinking it was lucky I had change for him. He gave me a hundred. Don't see too many of those in Hackensack."

"I see. I can't help but notice that you wear trifocals. How well do you see, Mr. Neswitz?"

"I, uh . . . I see fine with these." Neswitz pushed his glasses up on the bridge of his nose.

"When is the last time you had your vision checked?"

"A year ago last August."

"That's a pretty long time for someone of your advanced years, isn't it?"

"I don't think so, and you make me sound older than Methuselah. Every day I have the responsibility of filling over fifty prescriptions and I haven't made a mistake yet. Never have and never will. I'm not senile and I see just fine with these specs."

"I apologize. It wasn't my intention to imply that either you or your eyesight were deficient." Dennard cleared his throat repeatedly. "I beg the court's indulgence. Obviously my larnyx is deficient." Titters rippled through the courtroom. He made a production out of turning his water glass right-side up, pouring water from the carafe, and sipping slowly.

Judge Alexander doodled on the pad before him. "Could we please proceed, Mr. Dennard?"

"Yes, Your Honor. Mr. Neswitz . . ."

All eyes were riveted on the spectator as he stood gagging, then bolted from the courtroom, dropping his briefcase as he ran. As the bailiff picked up the spilled contents, Dennard turned back to the witness. "Mr. Neswitz. Would you indulge me by describing the man who just dashed from the courtroom?"

"I, uh . . . Well, he's tall. I think his hair is brown, a little too long. I didn't get a very good look."

"Are you telling me that when a disturbance such as you just witnessed occurs, you don't observe the person causing it?"

"I didn't say that. It was just confusing, too much going on."

"And isn't there a lot going on when you are trying to close up for the night, Mr. Neswitz? Don't you count your money, fill out your deposit slips, separate your charge records, lock the safe, secure your narcotics, turn off lights, think about what you are going to do when you get home, answer the phone? Wonder what you would like to eat, or about stopping off for a cool one? Think about taking ice cream to your invalid wife? Your wife is an invalid, isn't she? I mean, aren't you always concerned about her welfare when you are away?"

"I . . . of course. Most men would be." Neswitz leveled a righteous look at Michael.

"The point, Mr. Neswitz, is that you are preoccupied a good deal of the time, as you were on the night of October twenty-fourth, when you allege that the defendant purchased saline solution from your pharmacy." Dennard crossed his arms and paced the length of the jurors' box. "You can only vaguely describe the gentleman you just saw, but you can clearly, and without hesitation or question, testify under oath that the defendant is definitely the purchaser of saline solution out of the over fifty customers that you processed that day. Now, multiply that by the one hundred forty-seven days that have intervened since then. Mr. Neswitz, that's over seven thousand, three hundred fifty customers. Of that number, how many could you identify? How many could you identify and say with certainty what it was that each purchased?"

The DA decided it was way past time to interject. "Objection, Your Honor. Mr. Dennard is deliberately confusing the witness by distorted conjectures."

"I withdraw the questions. I am through with the witness."

"The witness is excused."

"The prosecution rests its case, Your Honor."

"Then call your first witness, Mr. Dennard."

"If it please the court, I call back into the room the gentleman Mr. Neswitz could not describe."

A collective murmur rustled through the spectators' gallery.

"Bailiff, please bring the witness back in."

Mr. Edward Jennings was summoned from the hallway and sworn in.

"Did you three weeks ago have an occasion to fill a prescription from Neswitz Pharmacy?"

"I did."

"And can you tell me at what time of the day you had this prescription filled?"

"I can. It was right before eight o'clock."

"And who waited on you?"

"The owner, Mr. Neswitz."

"And can you tell me what this prescription was?"

"Yes, sir, it was parapectolin."

"A controlled substance, is that right?"

"Yes, sir."

"Did you have to sign for that substance?"

"Of course. Mr. Neswitz opened a register and asked me to sign."

"Did anything unusual occur?"

"Yes, sir, I had my right hand—I am right-handed—in a sling, and I signed the register with my left hand. Mr. Neswitz had to hold the register for me."

"And how much time would you say this procedure took?"

"It was eight-fifteen when I left. I apologized for keeping Mr. Neswitz past closing. I waited while he locked up and walked with him to where our cars were parked."

Dennard faced the jury. "And under whose instructions did you make this purchase?"

"Yours, Mr. Dennard."

"I thank you, Mr. Jennings. You've been most

helpful." He addressed himself to his colleague. "Your witness, Mr. District Attorney."

"The state declines at this time."

MISTRESS TO BE CROSS-EXAMINED BY PROSECUTION TODAY.

You could hear a pin drop in the courtroom as Evie again took the stand and was reminded she was still under oath. "Miss Afton, have you or have you not been intimately involved with the accused for several years?"

"I have."

"Is it also true that you demanded that he divorce his wife and marry you? That you would end the affair if he did not?"

"Never."

"But you would have married him had he been free?"

"Yes."

"And Michael knew this?"

"Objection, Your Honor." Ralph Dennard stood and crossed to the center aisle. "The witness cannot possibly testify as to Mr. Christian's state of mind."

"Objection sustained. Rephrase your question, Mr. Prosecutor."

"Very well. Did the defendant ever say or imply to you that he wished the deceased dead?"

Evie turned to the jury. She moved not a muscle, batted not an eye as she perjured herself. "No, sir, he never said or implied anything other than that he wished she was a better mother to Justin. That was his only complaint in all the years."

"But you had complaints, didn't you, Miss Afton? Isn't it true that you schemed and persisted in publicly flaunting this back-street affair? Isn't it true that you shamelessly tried to take another woman's husband and son? Isn't it true that you compounded Barbara Christian's medical and emotional instabilities and sabotaged her marriage by your wily manipulation of her husband?''

Dennard threw up his hands in exasperation. ''Your Honor, the prosecution is harassing the witness. Could we have him direct one question at a time and perhaps pause so that the witness might answer?''

''I agree, Counselor. The prosecution will please allow the witness to answer.''

''There's only one question I would pose to Miss Afton; one answer I would like from her. And this time I would like the truth.''

''Objection, Your Honor. The prosecution is again badgering the witness.''

''Overruled. The witness will answer the question, please.''

Eve turned to the judge. ''I haven't heard it yet, Your Honor.''

''Very well. Address yourself to the point, District Attorney.''

''I ask you again. Did the defendant, Michael Christian, ever say or imply to you that he wished Barbara Christian dead?''

She dredged up every shred of credibility she possessed and once more faced the jurors' box. ''And I tell you again: no, he did not.'' She didn't dare look at Michael.

The DA played to the jury, looked at them incredulously, shrugging a silent ''I hope you're not gullible enough to believe a murderer's mistress.''

''Your witness, Mr. Dennard.''

Jesus Christ, this was a damn dog and pony show. ''I have no questions at this time, Your Honor, but I do reserve the right to recall.''

''Very well. You may step down, Miss Afton.''

Days stretched into weeks as Dennard relentlessly hammered home his theory of suicide and sick revenge before a packed courtroom. Throughout New York, from Bonwit's to Bergdorf's, from Bloomie's to The Russian Tea Room, from Hammacher Schlemmer to F. A. O. Schwartz, every coffeehouse, every restaurant, every boutique, every beauty salon and barbershop, every home, buzzed with the trial's latest disclosures. There was already talk of a movie. Michael was approached to sell the rights to his story. Daily, women thrust flowers, love letters, hotel keys at him as he came and went from the courtroom. The kooks pelted him with curses and evil wishes. And always the press was on hand to document the Michael mania.

SURPRISE WITNESS FOR DEFENSE. BABS'S SHRINK SAYS HER CONFIDENCES SURVIVE HER DEATH.
  BABS'S PSYCHIATRIST FORCED TO LAY IT ON THE BENCH.

"I want it stated for the record that Dr. Heinschill has petitioned the court to show adequate need for disclosure and the court demonstrated same. Dr. Heinschill, in accordance with his ethics and code of confidentiality, reserved the right to disclose only that information relevant to the legal question at hand, and, as such, must be considered an adverse witness."
"Let it be so stipulated."

BABS'S SHRINK REVEALS SHE WANTED TO PUNISH MICHAEL!
  DENNARD PREDICTS AN ACQUITTAL.
  PROSECUTION CONFIDENT OF CONVICTION.
  CLOSING ARGUMENTS TO BE HEARD TOMORROW.

Lauren and Savannah arrived in time to have dinner with Evie, Michael, and Justin at Eve's apartment. They dared not venture out for fear of being mobbed by reporters. For once, even Lauren had no quips for the press. This was serious, really serious. They'd talked all around it, talked about Cayman, about the twins, about books, about the past, because they couldn't talk about the present—it was much, much too sensitive a subject—and they damn sure couldn't talk about the future. It was much, much too tentative.

Mrs. Brighton sat soaking her feet in Epsom salts and sipping chamomile tea from a Spode cup. She had done her duty and salved her conscience. The verdict was in the hands of God and the jury.

Della Stearns Mendall sat in the conference room at Fenwick, Foster & Baltins, a battery of legal eagles surrounding her.

"If Michael is acquitted, we petition for legal guardianship of Justin and, on his behalf, sue for wrongful death of the mother. If Michael is found guilty, it is arranged that Judge T. Oliver Bailey will sign a court order, and at the same time that we serve Michael and Justin's appointed temporary guardian, Eve Afton, we will seize custody of the child."

Around the table pens hastily sketched out judicial procedures.

Sultan scratched in the potting soil of the ficus. Mrs. Brighton hoisted her feet from the soaking pan and dripped Epsom salt solution across the hardwood floor. "Naughty Sultan. Look at this mess."

Gus Lamonte had just turkeyed in his bowling tournament when the call came. *What in the hell did that limey bitch want now? Damn right it was a matter of life and death—hers, if this was some kind of wild-goose chase or yet another of her endless theories.*

"The court is ready to hear final arguments in State of New York versus Michael Christian. Is the state ready?"

"I have vital new evidence to present before final arguments. We request the court's indulgence."

"The defense has not been apprised of this vital new evidence, Your Honor. I request the motion be denied."

The judge sighed. He wanted to get this over with and putter on the greens at Pebble Beach, where his wife had already been for two weeks. "You've had ample time to present your case, Mr. District Attorney. Unless you can demonstrate extenuating cause for presenting this evidence, I am inclined to agree with Mr. Dennard and deny your request."

"What I am about to present is conclusive, incontrovertible proof of Mr. Christian's guilt. I believe that we can shorten the court's time considerably."

"Very well. You may proceed."

Mrs. Brighton was recalled, whereupon she revealed her discovery, and the DA asked that the pair of surgical gloves and the empty syringe be entered as exhibits 58 and 59, respectively.

Gus Lamonte took the stand, paving the way for the lab expert's testimony that unequivocally substantiated traces of saline solution in the empty syringe.

"State your name and occupation."

"Lawrence Beckman, fingerprint analysis."

Dennard could find nothing objectionable in his unimpeachable slate of credentials. Discreetly he popped a Gelusil tablet in his mouth, thinking a nitroglycerin capsule under his tongue was more appropriate. He glanced at his client. Michael had not changed his expression or posture throughout the damning testimony. He'd had clients in shock before, but this wasn't the same.

The DA retrieved exhibit 58, identifying the surgical gloves. "Are these the gloves you examined last night?"

"They are. They have my tag on them."

"And will you tell the court what your scientific and learned examination revealed?"

"They bear the fingerprints of the defendant, Michael Christian."

Oh shit, he had buried the wrong pair of gloves.

Pandemonium erupted. Judge Alexander's bang of the gavel and call for order were ignored.

Eve jumped to her feet, screaming, "No, no, no, Michael! Are you mad?"

Lauren and Savannah rushed to her side, pushing her back into her chair, trying to shush her.

"Dear God, how could he have done this to us? At least before, we had a slim chance that maybe one day we'd be together. Now we have nothing, not even a shred of dignity left."

"Shut up," Lauren hissed.

Eve sat unmoving throughout the remainder of the morning as summations were heard and the judge charged the jury with their options and responsibilities.

At four P.M. Michael Christian was found guilty and sentenced to life imprisonment.

For the first time since the hellish ordeal had begun, Michael displayed emotion. Tears streamed down his face as his eyes met Eve's. *I love you*, he mouthed as the handcuffs were clamped about his wrists.

She stood as they led him from the court. "Michael. *Michael!*" She broke free from Lauren and Savannah, burst through the swinging gate toward Michael, and threw her arms about his neck before anyone could stop her. "I still can't walk away from you," she sobbed. "We'll appeal, we'll appeal."

The bailiff dragged Eve off Michael, handing her back to Lauren and Savannah.

It was over. The Camelot world she had entered so briefly was no more.

Wedged between her only allies, Eve relied on Lauren to deflect the microphones and questions.

"Can you give us your reaction to the verdict, Miss Afton?"

"Is Michael planning an appeal?"

"Do you believe the evidence against him?"

"What are your plans now?"

"Will you write a book about this?"

Their questions, their faces, everything was a blur. She did not notice the process server until Savannah attempted to shove him away. She was being wrestled, jostled. Lauren's tight grip upon her arm was broken. An official-looking document was slapped into her hand. "Hearing in ten days, Miss Afton. Justin Christian is now in his grandmother's custody."

The cameramen missed not one shot of her dazed face, the recorders not one anguished word.

"Not here, Evie, hold on a little longer. Della Mendall isn't the only one with Wall Street lawyers at her disposal. You'll get permanent custody of Justin. We'll see to that, won't we, Savannah?"

"All for one and one for all." Savannah shoved harder against the stampede of salivating jackals.

CHAPTER NINETY-TWO

It was a bloody battle, a mudslinging free-for-all, a cat-clawing contest. No quarter was given, no mercy shown. Evie was fighting for a child she dearly loved, the only part of Michael left to her. Della Mendall was forced to become co-plaintiff in Michael's suit contesting Barbara's will. Justin was her excuse and the means by which she intended to wrest the remaining forty-nine percent of Stearns & Mendall ownership from the Juvenile Diabetes Foundation. Accusations, vile and bitter, abounded. Ruses, wily and loopholed, proliferated. No tactic was overlooked. The custody proceedings gave new meaning to the word *unfit*. Witness after witness revealed Eve and Della to be worthy opponents. It was a toss-up who was smoother, quicker, slicker, smarter—*dirtier*.

Fenwick, Foster & Baltins produced a complete dossier on the activities of Moni's Place and her association with underworld crime figures, presenting as exhibit 304, Silver's photograph of Moni, Eve, and Marcus Anovese exiting the Flamingo Palace. Exhibits 305 through 467 revealed Eve's like-mother-like-daughter proclivities. Exhibits 468 through 490 chronicled instances of intoxication or the purchase of supplies to achieve same. America's leading romance writer was indisputedly a Scotch-dependent whore.

In the end, the outcome rested on the statements of Babs's shrink and Eve's character witnesses. Dr. Heinschill's legal obligation took precedence over the code of confidentiality. Under qualified immunity, he approached the attorney appointed guardian *ad litem* for Justin and opened his records of Barbara Christian's early sexual abuse at the hands of her mother, Della Stearns Mendall.

Lauren, Eve, and Savannah were conferring with Eve's lawyer in Blackwell & Blackwell's offices. "Our only hope is to put the countess and Mrs. Boudreaux on the stand tomorrow. The character witnesses for Mrs. Mendall have withdrawn." He looked at Lauren. "Thanks to your influential intervention, their husbands have blocked their appearances. If the two of you can whitewash the black picture of Eve that Fenwick, Foster & Baltins has painted, we just might keep Justin from becoming a ward of the state. Do you think you can do it?"

"Since we've been covering for each other for over twenty years, I think it is safe to say we have some experience at this."

It wasn't the countess who worried the lawyer, but the spaced-out, easily intimidated Mrs. Boudreaux. He had his work cut out for him. It was going to be a long night.

He eased Savannah through direct examination, displaying her soft Southern ways to advantage, she was a lady who should not be subjected to this ugly scene. Thank God, she was doing great. Her Southern accent was like butter melting against freshly baked bread.

The Fenwick, Foster & Baltins lawyer was chomping at the bit. He perceived Savannah as the weak link and he was going to break the protective chain. "Do you have children, Mrs. Boudreaux?"

"Yes, suh. I have twin girls, darlin' little girls."

"And would you entrust their care to someone the caliber of which has been established in this courtroom?"

"Eve loves Justin, just as I love my girls. She would nevah do anything to harm that boy. It is reprehensible to me that you have suggested otherwise, suh."

"I didn't mean to offend you, Mrs. Boudreaux."

"Well, I understand. It's your job." Savannah cast her eyes downward.

"But, Mrs. Boudreaux, even if, as you claim, Miss Afton has Justin's best interests at heart, in all honesty, can you say that on occasion and in your company she has *nevah* comported herself in any but the most motherly manner?"

"Well, everyone has their moments. I mean, nobody's perfect. To the best of my knowledge, there was only one perfect person who ever walked this earth, and that was Jesus Christ."

"I am sure you are a good mother, probably an outstanding one—"

"Thank you, suh. I try."

"—so it is probably difficult for you to relate to this petitioner's basic unfitness, but let me ask you about your own mother."

Savannah blanched. "My mother was Mrs. Joshua Garland, wife of Evangelist Garland."

"I know. I've investigated your background thoroughly." He leaned forward. "I want to know about the days when your mother was plain old Norma Mae Owen. Isn't it true that your own mother, like Miss Afton, went from bar to bar, man to man? Isn't it true that you were often deserted while she yielded to the addictions of the flesh? Isn't it true that you still bear the scars of her neglect?"

"Objection, Your Honor. Counselor forgets Mrs. Boudreaux is not on trial."

"I believe this may be germane to the testimony. Objection overruled."

Savannah wrung her hands, her nails biting into her palms. "I don't know what you're implying. Why are we talking about my momma? It has nothing to do with what's transpirin' here today."

"It has everything to do with it." The lawyer pounded the front of the witness box. "We are talking about motherhood. We are talking about strength, fitness, morality, abuse. We are talking about an innocent child's future. Is there a child alive who deserves to be abused?" He slammed his fist again, then shook it in her face. "I will answer the question for you. No child deserves to be abused. Ever."

"I agree. Whyever are you shouting at me?"

"Because you intend to sit right there and perjure yourself to protect your friend. Your duty is to the innocent child, and you, Savannah Lee Owen Boudreaux, should know that better than anyone in this courtroom today."

Anxious glances were exchanged between the Vegas Pagan and Her Highness.

"What do you want from me?" Savannah's hands trembled as she clutched the stand.

"I want the truth. Have you or have you not ever seen the petitioner, Eve Afton, in a state of extreme intoxication? Have you or have you not ever been privy to immoral behavior on her part? Have you or have you not the courage of your convictions, the courage to protect a helpless child?"

Savannah buried her face in her hands. "All right. Yes, dammit, yes. Are you satisfied?"

"Yes to each and every question I just put to you?"

Savannah nodded mutely.

"Please speak for the record."

"Yes," came her muffled reply.

"No further questions. You may step down."

Eve cursed beneath her breath as Savannah ran from the room. She squeezed Lauren's hand as Lauren passed by to take the stand. "You're all I've got. Don't let me down."

Lauren did beautifully. Upon her testimony, Lizzie Borden would have been granted custody of Justin. The Fenwick, Foster & Baltins lawyer didn't rattle her—until he put her on her honor. "You have never made a secret of your life-style and playgirl escapades. Do you honestly believe the whirlwind life, the high life you and Miss Afton are a part of provides an environment conducive to a child's proper development?"

God. What should she say? Eve had amended her ways; Lauren had simplified her life. But they weren't permanent behaviors. She lifted her head, telegraphing her regrets to Evie. "No, I do not."

Eve sat stone-faced. They, who had lied their way through life and fiction, had betrayed her.

Unable to bear hearing the judge make Justin a ward of the state, she rose from her place at the table and walked out of the courtroom.

Lauren and Savannah ached to explain their defection, but now was not the time. Evie needed to be alone.

Bereft of Michael and Justin and on the verge of a nervous collapse, Eve went home to Moni.

It was the coldest and bitterest of winters in the Rockies and the coldest and bitterest of women who sat before a flaming fire and blazed scorching words across her blue-screened monitor.

CHAPTER NINETY-THREE

In the summer of 1987, Eve finished her novel, *Fast Friends*, chronicling the secret lives she, Lauren, and Savannah had led. It was an exorcism, an indictment of their characters, written with no what ifs, no compassion, no care for the repercussions. They had judged and been misjudged; had misunderstood and been misunderstood; had denied and been denied; had loved and lost; had failed and triumphed; had known heaven and hell and recounted it for millions of readers and millions of dollars.

When *Fast Friends* arrived in New York, it incited a near riot. Every major house wanted their name on the scandalous roman à clef. An auction the likes of which hadn't hit the publishing industry in years revved up enthusiasm and hiked the bids. Negotiations were underway for miniseries rights before the final, staggering sum and fortunate house were announced.

A year later, Eve Afton was the number-one best-selling author in the country. She was again heavily into Scotch and loveless encounters, with only Justin's now and then phone calls or letters having any meaning for her.

CHAPTER NINETY-FOUR

Dusk was making its usual descent a few miles outside Macon, Georgia. Magnolia boughs swayed lazily as lavender light filtered into the converted ballroom of the antebelleum mansion. Autumn breezes carried enticing fragrances of gardenia, honeysuckle, and jasmine into the still room. A white Angora cat sprawled atop the Bösendorfer piano suddenly stood, arching its back, and listened to the wind; then it catapulted out the doors, knocking a fourteenth-century pitcher to the floor.

"Liar! Liar! Liar! It's not true, you vicious bitch! I'm not. I can't be." Savannah hurled the damning book across the room. Vaulting to her feet, she reached inside the teakwood box for her private stash, her heart palpitating wildly, her molasses-colored eyes filled with panic.

Jesus H. Christ! So what now, now that the whole fucking world knew nearly every nitty-gritty detail of her life? She flicked her eighteen-karat-gold lighter and lit the joint, dragging deeply of the select Sinsemilla. Out of habit, her fingertips traced the familiar inscription: *All for one and one for all, Love, Evie.*

Instantly the lighter dropped from her hand. "Screw you, Eve Afton, and screw your book." The threat from the lips of the First Lady of Psychological Thrillers resounded more hollowly than the distant echo of her ancestors' Confederate war whoops. And at the moment, Savannah was obsessed with her bloodlines. Her heritage and the refinements of southern gentility, in particular, had been greatly expanded upon by her mother to all who would respectfully listen, though Norma Mae couldn't begin to pronounce *gentility*. In fact, if Eve's intimation was true, Momma hadn't even learned her colors, like basic black and white. All Norma Mae had known how to do was lie and fuck. All Eve knew how to do was lie and fuck over.

The grass worked its magic. As her heart rate slowed, her mind dared to dwell on the abhorrent chapter that triggered this latest outburst and the long-suppressed memories of her mother: *White Lilies and Black Orchids!*

Friends and traitors.

Smiles to your face and knives in your back.

The past rammed down your throat, the future up your tush.

It made no difference how rich or famous you became, recollections—true or false—had the power to haunt and hurt, the potential to immmortalize or victimize. The best seller *Fast Friends* would certainly do the latter to her. Eve had damn sure guaranteed that.

"Your mother should've done us all a favor and smothered you at birth, Evie." The frail champagne blonde collapsed into her favorite brocade chair. If only she could sleep a night through, she might, *could* think clearly. Even the sleeping pills the doctor prescribed for her chronic insomnia and depression had not granted her one minute's escape from the terrors that kept her pacing and plotting, typing and smoking, throughout the wee small hours. The faint purple half moons beneath her eyes bore testimony to her trauma. She buried her sallow face in her hands. "Fuck, I gotta have some rest—gotta think straight, gotta get straight. Everything is so scrambled."

Picking up her ever-present mug of coffee and cream, Savannah stared blankly into the caramel-colored liquid. Then, the same as Momma used to read the coffee grounds in the bottom of her cup, Savannah realized the full significance of the toffee color. Brown sugar.

"Momma, oh, Momma, am I? Am I? Did you? Did you? Is he my father? Was he what Eve said? Were you worse than I knew? And am I tainted? Answer me, Momma, just once, answer me truthfully. Did the pimp in Philadelphia father me? Did he become the corrupt congressman in Washington who sent black orchids and white lilies to your funeral because you made him crazy, Momma, just like your wild ways and fanatical crusades made me crazy, Momma? I remember every tacky tent, every stinking juke joint, every squeaking bed, every stinging slap, every change of schools, every cheap motel room, every smoking old car, every lousy town.

"I hated you then and I hate you now. I will never admit that you were what you were and I am who I am. Never, ever. So what do I do, Momma? Tell me! You always had all the answers, all the lies. How do I discredit what can be documented—the reality of my drug abuse and bouts of nymphomania, followed by guilt, then thoughts of suicide? Who was it I wanted to kill, Momma, me or you?

"Thanks to your actions and my stupidity, Evie didn't spare me a thing, didn't leave me an out. You were the one who was so good at timing and dramatics; you were the one who could make the obvious obscure and the repulsive seductive. How? Help me. Jesus! Just once, let me be smart, let me be like the lemonade you relished. Let me quench their curiosity and never satisfy their thirst."

Beau! Oh, God! Beau. How would he react? Even if she succeeded in hiding the book from him, it was a goddamn certainty he'd eventually get wind of it all. Holy shit! Nine tenths of the encounters Eve so accurately chronicled Beau never even knew about. Savannah had blatantly lied to him about the other tenth, and he'd believed her. This time he wouldn't. This time he would walk out of her life for good. He would be gone and she would be alone, permanently alone with a spitting cat, a house that moaned with the melancholy wind, and ghoulish nightmares, alone with the need to be held, loved, protected. More than anything, she couldn't tolerate this. She had tolerated much—much too much—but not this rejection. It was one too many.

The thought of being abandoned by Beau drove Savannah wild. *To hell with Norma Mae, to hell with appearances, to hell with trying to whitewash a rotted life.*

A madwoman, perched on the edge of a black hole, she pitched pillows and ashtrays about, toppled lamps, knocked paintings from the walls, ripped down draperies, until, physically spent, she crumpled to the floor, sobbing, cursing, clawing the sheer negligee from her thin body.

You're not alone. We're here with you, just like we've always been. Your momma's gone; Beau will desert you. There's no one. Just us. Listen to us. Haven't we always helped you when others couldn't or wouldn't?

The voices were back. It had been years since she had heard them, years since they had intervened. The voices she could trust. They hadn't let her down then and they wouldn't now.

"I swear you're gonna rue the day you ever made fast friends with me, Eve Afton." Savannah jabbed her hands through her hair, a gleam in her eyes. "Lucky for me you couldn't trumpet what you didn't know." Christ! Momma had been right—never tell, pretend it never happened. "Your fiction falls far shy of reality, Evie. You've no idea what I'm capable of, but you'll soon realize, oh, yes, you will."

That's it. Tell her, tell her. Let her know the fear and pain and terror you have known.

Unsteadily, Savannah dragged herself to her feet and crossed the room to her cluttered desk. Her disheveled hair fell over her face as she bent to slide open the desk drawer. Dazedly she withdrew the .38, then lit another joint and inhaled several tokes, flicking ashes onto the Persian rug beneath her bare feet. At first the revolver felt bulky and unnatural in the hand that once wielded an ice pick, but Savannah had written scores of violent scenes and wasn't the squeamish type.

CHAPTER NINETY-FIVE

Lauren flipped her diamond-studded Cartier sunglasses onto the bridge of her nose and surveyed her private beach and the Caribbean. After five back-to-back best sellers, she guarded her privacy, making little contact with the outside world, the one exception being her dear friend, Maxine, who owned The Bug Man Beach Shop. The nights of debauchery and life on the wild side were behind her. Finally she'd gotten it together. Finally she'd managed to live a few years without creating an international scandal.

Everything moved slowly on Grand Cayman, and Lauren liked it that way. She didn't care who was number one on the *New York Times* best seller list. Except . . . A warm smile crossed her face as she picked up Evie's book. So she'd finally done it, quit wasting her talent on simple plots and simple heroines and wrote her way to the top. Lauren fingered the cover, remembering the good times, the bad. They'd all made it—she, Evie, and Savannah Lee, and they'd remained friends, and it was the friendship that was finally most important. Lauren opened the slick cover of *Fast Friends*.

In Part V, *The Winter of Destiny*, Eve recounted a fairy tale of innocent love stained with the mortal sin of incest. The blood drained from Lauren's oval face, the phantom blow to her gut bleaching her bronzed skin. Confidantes and confidences, friends, falsehoods, and facts, life and lust, truth and trash—Eve had capitalized on it all.

"Dear God! Not again!" *Not now.* She'd gone around the world and fucked a million men. She'd written novels that steamed the glue off their bindings. She'd lost her mind and lived only where things were not real, where she didn't care, where nothing mattered because she couldn't bear to feel or risk the pain.

Before Remni, life had held little meaning; after Remni, it had been a living hell. She'd tried to forget the best way she could, and when others looked at her and saw the glitz, the glamor, the success, they'd envied her. Not one person had known or understood the private anguish of the darling of the jet set. Until she had told Eve. It had taken years for her to come to terms with herself, years to find peace, and with the peace had come, at long, long last, self-acceptance. She'd even begun to feel again.

How could Eve have chosen this particular time to betray her? She hadn't even bothered with more than a cursory disguise of their names, and the altered spelling was probably accidental at that. Eve couldn't spell *shit* if she was crotch-deep in it. She'd talked to Eve only weeks before and Eve had not breathed a word about *Fast Friends*. Lauren had come across the book in Georgetown this morning, a pyramid of hardcover gloss on display. No, true to Evie's naturally manipulative nature, she had not forewarned her of the public assassination.

Was this retribution for Lauren's testimony at the trial? She should have known. Past experience should have taught her that whenever Evie felt attacked, she retaliated with her claws unsheathed. Should she have given Evie credit for being able to understand or forgive? Of course not. Nothing but lies and lurid, lurid libel. But this smut? How could she have done something so cruel, let alone to one of her dearest friends? Why? Why now?

Utter bewilderment gave way to anger. That Eve had exploited her private anguish for profit and personal acclaim was unforgivable; that she had no doubt seriously jeopardized Savannah's always tenuous hold on life was unconscionable. The devious bitch! She shouldn't have expected better from the daughter of a whore. If she could get her hands around Eve's traitorous little throat at this moment she would strangle the life from her. Of course, she'd probably have to stand in line. But there was another way. If Eve had, indeed, done this for financial gain and a chance to bask in the limelight, then Lauren could easily accommodate her. She'd concede Eve her moment of glory, but it would cost her dearly—every blessed cent she'd earn on that piece of crap. Lawsuits were expensive, and she could better afford it than Eve.

Then, too, there was the other matter, the wild, unspeakable summer and the one small thing Evie neglected to include about herself.

CHAPTER NINETY-SIX

Eve Afton's limo slowed to a stop outside the Sherry Netherland Hotel, her home away from home now that New York no longer held a permanent lure. With a knowing look, the chauffeur delivered her into the doorman's care. Following tonight's late night celebration at the Manhattan Ocean Club, she was blitzed out of her mind. Sucking a breath of crisp October air, Eve snuggled her cheeks against the collar of her new Galanos-designed, Dion-made sable, cast her faceless paladin a stage smile, then allowed him to guide her staggering steps into the lobby. She wasn't so drunk that she missed the concierge's look or the sense of disapproval emanating from the arms that supported her across the marble foyer and into the elevator.

"Can you make it, Ms. Afton?"

"Haven't you read my books, Frankie? Making it is my specialty—anyone, any place, any time."

Ignoring her thinly veiled come-on in anticipation of tomorrow's apologetic gratuity, Frankie punched the button, and the door closed. True to her word, Eve not only found the correct floor, but her suite as well. Inserting the key in the lock wasn't so easy, but finding the bottle on the nightstand was no problem. Slowly the sable slid from her numb body; resolutely her hand clasped the fifth; miraculously the smooth Scotch flowed down her throat and into her aching heart.

Collapsing backward onto the bed, Eve raked a hand through her ultrashort, very chic copper hair. Then, lossening the silk tie at her throat—the very *proper* silk tie—she sighed and unfastened the top few buttons of her André Laug blouse.

Why hadn't she heard from them? Surely they'd read the book by now. It was torture, the waiting, the wondering—even worse than anticipating the reviews, even worse than deciding if *Fast Friends* should have gone to print at all. What were Lauren and Savannah thinking? Eve shuddered. Why hadn't she thrown the manuscript into the trash upon its completion? Her purpose had been served. She had wanted revenge for their oh so righteous defection at the most crucial time of her life, but her pain had been vented, all their actions explored with the writing. Except one—her insidious obsession to bring people to their knees, to gain her the respect and power as an author that she lacked as a person. Evie knew her fast friends, her dear fast friends probably wanted to kill her now.

She justified her disloyalty as easily as she had justified her word-processed margins. What would they have had her do? Ask permission? Take out an ad in *Publishers Weekly* and apologize? After all, it wasn't as though she'd excluded herself from the gut-spilling. Nor had she spared Michael, whose lust and love for her had brought fame and infamy. And who the hell's blood, sweat, and tears had been poured into the work? Not theirs! So maybe she should have consulted them first. Hah! And what would they have said? *Not no, but hell no, Evie.* Hadn't Lauren persistently badgered her to get off her butt and quit wasting her talent? To take a chance and go for all the marbles? And hadn't Lauren prostituted her talent and exploited others while climbing the charts? And wasn't it Savannah Lee who preached total dedication to the art, who'd contended that it wasn't a worthy effort if it didn't shake your peaches? So what the fuck did they *really* want from her?

Eve fumbled for the jangling telephone. Perhaps it was one of them. So often in the past, a thought would bring a call from one to the other.

But it wasn't Lauren or Savannah. It was the British playwright with whom she had flirted outrageously at the party. He wanted her.

"Are you lonesome, love?"

"Is lonesome synonymous with horny? Why not? Come on over. I'll leave word at the desk."

Eve eased the receiver down, a cold, detached expression on her face. When did acceptance come? She was so tired of adapting. Only on the rarest of occasions had she dropped her guard, been genuine, and it was always when sharing the highs and lows with her dearest friends. And where were they now? Sweet Jesus, where were they now?

The unsuspecting playwright hurriedly peeled off his clothes. He was hot to have the sultry redhead who'd stormed his senses as easily as she soared up the charts. Men found Eve irresistible, and this late night visitor was no exception. Like all the others, he wanted to plumb the depths of her mystique, discover the secret of Eve.

Tonight of all nights, Eve could be had. She spread her Neiman-Marcus sable upon the bed and enacted a ritual she had witnessed and perfected to a science. . . .

Tease as you undress. Murmur nice or nasty enticements according to their needs.

He was sweet and so were her words. An angel beckoned him to heaven, but it was the Vegas Pagan who pushed his naked flesh back upon the fur. She began at his feet. She was his supreme subject, his alone. She sucked his toes, her hands gliding up his muscular leg, caressing his sensitive inner thigh. In an excruciatingly slow movement, she slid her body up the length of his, her hardened nipples brushing against his stimulated flesh. She stopped to smile at him, a strange beguiling smile. His eyes were glazed, his hard cock primed for her pleasure, and she knew he was totally hers. Once again she had made a slave of a man. Once again she had the power.

You make love like a whore. Impaled by Michael's long-ago words, Eve recoiled. In one fluid motion, she was off the man, off the bed, handing him his pants. "You're on my coat. I need it."

"What the hell is going on?"

"Out. Just get out. Now."

"You can't be serious. We've only just begun."

"Wrong, sweetheart. Maybe another time."

"You're a bloody lunatic."

"And you're a goddamn bore." Eve pulled Calvin Klein jeans over her bare ass and jerked her coat from beneath him. Not bothering with bra or blouse, she wrapped the sable around her slender form and stormed out of the suite. Once more she managed to reach the lobby and locate the familiar night manager.

"I've got to send a telegram. Immediately."

"Of course, Ms. Afton."

She hastily scribbled a barely legible message:

LAUREN BENNETT
GRAND CAYMAN ISLAND
BRITISH WEST INDIES

SAVANNAH LEE BOUDREAUX
MOSS MARLE PLANTATION
MACON, GEORGIA

HAVE RESERVED A TABLE IN YOUR HONOR AT THE NEW
ENGLAND CRITICS AWARDS BANQUET ON THE TWEN-
TIETH.
THIS YEAR'S RECIPIENT BEGS YOUR ATTENDANCE
AND FORGIVENESS.
ANOTHER NECESSARY REUNION. ANOTHER HEARTFELT
PLEA.
PLEASE COME.
LOVE, EVE.

Back in her suite, Eve collapsed on the bed. The room spun
dizzily. "Should've dumped the book. Too late . . . too
late now."

Would they show up, or would two empty chairs mock
her? "Who the hell cares? . . . *I do. Oh, God, I do . . .*"

CHAPTER NINETY-SEVEN

Lauren arrived in New York and called her lawyer. "Hold the summons until I return to Cayman. Let it be a surprise."

Savannah packed her .38. *It is time for atonement*, the voices told her.

She kissed Beau good-bye at the airport. He'd been so good to her. He really deserved better. *Don't tell him. He'll try to stop you, and it's too late now.* As she boarded the plane, she turned, giving him a final, lingering look.

Eve was dressing to attend the New England Critics Awards banquet, at which she was the honored speaker. Her jade green gown plunged in a V to the waist, front and back. She certainly *looked* the part—the mistress who drove a man to murder and the author who betrayed her friends for profit and fame.

Lauren and Savannah hadn't answered her plea. She didn't know if they were coming, but still she had reserved their places at a front-and-center table. A chance to explain was all she asked, just a few private moments. Not at all sure she'd be granted the opportunity, at the eleventh hour she revised her speech to include a public explanation of a very private matter.

CHAPTER NINETY-EIGHT

As Evie approached the podium, Lauren, sleek, tan, clad in a one-shouldered black sequined gown and trailing a raven ranch mink coat behind her, opened the double doors of the hotel's ballroom, stealing the show and the applause. Smiling warmly to all, she regally proceeded to where Lee Boudreaux was intently straightening yards and yards of her pale peach chiffon evening dress. Lauren finally looked at Evie, then mocked her dear, dear friend with an exaggerated acknowledgment.

Under her breath, Savannah muttered, "Don't you think you're overdoing it a bit? The bitch doesn't deserve anything."

Lauren smiled graciously and bent to kiss Savannah's pale cheek. She sat, looking expectantly at Eve.

After making the usual remarks, Eve launched into her speech.

"I'm sure many of you have speculated about the heroines of *Fast Friends*. No, they are not typical, at times not likeable, perhaps even despicable, but they are not shallow, they are not hypocrites, they are not cowards. They are mortal, with all the flaws and frailties the word implies. Yet they are survivors, women who challenge life and have no qualms about risking it all in the belief they will win in the end. Yes, they misused and abused, but no one more than themselves."

Lauren was pensive. Savannah fidgeted, torn between Eve's voice and those ringing in her head. *She's trying to excuse herself. Don't listen. You know what you must do.*

"Their heartaches and successes are legion—they lived them, they shared them, they coped with them between books, between the lines. They were betrayed by mothers and fathers alike, used by friends and lovers. There were no heroes, no knights on white horses to rescue them." Eve looked directly at Lauren and Savannah Lee. "It was all for one and one for all, always. And it always will be for women like them. Kindred spirits, bound by heart and pen, they lived life hard and fast, high and low, but it cannot be said they didn't have guts, daring, style, and substance."

The audience broke into applause, reclaiming Eve's attention. Lauren nudged Savannah. "Smile and clap if it kills you."

Soon this will be over. Soon we'll see who really has guts, daring, and style.

Lauren glanced at the white beaded bag Savannah placed on the table. What in the name of God was she doing carrying that outdated bag again? And what in the hell did she have in there? Her old shack-sack?

Eve was grateful when Savannah and Lauren approached the dais and offered their congratulations, inviting her to join them for a private celebration in Lauren's suite at the Helmsley Palace after the obligatory autographing. She hadn't thought it would be so easy to obtain their forgiveness and her exoneration. It was almost too easy.

The seal was barely broken on the bottle of Grand Marnier before the claws were unsheathed.

"You goddamn bitch," Lauren shouted. "What the fuck did you believe you were accomplishing? Haven't you had enough notoriety, and if you needed money so badly, why in the hell didn't you come to me? Well, my dear fast friend, you have closed all doors behind you, because I wouldn't give you a nickel if you were starving. In fact, I intend to sue your ass straight into a welfare line."

"I didn't do it for money," Eve shot back. "It was something I had to write. You've been exploiting people for years, but now, suddenly, when it's your life being chronicled, you're outraged. How convenient."

Lauren flung the remainder of her drink in Eve's face. "I'll tell you why you did it, you little hypocrite. You did it because you've been fucking people over for years and we're the only ones left to be had. You just never could stand it that I had respectability and you were cheated out of it. You want to drag us all down to your level, and I don't go that low."

Eve grabbed a napkin, dabbing ineffectually at her face and dress. She calmly refilled her glass and Lauren's. "If you're intent on throwing good liquor all over the place, I hope to God you have a full stock, because I think this is going to be the longest night of our lives."

For one or all, it may be the last. Savannah sat mute, clasping and unclasping the beaded bag.

Lauren slugged down the refill. "I can't believe you would tell the intimate details of our lives without even *attempting* to disguise us. What I told you about Remni was in the strictest confidence. How dare you tarnish his memory—let alone what you have inflicted on Beau! The whole fucking world knows about Savannah's nymphomania now. Are you proud of yourself? You should be. You did one hell of a hatchet job on us."

"Well, at least you finally admit that I can write something other than tripe and trash."

"I was just going to ask who ghosted it for you."

"Fuck off, Lauren. I'm only going to take so much of your crap tonight." Eve began to pace.

"Fair's fair, Evie. We've damn sure been swallowing yours since that book came out."

"You asked why I did it. Well, if you'll shut up for a goddamn second, I'll tell you."

"Oh, I'm sure you'll have an excuse. You always do." Lauren stared her down.

"It was time, Lauren, time to face up to what we have done, what we've become. If we never examine it, how are we to understand it? We can't keep glossing over mistakes and tragedies, can't keep covering past tracks, or we'll lose our grasp on the future. If I had glossed over this, it would just be perpetuating the vicious cycle. As it was, I didn't say for certain that Savannah is half black. She is, you know."

Savannah Lee leapt to her feet, screaming. "You're not only an asshole, you're a liar!"

"I saw them together—Norma Mae and the congressman. They were getting it on right in his office on the desk. I heard what they said. He asked if you were his and her answer was 'oh, probably'. Are you forgetting the black orchids and white lilies he sent to your mama's funeral? They'd been fooling around for years. If you don't believe me, I can put you in touch with him. He'll verify your black blood."

Lauren was beyond mad. "One thing's certain, you megaslut. We don't need anyone to verify your black heart. All for one and one for all, huh? What a joke."

"You're pretty good at forgetting the pact, too, Lauren," Savannah accused. "I recall asking you for an introduction to your producer, but you were too busy, too swollen with your own success to bother, just like you were too wrapped up with Remni and becoming the Countess Bailesti to take the time to answer one goddamn letter. Oh, you're not without blame either. Far from it."

Eve snorted. "Oh, come off it, Savannah. You've done your share of reneging. You haven't once come through in a crisis, not really. You claim to deal with reality in your books, but when it gets down to the nitty-gritty, you're a weak sister. And let's not fail to mention that when *darlin'* Beau came onto the scene, you no longer needed us. But you sure as hell threw it up to us, your adoring husband, precious children, and phony contentment. Fuck! You were out balling every stranger in every new town. Just who's kidding whom here?"

"Evie, you neglected to mention her pseudo-literary claims that *she* never failed to flaunt each and every time one of our books came out."

Savannah reached down, picked up her bag, and clutched it to her chest. "Well, at least I didn't drive the men in my life to kill themselves, or someone else. Can either one of you say the same?"

Lauren slapped Savannah's face. "Don't you ever, if you value your life, say something as cruel as that to me again."

Savannah's hand snaked into her purse and withdrew the .38. "I've had it with the two of you. You think you're so fucking smart, think you know everything, think you can control everyone's lives on and off paper. You've been telling me what to do ever since Bulwer-Lytton, and I'm sick to death of it. You don't tell me anymore. This is my scene. I'll write the script, I'll direct it. For once, the two of you are going to pay attention to me. And, judging by the disbelief on your faces, I do believe at last I have managed to usurp center stage."

"Is that for real? Is it loaded?" Eve backed off a couple of steps.

"Put the gun down, Savannah Lee. This has gone far enough," Lauren ordered.

"Oh, it hasn't even begun. You accuse me of not facing reality; neither of you knows what reality is. Do you know I've killed before? No, of course you don't, or Evie would have put *that* in her book too. Not with a gun, with an ice pick. Are you shocked? Am I making believers of you? You think I don't know you've secretly laughed at my work, thought I preyed on people's fear? I've been the prey. I've known the fear. And now you, you are the prey, you will know fear. And reality. In reality, not a one of us deserves to live.''

"Let's talk about this, Savannah. You're becoming hysterical. If you'll give me the gun, I promise you we'll never, ever breathe a word of what went on up here tonight.''

Lauren's voice was soothing and persuasive, but not persuasive enough to still the voices: *They play with life and think they know it all. It's your mission to redefine reality for them.* "No."

"You're mad at me, not Lauren. Let's discuss it and excuse her from this lesson.''

"Don't get heroic now, Evie. It's all right. We've been in worse tights.'' Lauren gazed compassionately into Savannah's eyes. "Ice pick and reality, Savannah. Tell us.''

"At thirteen I was raped by a scum called Skeeter. Brutally raped. Voices told me he deserved killing and they're talking to me now. They're saying none of us has a right to live.''

"We're not responsible for Skeeter. We finally understand, Savannah. We're sorry. We'll help you any way we can. Don't do this. We do love you, Savannah. We get mad, we say things we shouldn't, but we care, and we've been there, and we're here with you, for you, now. Listen, Savannah, not to the voices, but to us. You deserve to live, we all deserve to live. We'll help you.''

Savannah brushed the tears from her cheeks with her free hand. "It's too late . . . too late for all of us.'' She cocked the hammer. "Forgive me. I should have loved you as much as you and Beau love me. But I can't love. There's too much hate.'' Savannah's anguished eyes lit on Evie.

"If you just hadn't done it, just left it alone, we could've gone on, but you had to have the last word, and now I have no choice."

This was it! Lauren and Evie concluded at exactly the same instant. They rushed Savannah. A shot rang out, then another.

Evie slumped to the floor, blood spurting from her chest. Savannah gripped the gun, her finger again tightening on the trigger.

"Give it to me, Savannah." Lauren reached for the .38.

"I didn't mean to do it," Savannah wailed.

"I know, I know. It will be all right, give me the gun."

Savannah slowly relinquished the .38. The weapon safely in her hand, Lauren collapsed at Evie's side, listening for a breath, a hope of life. Savannah began screaming.

"Shut up and listen," Lauren yelled, "security will be here any minute. We can cover this up if you will keep your head. We've got to get help for Evie before I can take care of you. She's going to make it, and so are we." Lauren transferred the gun to her right hand, imprinting it, then placed it in Evie's right hand. "All our fingerprints are on it, Savannah—all for one and one for all. Say nothing, let me do the talking. Understand?"

Savannah nodded dumbly. Lauren would take care of it. She always had, she always would.

"I know you would want me to do this one last cover-up, Evie," Lauren whispered when the knock came at the door. "We'll survive this, too. I have to believe we will."

FREE!!
BOOKS BY MAIL
CATALOGUE

BOOKS BY MAIL will share with you our current bestselling books as well as hard to find specialty titles in areas that will match your interests. You will be updated on what's new in books at no cost to you. Just fill in the coupon below and discover the convenience of having books delivered to your home.

PLEASE ADD $1.00 TO COVER THE COST OF POSTAGE & HANDLING.

- -

BOOKS BY MAIL
320 Steelcase Road E.,
Markham, Ontario L3R 2M1

IN THE U.S. -
210 5th Ave., 7th Floor
New York, N.Y., 10010

Please send Books By Mail catalogue to:

Name _____
(please print)

Address _____

City _____

Prov./State _____ P.C./Zip _____

(BBM1)